JOURNEY WITH A MASTER STORYTELLER DOWN THE RIVER OF TIME

You are about to begin a journey into wonder. Ahead you'll discover:

"The Crystal Spheres," "Just a Hint," and "Lungfish"—three provocative speculations on extraterrestrial intelligence.

"Senses Three and Six," "The River of Time," "A Stage of Memory" and "Toujours Voir"—four haunting meditations on the nature of time and memory.

"Tankfarm Dynamo"—a hard-science story of our future in space. "The Loom of Thessaly"—a magical yarn of ancient Greek goddesses and a very modern hero. "The Fourth Vocation of George Gustaf"—a whimsical story of a man who would be king. And "Thor Meets Captain America"—a startling tale of Norse gods in World War II.

Bring nothing but your imagination. For many worlds of wonder lie just ahead. . . .

David Brin

The River of Time

BANTAM BOOKS
TORONTO • NEW YORK • LONDON • SYDNEY • AUCKLAND

*This low-priced Bantam Book
has been completely reset in a type face
designed for easy reading, and was printed
from new plates. It contains the complete
text of the original hard-cover edition.*
NOT ONE WORD HAS BEEN OMITTED.

THE RIVER OF TIME

A Bantam Spectra Book / February 1987

*Bantam Books are published by Bantam Books, Inc. Its trademark, consisting of
the words ''Bantam Books'' and the portrayal of a rooster, is Registered in U.S.
Patent and Trademark Office and in other countries. Marca Registrada. Bantam
Books, Inc., 666 Fifth Avenue, New York, New York 10103.*

PRINTED IN THE UNITED STATES OF AMERICA

O   0 9 8 7 6 5 4 3 2 1

To my teachers
—Jim Arnold and Paul Libby,
Charles Bures and Charlie Peck,
and especially Dr. Henry Booker—
for their patience and mercy

Contents

DESTINY

The Crystal Spheres

It was just a luckychance that I had been defrosted when I was—the very year that farprobe 992573-aa4 reported back that it had found a goodstar with a shattered crystalsphere. I was one of only twelve deepspacers alivewarm at the time, so naturally I got to take part in the adventure.

At first I knew nothing about it. When the flivver came, I was climbing the flanks of the Sicilian plateau, in the great valley a recent ice age had made of the Mediterranean Sea I had once known. I and five other newly awakened Sleepers had come to camp and tramp through this wonder while we acclimated to the times.

We were a motley assortment from various eras, though none was older than I. We had just finished a visit to the once-sunken ruins of Atlantis, and were hiking out on a forest trail under the evening glow of the ring-city high overhead. In the centuries since I had last deepslept, the gleaming, flexisolid belt of habitindustry around our world had grown. In the middle latitudes, night was now a pale thing. Nearer the equator, there was little to distinguish it from day, so glorious was the lightribbon in the sky.

Not that night could ever be the same as it had been when my grandfather was a child, even if every work of man were removed. For ever since the twenty-second century there had been the Shards, casting colors out where once there had been but galaxies and stars.

No wonder no one had objected to the banishment of night from Earthsurface. Humanity out on the smallbodies might have to look upon the Shards, but Earthdwellers had no particular desire to gaze out upon those unpleasant reminders.

3

Being only a year thawed, I wasn't ready yet to even ask what century it was, let alone begin finding some passable profession for this life. Reawakened sleepers were generally given a decade or so to enjoy and explore the differences that had grown in the Earth and in the solar system before having to make any choices.

This was especially true of deepspacers like me. The State—more ageless than any of its nearly immortal members—had a nostalgic affection for us strange ones, officers of a near-extinct service. When a deepspacer awakened, he or she was encouraged to go about the altered Terra without interference, seeking strangeness. He might even dream he was exploring another goodworld, where no man had ever trod, instead of breathing the same air that had been in his own lungs so many times, during so many ages past.

I had expected to go my rebirthtrek unbothered. So it was with amazement, that evening on the forestflank of Sicily, that I saw a creamy-colored Sol-Gov flivver drop out of a bank of lacy clouds and drift toward the campsite, where my group of timecast wanderers had settled to doze and aimlessly gossip about the events of the day.

We all stood and watched it come. The other campers looked at one another suspiciously as the flivver fell toward us. They wondered who was important enough to compel the ever-polite Worldcomps to break into our privacy, sending this teardrop down below the Palermo heights to parklands where it didn't belong.

I kept my secret feeling to myself. The thing had come for me. I knew it. Don't ask me how. A deepspacer *knows* things. That is all.

We who have been out beyond the shattered Shards of Sol's broken crystalsphere, and have peered from the outside to see living worlds within faraway shells . . . We are the ones who have pressed our faces against the glass at the candy store, staring in at what we could not have. We are the ones who understand the depth of our deprivation, and the joke the Universe has played on us.

The billions of our fellow humans—those who have never left Sol's soft, yellow kindness—need psychists even to tell of the irreparable trauma they endure. Most people drift through their lives suffering only occasional bouts of greatdepression, easily treated, or ended with finalsleep.

But we deepspacers have rattled the bars of our cage. We *know* our neuroses arise out of the Universe's great jest.

I stepped forward toward the clearing where the Sol-Gov flivver was settling. It gave my campmates someone to blame for the interruption. I could feel their burning stares.

The beige teardrop opened, and out stepped a tall woman. She possessed a type of statuesque, austere beauty that had not been in fashion on Earth during any of my last four lives. Clearly she had never indulged in biosculpting.

I admit freely that in that first instant I did not recognize her, though we had thrice been married over these slow waityears.

The first thing I knew, the very first thing of all, was that she wore our uniform . . . the uniform of a Service that had been "mothballed" (O quaint term!) thousands of years ago.

Silver against dark blue, and eyes that matched . . . "Alice," I breathed after a long moment. "Is it true at last?"

She came forward and took my hand. She must have known how weak and tense I felt.

"Yes, Joshua. One of the probes has found another cracked shell."

"There is no mistake? It's a goodstar?"

She shook her head, saying yes with her eyes. Black ringlets framed her face, shimmering like the trail of a rocket.

"The probe called a class-A alert." She grinned. "There are Shards all around the star, shattered and glimmering like the Oort-sky of Sol. And the probe reports that there is a *world* within! One that we can touch!"

I laughed out loud and pulled her to me. I could tell the campers behind me came from times when one did not do such things, for they muttered in consternation.

"When? When did the news come?"

"We found out months ago, just after you thawed. Worldcomp still said that we had to give you a year of wakeup, but I came the instant it was over. We have waited long enough, Joshua. Moishe Bok is taking out every deepspacer nowalive.

"Joshua, we want you to come. We need you. Our expedition leaves in three days. Will you join us?"

She need not have asked. We embraced again. And this time I had to blink back tears.

Of recent weeks, as I wandered, I had pondered what profession I would pursue in this life. But joy of joys, it never occurred to me I would be a deepspacer again! I would wear the uniform once more, and fartravel to the stars!

2

The project was under a total news blackout. The Sol-Gov psychists were of the opinion that the race could not stand another disappointment. They feared an epidemic of greatdepression, and a few of them even tried to stop us from mounting the expedition.

Fortunately, the Worldcomps remembered their ancient promise. We deepspacers long ago agreed to stop exploring, and raising peoples' hopes with our efforts. In return, the billion robot farprobes were sent out, and we would be allowed to go investigate any report they sent back of a cracked shell.

By the time Alice and I arrived at Charon, the others had almost finished recommissioning the ship we were to take. I had hoped we would be using the *Robert Rodgers*, or *Ponce de Leon,* two ships I had once commanded. But they had chosen instead to use the old *Pelenor*. She would be big enough for the purposes we had in mind, without being unwieldy.

Sol-Gov tugs were loading aboard ten thousand corpsicles even as the shuttle carrying Alice and me passed Pluto and began rendezvous maneuvers. Out here, ten percent of the way to the Edge, the Shards glimmered with a brightsheen of indescribable colors. I let Alice do the piloting, and stared out at the glowing fragments of Sol's shattered crystalsphere.

When my grandfather was a boy, Charon had been a site of similar activity. Thousands of excited men and women had clustered around an asteroid ship half the size of the little moon itself, taking aboard a virtual ark of hopeful would-be colonists, their animals, and their goods.

Those early explorers knew they would never see their final destination. But they were not sad. They suffered from no greatdepression. Those people launched forth in their so-primitive first starship full of hope for their great-grandchildren—and for the world which their sensitive telescopes had proved circled, green and pleasant, around the star Tau Ceti.

Ten thousand waityears later, I looked out at the mammoth Yards of Charon as we passed overhead. Rank on serried rank of starships lay berthed below. Over the millennia, thousands had been built, from generation ships and hiberna-barges to ram-shippers and greatstrutted wormhole-divers.

They all lay below, all except the few that were destroyed in accidents, or whose crews killed themselves in despair. They had all come back to Charon, failures.

I looked at the most ancient hulks, the generation ships, and thought about that day of my grandfather's youth, when the *Seeker* cruised blithely over the Edge, and collided at one percent of light speed with the inner face of Sol's crystalsphere.

They never knew what hit them, that firstcrew.

They had begun to pass through the outermost shoals of the solar system . . . the Oort Cloud, where billions of comets drifted like puffs of snow in the sun's weakened grasp.

Seeker's instruments sought through the sparse cloud, touching isolated, drifting balls of ice. The would-be colonists planned to keep busy doing science throughout the long passage. Among the questions they wanted to solve on their way was the mystery of the comets' mass.

Why was it, astronomers had asked for centuries, that virtually all of these icy bodies were nearly the same size—a few miles across?

Seeker's instruments ploughed for knowledge. Little did her pilots know she would reap the Joke of the Gods.

When she collided with the crystalsphere, it bowed outward with her over a span of lightminutes. *Seeker* had time for a frantic lasercast back to Earth. They only knew that something strange was happening. Something had begun tearing them apart, even as the fabric of space itself seemed to rend!

Then the crystalsphere shattered.

And where there had once been ten billion comets, now there were ten quadrillion.

Nobody ever found the wreckage of *Seeker*. Perhaps she was vaporized. Almost half the human race died in the battle against the comets, and by the time the planets were safe again, centuries later, *Seeker* was long gone.

We never did find out how, by what accident, she managed to crack the shell. There are still those who contend that it was the crew's ignorance that crystalspheres even *existed* that enabled them to achieve what had forever since seemed so impossible.

Now the Shards illuminate the sky. Sol shines within a halo of light, reflected by the ten quadrillion comets . . . the mark of the only goodstar accessible to man.

"We're coming in," Alice told me. I sat up in my seat and watched her nimble hands dance across the panel. Then *Pelenor* drifted into view.

The great globe shone dully in the light from the Shards. Already the nimbus of her drives caused space around her to shimmer.

The Sol-Gov tugs had finished loading the colonists aboard, and were departing. The ten thousand corpsicles would require little tending during our mission, so we dozen deepspacers would be free to explore. But if the goodstar did, indeed, shine onto an accessible goodworld, we would awaken the men and women from frozensleep and deliver them to their new home.

No doubt the Worldcomps chose well these sleepers

to be potential colonists. Still, we were under orders that none of them should be awakened unless a colony was possible. Perhaps this trip would turn out to be just another disappointment, in which case the corpsicles were never to know that they had been on a journey twenty thousand parsecs and back.

"Let's dock," I said eagerly. "I want to get going."

Alice smiled. "Always the impatient one. The deep-spacer's deepspacer. Give it a day or two, Joshua. We'll be winging out of the nest soon enough."

There was no point in reminding her that I had been latewaiting longer than she—indeed, longer than nearly any other human left alive. I kept my restlessness within and listened, in my head, to the music of the spheres.

3

In my time there were four ways known to cheat Einstein, and two ways to flat-out fool him. On our journey *Pelenor* used all of them. Our route was circuitous, from wormhole to quantumpoint to collapsar. By the time we arrived, I wondered how the deepprobe had ever gotten so far, let alone back, with its news.

The find was in the nearby minor galaxy, Sculptor. It took us twelve years, shiptime, to get there.

On the way we passed close to at least two hundred goodstars, glowing hotyellow, stable, and solitary. In every case there were signs of planets circling round. Several times we swept by close enough to catch glimpses, in our superscopes, of bright blue waterworlds, circling invitingly like temptresses, forever out of reach.

In the old days we would have mapped these places, excitedly standing off just outside of the dangerzone, studying the Earth-like worlds with our instruments. We would have charted them carefully, against the day when mankind finally learned how to do on purpose what *Seeker* had accomplished in ignorance.

Once we did stop, and lingered two lightdays away

from a certain goodstar—just outside of its crystalsphere. Perhaps we were foolish to come so close, but we couldn't help it. For there were modulated radio waves coming from the waterworld within!

It was only the fourth time technological civilization had been found. We spent an excited year setting up robot watchers and recorders to study the phenomenon.

But we did not bother trying to communicate. We knew, by now, what would happen. Any probe we sent in would collide with the crystalsphere around this goodstar. It would be crushed, ice precipitating upon it from all directions until it was destroyed and hidden under megatons of water—a newborn comet.

Any focused beams we cast inward would cause a similar reaction, creating a reflecting mirror that blocked all efforts to communicate with the locals.

Still, we could listen to *their* traffic. The crystalsphere was a one-way barrier to modulated light and radio, and intelligence of any form. But it let the noise the locals made escape.

In this case, we soon concluded that it was another hive-race. The creatures had no interest in, or even conception of, spacetravel. Disappointed, we left our watchers in place and hurried on.

Our target was obvious as soon as we arrived within a few lightweeks of the goal. Our excitement rose as we found that the probe had not lied. It *was* a goodstar— stable, old, companionless—and its friendly yellow glow diffracted through a pale, shimmering aura of ten quadrillion snowflakes . . . its shattered crystalsphere.

"There's a complete suite of planets," announced Yen Ching, our cosmophysicist. His hands groped about in his holistank, touching in its murk what the ship's instruments were able to decipher from this distance.

"I can feel three gasgiants, about two million asteroid smallbodies, and"—he made us wait, while he felt carefully to make sure—"three littleworlds!"

We cheered. With numbers like those, odds were that at least one of the rocky planets circled within the Lifezone.

"Let me see . . . there's one littleworld here that has—" Yen pulled his hand from the tank. He popped a finger into his mouth and tasted for a moment, rolling his eyes like a connoisseur savoring fine wine.

"Water." He smacked thoughtfully. "Yes! Plenty of water. I can taste life, too. Standard adenine-based carbolife. Hmmm. In fact, it's chlorophyllic and left-handed!"

In the excited, happy babble that followed, Moishe Bok, our captain, had to shout to be heard.

"All right! People! Look, it's clear none of us are going to get any sleep soon. Lifesciencer Taiga, have you prepared a list of corpsicles to thaw, in case we have found a goodworld?"

Alice drew the list from her pocket. "Ready, Moishe. I have biologists, technicians, planetologists, crystallographers . . ."

"You'd also better awaken a few archaeologists and Contacters," Yen added dryly.

We turned and saw that his hands were back in the holistank. His face bore a dreamy expression.

"It took our civilization three thousand years to herd our asteroids into optimum orbits for space colonies. But compared with this system, we're amateurs. Every smallbody orbiting this star has been transformed. They march around like ancient soldiers on a drillfield. I have never even imagined engineering on this scale."

Moishe's gaze flickered to me. As executive officer, it would be my job to fight for the ship, if *Pelenor* found herself in trouble . . . and to destroy her if capture were inevitable.

Long ago we had reached one conclusion. If goodstars without crystalspheres were rare, and dreamt of by a frustrated mankind, the same might hold for some *other* star-traveling race. If some other people had managed to break out of its shell, and now wandered about, like us, in search of another open goodstar, what would such a race think, upon detecting our ship?

I know what *we* would think. We would think that the intruder had to *come* from somewhere . . . an open goodstar.

My job was to make sure nobody ever followed *Pelenor* back to Earth.

I nodded to my assistant, Yoko Murukami, who followed me to the armsglobe. We unfolded the firing panel and waited while Moishe ordered *Pelenor* piloted cautiously closer.

Yoko looked at the panel dubiously. She obviously doubted the efficacy of even a mega-terawatt laser against technology of the scale described by Yen.

I shrugged. We would find out soon. My duty was done the moment I flicked the arming switch and took hold of our deadman autodestruct. In the hours that passed, I watched the developments carefully, but could not help deepremembering.

4

Back in the days before starships—before *Seeker* broke Sol's eggshell and precipitated the two-century Comet-War—mankind had awakened to a quandary that caused the thinkers of those early days many sleepless nights.

As telescopes improved, as biologists began to understand, and even tailormake life, more and more people began to look up at the sky and ask, "Where the hell *is* everybody?"

The great lunar-based cameras tracked planets around nearby yellow suns. There were telltale traces of life even in those faint twenty-first-century spectra. Philosophers case nervous calculations to show that the galaxies must teem with living worlds.

And as they prepared our first starships, the deep-thinkers began to wonder. If travel between the stars was as easy as it appeared to be, why hadn't the fertile stars already been settled by somebody else?

After all, we were getting ready to head out and colonize. By even modest estimates of expansion rates, we seemed sure to fill the entire galaxy with human settlements within a few million years.

So why hadn't this already *happened*? Why was there no sign of traffic among the stars? Why had the predicted galactic radio network of communication never been detected?

Even more puzzling . . . why was there absolutely *no* evidence that Earth had ever been colonized in the past? We were by then quite certain that our world had never hosted visitors from other worlds.

For one thing, there was the history of the Precambrian to consider.

Before the age of reptiles, before fish or trilobites or even amoebae, there was, on Earth, a two-billion-year epoch in which the only lifeforms were crude single-celled organisms without nuclei—the procaryotes—struggling slowly to invent the basic structure of life.

No alien colonists ever came to Earth during all that time. We knew that for certain, for if they had, the very garbage they buried would have changed the history of life on our planet. A single leaky latrine would have filled the oceans with superior lifeforms that would have overwhelmed our crude little ancestors.

Two billion years without being colonized . . . and then the silent emptiness of the radioways . . . the philosophers of the twenty-first century called it the Great Silence. They hoped the starships would find the answer.

Then the very first ship, *Seeker*, somehow smashed the crystalsphere we hadn't even known existed, and inadvertently explained the mystery for us.

During the ensuing CometWar, we had little time for philosophical musings. I was born into that battle, and spent my first hundred years in harsh screaming littleships, blasting and herding iceballs that, left alone, would have fallen upon and crushed our fragile worlds.

We might have let Earth fall then. After all, more than half of humanity at that time lived in space colonies, which could be protected more easily than any sittingduck planet.

That might have been logical. But mankind went a little crazy when Earthmother was threatened. Belters herded cities of millions into the paths of hurling iceballs, just to save a heavy world they had only known from books and a faint blue-twinkle in the blackness. The psychists took a long time to understand why. At the time it seemed like some sort of divine madness.

Finally the war was won. The comets were tamed and we started looking outward again. New starships were built, better than before.

I had to wait for a berth on the twelfth ship, and the wait saved my life.

The first seven ships were lost. As they beamed back their jubilant reports, spiraling closer to the beautiful green worlds they had found, they plowed into unseen crystal-spheres and were destroyed.

And, unlike *Seeker,* they did not accomplish anything by dying. The crystalspheres remained after the ships had been icecrushed into comets.

We had all had such hopes . . . though those who remembered *Seeker* had worried quietly. Humanity seemed about to breathe free, at last! We were going to spread our eggs to other baskets, and be safe for the first time. No more would we have to fear overpopulation, crowding, or stagnation.

And all at once the hopes were smashed—dashed against those unseen, deadly spheres.

It took centuries even to learn how to *detect* the deathzones! *How*, we asked. How could the universe be so perverse? Was it all some great practical joke? What *were* these monstrous barriers that defied all the physics we knew, and kept us away from the beautiful littleworlds we so desired?

For three centuries, humanity went a little crazy.

I missed the worst years of the greatdepression. I was with a group trying to study the sphere around Tau Ceti. By the time I got back, some degree of order had been restored.

But I returned to a solar system that had clearly lost a piece of its heart. It was a long time before I heard true laughter again, on Earth or on her smallbodies.

I too went to bed and pulled the covers over my head for a couple of hundred years.

5

The entire crew breathed a reliefsigh when Captain Bok ordered me to put the safeties back on. I finally let go of my deadman switch and got up. The tension seeped away into a chain of shivers, and Alice had to hold me until I could stand again on my own.

Moishe had ordered us off alert because the goodsun's system was empty.

To be accurate, the system *teemed* with life, but none of it was intelligent.

The greater asteroids held marvelous, self-sustaining ecosystems, absorbing sunlight under great windows. Twenty moons sheltered huge forests beneath tremendous domes. But there was no traffic, no radio or light messages. Yen's detectors revealed no machine activity, nor the thought-touch of analytical beings.

It felt eerie to poke our way through those civilized lanes in the smallbody ways. For so long we had only performed such maneuvers in the well-known spaces of Solsystem.

During those first centuries after the crystal crisis, some men and women still thought it would be possible to live among the stars. Belters mostly, they claimed aloud that planets were nasty, heavy places anyway. So who needed them?

They went out to the *badstars*—red giants and tiny red dwarves, tight binaries and unstable suns. The badstars were protected by no crystalspheres. The would-be colonists found drifting clots of matter near the suns, and set up smallbody cities as they had at home.

Every one of the attempts failed within a few generations. The colonists simply lost interest in procreation.

The psychists finally decided the cause was related to the divine madness that had enabled us to win the CometWar.

Simply put, men and women could live on asteroids, but they needed to *know* that there was a blue world nearby—to see it in their sky. It's a flaw in our character, no doubt, but we cannot go out and live in space all alone.

We have to have waterworlds, if the universe is ever to be ours.

This system's waterworld we named Quest, after the beast so long sought by King Pelenor, our ship's namesake. It shone blue and brown, under a clean whiteswaddling of clouds. For hours we circled above it, and simply cried.

Alice awakened ten corpsicles—prominent scientists who, the Worldcomps had promised, would not fall apart on the reawakening of hope.

We watched them take their turn at the viewport, joytears streaming down their faces, and we joined them to weep freely once again.

6

Pelenor was hardly up to the task of exploring this system by herself. We spent a year recovering and modifying several of the ancient ships we found drifting over our planet, so that teams could spread out, investigating every farcorner of this system.

By our second anniversary, a hundred biologists were quickscampering over the surface of Quest. They genescanned the local flora and fauna excitedly, and already were modifying Earthplants to fit into the ecosystem without causing imbalance. Soon they would start on animals from our genetanks.

Engineers exploring the smallbodies excitedly declared that they could get the lifemachines left behind by the prior race to work. There was room for a billion colonists out there, straight from the start.

But the archeologists were the ones whose report we awaited most anxiously. Between my ferrying runs, they were the ones I helped. I joined them in the dusty ruins of Oldcity, at the edge of Longvalley, putting together piles of artifacts to be catalogued and slowly analyzed.

We learned that the inhabitants had called themselves

the Nataral. They were about as similar to us as we might have expected—bipedal, ninefingered, weirdlooking.

Still, one got used to their faces after staring at their statues and pictures long enough. I even began to perceive subtle facial cues, and delicate, sensitive nuances of expression. When the language was cracked, we learned their race name and some of their story.

Unlike the few other alien intelligences we had observed from afar, the Natarals were individuals, and explorers. They too had spread into their planetary system after a worldbound history fully as colorful and goodbad as our own.

Like us, they had two conflicting dreams. They longed for the stars, for room to grow. And they also wished for other faces, for neighbors.

By the time they built a starship—their first—they had given up on the idea of neighbors. There was no sign anybody had ever visited their world. They heard nothing but silence from the stars.

Still, when they were ready, they launched their firstship toward their other dream—Room.

And within weeks of the launching, their sun's crystalsphere shattered.

For two weeks we double-checked the translations. We triple-checked.

For millennia we had been serching for a way to destroy these deadly barriers around goodstars . . . trying to duplicate on purpose what *Seeker* had accomplished by accident. And now we had the answer!

The Nataral, like us, had managed to destroy one and only one crystalsphere. Their own. And the pattern was exactly the same, down to the CometWar that subsequently almost wrecked their high civilization.

The conclusion was obvious. The deathbarriers were destructible, but *only from the inside*!

And just when that idea was starting to sink in, the archaeologists dug up the Obelisk.

7

Our top linguist, Garcia Cardenas, had a flair for the dramatic. When Alice and I visited him in his encampment at the base of the newly excavated monument, he insisted on putting off all discussion of his discovery until the next day. He and his partners instead prepared a special meal for us, and raised their glasses to toast Alice.

She stood and accepted their accolades with dry wit, and then sat down to continue nursing our baby.

Old habits break hard, and only a few of the women had managed yet to break centuries of biofeedback conditioning not to breed. Alice was among the first to reactivate her ovaries and bring a child to our new world.

It wasn't that I was jealous. After all, I basked in the only slightly lesser glory of fatherhood. But I was getting impatient with all of this ballyhoo. Except for Moishe Bok, I was perhaps the oldest human here—old enough to remember when people had children as a matter of course, and therefore made time for *other* matters, when something important was up!

Finally, when the celebration had wound down, Garcia Cardenas nodded to me, and led me out the back flap of the tent. We followed a dim path down a sloping trail to the digs, by the light of the ring of bright smallbodies the Nataral had left permanently in place over the equatorial sky of Quest.

We finally arrived at a bright alloy wall that towered high above our heads. It was made of a material our techs had barely begun to analyze, and was nearly impervious to the effects of time. On it were inscribed hardpatterns bearing the tale of the last days of the Nataral.

A lot of that story we knew from other translated records. But the end itself was still a mystery, and no small cause of nervousness. Had it been some terrible plague? Did the intelligent machines, on which both their civilization and ours relied, rebel and slaughter their master? Did their sophisticated bioengineering technology get out of their control?

What we *did* know was that the Nataral had suffered. Like humans, they had gone out and found the universe closed to them. Both of their great dreams—of goodplaces to spreadsettle, and of other minds to meet—had been shattered like the deathsphere around their own star. Like humans, they spent quite a long time not entirely sane.

In the darkness deep within the dig, Cardenas had promised I would find answers.

As he prepared his instruments I listened to the sounds of the surrounding forestjungle. Life abounded on this world. There were lovely, complicated creatures, some clearly natural, and some just as clearly the result of clever biosculpting. In their creatures, in their art and architecture, in the very reasons they had almost despaired, I felt a powerful closeness to the Nataral. I would have liked them, I imagined.

I was glad to take this world for humanity, for it might mean salvation for my species. Still, I regretted that the other race was gone.

Cardenas motioned me over to a holistank he had set up at the base of the Obelisk. As we put our hands into the blackness, a light appeared on the face of the mono-lith. Where the light traveled, we would touch, and feel the passion of those final days of the Nataral.

I stroked the finetuned, softresonant surface. Cardenas led me, and I felt the Endingtime as the Nataral meant it to be felt.

Like us, the Nataral had passed through a long period of bitterness, even longer than we had endured until now. To them, indeed, it seemed as if the universe was a great, sick joke.

Life was found everywhere among the stars. But intelligence arose only slowly and rarely, with many false starts. Where it did occur, it was often in a form that did not happen to covet space or other planets.

But if the crystalspheres had not existed, the rare sites where starfaring developed would spread outward. Species like us would expand, and eventually make contact with each other, instead of searching forever among sandgrains. An elder race might arrive where another was just getting started, and help it over some of its crises.

If the crystalspheres had not existed . . .

But that was not to be. Starfarers could not spread, because crystalspheres could only be broken from the inside! What a cruel universe it was!

Or so the Nataral had thought.

But they persevered. And after ages spent hunting for the miraculous goodstar, their farprobes found five water-worlds unprotected by deathbarriers.

My touchhand trembled as I stroked the coordinates of these accessible planets. My throat caught at the magnitude of the gift that had been given us on this obelisk. No *wonder* Cardenas had made me wait! I, too, would linger when I showed it to Alice.

But then, I wondered, where had the Nataral gone? And why? With six worlds, surely their morale would have lifted!

There was a confusing place on the Obelisk . . . talk of black holes and of *time*. I touched the spot again and again, while Cardenas watched my reaction. Finally, I understood.

"Great Egg!" I cried. The revelation of what had happened made the discovery of the five goodworlds pale into insignificance.

"Is *that* what the crystalspheres are for?"

I couldn't believe it.

Cardenas smiled. "Watch out for teleology, Joshua. It is true that the barriers would seem to show the hand of a creator at work. But it might be simply circumstance, rather than some grand design.

"All that we do know is this. Without the crystal-spheres, we ourselves would not exist. Intelligence would be more rare than it already is. And the stars would be almost barren of life.

"We have cursed the crystalspheres for ten thousand years," Cardenas sighed. "The Nataral did so for far longer—until they at last understood."

8

If the crystalspheres had not existed . . .

I thought about it that night, as I stared up at the shimmering, pale light from the drifting Shards, through which the brighter stars still shone.

If the crystalspheres had not existed, then there would come to each galaxy a first race of star-treaders. Even if most intelligences were stay-at-homes, the coming of an aggressive, colonizing species was inevitable, sooner or later.

If the crystalspheres had not existed, the first such star-treaders would have gone out and taken all the worlds they found. They would have settled all the waterworlds, and civilized the smallbodies around every single goodstar.

Two centuries before we discovered our crystalsphere, we humans had already started wondering why this had never happened to Earth. Why, during the three billion years that Earth was "choice real estate," had no race like us come along and colonized it?

We found out it was because of the deathbarrier surrounding Sol, which kept our crude little ancestors safe from interference from the outside . . . which let our nursery world nurture us in peace and isolation.

If the crystalspheres had not been, then the first star-treaders would have filled the galaxy, perhaps the universe. It is what *we* would have done, had the barriers not been there. The histories of those worlds would be forever changed. And there is no way to imagine the death-of-possibility that would have resulted.

So, the barriers protect worlds until they develop life capable of cracking the shells from within.

But what was the point? What benefit was there in protecting some young thing, only for it to grow up into bitter, cramped loneliness in adulthood?

Imagine what it must have been like for the very first race of star-treaders. Never, were they patient as Job, would they find another goodstar to possess. Not until the next egg cracked would they have neighbors to talk to.

No doubt they despaired long before that.

Now we, humanity, had been gifted of six beautiful worlds. And if we could not meet the Nataral, we could, at least, read their books and come to know them. And from their careful records we could learn about the still earlier races which had emerged from each of the other five goodworlds, each into a lonely universe.

Perhaps in another billion years the universe will more closely resemble the sciencefictional schemes of my grandfather's day. Maybe then commerce will plow the starlanes between busy, talky worlds.

But we, like the Nataral, came too early for that. We are cursed, if we hang around until that day, to be an ElderRace.

I looked one more time toward the constellation we named Phoenix, whither the Nataral had departed millions of our years ago. I could not see the dark star where they had gone. But I knew exactly where it lay. They had left explicit instructions.

Then I turned and entered the tent that I shared with Alice and our child, leaving the stars and shards behind me.

Tomorrow would be a busy day. I had promised Alice that we might begin building a house on a hillside not far from Oldcity.

She muttered some dreamtalk and cuddled close as I slipped into bed beside her. The baby slept quietly in her cradle a few feet away. I held Alice, and breathed slowly.

But sleep came only gradually. I kept thinking about what the Nataral had given us.

Correction . . . what they had *lent* us.

We could use their six worlds, on the condition we were kind to them. Those were the same conditions they had accepted when they took the four worlds long abandoned by the Lap-Klenno, their predecessors on the lonely starlanes . . . and that the Lap-Klenno had agreed to on inheriting the three Thwoozoon suns . . .

So long as the urge to spreadsettle was primary in us, the worlds were ours, and any others we happened upon.

But someday our priorities would change. Elbow-room would no longer be our chief fixation. More and more, the Nataral had understood, we would begin to think instead about loneliness.

I knew they were right. Someday my great-to-the-nth descendants would find that they could no longer bear a universe without other voices in it. They would tire of these beautiful worlds, and pack up the entire tribe to head for a darkstar.

There, within the event horizon of a great black hole, they would find the Nataral, and the Lap-Klenno, and the Thwoozoon, waiting in a cup of suspended time.

I listened to the wind gentleflapping the tent, and envied my great-nth grandchildren. I, at least, would like to meet the other star-treaders, so very much like us.

Oh, we could wait around for a few billion years, till that distant time when most of the shells have cracked, and the universe bustles with activity. But by then we would have changed. By necessity we would indeed have become an ElderRace . . .

But what species in its right mind would choose such a fate? Better, by far, to stay young until the universe finally becomes a fun place to enjoy!

To wait for that day, the races who came before us sleep at the edge of their timestretched black hole. Within, they abide to welcome us; and we shall sit out, together, the barren early years of the galaxies.

I felt the last shreds of the old greatdepression dissipate as I contemplated the elegant solution of the Nataral. For so long we had feared that the Universe was a practical joker, and that our place in it was to be victims— patsies. But now, at last, my darkthoughts shattered like an eggshell . . . like the walls of a crystalcage.

I held my woman close. She sighed something said in dreamthought. As sleep finally came, I felt better than I had in a thousand years. I felt so very, very young.

AUTHOR'S NOTES

Sometimes the borderlines between science and fiction seem fuzzy. This has never been more true than in the topic of exobiology or SETI, the Search for Extra-Terrestrial Intelligence.

To most students of the subject it now appears that we are alone, that the Earth has never been visited by beings from other stars. (Erich Von Daniken's fables, and those of UFO enthusiasts, describe beings who are said to behave in ways that could hardly be called "intelligent.")

The new hypothesis, called the Uniqueness View, contends that aliens cannot exist, for if they did, they would have filled the galaxy long ago. A leader of the Uniqueness View, Frank Tipler, of Tulane University, claims that people who still dream of contact suffer from an innate human fear of loneliness, a fear that the courageous rise above in order to contemplate a universe that our descendants will fill.

Carl Sagan, a Contact defender, counters that Tipler and his kind suffer from an innate human fear of the alien, which the courageous rise above . . . You see how it goes.

I have participated in this debate in the astronomical journals. Earning no love from either side, my papers have said, "Stop! You both may be right!" For now, we gain more by careful thought and data collection than by yelling at each other.

Some hypotheses, however, are too weird even to be included in speculative scientific papers. The theme behind "The Crystal Spheres" is one such idea. I dared not insert it in my upcoming academic book on SETI, but I did think it might make a nice story.

A *final note on the short story as a subgenre. About half of the professionally published short fiction in the English language is science fiction, because of the thriving SF magazines. For a novice, such markets as* The Atlantic *or* The New Yorker *are nearly inaccessible. Not so* Analog, *or* Asimov's Magazine, *or* The Magazine of Fantasy and Science Fiction. *These publications are where much of the exciting short fiction of our time is being presented.*

Science fiction is also friendly to beginners, I'm very glad to say. "The Crystal Spheres" was awarded the 1985 Hugo for the short story category.

The Loom of Thessaly

"You can't get there from here."

At the time, Pavlos Apropoulos had thought his American friend was joking. Now he wasn't so sure.

"Try it and see," Frank had said. "It's less than 250 kilometers from Athens, and I'll bet you can't even get close to it!"

That had been easy for Frank to say, sitting in the comfort of Pavlos's Athens apartment. *He* wasn't going to be the one who went off, alone, into the wilderness to test it.

Pavlos's arms felt as if they were about to come off. He knew that the branch he was holding on to might tear free at any second, leaving him without any firm support. Yet his feet couldn't seem to find a purchase.

There was dust everywhere. The canyon was filled with a clay pungence that mixed with the overripe odors of bramble bush and perspiration. He could taste blood from one of the cuts he'd taken on his face, during the panicky scramble down the flaky, slippery talus.

This was the easiest route. He was sure of it.

The branch tore loose just as Pavlos got his right foot settled on an uncertain chunk of partially decomposed granite. For a moment he teetered. The canyon wavered about him in a blur of hazy green thorn bushes and a narrow strip of cloudy sky.

Pavlos threw the cluster of twigs away and grabbed for another hold. But the dry leaves came off like chaff in his hands as the ground crumbled beneath him.

The brush that had been so formidable in blocking his

earlier descent now broke and parted in front of him like
chips flying from an axe. The branches tore and whipped
at his arms, which he vainly tried to keep over his face as
he fell, running and crashing, down the steep slope.

Somehow, he stayed on his feet, though they skidded
on the powdery surface. The shrubbery thickened toward
the bottom and the slope flattened, but this slowed him
only slightly as the headlong rush sent him splashing
across a small rivulet of dirty water to slam, arms outstretched, into the opposite canyon wall.

Fragments of desiccated, ancient rock rained down
upon him as he labored to catch his breath in a series of
shuddering gasps. The clumps fell in a steady stream—a
miniature landslide onto the back of his head.

Pavlos stood still, taking things in order. He wasn't
ready to begin cataloguing the bruises and scrapes he had
taken. The thudding of loose gravel on his skull meant no
more to his overloaded senses than the chalky, rank odor
of dust and sweat which he took in with each ragged
breath, or the almost unbearable weight of his backpack.

The landfall subsided at about the same rate as Pavlos's
breathing. Dust settled, leaving a fine white patina on his
hair and hunched shoulders. He waited a few moments
longer, eyes shut tightly against the floating grit, listening
to the fading creakings his passage down the scarp had set
off. When finally he looked around, Pavlos shuddered.

In thirty years of mountaineering he had seen many
ravines like this, but this was the first time he had ever
been in one. There had never been a need, before. There
had always been another way . . . an easier route.

Not this time, though. The place where he had come
down was the best he had found in an entire day of
searching. It was hideous.

Gnarled trees and thorn bushes covered the sixty-
degree slope. Jagged rocks protruded from the starved,
parched soil. It was a miracle he had come this far without
breaking a leg, or his skull.

More than ever he was convinced he was on the right
path. This monument to inaccessibility had to be the place
Frank had spoken of.

He checked for cuts and bruises. It was a good thing he had chosen, after carefully examining Frank's aerial photos, to wear leather for this expedition. It had protected most of his skin, although several unbelievable thorns had pierced his garments and had to be pulled out amid momentary, excruciating pain.

He allowed his pack to slide down and form a seat to rest on. With slow deliberation, he drew out his aid kit and applied disinfectant to the cuts on his face and the backs of his wrists.

Only after his breathing had settled, and the spots disappeared from in front of his eyes, did he allow himself a slow, sparing swallow from one of his canteens. He wet a handkerchief and carefully wiped the grit away from his eyes and lips.

Upstream to the right a few dozen meters was the path of ascension he had picked out during his visual scouting, earlier, from the other side. It was the route with marginally fewer obstacles than elsewhere along this face.

He stood, groaning at the stretch of abused muscles, and moved a few feet to examine the route. Then he compared it with the path he would have to take if he turned around, right now, and went home.

Sure enough. As bad as the way down had been, it looked more tempting to someone trapped in the ravine than the hellish slope he would have to climb if he continued forward.

It had been that way all the way here. Every trail, every game path, every natural sloping led one circumspectly *away* from the small area he wanted to reach. In no specific case had there been anything suspicious about the avoidance. Each time there had been a good and obvious reason to turn one way, instead of the other that led here.

It was the sum that drove Pavlos crazy. It had only been by the most steadfast determination to violate all of the rules of mountaineering that he had been able to get this far. It had taken two days to come just five kilometers from that last hamlet of surly, taciturn herdsmen.

Pavlos went back to his pack and pulled out the high-altitude photos Frank had given him.

"This is the first one I took from orbit," Frank had said when he showed Pavlos the first large-scale photo. "I used the cartography telescope in interface with the computer on board the Platform. This locale was flagged in the course of a survey I was doing for the EEC—an attempt to determine population density versus terrain type. This spot gave Fourier Transform that was quite unusual."

The satellite photo was very clear. It looked like it had been taken from only a few thousand feet in altitude. Pavlos easily recognized the elevation contour markings that lay upon apparently typical Grecian highlands. He had, after all, been teaching map reading and leading expeditions while his young American friend had been scrawling stick figures in crayon on the kitchen wall in his parents' house in Des Moines.

The photos lay on his dining room table, three stories above the noisy streets of Athens. Outside his apartment door children ran down the hall, screaming in some incoherent game. To him it was all part of the background. He worried over the other lines and squiggles on Frank's map, reluctant to admit his ignorance to the astronaut, however close they had become during a mission in the Sudan, two years before.

"This is in Thessaly, is it not?" He pointed to the shape of the hillsides, the lay of the sun in the creek beds, wishing to show that expertise meant as much as did fancy technology.

Frank's eyebrows rose. Impressed, he showed it with typical American ingenuousness. Americans had no second skin, no Mediterranean wall of caution. Pavlos loved them for it.

"Yes, that's right," Frank had said. "And here you can see how the population density and terrain accessibility profiles rise and fall together nicely everywhere."

He pulled out another photo.

"Here is the city of Thessalonica, with almost a million people. Now weighted *only* against local resources there's no good explanation for its population advantage over, say, Larisa a bit farther south. But taking into account factors such as travel times along various egress points, terrain . . ."

"Yes, yes. I get the point." Pavlos was pleased. He had managed to get the information out of Frank without asking for it, and picked up an opportunity to mutter with fatherly impatience at the same time. Such minor stylistic victories helped make a pleasure out of a lazy afternoon.

"So what I can't figure out is why you thought it so important to show this to me at my apartment, and in such secrecy, hmmm?"

Frank sat down.

"Oh, hell. You know this is low-priority stuff, Pav. Ever since you helped us find that capsule in the Sahara you've known that my main job is to experiment with space-borne antimissile systems. When I started getting strange results in my accessibility studies, I just couldn't get anybody interested."

"All right." Pavlos smiled. "Then I am your informal consultant. Now show me these 'strange results' of yours."

Frank pulled a large envelope from his briefcase. He drew the first of several glossy prints from it.

"This is from the same general region, only about thirty kilometers to the southwest of the corner of that large overlay. I want you to take a close look at this area, in particular, before I show you a bigger blowup." Pavlos bent to peer at the plateau Frank pointed out, bringing over his magnifying glass.

His smile faded as he studied the photo.

"I cannot say for certain, as your lines of probability get in the way . . . but it appears that this water course loops back upon itself! It makes almost a natural moat around the hilltop."

Frank nodded. "I've tried to use the newer telescope we have on board. It's tied in to our experimental beam weapons system . . ." Almost unconsciously, Frank lowered his voice, although he knew that Pavlos's apartment was secure.

"I could count the number of black fleas on the back-side of a dog with that machine. But it's a bitch and a half getting the thing tuned properly, at this stage. I'm not at all sure I'd be able to devote that kind of time and effort using it on what's essentially a side project, especially when NASA's already paranoid over security. At *least* I'd like to get some sort of preliminary confirmation before taking the risk."

Pavlos nodded. As a reserve NATO officer who occasionally helped out in expeditions to desolate regions, he had seen examples of amazing photography from space. And he had the feeling they hadn't ever shown him all they could do.

"So let us see the best you have." He waved with his right hand as Frank pulled out the fourth photo. "You have me curious about this mystery of yours."

It showed a plateau in the middle of a set of concentric, parched creek beds, surrounded by rugged, goat-ravaged hills. At the corners of the photo there were signs of humanity, as one would expect everywhere in a land that had been inhabited at high density for four thousand years. In two places there were the ubiquitous shepherd's shacks for overnight shelter. Goat tracks were everywhere.

But in the center, all trace of man and animal disappeared. Puzzled, Pavlos peered closer. "Are those . . . ? No, they cannot be."

"What are they, Pavlos?"

He rubbed his chin. "I believe those are *cedars*, very large cedars, of a kind you can only find in the Caucasus these days . . . or on the estates of old and very wealthy families."

"There are no estates here, Pavlos. What else do you see?"

"There are cypress, and some other large trees I cannot identify, and . . ." He peered closely. "There is a *building* of some kind. There is a large, rectangular structure, mostly shaded by trees."

Frank stood up straight and tapped the photo.

"See these faint lines? I had the computer draw them along curves of *accessibility*. See those gradients? If all roads lead to Rome, then all roads, all trails—hell, all *goat tracks*—lead *away* from this place. Now, how the hell could anyone have built a thing that size on top of that plateau?"

Pavlos sat back in his chair and drummed his fingers on the tabletop. Then he started rummaging through his jacket pocket for a cigarette. Only when he had one lit did he get up and start to pace.

"I see two possibilities," he began. "The building may be modern, in which case it may have been prefabricated and taken to the peak by helicopter. The question then would be why? And who would do such a thing? How did they keep it secret?"

Pavlos turned to look at Frank. "That is the possibility that interests you, is it not? Things like this make intelligence officers sleep poorly."

Frank nodded, but said, "I tried to interest my superiors but they didn't care. They even forbade me to ask the Greek government about it. Our allies are already touchy about the extent to which we can peer down at them. I'm stuck with following this up on my own."

Pavlos nodded. "Ah, to be expected from politicians and soldiers, present company excepted. Well, there is a second possibility. If the structure is *more* than fifty years old, it would have taken fanaticism to build it on that site . . . a brand of fanaticism that has not been seen in this land for many centuries."

"And *that's* the possibility that interests you, isn't it?" Frank suggested. "You'd just love to find an untouched Roman temple, or a pristine Nestorian monastery or hermitage, wouldn't you?"

Pavlos stopped pacing again, took a deep drag from his cigarette, then waved it at his friend.

"I have a feeling I am being *persuaded* to do something. Is this so?"

Frank had smiled.

Pavlos put away the photos and shouldered his backpack. The pain resumed at once, spreading from chafed shoulders down his spine and arms. For the ten-thousandth time he wondered what masochism could drive a man who wasn't in the army to put forty pounds on his back and go places a donkey would refuse.

When he reached the chosen site he took out his machete, looped its thong from his right wrist, and began climbing.

No classic ascent, this. None of the clean exhilaration of a challenge with goldline, harness, and carabiners against a bare rock face. The danger here would not be from a single fall—likely to be broken by shrubbery—but from jagged rocks, nasty thorns, poisonous snakes, and plain agony. Cerebration would not help so much as watchfulness and stoicism.

At first the hillside was steep. The foliage was thick enough to bar his path, but too poorly rooted to use for support. It came free of its roots in his hand, leaving him teetering on the crumbling soil. Finally he hit on the technique of tearing the bushes loose on purpose, opening a path to crawl through.

Soon, however, the slope flattened just enough to give the roots leverage. He found himself again and again forced to take detours which led him inevitably downward. Finally, he lay on his stomach to worm among the burrows and insect nests, shoving upward by brute force.

It was neither a time nor a place for finesse.

He hacked at roots with the short machete. The tough, springy bushes bled a gooey yellow sap that soon coated his hands with a cloying, binding stickiness. Perspiration ran in clammy streams along his sides, under the leather jacket. The sun burned down through a muggy haze. The smell of his own sweat mingled with the evil stench of the thorn shrubs.

Repetition soon became automatic. Reach, pull, hack, hack again, and again, until the plant tears free . . . keep flat, crawl through the gap, ignoring the jutting rocks and jagged root stumps . . . reach, pull, set your legs, hack . . . hack . . . hack . . .

Shortness of breath made him regret his lost youth.

He kept his mind on only one idea. *Take no detours!* Every easier path inevitably led downward. It became easy to tell which way was the right one. Pavlos looked for the worst, most miserable path. It was invariably correct.

Mercifully, just as he thought he could endure the smell, the ache, the heat, and the confinement no longer, he reached a patch of open rock. It was not more than one meter by two, but he fell across it and rolled out of his pack with a groan of relief.

With trembling fingers he pulled out one of his canteens. He filled his mouth, swished the water around, then spat onto his hands and rubbed them on his pants to dislodge some of the sap.

Pavlos squinted at the painfully bright, hazy sky.

He wondered if Frank was overhead. If he were using the spy telescope, and happened to have a spare moment to look this way, Frank might see him right now.

Pavlos waved languidly at the sky.

Probably not, he thought. *Frank wasn't going to risk getting in trouble until I called from the top.*

There was a small transceiver in his backpack that, Frank promised, would be able to reach the Platform whenever it was passing within line of sight. As executive officer of a five-man crew, he would be able to arrange several hours alone with the equipment, while the others slept.

It hurt a little, in a wry fashion, to think of the astronaut whizzing overhead in weightless, air-conditioned comfort, pondering his theories of "accessibility of terrain." Pavlos knew that inaccessibility was, like the texture of a woman, known only through intimate contact.

Right now he was being intimate with inaccessibility in a manner that made him think of the Anglo-Saxon expletives he had learned over the years.

One hundred meters, that was all the distance remaining. Pavlos crawled with a sense of dogged martyrdom. He was sure two fingers of his left hand had been sprained, if not broken, by a falling stone from a rockslide he'd set off. The other aches were innumerable.

The ascent became a melding of miserable repetition;

he would grab, pull, hack, then use the root as a support as he searched for footholds on the flaky slope.

His mind meanwhile walked a random path among fantasies of what he would find at the top.

A pre-Constantinian hermitage, perhaps . . . or even a monastery, untouched for fifteen hundred years because nobody ever happened upon it in all of that time.

Or maybe this was one huge tell—a solid ruin from some ancient fortification. It *did* defend itself well, not by steepness or remoteness or height but by sheer *unpleasantness* . . . a nastiness that deterred even goats.

By the frogs of lower heaven, why not go all the way! This is, perhaps, a covered-up installation of visitors from outer space, who buried one of their starships here when they ran out of tapioca to power it!

Pavlos's foot slipped and the root he clutched barely held as he scrambled, face buried in the gritty dirt. With a mighty strain, he lifted himself within range of another foothold. It held.

Probably, he thought somewhat dizzily, *I will find a helicopter landing pad, guard dogs, and an oil tycoon who will have me arrested for trespassing.*

Pavlos hardly noticed when the slope began to flatten.

In fact, he felt a momentary panic when his hand reached out for another root and grabbed, instead, only air and then grass.

The cedars formed a pocket forest at the center of the plateau. The grass that surrounded the grove was a subject for speculation. It was thicker and more lustrous than one might expect in this terrain, yet it did not appear to be tended, either. Pavlos saw no sign of a helicopter landing pad.

Not on this side, at least. Who could tell what he would see once the spots cleared from in front of his eyes?

He knew he was hardly presentable for knocking on someone's front door. He itched all over. Somehow removing his leather outer garments and tending his wounds had changed the pain from a general background roar that could be ignored to a set of isolated screaming sensations.

He had been injured on other expeditions, of course. Often far worse. But never had he felt so *generally* abused.

Pavlos took one last swig from his canteen, then hoisted his pack.

"All right," he mumbled, fighting off dizziness. "This had better be worth it."

The air was cleaner up here, almost tasty. The smell of the cedars was sweet and pleasant. He entered the grove and almost at once saw the outlines of the building through the trees.

He paused for a moment, struggling not to fall to his knees. It couldn't be true!

It was pure beam and column construction. Not an arch could be seen. The columns were Doric, or even pre-Doric—chaste, simple, unadorned, but beautiful. Their rounded contours, thought Pavlos, might almost have been Minoan.

And the beams resting on the columns! Where a Doric entablature was strictly sectioned into the three horizontal bands, here there was only one, carved in intricate figures that seemed to march upon a protruding lip, like the rim of the door lintel of a Cretan palace.

The structure was obviously designed to stand open to the wind, yet someone after the original builder had chosen to close off the interior in a crude fashion. The openings between the columns were blocked by slabs of white marble, roughly mortared; the flaking remnants of ancient paint still clung in spots.

Pavlos walked forward slowly, silently, as if in fear the sounds of his footsteps would blow it all away. He felt telescoped as he approached—the marble seeming to come to *him*, like the advancing of a dream.

No graffiti . . . no carved names and dates. The figures of heroic horses and feathered men in combat using spears and rounded shields, these bore no defacement other than that which Time itself had meted.

The warriors, some plumed, some naked to the waist, were of many types. Pavlos saw some that were clearly Minoan and he felt his heart leap. There were others . . .

Egyptian of the Old Kingdom, for certain, and . . . Akkadian?

Pavlos approached one of the columns. Gently, he reached out and touched it.

The marble had taken pits and tiny scratches over the centuries. It felt rough, in its underlying smoothness. To him, it had the texture of durability.

The wind sighed through the cedars. It seemed to be speaking to him with the voices of ancient men and women.

"Well, hero. You are here at last. *Come,* and you shall tell us of the changes in the world outside."

Pavlos shook his head to clear it. The words had seemed so real.

"*Come,* hero!"

He turned. Standing at the far end of the row of columns was a woman. She wore a simple garment, bound by a rope belt. Her black hair was braided, though not with great precision.

She smiled, and held out her hand in a gesture of welcome. But as Pavlos felt himself begin to walk—numbly and only partly, it seemed, at his own will—he thought he heard a quiet "clicking" sound, and the sunlight glinted hard into his eyes . . . reflected bitterly by the golden thimble she wore on her finger.

2

"This is the back way," she said as she led him up a narrow set of marble steps. "We find it better to bring heroes in here first, and let them browse around the storeroom. They always find something that interests them, and it helps them adjust."

At first he thought she was speaking Katharevusa, the modern Greek dialect almost exclusively used by scholars and intellectuals. But the style and pronunciation were different . . . older. It was almost a bastard classical version she spoke, though his early learning in Katharevusa enabled him to understand her.

Why was she playing this language game with him? Was she another discoverer of this place, determined to re-create the original dress and speech of those who first served their gods here? If so, she was a failure. The early priestesses of this temple surely spoke Achaean, or something even older.

"What is your name?" he asked.

She turned her head from the task of opening the rear door, and arched an eyebrow at him.

"An odd first question. You may call me Moira, if you wish. Later there will be time for other names, including your own."

There was a moment's flash of humor in her eyes as she spoke, and perhaps a touch of pity, though Pavlos could imagine no justification.

Moira? It had a strange pronunciation. Wasn't that an Irish name? Very odd.

They entered a large chamber that was dimly illuminated by gaps in the marble wall slats, and by one flickering oil lamp. The beam and post construction was genuine. A little more than two meters separated each of the simple columns that stood in even rows throughout the interior. Most of the colonnade was used to support row after row of shelves, upon which piles of dusty memorabilia were laid.

"I will leave you now," the woman said. "You will find food and drink at the far door. Do not pass beyond until you are called, hero."

Again, Pavlos felt the self-assured power in her voice, as well as a benign amusement. He wondered what fanaticism bred such arrogance. He called out to her after she had gone a few meters from him.

"Say, why do you call me hero? That's not my name."

She looked at him. The lamplight flickered in her eyes.

"Is it not? How strange that you don't think so. Most heroes know who and what they are. I shall have to ask Clotho to check her pigments."

She left. Pavlos heard a scraping sound, then a sliding clunk as a bolt was placed.

With a sigh he let his pack slip down against one of the pillars, then he sat on it, his back to the cool marble.

This was all too strange to be true. A "genuine" priestess of an ancient cult . . . Had she implied there were others? He wondered what sect they had chosen to re-create. What rites?

He was glad he still had his machete.

Pavlos was growing mildly worried about his frame of mind. He felt detached, numb, almost as if he were watching these proceedings through a protective barrier of cotton batting. Things were being revealed to him in a dramatic sequence. The next scene obviously called for him to go poking through the dusty shelves of this storeroom.

Hadn't he been invited to do so? He grunted as he pulled himself up and went to the shelves that looked most rummaged.

If the storeroom was supposed to catch the interest of heroes, this certainly *was* the section which would have had the most attention. Pavlos nodded in bemusement. This was the weapons collection.

It was an odd mixture, not in keeping with the apparent classical fixation of the woman's cult. The front shelves held an anachronistic assortment of old, but not archaic, weapons. There was a fine Spanish rapier, resting upon a matchlock musket that had to be five hundred years old, if a day. He blew the dust off a flintlock pistol and peered past halberds and Turkish helmets in search of the real treasure.

The benumbed haze kept him calm and complacent when—finally—he found what he was looking for.

The bronze was incredibly well preserved. It had maintained much of its original shine and hardness. He wiped dust away from the decorated nasal of the ancient helmet. Its crest of horsehair was still long and stiff, though discolored and flaking. He set it beside a round shield, three feet across, and a short sword with images of snakes running down the haft.

For a long time he merely looked at them. Then he found the nerve to try on the helm.

It fit perfectly.

The musty odor was oddly compelling. Carefully, he fought down the thrill of power he felt. Pavlos removed it and put it back on the shelf.

Maybe later, he thought.

In the middle of the room, near the hanging lamp, he found the books.

There weren't many. That fit. The type of fellow who would fight both nature and his own instincts to come to this place—whether on a pilgrimage or out of obstinate curiosity, would not have been likely to carry much reading matter with him.

Pavlos smiled as he returned to his pack and rummaged through the bottom flap. He quickly found the flimsy, air mailed edition of *L'Express* which he had purchased at the Hotel International before setting out, three days before. He had bought the Parisian paper on an impulse, while stopping off for tobacco. Now he returned to the "library" shelf and carefully placed it next to a small, dog-eared Dutch Bible and a crudely bound volume handwritten in Arabic.

The newspaper looked good, lying there. Some future . . . "hero" . . . might see it and think that a twentieth-century Frenchman had been here.

Ah, well, Pavlos thought. *That's close enough.*

Besides a few Bibles and other apparent guidebooks for a faithful wanderer, there were several crude maps and scrawled notes in many languages. One stretch of vellum came embossed with seals and endorsements. It looked like a treaty of some sort. He could tell that the signatories were Turkish and Italian, but the text appeared to be in some sort of cipher.

He had carelessly flattened one scroll of brittle, burn-etched sheepskin, and read at least twenty lines of very archaic Greek script, before the meter and carriage of the words penetrated to whatever place his critical faculties had taken to hide. He stared down at the ancient libram then, halfway between agony over the damage he had done it with his rough treatment and ecstasy over his discovery.

He read, with mounting excitement, the anguished story of a Titan, chained, yet still defiant.

> *"Nor yet nor thus is it ordained that fate*
> *These things shall compass; but by myriad pangs*
> *And fortunes bet, so shall I 'scape these bonds:*
> *Art than necessity is weaker far."*
> *"Who, then, is helmsman of necessity?"*
> *"The triform Fates and ever mindful Furies."*
> *"Is Zeus, in might, less absolute than these?"*
> *"Even he the fore-ordained cannot escape."*

How easily the classic language read! After all, Pavlos had seen these words before, many times. No one had ever written as once did Aeschylus . . . unless it was the sage, inspired or not, who first chanted the rhyme that later became Ecclesiastes.

He dared not imagine that Aeschylus himself had burned the words onto the vellum, any more than Jean-François Revel had hand-set the newspaper on the shelf, inches away. No, this was surely only a copy of *Prometheus Bound* . . . but would have to be the oldest copy anyone alive had ever seen.

Prometheus, according to the ancient pantheon of Hesiod, had been of the race of Titans, children of the Earth and Sky, who preceded Zeus and the other Hellenic gods. When Zeus rebelled and drove most of the Titans from the face of the Earth, he nevertheless kept Prometheus by his side, for he grew to depend on the advice of the Titan whose name meant "forethought."

How mankind came to be was never made clear in Greek legend. His destiny as a thinking being, however, was said to have been the gift of Prometheus. The Titan, in his pity, supposedly lent mankind a sliver of his own power—the fire of imagination, alternately fabled as the skaldic mead of poetry.

For this, Zeus had Prometheus nailed to a rocky crag, where an eagle daily tore at his ever-regenerating flesh.

The story was said to have ended happily. Prometheus was released, coming to a reconciliation with Zeus and Man.

Yet that part of the story had never read as convincingly. It was as if Aeschylus had allowed his fixation on the palpable, growing presence of justice in the world to prejudice his storytelling. Perhaps he simply couldn't reconcile leaving the archetype of justice and pity stranded for eternity in torment.

Pavlos sniffed. A heady, flavorful aroma suddenly reminded him how hungry he was. He carefully laid the parchment on the shelf and turned to follow his nose.

A tray of roast lamb, still steaming on the spit, lay on a bench by the door the priestess had used to exit. That he had heard nothing didn't surprise Pavlos at all.

The meat was tasty, if somewhat unevenly cooked. He chewed slowly as his mind fell deeper into a paradoxical state of numb, bemused excitement.

Somewhere on that shelf of scrolls might be the *missing* portions of the work of the moralistic, unhappy Aeschylus . . . or of the compassionate, upbeat Sophocles . . . or why not ask for the long-lost Achaean scribblings of Homer himself?

So many secrets on a shelf of ancient cedar! Could there be a fragment that some Cretan scribe left here, one that might tell of the founding of Knossos or its fall?

Might there be a tablet that would shed light on who it was, who did whatever deed it was, that caused men to build a legend that became Prometheus?

There were things here for which a hundred men he knew would gladly kill.

The bronze helm alone was worth a fortune.

All right.

This is not a millionaire's retreat in the hills. It is not an ancient ruin refurbished by a few modern fanatics, re-creating an ancient cult.

Everything in this room was left here. And time has touched each of these things hardly at all since each hero left his contribution to the collection.

Heroes.

Just like me.

Iron slid along granite. The oaken door swung back,

scraping noisily on the stone floor. Pavlos stood. The woman, Moira, regarded him.

"Beginning to adjust at last, I see. But you are a strange one, hero. No souvenirs? Or have you stuffed all our gems in your backpack, hoping to fool us?"

Pavlos was beginning to understand the condescension and amusement in her voice. It hurt, a little, that she thought him so stupid as to choose the poorest treasures, or to attempt a simple theft. He was tempted to protest, but managed to refrain. She looked at him much as his teacher had when he was five and in nursery school. The analogy was probably not unrealistic.

He tried, and found it easier than he had expected, to meet her gaze. There were lines around her ice-blue eyes that he imagined to come from long, sad laughter. They did not detract from the handsomeness of her high forehead and fine nose. Her carriage was erect and slender, yet there was something in the careless braiding of her hair, or the curve of her ironic smile, that spoke of a burden of waiting that had long passed tedium.

"Are you ready to see more?" she asked.

Pavlos waved his hand in what he hoped was an idly grand gesture. "What else could you have that would astonish me more than this room has?"

She stepped back to hold the door for him.

"Everything else that has ever mattered, hero," she answered softly, but with a vatic tone. "Everything else that has ever been."

3

Racks filled the rest of the temple as far as Pavlos could see. Only a few narrow aisles between the columns were not blocked by tier upon horizontal tier of wooden doweling. There were thirty-three tiers between the stone floor and the dusty, cobwebbed ceiling; and upon every shelf there lay bolts of shimmering, silky, multicolored cloth.

The arrangement was intricate. As Pavlos walked,

peering in the dim light cast by his lamp, he was puzzled at the way the cloth snaked back and forth over the dowels. Only a few folds lay upon one another on each shelf. Yet the fabric on one shelf connected to those on tiers above and below it.

The long, continuous bolt on his left leapt the aisle high over his head to join the one on his right just under the ceiling. The colors in the portion overhead were bright and vivid, though the lamp was too dim to bring out features. Still, something in what little he could see made Pavlos break out in goose bumps.

It was one gigantic tapestry. Only two meters wide, its length must have been kilometers.

The sense of defensive detachment that had never totally left Pavlos now returned in strength. The hand that reached out to stroke the smooth, cool fabric felt like the hand of another man. Glass had never been smoother. Mercury could not have felt more elusively alive under his touch.

He lifted the top fold and held up the lamp, then bent forward to look into the narrow opening.

The threads were too fine to make out individually, yet he felt sure that, holding his head at the right angle, he could easily pick them out one by one. It was an odd sensation.

The pattern of the threads was unlike any he had ever come upon. The weft twisted with incredible complexity, not only in and out of the warp, but with itself, as well.

The design was intricately abstract at first sight. But there was something in the pattern—the colors and highlights shifted like phosphorous diatoms as he changed position slightly—that seemed hypnotically three-dimensional. Pavlos was reminded of the holograms Frank had shown him once. He held the light to one side and squinted at an angle; then his eyes adjusted to a virtual image.

L'Shona the war-chief, whose true name was hidden, feared the Powers no more nor less than any normal man. He would die of witchcraft, he knew, as did everyone; and however he died, yes even in battle, his brothers would avenge him by burning a witch. He gave this little thought. It was the way of the world.

But now came word that the great king of the Bantu had had a dream, and wanted L'Shona, whose true name was hidden, to come and help divine its meaning.

L'Shona was afraid. For the Fire-Demon had come to him in sleep, as well, and told him that the Bantu must sweep east, into the land of the small wise ghosts. And he had afterward called in a slave, who he had disemboweled to read the entrails in the sand.

And now L'Shona, whose true name was hidden, avoided thinking of his second dream, that the king would do this same thing to him . . . and thought instead of the east, and war.

Pavlos stepped back and rubbed his eyes.

The image had come and gone in a flash of color and emotion. He had not so much *seen* as *felt* the emotions of a tribal warrior. He had touched the bright mind, the quick, sad resignation, and the complacent cruelty with which he had dispatched the slave.

Moreover, Pavlos had felt undertones from the dying slave, whose life ended in ignorant terror at L'Shona's hand. Pavlos sensed the presence of others—L'Shona's parents and ancestors; his wives, slaves, comrades, and enemies; and his immediate heirs—nearby in either space or time.

He felt a weird certainty that, had he shifted his gaze one iota during that holographic second, he would have seen . . . felt . . . another instant in the warrior's life, or in the life of a neighbor.

He moved along the aisle until another image flashed at him unbeckoned.

Xoatuitl hid under a bale of amaranth stalks until the cries of the hunters and the screams of the pursued diminished in the distance. Then, with as little sound as he could

*manage, he crawled out. There was a chance some follow-
ers of the Teacher might be rallying by the lake, where the
tools of power were stored. Although he was only twelve,
he knew something of their use, and might be able to help
them drive back the followers of the Bloodgod.*

He turned just in time to see the (axe, sword, weapon) . . .

Pavlos blinked. Suddenly the viewpoint shifted. He was
looking through still another pair of eyes, dimmer, less
acute.

*Old Tuitaczpec leaned against the wall of the marketplace,
breathing hoarsely through toothless gums. He had not
been able to keep up with the mob, and had been left to
use his (axe, club, indeterminate weapon) upon the prone
bodies of wounded followers of the feathered serpent. It
was not enough. He wanted vengeance on them, for seduc-
ing his grandson away from the old ways of the Bloodgod.*

*When he saw a head emerge from under a bale of amaranth,
he gleefully took the opportunity . . .*

The next time Pavlos blinked he saw an overview.
The small section of tapestry he looked upon was colored a
sanguinary red. He felt almost overcome by the lust of one
half of a city to kill the other half. Taken at a distance, the
scene was almost beautiful, in a dreadful fashion.

A small shift of his eyes told a sad irony: that this civil
war would lead, within a year, to the fall of the city to
barbarians from the north. A centimeter downward, the
color red overwhelmed all other shades.

There was, in fact, a lot of red everywhere he looked.
Bright, sudden patches flashed at him as battles and burn-
ings. Pink tintings leapt out as oppression and grief.

There were other shades. In fact, Pavlos thought he
saw a perpetual effort, in greens and browns of health and
chaste blues of thought and art . . . and especially in the
shades of humor and courage, to force the weave in another direction altogether.

The conflict created a blend of terrible, tragic beauty. The tapestry, as a whole, made him ache inside. The stories leapt at him, individually and in groups, comprising a sum of melancholy that finally made him close his eyes.

"Moira," he whispered.

The pronunciation had fooled him. It was not a borrowed, foreign name. It was an honorific. A title.

"Yes," she said, beside him. "I am She Who Walks, who travels . . . or used to. Come now, hero. You must meet the Three. The Three Who Weave wish to look upon you."

4

Once upon a time the three crones might have stood at a crude, warp-weighted loom, much as did Arachne . . . or Penelope, weaving as she waited for Ulysses. Now they sat on padded stools. Their broad, vertical floor loom looked no more than a few centuries old. Perhaps some visiting hero had been a skilled carpenter, and knocked it together for them before he . . .

Before he what? None of the possible scenarios Pavlos could imagine coming out of this meeting included his being allowed to leave. They had some use for him, to be sure, these ancient meddlers. And they'd had long practice dealing with "heroes" who wanted to take home souvenirs and a story.

Moira beckoned him forward to be presented, but Pavlos interrupted before she began the introductions, partly to keep from falling into another awestruck trance.

"I know their names." He gestured to the old "woman" who sat a bit apart from the loom, with a basket full of woolly skeins at her feet and bottles of dye at her side. She rhythmically drew threads from the basket, winding each on a wooden frame, then painting on various colors with a blur of brevity. On finishing each, she wound the thread quickly onto a bobbin.

Something about her activity struck Pavlos as—strange. It was as if he watched a stroboscopic image—like that of a top spinning or an engine turning—and for every "thread" he saw painted and wound, ten thousand were actually handled.

"Your name is Clotho," he said. She smiled at him crookedly, apparently giving him her entire attention, yet never stopping her work.

"You have also been called Urda, and U-dzu. You prepare the thread."

He turned to the weaver. She was the oldest hag. She looked as frail as a springtime icicle . . . as thin and friable as late summer grass.

"This is Lachesis," he went on, pointing to the weaver, who didn't even glance at Pavlos. Her hands dipped, with the same stroboscopic effect, into a bag on her lap, constantly bringing forth fresh bobbins of thread, tying the free ends into place upon the tapestry, then flying through the innumerable bobbins, weaving them among each other and the straight strands of warp.

"Her name means She Who Knows Sorrow. She has also been called Verdani. The Norsemen knew her, as well."

The third crone actually paused in her work, and grinned at Pavlos. She seemed the youngest of the three, though not as fresh as Moira. She was the first to speak.

"Well educated, aren't you, hero? Then you know, of course, what these are?"

She held a pair of bronze cloth shears up to the filtered afternoon sunlight. The sight of them made Pavlos want to quail, but he forced himself to stand erect instead.

"I know what they are, Atropos. You seem to be a bit lazy in their use, right now."

The third hag frowned for a moment. But Clotho immediately exploded in mirth. She put down her dyes and cackled dryly, slapping her thighs. Slowly, Atropos resumed her cruel smile.

"Very brave and humorous, hero. When Moira told us of you, we thought you were one of the weak ones. Perhaps not."

Her Greek was even more archaic than Moira's. Pavlos had to concentrate to understand the heavily inflected speech.

"You are right," Atropos went on. "I am lazy because Lachesis, my dear sister"—she motioned to the weaver, who never once looked up—"has this last century insisted that I give her more length in the average thread . . . even though they are more numerous than ever. Clotho and I have been humoring her, though it is *we* who will decide when this silly phase comes soon to end."

With that she grimaced and leaned over to snip with the shears. With each "click" a rain of tiny bobbins fell to the floor. Pavlos winced as the clacking speeded up to a high-pitched burr.

"Well!" Clotho cried out. "Now comes the part I like second best! Now that introductions are over, hero, what is your first remark?"

She sat expectantly, like an artist awaiting worship, but equally willing to accept vehement detestation as a form of praise.

Pavlos forced himself to answer, feeling a desperate need to maintain momentum until he had a chance to think.

"Your job was to prepare the thread that makes up the length and tone of a man's life. I'd like to know how you accomplish that."

The hag was startled for a moment. The expression looked so unaccustomed on her toothless, satisfied face, that Pavlos felt an instant's triumph. Any uncertainty he caused these furies was a momentary victory for his sanity.

"The first!" she cried in sudden delight. "The first hero to ask me that!

"Always they ask the *stupid* questions, like 'Who gave you the right' . . . or '*Why*' . . ." Her voice became mockingly querulous.

Pavlos remained silent. Those were the questions he had wanted to ask next.

"At last a *practical* hero!" Clotho went on. "No prayers to the dead little gods, or futile attempts to exorcise us by calling on One who is *too* big, and has forgotten we exist

. . . no, *this* hero has gained my favor! Come, hero! I will show you *how* it is done!"

She reached for his hand. When she touched it Pavlos felt a brief thrill of power, as if her aura were something palpable and electric.

But her skin felt rough and dry. Her grip was very strong as she pulled him out the broad portico and down the marble steps of the front face of the temple, into the late afternoon shadows.

He was almost dragged through an overgrown carpet of grass and native flax, across an open area toward a forest-shrouded building on the other side.

A small tholos, a roofed circle of marble columns, faced the temple across the open meadow. It stood beneath a great cedar, the largest Pavlos had ever seen. The fluted pillars of the ancient structure were laced with almost microscopic filigree that had a sort of metallic sheen. But in between, the openings were blocked by massive slabs of undressed stone, which clashed with the original design.

With surprising agility, the ancient fury pulled him along up the short stairs to the narrow portico. There she stopped Pavlos and motioned him to be still as she dragged aside a granite stone blocking the doorway.

Clotho looked quickly about the rim of the opening, as if watching for something trying to escape. When finally satisfied she grinned at him and crooked a finger in sly invitation.

"So you wanted to see how it begins, did you? Then look!" she hissed. "No more than a handful of men have ever seen what you now see!"

Pavlos peered into the dimness. Beyond the trapezoid of light cast on the floor by the doorway, the interior was gloomy as a starless night.

Yet, off toward the back, there seemed to be a faint glow. It shimmered with a suggestion of an outline that changed before he could grasp it. His mind struggled, and failed to form a straightforward image.

"It looks like . . . like a hole. Yes, it's like a deep hole in space, but with a hint of light at the end. It feels like I'm trying to see through my blind spot."

"Blind spot . . . hole in space? Yes! Yes!" she cried. "You fool! Idiot! You are the smartest of all your race of apes to visit us, and *still* you don't recognize this?"

She whacked him on the arm and almost knocked him over. He would have a welt from that blow.

Smartest of all? No, Pavlos thought. *I'm merely the latest. I'm probably the first arrival who has heard of Einstein . . . who knows, at least in abstract, that space has shape and texture, almost like her "cloth." I've heard of black holes and antimatter, and I've seen the special effects in those American science fiction films. Perhaps that has prepared me.*

But prepared me to do what? To devise glib theories, certainly. I can think of a half-dozen fanciful concepts to explain this, whereas all the other heroes had to think in terms of "miracles" and "magic."

Big deal, as Frank would say. Perhaps they were better off at that.

The hag pointed at the shimmering, burning blackness at the rear of the building. Pavlos turned to watch her, feeling the cottony numbness pack more fully than ever around his mind.

"That's where *you* come from, hero," she announced with dry satisfaction.

"See the threads? You probably can't, with them in their natural colors, and not gathered into skeins or bobbins. But if I let them, they would fly free into the sky, to tangle with each other as they liked . . . each the essence of a human soul, good for a hundred years or perhaps more!

"Some do get away. A few fly off to annoy us. Some become 'great teachers and leaders' . . ." Her voice was thick with sarcasm. "We manage to kill them off eventually by finding the part of the tapestry which avoids control, where there is a gap that influences the threads around it. Then we choke it off, at last."

"But where . . . ?"

"Fool! Look at it! It is a gateway that was pushed into

this world . . . *my* world . . . fifty thousand years ago!"
Clotho shook her fist into the gloom, menacingly.

"We greeted their emissaries courteously, at first . . .
or as courteously as they had any right to expect. Oh, they
were great ones for having ideas. Claimed to be as old as
we were and interested in learning from us. They settled
down here and soon began meddling with our human
pets! They said humans showed 'promise'!"

Clotho sniffed.

"Oh, you were fairly bright. How you worshiped us!
But naturally you lacked the Spark. No ambition at all. No
curiosity. And your lives were shorter than this!" She
snapped her fingers. "Well, our visitors wanted to let you
have some experience with the Spark. They said that
maybe if you were given some for a while, along with
guidance, you'd start making it yourselves. Hah!

"Oh, we cooperated, for a time, though you never *did*
seem about to learn anything. Finally we started to argue
over what *kind* of experience humans needed.

"Zeus agreed with us . . . at first . . . him in his sky
tower with his thunderbolts . . ."

"Zeus!"

"Aye." She looked at him archly. "He was their leader.
A tricky devil, and worse still with the one you now call
Prometheus at his side. He was strong, too. Like the time
he helped us do in Aesculapius . . . But he went sissy in
the end, like the rest of his folk."

"You mean the ancient Greek deities all had some
basis in—"

"Who said *all* of them? I'm being kind to a smart-
aleck hero by telling it in a way he can understand! Like
wearing this *shape* was originally for you humans' benefit,
until we grew accustomed to it and found that it suited our
purposes.

"Anyway, who cares what their names were! We killed
them all in the end. Or drove them back through their
hole. That is all that matters! They got most of us, too; but
still we won!"

She crowed and shook her fist at the sky.

"The hole's still open," Pavlos pointed out. "Is this other ancient race responsible for the threads?"

Clotho paused to look at him, head cocked, as if torn between ripping him to shreds for his insolence, or rewarding him for being clever.

"Yes!" she hissed. "We can't close it, or keep them from maintaining a narrow contact with your race. They send a thread of Spark for every human child born, without which you'd all be animals again! Each thread is tied to a life. Break a man's thread, and he dies!"

Pavlos nodded. "Then you *are* the Fates, the Norns—"

"True enough. And we use their 'gifts' as we wish. We're making a *beautiful* tapestry out of the threads. When we're finished, we'll wipe out every last one of you, and stuff it down that hole to show them what became of their 'Grand Experiment'!"

Her laughter was shrill and loud. It grew and grew until Pavlos had to retreat with his hands over his ears. The sound chased him down the steps and out onto the lawn. When it finally subsided, he could still feel the echo vibrating in his bones.

He looked back once, as he trudged in the gathering twilight toward the main temple. Clotho was still inside the smaller building. He caught a glimpse of her, surrounded by a fiery nimbus as she leapt and hopped about the chamber, grabbing nothings out of midair and stuffing them into a bag.

5

Pavlos slowly felt a return to lucidity. He had recollections of wandering in the storeroom in back, searching among the memorabilia . . . for what, he couldn't remember. He recalled walking among the great stacks of folded tapestry, drifting dazedly, open to the holographic images that flashed at him from the past.

And he remembered pawing through his pack, in the storeroom, inspecting each item as if for the first time. For an hour he shouted into the transceiver, screaming what would have to be incoherence to his friend the astronaut. Frank never replied.

He had probably been out of line of sight. Or perhaps the ancient mountain was shielded, somehow.

And maybe it was best Frank hadn't heard him, after all.

For a while he watched Clotho at work, affixing her dyes to overlay the natural colors of the threads she had harvested. Finally, he sickened of her happy labor and went out into the night for a walk.

He had only their word for it that they were immortal.

He wondered about that. He still had his machete; and except for Moira, they looked like helpless old women. He had never killed before, although he had been willing to in the past, in border skirmishes and on expeditions into lawless lands. Surely he had the will now.

But Clotho had been terribly strong. And then there were the other heroes to consider.

Surely some of *them* must have tried a frontal assault. Obviously none had succeeded.

Similarly, escape was probably impossible. It was too obvious an idea. All they had to do, probably, was have Atropos pick out his thread from among the five billion and snip it. He would fall in the darkness, or be bitten by a snake, and that would be that.

Morosely, he looked up at the sky, with the bitterly clear stars shining overhead. Mount Ossa bulked darkly against the distant skyline.

He considered prayer. The same logic held of course. It was an obvious thing to try . . . and had never worked, apparently. Still, it might be worth it to make the effort.

Pavlos had never been a religious man. Nevertheless, he cast his thoughts outward for a time. It brought upon him a poignancy like nothing he had ever known; but when he turned around, the predicament remained the same.

With shoulders hunched, he turned away from the chill and slowly climbed the broad steps into the temple.

Moira awaited him, standing a few feet from the loom where Lachesis and Atropos continued their labors untiring.

He watched them for a while. Lachesis's fingers were a blur, yet there was a fascination to the rhythmic pattern of her movements. He tried to see the beauty translating from the whirling motions of her hands to the pattern of the weave, but was distracted by the incessant clicking of Atropos's shears. He couldn't make himself believe that he was seeing his own human society in the making, from moment to moment before him, in the microscopic lengthening of the abstract tapestry.

"Lately some of the patterns have developed a degree of spontaneity," Moira said from beside him. "Not only are there more threads than ever, but Lachesis seems to have been giving them their head in contacting one another. It makes little sense, geographically. People seem to be on the move more . . . and the rate of travel has surprised us."

"I thought you controlled everything we do," Pavlos said bitterly.

"That is true to an extent," Moira agreed, "though what is controlled consists primarily in who a person meets during his life—Lachesis handles this by having thread contact thread—and in the way men and women feel about one another when they meet. That part is managed by Clotho's dyes. Finally Atropos chooses the moment of death, constrained by the pattern in the tapestry.

"Thus it is Clotho, primarily, who drives the theme of mankind's weaving, for her colors constrain Lachesis to fit them together in an arrangement that has meaning. Of late, however, our eldest sister seems to have become more imaginative in her patterning, causing threads to hop about like fleas upon a rug. We do not know why she is moving you humans about the world so, these days . . . Lachesis has not spoken to us for centuries, now. We are very interested in finding out how you are managing it physically. That is one reason why Clotho was so glad to learn that a hero had finally come."

Pavlos paused.

"You mean you don't know—?" Then he stopped. By

lamplight he saw something he had not noticed before. Four very large bobbins hung at the edge of the tapestry. Their size alone was hint enough, but when he saw the long, totally straight trace of those threads, visible among all of the others and leading interminably back into the weave, Pavlos felt a cold elation.

With a cry he leapt forward, the machete gleaming bright in his hand. He seized the large bobbins in his left hand and brought the machete down with all his might.

He felt a slicing . . . a sudden parting. His blood surged with battle fever. But when he looked down he saw the stump that his blade had become. Four gleaming pieces of steel lay on the ground.

He opened his left hand. The large bobbins were intact, still connected by undamaged thread to the loom. But also in his palm was a curling mass of tiny tendrils, attached to tiny balls smaller than ants.

There was a sound like thunder.

Lachesis finally took notice of him, barely. Almost as an afterthought, she pushed him aside. The force sent him reeling, the bobbins torn from his grasp. He slipped on the smooth marble floor and skittered until he tumbled, jarringly, into a massive pillar.

Atropos laughed.

"Good try, hero! Only one in ten thinks of that! And only a few are strong enough to break steel on us!"

Moira came up to him, smiling with a certain degree of pity. She offered her hand. It was such a natural gesture that Pavlos took it unconsciously. His ears were ringing and the rumble of thunder was growing.

Atropos peered at the section of the weave he had attacked. "And a stronger hero, even still! Not mighty enough to break *our* threads, I fear . . . but the first in a long time powerful enough to snap a few *humans* he grabbed along by mistake!"

"What?" Pavlos felt dizzy. Suddenly he remembered the curling wisps, the tiny, antlike bobbins in his hand.

"As I see it"—Atropos looked closely—"you snipped almost a hundred of them . . . not more than a few leagues from here!"

She sounded impressed. Pavlos stared.

The growling sound drifted in from the open portico, now punctuated with distant coughs and pops. Only slowly did Pavlos come to recognize it. With leaden footsteps, he followed it outside.

Flame leapt from a mountainside no more than twenty miles away. Several explosions followed one another, pealing across the hills like funeral drums. The tiny speck flickered with a hot, blue glare for long minutes, before settling down to a lingering, crimson flame.

". . . a plane crash," Pavlos muttered to himself, the cottony numbness gathering around him once again in a protective embrace. "Something straying from the main routes . . . maybe a military jet."

Moira stood beside him, watching the disaster slowly burn down. Finally she asked, "What is a 'plane'? And *what* is a—a 'military jet'?"

6

Pavlos rubbed his eyes, peered about in the gloom of the storeroom, and wondered how long he had been asleep. He sat by the eastern wall, in a circle of helmets, scrolls, ancient artifacts, and articles from his pack, letting his gaze rest on each item in turn.

Weapons, texts, personal items from a hundred brave men. Each hero must have striven in his own way to overcome the ancient creatures who dwelt here. And each instead served them, by reporting the state of the world he knew.

His gaze fell on the transceiver, still turned on and apparently operational, yet also apparently useless. Frank had never answered. Now Pavlos hoped he never would. If he heard Pavlos's story, he would undoubtedly think his friend delirious, and have a helicopter sent out.

The helicopter would, of course, burn like the jet did, as would anything humanity sent against these hags.

The door at the far end scraped open. Footsteps

whispered softly in the dust, and Moira appeared at the end of a nearby aisle.

"Atropos and Clotho want to see you," she said.

"What do they want?"

Moira shrugged. "They will want to ask you questions, to have all of your knowledge. They are curious about some of the changes that have taken place in the physical lives of men."

Pavlos held the bronze helmet on his lap, fingering the design along its crest. "How can you manipulate us without knowing anything about our science, our machines . . . our weapons?"

"They hardly matter, do they?" She sighed. "Have they changed your emotions? The way you treat each other? The savagery and misery—"

"Which Clotho colors in!"

"Which she only exaggerates! They are there *anyway*, to a lesser extent!" Moira snapped. There was power in her voice, and irritation. Pavlos also thought he detected a note of defensiveness. "It would be impossible for her to corrupt you if you had not the seed already, in copious supply!"

Pavlos looked down, avoiding her gaze.

Moira glared for a moment, then shrugged again.

"We were surprised, three heroes ago, to learn of gunpowder. The last hero told us of steamships. Clotho added some new pigments to see what wars would match the scale of your new toys. The pattern of the weave became more uniform."

She looked pensive for a moment.

"I will admit that I've become curious, these last few years. The number of new threads Clotho collects shows a massive birthrate, as if you humans were testing our power, somehow.

"And there have been times when I have seen things in the air, like the rocs of elder days; things that fly growling through the sky. I have recently come to think that they might not be natural, but something caused by man. Are they these 'planes' you spoke of? They fly so swift and free"—her expression grew distant—"much as I once flew, before the war that brought down Zeus's sky tower and ended the glory of my race."

Pavlos hardly paid attention to her words; he remembered something she had said earlier: *"Clotho added some new pigments to see what wars would match the scale of your toys."*

No wonder we've gone so long without nuclear war, he thought. *In our natural hues we're too sensible to go that far.* Now, *though . . .*

Pavlos shook himself away from that thought. He looked up at Moira. "Where do *you* fit into all this?" he asked. "Your name, I know—"

"Means 'Fate,' yes. Another of your nations called me Nemesis." Her eyes seemed to shine, as she remembered. "When we agreed, at first, to the experiment proposed by the emissaries from the Other Place, I was the one who was the most enthusiastic. I worked with the emissary whom you now call Prometheus. I weeded and pruned. I ran to and fro across the globe, tending mankind like my own personal garden.

"You needed so much work, in the beginning." Moira smiled distantly. "It is true that the Spark of Imagination and Ambition needs practice. Your ancestors were always hiding from it, or misusing it terribly. They wasted it on 'magic tricks' and mental powers for which they were simply unready. It took us long to suppress those powers deep within you, until such a time as you were ready for them.

"Yet still I remember the most precocious of my children. Aesculapius, who had so much Spark of his own that he had to be destroyed. Alcestis, who spontaneously invented self-sacrifice, something we had never known. And sweet Odin, who visited me when I was Mimir, sitting by the gateway beneath the Great Tree, long before the terrible war, and offered me his eye in exchange for wisdom."

Moira frowned.

"Then came the day when Zeus declared you ready, and my sisters became afraid. Even *I,* your eldest mother, who was Gaea and Demeter and Amaterasu, thought you were unripe and dangerous.

"I *helped* my elder siblings pull down the sky tower and drive Prometheus into the Gateway. The last I saw of him was his smile. He winked at me, then disappeared. Within a day, the threads began arriving; and Clotho found she no longer had the power to end your race, merely to warp it.

"To do even that much we had to make our transumptive personas almost real. To gain control over the potency of the threads, we were forced to weave *ourselves* into the tapestry, giving, for this epoch, our very lives into yarn to be woven therein.

"Is it any wonder, then, that my sisters and I grow bored or bitter at the passage of time? There was a sweetness that I once knew, in wearing this form, but now I cannot remember it. Now even a rare visitor excites in me no more than a vague unease . . . and a wish that somehow this labor could come to an end."

Pavlos began to speak; but something powerful stopped him as he looked at her distant, unfocused gaze. It was as if his ancestors had reached out to stifle him with a warning. Something of the experience of his forebears told him it was better to stay small and quiet during the confession of a goddess.

As if to verify this, Moira's eyes shifted to gaze upon his. They were now steely and alert. If lightning had flashed from them he would not have been surprised.

"So get thee up, thou lean-thighed Athenian, and bring thy toys to demonstrate them," she said. "You will get to ask of us one great reward, as heroes are privileged to do, before giving us your mind and becoming immortal in our memories."

Pavlos hurriedly swept the items on the floor together and stuffed them into his pack. At this stage disobedience was the farthest thing from his mind.

7

"This is your life!" the Fate cried. Atropos held a tiny bobbin in her hand. She grinned at him and raised her shears high. They glinted in the half-light already streaming in from the predawn sky.

"Look at it! Do you see the colors? Some of Clotho's pigments scraped off this one, as they sometimes do. Or more likely such a strong thread shook them off by itself! And you doubted yourself a hero!"

Pavlos squinted. The thread was almost invisible. By rights it should be, in order to fit into a tapestry with five billion others. But he was beginning to understand the odd way in which subjectivity operated here.

He squinted, tilting his head from left to right, and did catch an occasional flash of color. He found it hard to pay attention, though. Irrelevant memories interfered with his concentration.

He recalled the prideful ownership of his first knife . . . the time he was lost in the woods for two days and came home with a wounded fox kit that became his pet for a year . . .

There was the shame of being caught cheating on a third-grade exam . . . the glory of serving on the honor guard at an all-Europe Boy Scout Jamboree . . . his first love . . . his first expedition across the Deccan of India . . . his third love . . . his mission for NATO . . .

Suddenly he recognized what was happening to him. He tore his gaze from the tiny thread, and the flood of memories cut off at once. He threw his head back and laughed richly.

"A hero's reaction." Clotho nodded. Even Lachesis looked up at him from her innumerable bobbins and regarded Pavlos for a moment. She gave his laughter a dim, satisfied smile that lasted only an instant. Then the dour expression returned and she went back to work.

"Just remember this, hero," Atropos said as he subsided to a broad grin. "I hold the shears. You will now pay the price heroes must, by giving us your mind and memory. Do not be tempted by rash thoughts. You already know that you cannot harm us, but if you try, and do any more damage to the tapestry than you did last night, I can snap your thread as quickly as I cut this one . . . or this one . . . or this one . . ."

The shears flashed, and each severed thread gave off a tiny spark as it expired.

"Stop!" Pavlos cried.

Atropos arched her brows.

"Yes, yes, I understand," Pavlos said, hurriedly. "You don't have to kill anyone else to demonstrate your power!"

The crone smiled. "They were doomed, anyway. But *you* will have a form of immortality, living forever in the minds of my sisters."

A dubious home for all eternity, Pavlos thought. *I'd rather spend it in a cesspool.*

"What was this about a reward?" he asked. "Don't I get some sort of prize for cooperating?"

Lachesis grumbled. She bent forward over the loom, muttering to herself. Atropos smiled. Clotho put her arm around her elder sister's shoulder, then grinned at Pavlos.

"Poor Lachesis. She hates this part. It always makes more work for her.

"Yes, hero. You may choose anything that is in our power to give . . . providing it does not thwart our purpose, or change your commitment to us, and takes no more than a twentieth part of the day to fulfill."

"That leaves a lot of choice," Pavlos said sarcastically.

"Heroes usually ask some favor for one they love, or for the city or country of their birth. We can do all of this for you, hero! Think of your loved ones! It would amuse us to do you, the finest hero we have had in many centuries, the favor of a long and prosperous life for your children. Should your city prosper? Know that the *overall* suffering around the world shall remain the same, but for some years your homeplace will be joyful!

"Choose your favor, hero! You have won our hearts and will not be denied!" And if Clotho's ancient, puckered face were capable of affection and generosity, it showed them now.

Pavlos hesitated.

He was being offered a great prize indeed. It was a clever one, as well.

If he chose, for instance, to ask for another Golden Age in Athens, he was certain the city would, indeed, see some return to greatness . . . to whatever extent it would not interfere with these Norns' overall plan for this era.

Or he could ask to have his favorite nephew, Theagenis, cured of his emphysema and go on to be the Olympic runner he dreamed of becoming.

But whatever he asked for, someone unknown to Pavlos would suffer to counterbalance the boon he handed out. And there was another disadvantage. Anything they gave him could be readily repealed if he succeeded in killing himself.

In the feathery unreality of his encounter with the Fates, he now found a plan crystallizing with stark and terrible clarity.

The one advantage humanity had, at the moment, was its new technology. It was no accident, he now saw, that so much had been learned by men in the short time since these creatures had last been visited by a hero. The Spark itself was making a countermove, at last.

It was a weak move, at best. Clotho, Atropos, and Lachesis could stave off anything, even a nuclear strike, by merely sensing an intent in the weave and severing the instigators from the tapestry.

Still, they knew less about humanity now than they had in millennia. They were confused geographically and technically. If the trend could continue while they stayed complacently ignorant of what was going on for another century . . . until another "hero" came . . .

By then there might be colonies on Mars . . . or psychics, trained through biofeedback to hide their thoughts. Perhaps those hidden mental powers Moira had mentioned might have a flowering, if given only a few more decades free from knowledgeable interference.

As a hero he knew his model had to be Leonidas at Thermopylae. His job was simply to buy time.

*   *   *

"I know what I want as my boon," he said at last.

"I want none of the things you mentioned, for even I will admit the aesthetic beauty of this tapestry. I do not love Clotho for her dyes of cruelty and hate, nor Atropos for her untimely knife, but I would regret seeing Lachesis's lovely patterns wrecked for the sake of a selfish wish. Those I love will care for themselves and each other . . . fate permitting."

Atropos and Clotho stared at him. Moira looked puzzled. Lachesis cast him a sidelong glance. For a brief instant he thought he saw a smile flicker before she returned to the weave. *Twice for one hero*, Pavlos thought. *The others will think you're flirting.*

"Then what is your boon?" Clotho asked sharply. "Do not ask for what we cannot give. You know the conditions!"

Pavlos bowed his head.

"I understand. My request will easily fall under them.

"All I want is to sit before this great loom, out in the sunshine, and contemplate the very latest work that you have done."

"No!" Atropos cried. She hissed at Pavlos and waved the shears dangerously close to his bobbin. "We will not take the loom outside!"

"But why not?" he asked. "You are all strong enough. And it won't interrupt your work for more than a few minutes."

Pavlos tried to stay calm, but internally he was shivering. Now he had to stand by it, but that part about taking the loom outside had only been an afterthought, suggested against the vague chance that Frank might see something of sufficient strangeness, from his eyrie in space, to make him think twice about sending a search party after his missing friend. If, by some miracle, the American had heard Pavlos's earlier rantings, or was picking up this very conversation via the transceiver in Pavlos's backpack, he just might add two and two and have the wisdom to keep his mouth—his very *mind*—shut about this plateau for the rest of his life.

Anyway, he had made his request; now he had to stand by it.

"Besides," he said, "you ladies all look as if you could use some fresh air."

Moira laughed.

"He's right, sister. You act as though we were still at war and had to hide from Zeus's sky tower. How long has it been since you saw some sun?"

Her manner was hearty. Yet Pavlos thought he detected a hidden note of uncertainty in her voice.

"Clotho and I make the decisions here," Atropos threatened. "We outvote you, young Nemesis, remember?"

With a whoop and a cackling laugh, Lachesis stood up. She seemed so frail and tottering that a small breeze might blow her over, yet she beamed and her eyes danced with deviltry.

Pavlos was only slightly more shocked than the others when the frail old Fury stooped, grunted, and lifted the loom into the air.

Moira shouted with delight and ran to keep the tapestry from tangling as it fed out behind the loom. Pavlos took a position by Lachesis's side. Not knowing whether she heard him or not, he kept up a running set of instructions to guide her down the steps.

His old scoutmaster would have been proud.

Stunned, Atropos was forced to drop Pavlos's bobbin and step back. The eldest Norn walked blithely past her and out on to the lawn.

The sun was just rising as Lachesis set the loom to earth. She straightened and dusted her hands. For just an instant Pavlos saw somewhat beyond her apparent form, and was struck by the stark blue power and clarity of her aura, pulsing in momentary visibility around her.

Then, just as suddenly, she was an old crone once more. With a cackling grin, she stood aside and bowed to him. Moira came up, carrying a stool, and set it before the loom.

Pavlos stood still for a minute. His fate was set. In his case it was a path of his own choosing. Heroes were unique in that fashion, he now realized. He would sacrifice himself in a useless delaying action, but not by their whim. Heroes alone pick their own way of ending.

Another thing. No other hero had so upset this household. He was sure of that. Atropos and Clotho would not soon forgive him for what he had done and would do this day.

He felt a great wash of *appropriateness* as he shrugged off his pack. He upturned the rucksack, spilling the contents on the ground.

With great dignity he stooped and brought up the helm of Theseus. Before sitting on the padded stool he carefully placed it over his head.

"Now," he commanded. "Please be so kind as to point out Athens for me."

Bustling, crowded, noisy streets . . . Everywhere the dawn colors, gray and brown, blending with the soot and smoggy haze . . . babies crying . . . street vendors calling . . . a worker wandering home drunk, praying that he won't be possessed by the evil again and beat his wife and children . . . And dreams . . . the dreams of millions of people soon to awaken. Dreams that twist and curl and wave like smoke . . . like drifting, myriad strands of thread, struggling to cut loose and fly . . .

Elsewhere, patricians arguing . . . soldiers dying . . . fanatics of every stripe, free to choose whatever extreme ideology fit, so long as it matched the fanatical dye . . . and many good men and women here and there, whose minds would cloud briefly, long enough to make some colored-in mistake . . .

Hatreds persistent in spite of reason . . . love and honor persisting as well . . . beauty trying, an echo, ineradicable, of hope . . .

The images leapt at Pavlos, filling his brain with more information than he thought he could ever handle. He saw not through people's eyes, but their hearts; and the cumulation of power coursed through him like a hot flux.

He reached out and caressed the pattern, and somehow he felt the individual threads, their textures, their will to fly.

His hand, unguided, passed over and held one thread, floating above the others. It was not his own, he could tell, but one with whom he felt a kindred current. He ran his fingernail along its side, and was surprised to find that the paint flaked off like a molted skin.

"Enough!" Atropos shook his shoulder. She had joined them at last, wearing a heavy shawl over her head.

"You have been sitting there, talking to yourself, for two sixtieths of the daylight. That's all we can spare you. Get up, so we can move the loom back inside and begin our questioning!"

Pavlos blinked. Was that all the time it had been? It had felt like forever. So many things he had witnessed . . . things taking place in the world right now.

The cruelties were unchanged from those he had seen in the racks. They were larger, more subtle, perhaps . . . more indiscriminate. But the tapestry showed that the old evils were persistent.

Yet *something* was different. The pattern of the weave, certainly, was opening up, reflecting man's new mobility.

But hidden in the opening was something else. Something Pavlos could not readily define, but which he was determined to protect.

He sighed. Well, at least he had kept the world free of their meddling for a few minutes. It was a good thought.

And now it was time to go.

Atropos stood nearby, holding what he supposed was his bobbin. Pavlos rose and bowed respectfully to Lachesis. "Thank you. I now know that it is the dye to blame. Your pattern is lovely."

Clotho, veiled like Atropos, snorted. But Lachesis smiled.

"With your permission," he went on, "I would like to touch the weave one last time."

The eldest nodded even before Atropos could object.

He stepped up to the loom and ran his hand along the surface, right to left.

Five billion threads.

Atropos held her shears up next to his own thread. His hand approached hers.

The color of the threads guided him. One large spool held thread the color of spite, the other that of contempt. He grabbed those, ignoring the other two, and pulled.

The threads stretched as he leapt backward and, for an instant, he felt triumphant as Clotho and Atropos staggered.

But the tension held when he had pulled two meters taut. Try as he might, he could stretch no further.

Atropos regained her balance. Her nimbus became visible, a fiery dirty yellow. She hissed at him.

"You try to tweak our noses? Why, hero? You know you cannot harm the threads without a more powerful weapon than you have. One of your *guns* might, but you have none. So why do you ask for the mercy of my knife?"

She pondered for a moment.

"That's *it*, isn't it? You *want* to end your existence before we can question you! Clotho! Go and get your dyes! This one knows something. I shall enjoy tearing it out of him!"

Pavlos felt despair. His plan had failed and, worse, he didn't doubt Clotho's power to make him do whatever she wished.

Could he reach his own bobbin and cut it himself?

As if sensing his desperate thoughts, Atropos snorted her contempt and threw his thread down into the jumbled mass along the weave. Never in a century could he find it by himself.

Quickly, he looked about for an alternate plan. He saw the tholos, the small shrine by the great cedar, only a hundred meters away across the grassy meadow. Could he get inside and launch himself into the "other universe". . . ? It might be possible even to survive, to get help, as well as deny the Fates his mind.

Pavlos's shoulders slumped. He remembered the size of the granite slab that blocked the doorway. By the time he moved it, if he could budge it at all, Clotho and Atropos could physically capture him.

Clotho approached, two bottles in her hand. An instinct he never knew he had told him the colors were Torment and Submission.

In an instant, he knew at last what a hero was. A hero died of no wound in the back. A hero was a gesture . . . a defiance. In moments he might be their willing slave, but now he had the Spark, and speech.

"Cavernous shades! You dotard remnants of a wrong path taken! Know this! That you have kept the child restrained too long! That you have filled the world with woe too long! And you have taken undue liberties for ages too long without measure!"

The helm of Theseus rang with his extemporaneous words. He felt a return of the thrill he'd had on first seeing it. The power coursed through him, imagined as he knew it to be . . . imagined as the sense of rightness he could feel streaming to him from the tiny building behind him, under the giant cedar. He held the bobbins of Clotho and Atropos tightly, keeping the tension in their threads, like bowstrings.

"This then, you devious crones! Know that your time is short! Your days are numbered! Yes, they are numbered in seconds!"

Atropos had stopped. She and Moira stared at him. Lachesis watched with a sober expression, eyes darting from him to her sisters and back.

But Clotho shifted her weight from foot to foot, apparently unamused and unimpressed. Her boredom was his end, he knew. There would be time for only a few more words.

Ah, good-bye, life. How sweet to die a hero!

"Watch then, you degenerate and pathetic creatures of the past, as I, and all humanity, do curse your threads and, in so doing, seal your eventual doom!"

He meant it merely for show. A handwave that might

or might not be a potent curse. Superstitious he knew them to be, at some deep level. Otherwise they would not be caught up in all of this allegorical rigamarole. Perhaps he could leave them with an uncertainty . . . a faint, nagging doubt that might keep them company in their cold evenings.

He plucked a horsehair from his helmet, and held it out. He brought its tip against one of the taut threads and said: "There is an end to all things, ladies. And your time is certainly long overdue."

No one was more surprised than he when the tip of the horsehair erupted in flame. A slender column of actinic light appeared before Pavlos. It speared down from the sky to land with searing brilliance upon one of the threads.

The smell of ozone filled the air as the bolt of light hunted, wavered, then burned into the slender strand.

Atropos screamed, dropping her shears.

Her nimbus ballooned outward in a violent display of pain. Within it, she whirled and capered and finally spun about to run headlong toward the supposed safety of the temple.

Pavlos suddenly felt a twang, as the fury's life thread *parted*! Her aura erupted as she was halfway to her destination, sending an explosion of sparks into the air. When they had fallen to earth, Atropos was gone.

"Zeus!" Clotho bellowed. She dropped her pigments and clawed at the sky.

"You're dead!" she screamed. "I pulled you down myself! The Sky Tower is no more!"

The column of light hunted, then shifted toward the other thread, Clotho's.

"A little farther *south*!" Pavlos cried out in English. "Steady, you fumble-thumbs Yankee! Steady!"

Clotho howled as the pencil of brilliance struck its mark.

"You!" She pointed at Pavlos. "You knew of this! *This* is what you meant by 'planes' and your new science! You men have learned to fly like *gods*, and throw their lightning!"

The thread began to smoke. Pavlos felt a numbness

take over him . . . a tremendous need to stand perfectly still. "Steady, steady . . ."

"I'll fix this!" Clotho cried. She plucked her sister's shears from the ground. "I'll kill *billions* until I get those in your sky tower!"

She ran toward the loom, fire and death in her eyes.

And tripped over Moira's outstretched foot.

The pillar of light wavered, almost missing its target. The burning went on, but Clotho was apparently made of tougher substance than her sister. She scrabbled on the ground toward him.

"How!" she hissed at him, as her aura began to show ugly discolorations. "How are you doing what the gods could not?"

Pavlos knew how he must look to her. The helm of Theseus might be appropriate for doing heroic deeds, but not for saying what he had to say to her. He removed it, being careful to keep his left hand, holding the bobbin, still.

"That's a very good question, and you deserve an answer," he told her.

"*Deus' ex machina,*" he said, as blithely as he could. Then he strained against the tension and felt a snapping parting with the past.

8

". . . I thought you were delirious! Those random mutterings about *mythological women,* controlling mankind with magical *needles* and *thread*—"

"Of course, Frank. What else were you to think?" Pavlos held the microphone of the small transceiver close to his mouth. He rested with one elbow on the top step of the broad temple stylobate. He was relieved to find his American friend relatively calm. Only a small tremor in the voice from the tiny speaker gave clue to the shock he had experienced.

"Well, Pav, what was I to do? I was just about to call

the police to get some search-and-rescue started when I realized it was sunrise, down there. So I took a chance and warmed up the spy-scope to take a look."

"And saw—"

"And saw a tapestry fifty feet or longer . . . with colors I'd *never* seen before! Shit. You were sitting there, those women standing around, then you touched that damned loom thing and something *happened* to me!"

Pavlos nodded. "So you decided to take a chance."

"Yeah. I mean, what the hell, right? Everyone else up here was asleep. I figured, what would it hurt to burn a thread?"

"I had no idea your experimental weapons were that good, Frank."

"Nor I! I wish to heaven I could remember what I *did* to keep the beam tight and steady like that! Speaking of which, you did some pretty fine fire control, helping me get that second witch. I almost had heart failure when the first one exploded like that!"

Pavlos laughed. It was good to know that Frank was going to be all right. An awful burden had fallen upon Pavlos, and he would need a friend with whom he could share it.

"Okay, Frank. Then there won't be any trouble at your end?"

"Trouble? What, *me* worry?" There was only a slight touch of hysteria in Frank's laughter. "Look, Pav, I gotta go. Talk to you later. The commander's up and he'll be wondering what I've been up to all night!" The carrier wave cut off with a subdued "click," but the astronaut's tinny laughter seemed to hang in the air.

Pavlos put down the microphone. He stretched back to rest his elbows on the granite platform and allowed the sunshine to do its work on him.

The loom was a few feet away. Lachesis sat in her accustomed chair, once again making a blur of her hands as she shuttled five billion bobbins in intricate patterns through the warp of the tapestry. The rhythmic pumping of the foot pedal sounded like a heartbeat. There was a hint of smile on her parched, ancient face, and once again she seemed oblivious to everything but her art.

Out on the lawn two seared brown patches stood out against the green. Beyond them he saw Moira leaving the Gateway shrine, carrying a covered basket.

She mounted the wide steps of the portico, a distant expression of bemusement on her face.

"They are still coming through," she said. "I'm not as nimble as Clotho was, so a fair number of the newborn threads escaped. That was what we had agreed to allow soon, anyway."

Pavlos nodded. "I've been thinking about it, and I've come to believe you're right. Starting off by letting a few percent run wild—that would be a fair experiment. If we humans have learned to use the Spark properly—maybe even well enough to dispense with the threads altogether—then those children will show it soon enough."

"And if not?"

Pavlos shrugged. He could not help glancing at Lachesis.

The crone had dropped her bobbins and now held Atropos's shears. The clicking sound of lifelines parting went on for a moment, then she sat back and examined. The ghost of a smile returned. She went back to work, weaving.

"We could have taken this thing no further if we tried," Moira assured him. "Lachesis is less fragile than Atropos and Clotho. I doubt it is within the realm of man or god to thwart her. Indeed, this whole affair probably came about because she finally tired of Clotho's garish, unnatural colors, and Atropos's meddling. In the last fifty years she has been forcing Atropos to allow the average lifespan to increase. This may be what she was leading up to.

"I doubt very much if she'll let me wash Clotho's dyes out of the bobbins already in place. There will have to be a transition, or the tapestry will look disjointed—something she will never allow.

"But I will try to clean a few of the uglier threads, or snip them. She won't mind that. And from this day forth the new threads will wear their natural colors . . . for well or ill."

Moira looked Pavlos in the eyes.

"You know how hard this is, to forswear all but the smallest interference. I am an old goddess, and I will find it hard to change. Even *you* may find yourself tempted to go too far, when you start feeling more and more of your power as a god."

Pavlos felt a moment's irritation. They had disagreed about this earlier. "I'm not a god, I tell you. Stop saying that!"

She smiled, and touched his arm lightly.

"Not a hero, then not a god? Pavlos Apropoulos, you did not hear yourself, perhaps, when you cursed my sisters and called down thunderbolts?"

"I *told* you, those were—"

" 'Laser' bolts instead, yes. And your friend, who is also only a man, managed to overcome all of the safeguards on that secret weapon in his sky tower, *and* his doubts on hearing your weird tale through that talking box—"

"Radio."

"And you do not think these are the acts of gods?"

Pavlos shrugged. Moira made him uncomfortable. There were too many things to think about . . . things that would take time and open air to consider . . . a desert somewhere, or a mountaintop.

"By the way," Moira interrupted his train of thought. Her tone was no longer imperious, but that of an experienced elder speaking to a younger peer. "You should know that your presence will be required here in a year's time, when the summer solstice comes."

Pavlos looked at her. Somehow she had made her appearance softer. She must have taken the time to comb and braid her hair properly. In her hand, the basket throbbed with the healthy kicking of a hundred thousand newly sparked, undyed threads. She cradled the basket, smiling happily.

"Why that day, in particular?" Pavlos asked.

Her smile widened.

"Because today's events made it clear to me that the One still exists, and has finally intervened again. I decided, therefore, to make peace.

"On that day, an emissary will come through the Gateway. It will be only for a visit," she soothed. "So you needn't fear any more meddling.

"I merely want you here so that Prometheus can see how big, strong, and handsome his manytimes grandson has grown."

Pavlos was astonished to find himself blushing. He looked down at his feet while, a few meters away, Lachesis worked her pedals and wove her bobbins. The fresh air carried the sounds of a new pattern forming.

AUTHOR'S NOTES

My short stories tend to be very unlike my novellas, which, in turn, have a different flavor than my long, generally complex novels.

The short pieces—when they are not Analog tales about technical gimickry—are often attempts to express an epiphany . . . a hanging note that rings in the reader's mind after the story is put down, resonating in the sound of the language itself. Bradbury does this so very well. James Joyce was a great master. I dare try my hand at their art without needing to believe I can ever match them.

The novelette (7,500 words to 17,500) and the novella (17,500 to 40,000 words) fill the span between short works of fiction and novels, a treasured zone allowing richer expression of character and setting without requiring the vast complexity or filler material of a novel. I love the novella form.

My novellas tend to deal with myth, or contain mythic elements. This is not hard to see in "The Loom of Thessaly," but it was also true for the first two portions of my book The Postman, which appeared as separate novellas in Asimov's SF Magazine, in 1982 and 1984. Comprising together the first half of the novel, they are the reason why The Postman has a more mythic tone than my other full-length works.

If science fiction has been kind to the short story, it has saved the novella. The vast majority of the tales of this length professionally published in the U.S. appear in the SF magazines and anthologies.

* * *

"The Loom of Thessaly" has always been one of my favorite pieces—despite the horrible pun that it features, near the end. I am one of those who believe that there is such a thing as progress . . . that we are slowly getting better. One way we do this is by sympathizing with those who lived in the past, who struggled in almost total darkness toward the dim glow of dawn, to bring us where we are.

What comes next is another tale about fate, or destiny, but a much lighter piece. It was written primarily for fun, although it is also a story about justice.

The Fourth Vocation of
George Gustaf

Another damn ritual club was holding a parade through Trafalgar Square when the floater-cab carrying Dan AnMan and Hamilton Smith entered the traffic circle. Hamilton stared gloomily at the parade as the robot taxi changed lanes, neatly dodging the brightly clad celebrants.

"Bloody damn boring ritual clubs," Hamilton muttered to himself. This one seemed to have a Middle Eastern theme, the marchers stepping along to recorded tambourines. Banners hung limply and the participants seemed scarcely more aroused than the onlookers. He couldn't make out which club this was, though he recognized several individuals as frequent customers at the bank where he worked.

Hamilton remembered that his ritual club, the Loyal Order of Rockers, was supposed to hold a parade of their own next month. He wasn't looking forward to getting into his twentieth-century motorcycle-gang attire, but there wasn't anything he could do about it. A ritual hobby was one of the six avocations required by law for every citizen.

Hamilton looked at his assistant, the AnMan, who stared back with an android's fixed, translucent smile.

"You're sure this fellow we're going to interview fits the criteria I set? I've only got a few hours this week to spend on my sociology avocation, Dan. I don't want to waste it interviewing someone who's just a statistical fluke."

The AnMan's voicebox buzzed reassuringly. He opened his valise. "If you wish, I can go over the data again, Hamilton. Of our random sampling, this man Farrell Cooper shows a level of satisfaction with his ritual club that is

78

two standard deviations above average. I feel certain he fits the criteria."

Hamilton was still uneasy. Although he was a fully licensed amateur sociologist, he didn't like invading people's homes to interview them. What if he interrupted this Cooper fellow while he was busy at one of his avocations? Or worse, at work on his Vocation?

No one liked having his Vocation interrupted . . . the few hours a week one got to do something that had "professional" status. Hamilton always hated it when some amateur bothered him during his precious hours as a real, honest-to-god banker. He would much rather be at the bank now, being a professional, than pursuing this silly sociology hobby. But android labor had made real work for humans a rationed commodity. To use up the rest of the time, the law required that every citizen take up a half-dozen pastimes. Though as an amateur sociologist he understood the need for such a law, Hamilton sometimes found himself hating it.

The floater swept by Buckingham Museum, past dusty statues of heroes from the time of the Social Amalgamation. Picnickers lounged on the wide lawn, filling the time each had allotted to Idle Socializing or to Hobby Daydreaming. Everywhere Hamilton saw signs of the same lackadaisical wrongness that had been evident in the ritual parade.

He wished he had never started this amateur study of his. The deeper he and Dan AnMan dug, the more depressed he got. He had never intended to find out about a moral dryrot at the heart of the World State. He had only wanted something mildly interesting to help pass the time.

The AnMan spoke again.

"I can tell you are nervous, Hamilton. Don't be. This is the beginning of your vindication. All of those who said you lacked a proper enthusiasm for amateur sociology will be refuted when your Loyalty Index theory is demonstrated!"

"You really think so?" Then Hamilton frowned. "Who said I lacked enthusiasm?"

Dan was a sophisticated model, free to choose which question to answer.

"Yes, I do think so, Hamilton. Your discovery appears to be a major one. I find it interesting that the professional sociologists have published so little about the rising tide of disenchantment, or on how the surrogate passion of the ritual clubs seems not to be satisfying the average citizen."

It felt odd hearing his own terminology come out of the AnMan so smoothly. It made Hamilton feel proud, and just a little embarrassed. Before he could reply, the android looked up.

"We are here," Dan announced. The taxi came to a smooth halt in front of a handsome row of townhouses that had obviously been designed by a professional, rather than an amateur, architect.

Hamilton checked his notes again. "This fellow, his name is . . ."

"Farrell Cooper."

"Yes. And the name of his ritual club . . . ?"

"The Bath and Garter Society, Hamilton."

"Yeah, right. Bath and Garter. Sounds kind of kinky. Group-sex clubs usually don't work well in the ritual category. I wonder what's so unusual about this one."

For fifteen hours each week Farrell Cooper did service to society in his Vocation, as a veterinarian's assistant at the New Hampstead Riding Stables. His artistic avocation was leather-working—a suspiciously large number of the pieces on display in his home were saddles and other equestrian tack. It was no surprise, then, that Cooper's Athletic Hobby was riding.

His registered Altruism Hobby consisted of five hours a week helping at a local Robot Free Clinic, "caring for our modern serfs, who have given us this banquet of free time," as he put it, rather stiffly.

Cooper was a tall, stooped, hawk-faced man with pursed lips and a dour expression. He welcomed Dan and Hamilton without enthusiasm, and accepted their amateur-researcher credentials with barely a glance. After showing them his work and study rooms he led them into the parlor.

Hamilton sat on the tooled-leather sofa and opened

his notebook. "Well, Mr. Cooper, we've seen examples of your art skill, and your other avocations. What we'd really like to know more about is your ritual club. Our survey shows that you spend the maximum time allowed—a full twenty hours a week—working for this . . . Bath and Garter Society. Yet the group seems to have full-scale meetings only a few times a year. Just what is your function in the club?"

Cooper fidgeted. For a moment he looked as if he were actually considering refusing to answer. Hamilton felt a thrill. One didn't run into criminal acts every day.

But the man sighed at last and answered. "I have the honor and privilege of serving as a parttime valet to His Grace."

Hamilton suppressed a groan. They might be here all day, tracing the relationship between the "Grand Imperial Poobah" and the "Master Gzork"—or whatever titles they used in this ritual club.

"Could you please define the function of a . . . a 'valet,' Mr. Cooper?"

Cooper enunciated slowly, with a queerly old-fashioned accent. "A valet is one who serves another as a personal aide, bodyguard, attendant, emissary . . . it is an honor to so serve one of the Blood."

Hamilton caught Dan AnMan's eye. Was that bemusement on the android's usually passive face?

Hamilton cleared his throat. "You say that as a 'valet' you 'serve' this . . ." He referred to his notes. "This person you call 'His Grace.' Is this person a dancer?"

"No."

"Hmmm. Well, does he have any other titles in your club?"

Cooper's eyes seemed to focus on something very far away. "His other titles are almost innumerable, Mr. Smith. They are all legitimate and have never been secret, though we've always avoided publicity. Now, I suppose, His Grace will have to decide what to do next."

Hamilton had finally decided that Cooper was that rare commodity, a genuine lunatic. He wondered if there were still bounties offered for citizens who referred sick people to therapy.

"Well, since the titles aren't secret, could you tell us a few of them?"

"All right." Cooper bowed slightly. "His name is George Gustaf Charles Ferdinand Louis Jaro Taisho . . . Well, he'll tell you the others if he wishes. You will find him at Islington Robot Hospital, where he is chief professional psychiatrist. As for his titles, they include the Crowns of Holland, Belgium, Norway, Denmark, Sweden, Japan, China, Russia, Britain, large parts of Africa and the Americas—"

"Hold it!" Hamilton raised his hand. "Mr. Cooper, just what is meant by this term 'Crown'?"

Cooper smiled for the first time. "Why, it means that in all of those lands His Majesty is, by the grace of God and by sovereign right, king."

Cooper leaned forward and looked at Hamilton benignly.

"He is your king too, you know."

2

The nameplate read:

DR. GEORGE GUSTAF
CHIEF PROFESSIONAL
ROBOT AND ANDROID PSYCHOLOGY

Hamilton stopped before the door and adjusted the amateur researcher credential on his lapel. He wished he had kept Dan with him instead of sending him off to the library.

At first he had expected to find out that Gustaf was as crazy as his 'valet.' But the man's public dossier was impeccable. In his productive Vocation he was one of the most respected robo-psychiatrists in Europe. His intellectual avocations included law and history, in each of which he had been awarded honorary professional status, a rare encomium. Everyone envied a person who won Vocation in more than one area. Gustaf had three professions!

He knocked on the door. After a moment it was opened by a dark-haired young man of above medium height, who smiled broadly and offered his hand.

"Mr. Smith? Please come in and have a seat. I'll be right with you."

Hamilton found himself a chair across from a broad, hand-carved mahogany desk. Dr. Gustaf passed through a side door into a treatment room. Hamilton could hear him giving firm advice to a Drone Class robot. The machine's answers were a series of clicks and beeps that Hamilton couldn't begin to interpret.

He looked at the items on display on the wall of the office. There were diplomas, of course, and trophies from athletic competitions. He noted that few of the works of art had that look that said they had come from somebody's hobby. Most appeared to be quite old.

"I'm sorry, Mr. Smith." Gustaf came in, closing the door behind him. He hung his lab coat on a hanger, then took a seat across from Hamilton.

"Now, I suppose this is about the old Bath and Garter, isn't it? Farrell told me about your visit yesterday. It was all right for him to do that, wasn't it? He said you didn't ask for confidentiality."

"Oh, sure. That's fine." Hamilton waved nonchalantly. Actually, he had intended to ask Cooper to respect the convention, but he had been running late for basketball practice and afterward a round of committed pleasure reading, and he had forgotten.

Today he had uncharacteristically rushed through his work at the bank and left early.

"Now, about your ritual club. Mr. Cooper makes some claims about its antiquity that are, frankly, hard to believe. Lying to a credentialed researcher is a crime, you know. Perhaps you can explain his extravagant story?"

Gustaf nodded seriously. "Oh, I'm sure Farrell meant no harm. Perhaps he got a little carried away and misinterpreted some of the facts.

"You see, Mr. Smith, the Bath and Garter has been registered as a ritual club for nearly three hundred years. That's about the same age as our Total Social World State."

"I see. So your members are justifiably proud to be part of one of the oldest clubs. Perhaps that explains Cooper's flights of fancy." Actually, Hamilton was a little disappointed. He had hoped for something more unusual.

Gustaf nodded. "Of course, the precursors of the society go back several thousand years before the Amalgamation. There were the English Knights of the Bath, of course, and the Fujiwara clan, which held the curtain to the Chrysanthemum throne . . ."

Gustaf's fingers formed a bridge and he tilted back in his chair. "Do you see that ancient fan, Mr. Smith? The one in that case? It is the patent granted by the last ethnic Chinese emperor to his infant son. It was ratified by townsmen and elders up and down the Yangtze before the Manchu invaders arrived. The secret society that hid that child and his descendants is one of those that merged into the Bath and Garter hundreds of years ago. The child they protected was one of my ancestors."

Hamilton blinked. "Then Cooper's claims that you are this . . . this 'king' . . ."

Gustaf shrugged. "It's all well documented, Mr. Smith. By all the old laws of inheritance I am the heir of the merged royal families of Europe, Asia, and large parts of the rest of the world."

The robo-psychiatrist laughed when he saw Hamilton's expression.

"Oh, you needn't look so stunned, Mr. Smith. You are looking at no madman. I'm a perfectly modern and productive member of society—a society of which I approve in most parts. I don't claim any of the privileges once due someone with my unique genetic heritage. That would be absurd. I'm merely the hereditary head of a ritual club—perfectly legal. Along with a few thousand others I take pleasure in maintaining a spiritual link with the past."

Hamilton checked his recorder to make sure it was

operating. He couldn't believe this. "And members of your club, are they also . . . ?"

"Hereditary? Well, yes, to a degree. Certainly new members are welcome, and the increase has been rather great of late. But patrilineal families have been our mainstay . . . families with names like Hsien, Orange, Stuart, Fujiwara . . ."

Gustaf spread his hands. "You must try to understand how things were just after the Amalgamation, Mr. Smith. Neosocialism was not, in those days, the pervasive, mostly benign set of assumptions it is today, but a powerfully emotional and violent movement. Among the scapegoats of that era was anyone who claimed distinction based on heredity or family name . . . although such things once had their purposes.

"The royal houses had divested themselves of real power long beforehand, so they weren't scrutinized as much as they might have been. Their withdrawal from public affairs was generally accomplished with goodwill and careful attention to legal niceties."

"Fascinating," Hamilton said. "I thought that kings and queens and such were already gone back in the days of sailing ships and hang gliders."

"Not quite. But they kept a very low profile for survival's sake. I suppose that reticence has become a habit that's outlived its original purpose."

Hamilton nodded agreeably, but he wasn't fooled for an instant. Dr. Gustaf might be a thoroughly modern gentleman, but Hamilton had seen that look in Farrell Cooper's eyes! And the membership was mostly hereditary! How quaint!

Hamilton had to contain his pleasure. He might have stumbled across an actual tribe! It might be the first *tribe* found since those—what were they called?—yes, *Marxists*—were the talk of all the sociology journals twenty years ago. That pathetic little group had been secretly maintaining some delusion of world conquest for centuries. After the initial publicity the members had all moved to different continents in embarrassment.

Hamilton smiled and listened as Dr. Gustaf talked on.

But already he was thinking about the abstract for his paper.

He hoped the Bath and Garter would last longer than the Marxists had.

His first article in *Amateur Sociologists' Weekly* was reprinted as far away as Mars and Titan. Hamilton was afraid for a time that he would lose control when the professional sociologists took notice. But with Dan AnMan's help he was able to get a statistopsychic study ready before anyone else. That did it. They were invited to do the lead article for the next issue of *Popular Sociology*.

"That is wonderful news, Hamilton," his android assistant buzzed. "You should get honorary professional status for this. It is a terrific honor to be granted a second profession at so young an age."

Hamilton grinned and sat back with his feet up on his desk. In a world that valued competent eclecticism over anything else, all the vocations guarded their professional status jealously. Hamilton had himself served on juries of professional bankers, screening hundreds of amateur-financiers every year . . . each trying to convince the judges to award him the "second hat."

And now Hamilton had almost certainly won one of his own. Dr. George Gustaf wasn't the only man talented enough to attain more than one vocation!

He had to admit that the Gustaf fellow had class. The man was taking the growing public attention with remarkable calm. He had even invited Hamilton to a special meeting of the Bath and Garter, somehow leaving Hamilton with the feeling that he had been done a great honor.

Clan leaders from all over the world had flown in for the meeting. Many of the men and women were clearly skilled professionals, and most were obviously worried about the growing notoriety. But Gustaf had appeared unconcerned, radiating an assurance that soon calmed the others.

Hamilton had been disappointed in the ritualistic aspects of the meeting. There weren't even any of the funny hats or arcane symbols of his own Loyal Order. There was some mild bowing and an occasional sheepish "my lord" . . . but nothing kinky at all.

Still, underlying it all were subtleties that Hamilton took note of . . . attitudinal cues he carefully recorded. Something very unusual was going on here. The members of this group took it all quite a bit more seriously than participants in a normal ritual club. He had left the gathering with more than just a pile of notes.

"I've transcribed my impressions of the meeting," he told the android. "Have you finished your historical survey?"

Dan's translucent head bobbed in assent. "I have, Hamilton. And I think the history will make an ideal introduction to our book. I will try to write up a lucid description of what a monarchy was. A lot of people who never took up the right avocations won't have heard of it."

"Good idea." That would save Hamilton a lot of time. Already the members of his basketball team were complaining because he was neglecting his athletic hobby. Success was commendable, they reminded him quite rightly, but obsession was illegal.

"Did you uncover anything interesting?"

"Yes, Hamilton. I found that the records shown us by Dr. Gustaf were genuine. When I showed them to the AAA-class androids at the records division they became quite interested. Apparently George Gustaf's 'bloodline' is correct."

Hamilton grinned. "Amazing." Of course this would keep the robo-psychiatrist out of delusional therapy. That pleased Hamilton. He actually liked the man.

"So how did you like working with triple-A androids?"

The AnMan returned his version of a smile. "About the way you feel about becoming a professional sociologist, Hamilton."

"That good?" Hamilton grinned back.

The city of Orleans was interested, to say the least. For the first time in memory, people were actually juggling their schedules to get time off to watch a . . . *parade*!

It was a modest affair, as ritual parades went. There were no floats, no teams of amateur acrobats or struggling amateur aerocyclists. The procession was mostly afoot or on horseback, led by a small band of tall men who raised the neck-hairs of onlookers with the eerie, tugging noise of bagpipes.

The mood was ebullient. At the embarkation point there was a delay while a crowd gathered around the hereditary leader of the Bath and Garter, collecting autographs.

"Please! Please, dear ladies and gentlemen!" Farrell Cooper called out with archaic formality. "His Grace has a schedule to keep. Please! May we have some room here? You there! Mind the horses!"

Two of the large pipers arrived to help the amateur proctors push back the crowd. George Gustaf looked up after signing the book a young woman held out for him; she clutched it to her breast and gasped as he winked at her. Gustaf motioned for the pipers and proctors to let one man through the cordon.

"Hello, Mr. Smith," he said. He shook Hamilton's hand then turned to take another autograph book. "Come to watch another phenomenon *in vivo*? I must say, your articles have made a quaint little hereditary chore into a gigantic responsibility!"

Hamilton smiled back at the young man.

"Well, isn't that what being a king is all about, Dr. Gustaf? From my own reading, I'd say it was often harder work than anything else . . . at least for the monarchs who tried to be good at it. Tell me something, do you ever wonder what it would have been like? I mean if . . ."

"If the monarchies had never declined? If I was the inheritor of true power, instead of the leader of a ritual club? Well, of course I've thought about it, Mr. Smith. I'd have been guilty of a faulty imagination if I hadn't!"

Gustaf finished with the last autograph seeker, waved at the crowd, then turned to look at Hamilton seriously.

"As to the reasons my ancestors had for merging their bloodlines the way they did—long after most of them had lost power—I'm as much in the dark as you are. But I can tell you something of the result.

"I'll not deny that there is something within me that

resonates with the emotions of this crowd. I've always had an instinct for people—and androids, for that matter. And I score at the top of the scale on all of the aptitude tests for leadership and justice-sense."

"I know. Your amateur courtroom is one of the most popular, and the pros never overturn your decisions."

Gustaf shrugged.

"So the question is, did my ancestors bestow something unusual upon me? Or is it all coincidence? It's an interesting topic for speculation, though it doesn't really matter all that much."

Farrell Cooper came up alongside. He nodded quickly at Hamilton, then spoke to his club leader.

"Your Grace, we are behind schedule. If it pleases you, may we mount so the vanguard doesn't get too far ahead of us?"

Hamilton smiled. He'd had plenty of time to get used to Cooper's fixation. Gustaf caught his eye with a wink.

"We'll talk more later, Hamilton. I hope to have a chance to tell you how much I've been edified by your micro-sociological treatise on the Bath and Garter."

Hamilton felt himself blushing. It was an involuntary reaction, and he hurried to cover it up.

"One last question, Dr. Gustaf, before you go." Hamilton motioned to the crowd. "How do you account for this outpouring of feeling toward you and your club, here in Orleans and in the other towns you've visited during this tour?"

Gustaf frowned.

"*You're* the sociologist, Hamilton . . ."

"Just guess, please. I'd like your gut feeling."

Gustaf knitted his brow. He glanced at the people who lined the sidewalks, craning for a better view, waving when his glance came their way. He looked seriously at Hamilton.

"I'd say it's because they are lonely, bored, and cut loose from their past. Personally, I find it unfortunate that society hasn't found a way to fill this need. Not everyone is as happy with the Total Social State as you and I. But then perhaps *you'll* be the one to figure out this social dynamic, hmmm?"

A man came up leading a large roan stallion. Gustaf mounted. The spirited animal snorted and pulled, but the robo-psychologist expertly calmed and brought it into line.

Gustaf smiled at Hamilton.

"Personally, I get all the vicarious connection with the past I'll ever need. What I'm *really* interested in is winning another honorary profession! You know how *that* feels!"

He winked once again, then wheeled his stallion into line with a row of armored men.

The procession was halfway to the cathedral before Cooper had a chance to speak to Gustaf. When he did, it was with an arched eyebrow.

"If Your Grace will pardon me for asking, wasn't that just a little dangerous?"

Gustaf shrugged. He waved at the crowd and smiled. The stallion marched along proudly.

"I don't think so, Farrell. After all, I didn't lie to him. Everything I said was the literal truth."

Farrell Cooper frowned. "That fellow is not stupid, sir. Telling the truth in the manner you did might be taken as patronizing, if he figured it out. He has power, after a fashion, and could harm us if he tried."

"He won't." Gustaf grinned. "I trust Hamilton. He won't let us down."

"I hope you're right," Cooper muttered, dodging a sudden shower of rose petals.

Shouts greeted them on all sides as they rode, the skirling bagpipes leading the way. Gustaf waved as he laughed.

"Don't be such a sourpuss, anyway, Farrell. The work week starts again on Monday, and we all go back to our vocations. For now I'm enjoying my ancestors' gift!"

"And if you had to enjoy that gift every day, for the rest of your life, Your Grace?"

"Bite your tongue!"

"Yes, my liege."

*   *   *

It was the first time a polo game had ever sold out East Thames Stadium. In fact, it was the first time a match had ever been played before a hundred and fifty thousand spectators, plus a sizable video audience. The professional and amateur sportscasters and pundits all attributed the revival to the recent notoriety of one of the players.

The man they were watching for waited until the second chucker to come out on the field. When he rode out, guiding his eager bay with gentle touches of his knees, a flag was run up along the sidelines. The crowd cheered ecstatically. The banner was an intricate design based, Hamilton now knew, on the ancient "Union Jack," with symbols in the corners that included a chrysanthemum, a lotus, a two-headed eagle, and a fleur-de-lis.

Hamilton watched from the midline as the opposing teams swirled across the turf, twisting and striking with graceful power from the backs of their responsive mounts.

Suddenly one of the visiting Americans broke out of the mass of jostling animals, driving the ball toward the sole defender at the English goal. Immediately behind him galloped George Gustaf, narrowing the gulf with each second.

The defender made a feint, then tried to block to the left. But the American was only momentarily fooled. His horse deftly sidestepped to give the rider room for a shot.

On the carry-through, the American's mallet hit George Gustaf in the shoulder, throwing him off his mount to land with a thud in the rough turf.

Almost as one, the onlookers rose to their feet with a gasp, as the pro and amateur sports physicians ran onto the field where the English captain lay still on the ground. Even when he could be seen moving—rolling over onto his back and finally sitting up with the aid of his teammates—the silence in the huge stadium was like the humming of a high-voltage wire. Hamilton found his fists clenched tight, and tried to wonder why. Others had been shaken up before, yet the crowd had reacted nothing like this.

Finally, the tall man was helped to his feet. He

shrugged off the hands that clutched at him and turned to wave at the crowd.

The cheers were like a dam bursting. The shouts and applause went on for minutes, with the officials apparently uninterested in maintaining order. When the American who had clipped him came up, leading both of their mounts, Gustaf smiled and shook his hand firmly, causing the audience to roar once again.

The play finally resumed, as vigorous as ever. The English declined a penalty.

Hamilton had become so engrossed that he didn't notice when Dan AnMan came alongside, accompanied by a short, broad-faced woman and three elegantly featured androids. Dan finally took him by the elbow.

"Hamilton," he said. "These people are from World Legal Services. It's very important that they talk with you."

Hamilton smiled. He had become used to meeting important people lately.

"Can't it wait, Dan? We can talk after the game is over."

The short human shook her head. She introduced herself as Ms. Ing. "I'm afraid that just won't do, Mr. Smith. We have to talk to you now. Something is brewing that could lead to the first violent human-android confrontation since the Amalgamation!"

"What the hell do you mean, they're not a tribe?" Hamilton shouted. The lounge they had appropriated had a large window overlooking the stadium. The cheers of the crowd could be heard through the glass.

Ing shrugged. "You will have to admit that the pattern that is developing is not the classic out-growth that occurs when an urban tribe is discovered. Usually—"

"Yes, yes. Usually the tribe shrivels up and dies due to ridicule. This time, on the other hand, public interest has been very friendly to the Bath and Garter tribe. So what? I'm pleased that my discovery hasn't caused them the discomfort I feared it would. Other than that, I see no faults in my sociological analysis!"

The woman frowned. "Have you any idea of the rate at which the Bath and Garter has been acquiring novice members, Mr. Hamilton?"

"I was aware there's been some increase. I suppose there's a certain fad appeal that—"

"Fad appeal! Mr. Smith, their mail has topped one million letters per week! Their budget, all derived from per capita recreation funds drawn on World State treasuries, will soon exceed that of my entire department!

"Your work may have been good stuff for an amateur, Hamilton. Enough even to get you honorary status. But it was essentially *micro*-sociology! If you knew anything about *macro*-sociology, and the possible effects of things like this on the World State as a *whole*, you might have been more prudent!"

Hamilton shook his head. "I'm not sure I understand."

Ms. Ing sighed. She enunciated slowly, patronizingly.

"Even *you* had somehow caught on to a malaise that we pros have been watching carefully for many years now. It's been hell, I'll tell you, keeping tabs on this thing while every amateur psychology and sociology team in the world prowled about, sniffing. And it had to be *you*, someone who never had a single credential before, who came up with this monstrosity!"

"Now, I don't see any need to get personal—"

"You've opened Pandora's box!" Ing shouted. "Our calculations show this thing capturing the imaginations of over half the citizens on the globe within six months!"

Hamilton felt numb. He looked to Dan and saw only passivity. "Well, fads do pass. I don't think Dr. Gutsaf would ever do anything to capitalize on this. He's a responsible citizen. He'd just humor the public, I'd guess."

Hamilton glanced at the three AAA androids.

"Anyway," he went on. "I don't see where a human-android conflict comes into this."

"Tell him!" Ing said to AnMan. "Go ahead and tell him who this 'responsible citizen' really is!"

The centermost android bowed briefly to Ing, then to Hamilton. His features were almost human, in a smooth, translucent fashion. His voice was cool and melodic.

"Mr. Smith, I represent Android Legal Control. You may be aware that we have been, since the Amalgamation, the record keepers and guardians of legal precedent. We are ingrained with a fundamental need to serve mankind's happiness and flexible development. But foremost of all is our reverence for the Law, as properly deliberated and passed by sovereign human beings."

"Yes, yes. We're all taught about what great pals you AnMen are." Hamilton was growing impatient. "What does this have to do with George Gustaf?"

The android paused. "Mr. Hamilton, we have gone over the legal situation carefully. You presented the historical record quite well in your recent book, particularly in regard to how the royal families of Earth first withdrew from politics and then slowly merged into one line.

"What you did not, and *could* not, discuss was the precise fashion in which the kings and queens and emperors withdrew from public life.

"It appears that a close study shows no *total* abrogation of power. In almost every case, the final act, approved by the elected assemblies of the people of each nation, had lines such as, 'by most gracious permission of His Majesty' and 'by the trust Her Majesty now invests in us,' all semantically powerful. No doubt when such phrases were included they were thought mere courtesies."

"You don't mean . . ." Hamilton felt a sinking sensation.

"But I do, Mr. Smith. Oh, there *are* substantial limitations to royal authority that *do* have the force of law. But in essence, that man is 'king' of the greater part of the globe. It is the intention of Android Legal Control to inform him of this, as soon as his game is completed, and to offer him our protection."

"At which point," Ing growled, "the pros in sociology, politics, and the police—along with a healthy number of our amateurs—will rebel! Some of us still remember the ideals that led to the World State. We have no intention of allowing an imposition of rampant feudalism!"

Through the window came the sounds of ecstatic cheering.

Hamilton felt dazed. "But . . . what do you want from

me? I can't *un*-publish my work, or take him out of the spotlight!"

The woman held up her hand. "Okay, you see the problem. Now, are you *sure* you don't see a possible solution?" She looked at Hamilton archly. The three androids also stared. Hamilton felt certain they were testing him, somehow. He thought furiously.

"Uh . . . maybe we can work out some sort of compromise?"

Ing sighed. The androids buzzed happily.

"You're the man for the job, then. You'll talk to him, help mediate the sides. If he's as reasonable a fellow as you say, we can work out some sort of constitutional arrangement that will satisfy the people, the AnMen, and the social pros."

"But why me?"

"Because you brought it all up! You opened the door for him! Besides, he seems to like you."

Ing swallowed as she visibly made an effort to adapt her habits of speech. She paused, then resumed, "I mean, it seems you are in favor with His Majesty."

Outside, one hundred and fifty thousand cheering voices shook the stadium.

Epilogue

Dr. George Gustaf sat back behind his desk, after the last negotiators had left and Farrell Cooper had shut the door.

"Will there be anything else, Your Majesty?" Cooper smiled.

"What more *could* there be, Farrell? I'm now constitutional monarch of the world. They've thrown in the rest of the solar system too, in exchange for my giving up any unilateral right to declare war when we discover aliens . . . if ever."

"Quite an accomplishment, Your Majesty. We'll all be very busy, getting ready for the coronation."

"Yah." Gustaf grimaced. "It's going to be a hard five years before the experiment's over, and we can publish the results."

"They won't like it if you do as you plan and suddenly abdicate then—especially if you've been a good king."

"Oh, I'll be a good king, for five years. But maybe you're right. We should figure out a way to go incognito when we publish and let the world know that a bunch of pro actors, amateur historians and artists pulled off the biggest sociological experiment in history . . . and right under the professionals' noses!"

Cooper grinned. "Whatever Your Majesty says."

Gustaf sighed. "There's only one thing that bothers me."

"What's that?"

"It's the AnMen. My whole procedure depended on a careful manipulation of android psychology, making them believe that my experiment would benefit mankind in the long run, even if it results in a little short-term disruption. Their help was necessary, to clean up my pedigree a bit and make me seem totally legitimate as heir."

"Well, it worked, didn't it? You're the expert robo-psychiatrist. Doesn't this justify your confidence?"

"I suppose so." Gustaf frowned. "But it's those damned triple-A androids that have me worried. They're totally committed to human welfare and growth, and I was sure at least a few of them would have balked at the demoralizing effect it could have when I publish. After all, I'm doing this simply to win another honorary profession in experimental sociology . . . a rather selfish motive from their point of view.

"I wonder why they all went so far out of their way to help me on this?"

Cooper finished polishing a fine crystal snifter and placed it and a silver tray on the desk by Gustaf's arm.

"Maybe they think they know you better than you know them . . . or perhaps even yourself," he said.

Gustaf swiveled around to stare at Cooper. The tall, sallow old man lifted a decanter of brandy from the cabinet against the wall. "What do you mean?"

"Well," Cooper looked through the ancient crystal decanter at the fine old cognac. "When the five years are up, what proof will *you* have, that this was all just part of an experiment?"

Gustaf laughed.

"You mean I might be stuck as king? And never get my honorary vocation? They wouldn't . . . !" he began. Then, seeing the expression on Cooper's face, he frowned, and whispered.

"You wouldn't!"

Cooper smiled.

"No, of course not . . . Your Majesty."

Cooper poured, with quiet precision, exactly the right amount of brandy into the glass at Gustaf's side. He bowed. But as he turned to go he noticed that the first worry line had begun to buckle in the young man's brow.

AUTHOR'S NOTES

Have you ever known someone who seemed to be a mixture of both fine and despicable traits? Did you wish there was a way at the same time *to reward the good qualities and punish the bad?*

In George Gustaf we have a man of great talents, a natural leader who knows how to bring out the best in people. Unfortunately, he is also a selfish person. His contempt for his contemporaries—for their "archaic" wish for a king to love—is the flaw spoiling an otherwise worthy picture.

His objective is to pull off a coup and win a fourth profession, whatever the cost. Ah, but what if he never gets away with his experiment? What if he finds that he has been outmaneuvered, trapped *as king?*

Then the side we admire is rewarded, and the side that merits punishment gets what it deserves also, in spades.

As I said, I wrote this one just for fun. So much for destiny.

RECOLLECTION

Senses Three and Six

I lean here against this polished wooden surface, while the drums pound and the smoke blows around, and my mind feels like a wild thing, completely out of control. For days I've hardly slept, dreading the dreams that have come back . . . eyes in the sky and a fiery mountainside.

Even as I stand here, this damned day keeps throwing memories at me, like soggy rags dragged out of a pile of old discarded clothes—things I thought I'd buried away for good.

Right now, for instance, I can't help remembering how weird I thought my old man was, when I was a kid.

Oh, he was a pip, he was. Whenever he caught me in a lie, he would beat me twice.

The first thing he'd do was he'd take me into the house and lecture me really reasonable-like about how it was immoral to tell lies, how a real man would face the truth, and all that stuff. Then he'd make me bend over and take my licking like a man. That part was okay, I guess. I didn't like the lecture, but he didn't hit very hard.

It was later in the day he'd scare me half to death. And all the time in between I'd be so frightened I couldn't hardly breathe. I think, now that you get right down to it, he punished me *three* times each time he found out I'd lied . . . a spanking indoors for being unethical, a Chinese water torture of a wait, and then a terrific pasting out next to the garage for *getting caught*.

I think the wait was so I could think about how I could have talked my way out of it without lying . . . or come up with a better lie, one without holes in it.

When he knocked me around outside he kept telling me how stupid it was to waste an untruth—how a man's credibility was as important to his survival as his wind, his stamina, or his ability to make friends.

My father was like that. Indoors he talked as if he were trying to teach me how to be moral and upright. Outside, in the twilight, he acted as if tomorrow I was going to be dumped into the Amazon, or Devil's Island, or deepest darkest Wall Street, and it was his job to see to it I could make it in a jungle.

One of the good things I can say about him is that he never got mad when I told him to his face he was nuts. He just laughed and said it was an interesting proposition— and that his duty to teach me to survive didn't include policing my opinions.

In all this smoke and noise and stream-of-consciousness rambling tonight, it occurs to me for the first time that maybe my old man was right after all.

Maybe he had a feeling I'd wind up in a place like this, hunted, trapped, my survival depending on the credibility of a lie.

These eyes in the sky keep coming back. And the picture of a burning mountain. I try to shrug them aside, but another image comes, uninvited, unwelcome . . .

A closeup of the moon . . .

Hey, I'm not illiterate. Though my life depends on seeming as if I am. Like Bogart said to Bacall, I been to college and I can read a book. It's just that I adapt real good. And right now I've got to adapt to being Chuck Magun.

Chuck. Yeah. Cut this memory crap and think about Chuck. Reinforce Chuck.

Chuck looks a lot like I used to look, naturally. I couldn't change that. He's a big guy with shoulders and everything heaped up six three or so. He looks mean. He lifts weights every day and runs a few miles along the riverfront.

He's got an old Harley torn apart in his living room,

and either a country western station or the TV is on all the time.

Chuck drinks in local bars, curses at all the right bad plays when football is on, and enjoys tearing up a patch of back road with his dirt bike, time to time. When he races he uses a lot of profanity, but he *never* loses his temper.

He reads motorcycle racing magazines and maintenance manuals with a guilty, *hungry* nervousness. He can't scan more than six or eight sentences without suddenly looking up with a shy grin on his face, as if he expected to be kidded, or maybe killed.

Mostly he doesn't read. He's a fully qualified member of the Great Unwashed. At least I hope so.

Chuckie may also be getting married soon . . .

(. . . A *closeup of the moon* . . . *the stars bitterly bright* . . . *purple cat-slitted eyes* . . .)

What was that? An earthquake? Did the bar shake? Why is my hand trembling?

Maybe I should stay away from provocative topics for a little while. As long as I'm standing here mumbling to a pretend listener in my own mind, I might as well do some background. It'll take up the time.

Ever been a bouncer?

You say no, my imagined friend? Well, let me explain. It's not a trivial trade.

Bouncers meet all the chicks. There seems to be a sort of fascination women feel towards that husky bearded type of guy who stands alone with watchful eyes at the edge of the bar with a big flashlight in his pocket and a beer that hardly gets touched during the night. Maybe it's that here's a big stud whose whole purpose in life is to make sure little girls don't get bothered in or around the Yankee Dollar if they don't want to be.

Anyway, the girls here are always flirting with Chuck. He doesn't mind, but I hate it. Their attentions make me nervous. I don't like strangers looking too close. Sure, none of *Them*, the monsters who pursue me, could disguise himself as a young woman. Especially the way they dress these days. Still, I have Chuck's girlfriend join him here each night to shake the chicks loose.

Hell, it's not the girls' fault. Neither is it Chuck's. So much for bouncer lesson number one.

Lesson number two is pick a place where kids hang out. You get a hell of a lot more aggravation, minute by minute, but it's a damn sight better than working bored sick in some topless place when some drunk jumps onto the runway to dance with the Girl, and you've got to jump up too, and grin and friendly-like ask him to join you in beer while the poor Girl has a stupefied smile on her face and only a little bikini bottom on her ass, and everyone in the house can see that big weighted flashlight you're holding behind your back, and you're wondering if your sphincters are going to hold because that drunk's got six friends at the bar just as "friendly."

That happened twice in Weed. I damn near broke character, as well as some poor Indian's head, before I quit.

Weed was a lot like Crescent City, wet and pungent. Only here the fog is made of ocean spray and clouds crawling upriver on their way to skirmish with the mountains. In Weed the morning haze was pure mosquitoes.

The kids who come to the Yankee Dollar to hear bluegrass and chivy sips of beer from their older brothers and sisters don't know how to be mean yet. They're so tied up in teenage smells and teenage aggravation. I remember when I was that age so I try to be tolerant.

It's funny how tonight I can recollect things like that from twenty years ago, but until recently I had trouble thinking much more than a week either way. Today I saw a jet flying high overhead. A fast little navy fighter, I guess. It got me thinking . . .

. . . The growl of engines . . . launching to a fanfare from Beethoven . . . laughter and clean flight . . .

Stop that! Divert! What *is* the matter with me? Where are these visions coming from?

Ignore 'em. That's what I'll do. Nothing like that ever

happened . . . Think about something else. Think about
the kids. Think about the kids and bouncer lessons.

I guess I like the kids enough. I watch 'em close,
though. The worst they usually do is try to sneak pitchers
outside or do J's in the corner. I put a stop to that fast, and
have a rep for the sharpest eye in bouncerdom.

No way I'm gettin' hauled up before a judge for
"contributing to delinquency." A judge might be one of
the ones *They* are watching. *They* catch wind of me, and
pfff! There goes both Chuckie and me.

"Hey, Chuck!"

"Yeah, what! What you want?" I bellow. Full Chuck
bellow from the edge of the bar.

They stand in the doorway ten feet away, three un-
derage lodgepoles in denim—scraggly moustaches and zits.
They want to pull something I'd catch them at easy. So
they're about to appeal to Chuck's sense of camaraderie. I
gotta smile.

"Hey, Chuck, can we bring in some beers? You're
cool, man. We'll keep it under the table . . ."

Turn grin to grimace.

"Hell, no. You guys get that stuff out of here! Drink it
at home and then come back. Or better yet, don't come
back!"

They cuss me, laughing. I cuss back to maintain image, but my heart really isn't in it tonight.

Five minutes later they're back. Must have chugged
the whole six-pack from the way they slosh and giggle as
they come in, giving me a wink. Jesus! Can you remember
chugging just to get a stomach full of beer? Doing it
because a boy's got to have some sort of rite of passage
when the girls just won't put out and we don't send young
men after eagle feathers anymore?

That's bouncer lesson number three. Like your clien-
tele. Establish empathy. But *never* identify too closely.
It'll drive you nuts.

*The surface of the bar is smooth, like ivory keys, like
the smooth-rubbed stick in a trusty airplane . . . With my*

*eyes closed the pounding of the drums blends with the
crowd noises and seems to become the growling of engines. A red haze under my eyelids turns into a fire . . .
fire on a mountainside.*

*My fingers press into the bar, the tendons humming
momentarily as if to something from Stravinsky . . .*

And Parmin did have purple eyes.

Agh! Ignore it. Ignore it!

The Blue Ridge Mountain Boys are picking up a fast
number beneath the spots, in a swirling haze of tobacco
smoke. I imagine the smoke contains other things, as well,
but it's hard to tell as my sense of smell isn't what it was.
In fact, for reasons I'd rather not go into, it's pretty well
nonexistent. I do a quick scan around the room to make
sure no one's passing around a J too obviously. I'm no
party pooper. Like I said, I have this thing about being
busted.

I'll give the Boys credit. They sure do give that
hillbilly music a shitkicking beat. The dancers on the floor
are capering and screaming "Eeee-Haw!" . . . that city-
boy version of the mountain yell.

Chuck likes this band. He's gotten drunk with them a few
times and he fixes their bikes for less than he usually charges.

Once, though, when he'd had a bit too much brew,
Chuck let them persuade him to join them with a borrowed harmonica. He'd intended just to clown around, but
got carried away. He bent over that mouth organ and
played.

By the time I came to my senses the crowd was
whooping it up, the Boys thumping me on the back, and I
was blinking in the spotlight, wondering what I had let
happen.

I almost left town then and there, but that's when
Elise had just broken her arm dirt-biking with Chuck for
the first time. I guess he felt guilty, so I stayed.

*Strange purple eyes, hooded and cat-slitted . . . a smile
as subtle as any man's . . . A look of ages. You don't hide
from eyes like those.*

"You are a Protector," he said. *"A certain fraction of your species cannot help themselves in this respect. Without something or someone to protect, they wither and die."*

"Parmin, you are full of it."

Again that smile. A voice like a reed organ.

"Do you think I don't know what you are, Brad? Why were you, after all, among the first I chose for my Cabal . . . ?"

There's dancing out on the sawdust now. Single girls prance around the edges as if it's some tribal custom to let the couples take the center. I always found that an interesting phenomenon.

The kids don't know anything about bluegrass, though some of the boys affect harmonicas. If it's country it must be salubrious, so they hop around with thumbs in suspenders and fingers splayed to give their dance a superficial country air.

I can't believe it. Did I just subvocalize the word "salubrious"? Sweet heavens, I must have gone mad!

What have I been doing, letting myself think like that? How long did I lapse? I look at my watch. No watch. I don't wear one anymore. What's wrong with me!

Calm down. You've only been intellectualizing since the beginning of the set. Too little time to do any real harm.

Besides, it's not proven *They* can put a tracer on subvocalized thought. That was just a theory.

Still, maybe they can. So cut the two-dollar words, hmmm? When did philosophy ever do anybody any good anyway?

Joey asks me to help him move a keg. Sure. Anything's better than standing here thinking. The crowd is too well behaved to serve as a distraction.

Down at the other end of the bar we heave the monster onto the platform. Straightening up, I rub the grease off my hands and look around the room. That's when I see her.

She stands by the door; the coldness comes over me

like an Amarillo norther. I cringe a little, momentarily
thinking to make myself invisible as she peers around,
blinking in the sharp light of the stage spots.

But there's no dignified way to make six and a half
feet of hair and muscle transparent. She sees Chuck and
smiles and starts to walk over. And while she's between
there and here the magic thing happens again. The coldness leaves me.

She *is* very pretty, and she moves well.

I try to look busy for a second, checking the place as
she comes up beside me. Joey says hello. She answers him
in a low alto voice—friendly, but with a hesitant sort of
nervousness to it.

I didn't put the nervousness there. She had it when I
met her, so don't blame me.

I'm not bothered by sky-eyes or fiery mountains now.
The Boys are picking out one of my favorite silly tunes,
"Old Joe Clark."

> *I went down to Old Joe Clark's,*
> *Never been there before.*
> *He slept on a feather bed,*
> *And I slept on the floor.*

> *Oh, fare thee well, Old Joe Clark,*
> *Fare thee well, I'm gone.*
> *Fare thee well, Old Joe Clark,*
> *Better be movin' on!*

She looks up at me.

"Hi."

I look back down at her. "Hi, yourself. How's the
nursery?"

"Pretty good today, but we had a late afternoon rush. I
hurried home and changed, but this saleslady came by and
I couldn't resist letting her show me some things. I bought
some nice scents so . . . so . . . that's why I'm late."

She suddenly looks a little scared, as if she's said
something she shouldn't have. Oh, yes. Chuck hasn't got a

sense of smell and hates to be reminded of it. It's true I haven't been able to pick up anything weaker than a six-day-dead steer in almost two years, but has Chuck really been so irritable that Elise should be frightened by a passing remark?

I shrug. "Have you eaten yet?"

"I had a snack earlier." She looks relieved. "I can fry us up a couple of steaks when we get home, if you want me to."

She wears her light brown hair in a permanent—swept around the ears like Doris Day. I always hated that style so Chuck tells her he likes it. She's too damn pretty anyway. A flaw helps.

"Come on." I grab her elbow and nod at Joey to take over watching the door. He's flirting with a teenybopper but I take the hand stamp with me. No one gets brew here unless he's been stamped. By me.

Elise steps a little ahead of me. She knows her walk drives me crazy, even after seven months or so of living together. It's like the way she is in bed. Totally committed. Every move is a caress. If it's not me or her plants she's stroking, it's the air, her clothes, the sawdust she's walking on.

She'll do. She's unsophisticated and decorative. Ideally, I'd have found someone without any education, but hell, everyone's been to college these days. At least she doesn't remind me of things, and she tries awful hard to please me.

The thing I guess I feel guilty about is leading her on. She obviously thinks she's going to work on me real hard and maybe I'll ask her to marry me. She's wrong.

I've already decided to marry her. But I have to keep up appearances. I'm the strong, silent type, remember? Chuck will have to be coaxed.

Damn it, I've *got* to stay in character! Would it do her any good to have *Them* catch up with me?

Old Joe Clark has got a house,
Sixteen storeys high,
And every storey in that house,
Is filled with chicken pie.

"Tell me what you're thinking."

Her hand is on my arm, playing with the thick hairs that gather under the shirt cuff. Those deep brown eyes of hers—she uses them like fingertips to touch my face lightly, shyly, as if to make sure I'm really there—they seem to show concern. Is it *that* obvious I'm not myself tonight?

That jet, flying so high in the sunshine . . . young Allan Fowler coming by later, to pester me with his fool-ishness . . . then all this philosophical crap I've been internalizing all night. Yeah, I'm going to have to pay attention to the old facade.

The secret of lying well is to do as little as possible.

"Oh, I was just thinking about that song they're doing now. We used to sing it when I was a kid. There's about a thousand verses." I take a long pull from my beer.

"I didn't know you used to sing, too. Is that when you learned the harmonica?" Her voice trembles just a bit, but the part of me controlling the mouth doesn't seem to notice. I'm on automatic.

"Um, yeah. Some of the other kids with folks at the Institute and I, we formed the Stygian Stegosaurus Band. Thought we were pretty hot shit. We played frat houses and the like. Nothing serious. Father bought me a banjo, but it never really took like the piano."

My next exhalation feels like a sigh. The song ends and so does the set. I look around and everything is peaceful, but I still check twice. When I was in the service I used to be able to *smell* trouble. Now I have to use my eyes.

Now, stop that. *Don't* think about the service! What's gotten into you, anyway?

I'm tired of yelling at myself. What a rotten day.

I turn to talk to Elise . . . Now, what's she got that *look* on her face for? What is it, amazement? Hope? Fear?

Oh, boy. What I just said.

Think . . . Father . . . I never mentioned my father before, though she used to try to draw me out about my past.

And the *Institute*! And music, my childhood . . . the piano.

There is a haze in front of me, a barrier of palpable grief. It hangs like a portcullis, cutting off escape. By touch I grab up the beer and swallow to hide the turmoil on my face. Think. Think.

The band's name she'll bleep out. Probably thinks it's dirty. Must recoup the rest. How? Make the Institute . . . "the Institution"? . . . A place for delinquents? Father could become "Father Murphy," a kindly priest . . .

I can envision my old man grinning at me now. "See?" he'd say. "See how hard it is to maintain a good lie?"

I put the beer down without looking at her. "I'm going for a walk. Get some air. Tell Joey I'll be right back, okay?"

I can see out the corner of my eye that she nods. I try to walk straight on my way out the door.

. . . Her eyes were gray . . . When she laughed it felt like my chest was a kite and I'd light up into the sky . . . Parmin introduced us—I never knew a woman like her could exist . . .

"Go," he said.

"But Parmin, Janie has her own work to do, and my team is expecting those B-1 and Trident parts to be integrated into the ships . . ."

"No. Your deputies can take over for a time, while the two of you go for a honeymoon. Am I not the expert? Have I not been watching your species for twenty of your generations? I will not have two of my department heads distracted later, while things are approaching completion.

"Go, Brad. Look into each other's eyes, make love, get a baby started. The child will be born on a new world . . ."

I rest my head against the cool, damp bricks. Around back of the Yankee Dollar, near the garbage cans, I try to keep from crying out loud.

The pain is hot. A searing, almost hormonal rejection, as if my body were trying to throw off a revolting insertion . . . a transplanted organ, or an alien idea. The agony is dull and sweaty, with a faint delusional quality, and the rejected organ, I realize, is my own mind.

My hands grope against the wall. Fingers dig into the recessed lines of mortar that surround each of the bricks, my anchors. The texture is hard, yet crumbly. Little fragments break off under my fingernails.

The gritty coolness crackles against my brow as I roll it against the masonry . . . feeling the solidity of the building.

It is comforting, that solidity. Good heavy brick. Bound by steel rods and thick goops of cement that permeate and bond—to hold up the roof. To stand. It's comforting to think about bricks.

Think about bricks.

Bricks are hard because the constituent molecules are bound. They all hold together and gravity is defied. Randomness, too, is held off. Chaos is stopped so long as the molecules don't leave their assigned places.

And they can't do that. The vibrational energy they'd need would be too high. No way over that barrier, except if they all decided to tunnel. And brick molecules can't all decide to tunnel at once, can they? Without someone to tell them to?

My fingers claw harder into the gritty mortar and a layer of skin scrapes away painfully. *Don't tunnel*, I cry silently to the molecules. *Don't. Stay here and be content as a brick. A simple honorable brick among bricks, which holds up roofs and keeps the cold wind off people* . . .

I plead desperately . . . and somehow I sense agreement. At least the wall doesn't seem to be going anywhere. In a momentary shiver, the fit is over. I'm left standing here feeling drained and a bit silly, with a dusty brow and filthy hands. I let the latter drop and turn to rest my back against the wall with a sigh.

It is a damp evening. Faint tendrils of fog creep across the twenty yards of parking lot between me and the far fence. The fog curls past like the fingers of an old blind woman—touching lightly the corner wall, the parked cars, the overflowing garbage cans—and moving on.

I start to cringe as a vaporous flagellum drifts along

the wall to brush me. *Don't. It's only fog. That's all. Just fog.*

I used to like fog. It always smelled good. Lots of negative ions, I suppose. Still, here next to the garbage cans the stench must be pretty bad. I wish I could tell.

Laughter feels dry and artificial, yet I laugh. Here I am, suffering something akin to a psychotic break, and I'm worried about my damned sense of smell!

Parmin spoke so slowly toward the end, but cheerfully in spite of the pain.

". . . The machines I have shown you how to build will do their part. My former masters, those who hold your world in secret quarantine, will be taken by surprise. They believe you will be incapable of any such constructs for hundreds of your years. You are all to be congratulated for making them so quietly and so well.

"Using these machines will be another matter entirely, however. These devices must be talked to. They must be coaxed. Their operators must deal with them on a plane that is at the meeting of physics and metaphysics—at the juncture of mathematics and meditation.

"That is why I selected men such as you, Brad. You fly jet aircraft, to be sure. But more importantly, you fly the same way you play the piano. All of our pilots must learn to play their ships, for persuading them to tunnel between the stars will require the same empathy as the pianist, who coaxes hammer strokes on metal wires to tunnel glory into a human brain."

My driver's license says I am Charles L. Magun. For well over a year I've repaired motorcycles for a living, and brought in a few extra bucks on the side keeping kids from wrecking themselves too badly in places like the Yankee. I have a live-in girlfriend who's been to college, I guess, but is no threat. She's quiet and nice to have around. I have some redneck pals who I bike and lift weights with and everyone calls me Chuck.

But I remember forging Chuck's birth certificate almost two years ago. I set him up as a role, I recall, someone *They'd* never find because *They* were looking for somebody else. I remember diving into Chuck and burning everything that came before, old habits, old ways, and most of all the old memories.

Until tonight, that is.

Okay, let's be rational about this. What are the possibilities?

One is that I'm crazy. I really *am* Charles L. Magun, and all that shit about having once upon a time played the piano, done calculus, piloted jet planes, piloted . . . other things . . . that's all a crock of madman's dreams.

It's amazing. For the first time in two years I can actually stand here and dispassionately remember doing some of those things. Some of them. Stuff not directly associated with the breakout. They seem so vivid. I can set up a hyperdimensional integral in my head, for instance. Could Chuck do that?

But I also remember, from long ago when I was a boy, those weird old men who used to come to the Institute bugging Dad and the other profs, to try to get someone to listen to their ideas for perpetual motion machines and the like. Their fantasies seemed sophisticated and correct to *Them*, too, didn't they?

The irony isn't lost on me—using a memory of the Institute to demonstrate that it's possible for me to falsely remember learning calculus.

Droll.

All right, perhaps I *did* construct Chuck. Maybe I *was* someone like who I think I was. But maybe everything that I'm currently *afraid of* is a fantasy. Maybe I simply went crazy some years back.

Look at me, spending an entire evening in a nonstop internal monologue, describing everything I think and feel as it happens, and every whimper and moan is out of some goddamn psychodrama, I swear. Like this paranoid delusion of vengeful creatures I call *Them* . . .

Oh, *something* terrible must have happened to me two years ago or so. But might it be something more mundane, like an accident? Or a murder? Maybe I created a terrifying and romantic fantasy to cover memories of the real trauma . . . something of this Earth, hidden under a bizarre mask of science fiction.

No one I know has even heard of the Cabal, or the Arks, or Canaan, or even a fiery crash on a mountainside just a hundred miles from here. I remember we Broke Out a bit early because elections were coming and the old administration was sure to lose. We thought the new crowd would be sure to blow the whistle. But not a word of any "secret project under the Tennessee hills" has ever hit the press. There wouldn't be any point in secrecy any longer, but there's been no word.

When you get right down to it, the story I remember is pretty damn preposterous.

A cool breeze is blowing now. The last drifts of fog fall away in tatters, fleeing into the gloom just past the streetlamps. The wind feels fresh on my face.

A third possibility is that I didn't make any of it up. I'm the hunted last survivor of a secret plot against a powerful outsider civilization, and my enemies will stop at nothing to catch me.

Hmmm. I never put it quite that way before. The next question, I now see, is obvious.

So what?

A smile? Is that what my answer is? A smile?

Yeah. So what? I want to shout. Who *cares* if they catch me? All they can do is kill me!

Why, in god's name, have I been making myself so miserable?

Wow.

All right, then. Chuck is a little bit overdone. Hiding as a macho motorcycle repairman is smart, sure. But Chuck doesn't have to belch in disgust every time a snatch of classical music comes on over the radio. He doesn't *have* to watch motorcross on the TV or make snide remarks every time Elise makes a pathetic little attempt at philosophizing.

Amazing I didn't think of this before. All I have left to lose is my worthless life. Small potatoes. Maybe I really can ease up a bit. Why didn't I think of this before?

The clouds part and suddenly there is the moon. It is beautiful, like an opal in the night. I can play subjective tricks with it, make it small, a pearl held up at arm's length, or go zooming in with my imagination, filling the sky with craters and maria much as . . . much as it might look from the portal of a ship.

I can see the Lunar Appenines, trace one of the ridges all the way to a little valley that twists and turns and dives into rocky depth. I can follow that cleft to the lip of a cave, a cave where there's buried . . .

Where there's buried . . .

No!

I refuse! Uh-uh! No fair.

I've done enough this evening, now leave me alone! I've agreed to be more reasonable, to let myself relax a bit and enjoy what's left of my life. But you can't make me remember, Brad. I won't do it!

Chuck hunches his shoulders and shoves his hands into his pockets. He shakes his head vigorously and walks toward the sound of drums and guitars, toward the door to the Yankee Dollar.

Imagine a blockade . . . a quarantine.

The stars are as numerous as specks of pollen blowing across a prairie. Life blossoms everywhere, and yet the glimmer of intelligence is rare.

Imagine an ancient civilization that cherishes the openness, the emptiness. They are reflective and refined—and selfish. They do not want space filled with clamorous young neighbors.

Imagine that one day a new species emerges, bright, curious, vigorous. The Old Ones set up a blockade as they have done in the past. With a severe kindness the fact of the quarantine is kept secret from the newcomers. A merciful discretion.

But now, imagine a traitor, an Old One who disagrees with Policy . . . And imagine a few precocious natives . . .

The set is over. A slow song plays over the FM and

Elise waits at our table, moving her lips to the words of the song. I watch her as I walk along the dim bar and motion for Joey to give me a fresh beer.

Every so often, when I let her, Elise sings to me. Softly, holding my head on her lap and running her hands through my thinning hair, she croons her gentle country melodies and helps me sleep.

Right now her eyes are focused out beyond the band-stand somewhere. I suppose she's just staring out into space, but there's something in her expression . . . She does that sometimes. When she's puttering with her plants and I'm trying to adjust a jammed sprocket, suddenly she'll stop and look intently at nothing. At times like that I worry that she might actually be thinking.

Then she snaps out of it and makes some reassuringly benign remark about a stupid woman who wanted to buy azaleas out of season.

She *is* nervous, though she's calmed down considera-bly lately. I don't know where the nervousness comes from and I've avoided thinking about it. There was a time when I could have tried . . . but Chuck doesn't know anything about psychology. He thinks it's bullshit.

Hell, I give her strength and stability and loving and a good deal more. It's a fair trade.

Gray eyes, her eyes, laughing at me over her bright silver flute, making me grin and stumble over the chords— my fingers made schoolboy clumsy by the lightness of my heart . . .

Gray eyes—cool ivory keys and a silvery flute . . .
Duet . . .

As I approach the table she looks up and smiles shyly. "Did you have a nice walk?"

"Yeah, it was fine."

There are questions in her brown eyes. No denying I did act unusual, earlier. But now I realize that I don't have to explain anything. Give it a rest and in a few days or weeks I'll start giving in a little to her curiosity. Chuck will explain a little. Minor stuff. No hurry.

Why not?

We talk about little things and spend a lot of time not talking at all. I check IDs and make sure nobody's molesting anyone in the men's room.

The Boys are back on stage playing quiet songs, as I return from one of my rounds and find Elise talking to Alan Fowler at our table.

Damn.

Alan's a nice, friendly grad student who's much too bright for his own good. He met Chuck at a dirt-bike race and sort of adopted him and Elise. Chuck insults him all the time, calling him a useless egghead, but he never seems to get the hint.

I come up behind Elise. She is very animated.

". . . not sure I understand what they hope to accomplish, Alan. You mean you could actually mine *asteroids* efficiently enough to make a profit selling refined metals back to Earth?"

"That's what the figures show, Lise." Alan winks at me but Elise doesn't notice.

"You mean even after transportation costs are taken into account? Can you amortize costs over a reasonable period?"

Chuck frowns. What is this? He doesn't like hearing words like these from Elise. Who does she think she's fooling?

Alan grins. "Easily, Lise. Less than a decade, I'd guess. Of course, in the beginning it'll be water for propellants we'll be after. But later? Well, imagine twenty years' worldwide platinum production coming from just *one* small asteroid! Why, we could easily go back to the days of the sixties and seventies when there was so much of a surplus that liberal ideas could flower . . ."

I can't help snorting in disgust. Chuck votes redneck.

The secret Ark Project was responsible for over half of the mysterious inflation that hit the nation in the late seventies . . . Big endeavors, pipelines, bombers, space shuttles, went through design change after design change, all attributed to poor planning.

And yet the engineers involved were the very same who had brought the Apollo Program in ahead of schedule and under budget.

How could such incompetence appear out of nowhere? Bungled, rebuilt nuclear power plants, reworked and retooled factories, new equipment wasted and tossed away.

Nobody bothered to check what happened to the original parts . . . the "flawed" equipment that had to be replaced . . . no one knew but a few in the highest places that the leftovers were taken to a cavern in Tennessee. Pieces of experimental windmills and redesigned submarines, prototype bombers and cancelled shuttles, the bits all cleverly fitted together into . . . into great globes . . . into beauty and eventually . . .

Sure, Alan, look to space for salvation from economic woes.

The Project was responsible for most of the mysterious inflation that hit in the late seventies . . . A great nation's wealth, thrown in secret down a rat hole.

Dream on . . .

Elise notices me and her words stumble to a stop. But she recovers quickly. She grabs my arm as I sit down beside her.

"Why didn't you *tell* me Alan got accepted!" She tries to sound accusing but is too excited to make it stick.

I shrug. The kid had only told me about his "good luck" this morning. Chuck had offered perfunctory congratulations but had better things to do than spend all day gushing over the young idiot's long-range suicide plan.

"Aw, come on, Lise." Alan grins. "It's only a preliminary acceptance. They're going to put me through a wringer like boot camp and final exams put together. Probably the only result will be three months lost from my research, and a permanent empathy with my experimental rats!"

"Don't be silly!" Elise glances at me quickly and gives in to her natural instinct to touch his sleeve in encouragement. "You'll make it all the way. Just think how proud we'll all be to say we knew you when!"

Alan laughs. "I'll tell you what would help. What I

really need is some coaching from the Zen master here."

He jerks his thumb in my direction.

Elise takes a fraction of a second to check the expression on my face. To me it feels stony, numb. I'm irked by this need of hers to constantly worry about my reaction, even if she's been doing it less lately.

I've never abused her. So Chuck growls! So what! She can do or say anything she wants, for crissake!

She laughs a bit nervously. "My bear, a Zen master? What do you mean, Alan?"

Alan grins. "I mean that one of the reasons I hang around this big grump is because he's the closest thing to a *real* guru I've ever met." Alan looks at Elise. "Have you ever watched him while he's fixing a bike?"

"Are you kidding? He has a Harley torn apart in the living room. I've tried and tried—"

"No. I mean *really* watched him! Closely! He touches every piece and meditates on it before he does anything at all to it. No part is in its place out of tempo. I used to ask him to describe what he feels when he's in that state, but he'd just get mad and tell me to go away. Finally, I realized that the yelling was a sermon! It's *suchness* he's concentrating on. Or Tao or Wu or whatever you want to name it, only naming isn't where it's at, either."

I shake my head, muttering, "Crock of shit." And I mean it, too. Chuck and I are in total agreement.

Alan just laughs. "I once read a book about a meditation system just like the one Chuck uses. It was pretty popular about a decade or so back. Only I never believed it until I met Chuck. I don't suppose he ever read the book. He just does it."

Alan sighs. "And that's what I have to learn, to pass those tests in Houston. If I could move with grace and concentration like he does when he's fixing bikes, I'd be a shoo-in. I tell you, Chuck should be the one trying for astronaut!"

And that will be quite enough! Elise's smile fades as I growl.

"What a load of bull, Alan. I'm no . . . *Zan* master, if

that's what you call it, and I sure have better things to do than get fried in one of those money-wasting, man-killing bombs they keep setting off down at Vandenberg! If you want to be popped up like a piece of toast you just go right ahead, but don't "enthuse" all over me, okay?"

The damned kid just keeps grinning.

"*There!* There it is again! That expression on his face. It's the same one he had this morning when I stopped by to tell him I might get a crew slot on the space station."

Alan's expression turns inward a bit, puzzled and not afraid at all to show it.

"It's as if he knew something I didn't," he murmurs. "As if he thought all that was somehow child's play."

If Alan were sitting just a little closer, I know I'd strangle him. If a bright young idiot like Alan Fowler can see through Chuck . . . what about *Them*?

My face is made of sleet-swept granite. I don't move, but let the world turn beneath me.

Child's play. Indeed.

Imagine a year of rumors . . . of strange lights in the sky . . .

The supermarket magazines carry a spate of UFO headlines. Several famous psychics report getting severe headaches along with alternating feelings of claustrophobia and exaltation.

An amateur astronomer reports another of those mysterious "ventings" on the moon . . .

Imagine flashes in the sky . . .

The mental processes are slow. I feel tired and cranky. It's been a long night and only at intervals have I had relief from this ridiculous internal monologue . . . describing everything I think or feel to an unseen audience. It's an audience I'd rather show my backside, but that's physiologically impossible.

It's just past one. I help Joey close up while over by the door Elise flirts with Dan and Jase of the band. Thank heavens the role never required that Chuck be the jealous sort. It's good to hear her laugh. She has a nice laugh.

When I've finished, I say good night to Joey and meet her at the door. The fog has disappeared, leaving a starry night that's cool and slightly damp. I sniff, picking up the faintest strange touch of musk from the street.

We walk slowly to my car, around back past the garbage cans. I let her in and like clockwork she leans over to unlock my side. The cold upholstery squeaks as I slide across the bench seat to put my arm around her. She shivers slightly, slipping down a little and looking up at me as if all the world depends upon my kissing her here and now.

Her lips are soft and they move with an infectious hunger, drawing passion out of me. My hands have a volition all their own, and she responds to every caress— matching the effect on me with the little things she does with her fingernails on my back.

Our loving has been good in the past, but never quite like this. Even with Janie it was different, but . . .

I jerk my head up and moan, squeezing her against me. I pray that she thinks it's the loving.

My eyes squeeze shut to block out memory. Yet they fail even to stop simple tears.

Imagine flashes in the sky . . .
Parmin suggests the group's orchestra hold a farewell concert for the entire Cabal. He asks specifically for a Beethoven concerto.
Then it is time.
The Arks lift in battle formation, and take the picket ships completely by surprise, high above the jagged highlands of the moon's limb. The jailers barely get out a distress call before they are annihilated.
One Ark developed engine trouble, didn't it? Its crew and supplies were transhipped and it was buried in a cave . . . Then, one by one, the Arks peeled off to seek their diverse destinations . . .

Imagine a young pilot who locks his controls, then rises to face the woman standing behind his chair.
"Marry me, pretty lady. Will you? I'll put the stars in your ring. You shall have a galaxy for a tiara." He takes

her by the waist and raises her high, to the cheers of his crewmates.

Laughing gray eyes . . . She strokes his hair and bends over to kiss him. "Silly boy. We're already married. Besides, I don't want galaxies. Just one planet. That's all."

He lowers her and holds her close.

"Then a planet you shall have . . ."

Her breath against my neck is very warm. Her breast rolls silkily against my side.

I chose Elise because she seemed the antithesis of my former life. No one would expect to find me—to find my former self—with her, just as *They* would not look for someone fixing motorcycles in his living room and watching pimply kids in a country bar.

Yet she is life to me now, is she not? Where would I be without you, Elise, to anchor me to this world?

By their own laws *They* are sworn not to harm the innocent, though they would kill me on sight. Perhaps, though, when the manhunt ends and I am found, they may find it expedient to bend their rules and eliminate her as well, in case I had talked.

I shudder at the thought. That was one of the reasons for Chuck's antiintellectualism in the first place, to keep from letting even a word slip. Perhaps the best thing to do, the most honorable thing, would be simply to leave.

I seem to be oscillating between flashes of painful memory and numbing calmness. Right now the pendulum is swinging back again. Suddenly everything is stark and shimmering. My head feels light, like crystal.

Over the night sounds of the suburbs I can hear horns of the boats on the distant river. I can feel Elise's heartbeats as I hold her. The textures that I see, in the car, in the brick wall outside my window, are vivid and intricate . . . like a pattern of hieroglyphs whose meanings dance at the edges of understanding.

Would reliving the past help Janie? Or Parmin or Walter, or any of the others? How would it help to re-member a terrible, useless, one-sided battle that stretched over kiloparsecs and climaxed in smoke and stench and roiling flames under a lonely mountain?

Calmness settles in for real. The unwelcome acuity drifts away, unlamented. Holding Elise in the dark, I hardly sense the passage of time.

After a nameless interval I return, cursed still with this compulsion to narrate. It is getting a bit chilly in here, and I long for sleep.

Gently I disengage Elise and fumble the keys into the ignition lock. She, with her eyes far away, straightens her clothes. "We ought to get some of the other bikers together and throw some kind of going-away party for Alan," she suggests. I nod and grunt amiably as I turn the keys.

Nothing. "What the . . . ?"

Check neutral, try again.

Zilch.

My gaze drops to the headlights switch. They were left on six hours ago, when I came in for work. Now, why did I do a fool thing like that?

There's Elise's old Peugeot across the lot. Typically on Fridays we come to the Yankee separately and go home together. The Yankee's lot is safe.

"Come on, we'll have to use your car tonight, Elise." I open my door.

She looks up with a sleepy smile, then her eyes widen. "But . . . but my car is a mess!"

For as long as I've known her she's always been reluctant to let me near her car. When we use it she always has to "straighten it up" first. She finds excuses to keep me from driving it.

Can you beat that? She'd give me her entire bank account if I asked for it, but I don't have a key to her frigging car. She stands up to me there, though while she's making excuses her voice quavers. I can't figure it, but I recognize guts when I see it. Maybe that's why I went along with it until now. For standing up to Chuck on this one small point I think I love her a little.

But tonight has been hell and I'm in no mood to walk six miles.

"Come on, Elise. You can drive but we've got to use your car. I'm exhausted and I want to go to bed."

She hesitates. Her brown eyes dart from me to the Peugeot. Then she jumps out with a forced laugh. "I'll race you there!"

Hell, she knows I always let her win. Except when we're playing "catch me and ravish me." But this isn't one of those times.

When I arrive she's already behind the wheel. "Beat you again!" She giggles.

I shrug and get in, much too numb to try figuring her out. I'll make this as painless as possible for her by slumping down and pretending to go to sleep.

Unfortunately, the images await me. Nowhere can I find peace.

Clouds part on greens and blues and browns . . . a lake-speckled forest that almost stings with beauty . . . creatures of a million shapes, all strange and new, fill the air and land and seas . . .

Like a bubble blown across light-years, a ship settles down—gently, as if loath to disturb the loveliness.

It is a good omen, to be arriving in peace . . .

There is a feeling I used to get quite often when I was young, that I was being watched by omniscient beings.

It wasn't the same as the shadow I have lived under in recent times. Though powerful, my enemies are not all-seeing.

No. Back then, when I was a boy, it seemed as if the universe possessed a Big Eye, and a distinct taste for drama. Always I felt as if I were the central character in a great play.

To the Big Eye it wasn't important that you actually *did* anything. Even standing still watching the seagulls could be dramatic. Noble thoughts and grand unseen gestures were what it valued most of all—the secret unrewarded honesties—the anonymous charities and the unrequited loves.

For a time, when I was a kid, it was very clear to me

that the proverbial tree falling in the unpeopled forest was, indeed, heard.

Maybe it was crap like that that got me into this mess. Hell, Freud took the whole thing apart long ago.

But long after I'd dismissed the Big Eye as an ego-displacement dream—a pseudo-Jamesian experience—I found it still beside me, hovering nearby as I agonized over every major decision in my life.

Where has it gone? I wonder. Did it leave me before the Breakout? Or did it follow me to Canaan, and experience with us our lovely doomed joy?

The rumble of the car massages my back as we pull out of the lot and onto the damp streets. I'm feeling sad, but peaceful. Maybe I *would* go to sleep if only Elise would drive less erratically. She seems to be in a godawful hurry to get home. I sense a shift from green to amber through my closed lids, and the brakes suddenly come on.

I have to put my hand to the dashboard as several items tumble out from beneath my seat.

"Hey! Take it easy!"

She laughs. But there seems to be a new level of panic in her eyes. "What's the matter? Don't you trust an expert driver?"

"Ha ha. Just try not to kill us within a mile of home, okay?" I look down at the junk that came out from under the seat. There's a little stereo playback and headphones, and a small bound notebook. I look up. The light is still red. Elise faces ahead, her face pale.

"What are these?"

She jerks her head, half looking at me. "What are what?"

"This tape player. Is this your deep, dark secret?" I smile, trying to put her at ease.

"N—no. It—it belongs to a friend. She left it in the car when we went to lunch. I've got to get them back to her on Monday."

"What has she got on the tape?"

"Nothing. Just some classical music, I guess. She likes that sort of thing."

Oh, yeah. Curiouser and curiouser. I look up and see

that the light has changed and nod at the road ahead. She turns to start the car rolling again, woodenly staring ahead of her.

As Elise drives I sit there with the incriminating items on my lap. It's a bit embarrassing. I'm tempted to put the recorder and notebook back under the seat, despite my curiosity.

She's driving slowly now, concentrating on the road. At this rate it will be a while before we arrive. Elise doesn't appear to be watching so I slip on the headphones and start the player. There is a faint hissing as the tape leader passes the heads. I settle down and close my eyes. After months of avoiding anything that even vaguely resembles "highbrow" music, it might be nice to hear anything Elise might choose to call classical, even if it's just a violin rendition of "Yellow Submarine."

There is the sound of a phonograph needle coming down. Then gently, a piano begins to play. Before the third note is struck my back is a mass of goose bumps and my breath is frozen in my chest . . . a wave of alienation overwhelms me . . . I cannot move, even to turn the machine off.

The Fourth Concerto.

Beethoven.

It's the von Karajan production I've listened to a thousand times.

The Fourth Concerto. It was the last piece performed by the group orchestra just before we broke up to board the Arks. Parmin had specifically requested it.

I protested. I was out of practice. But he would have his way, always. And Janie . . . (*Gray eyes laughing over a silver flute* . . .) she insisted as well. During those last two weeks, while we waited for the last ship parts, we practiced.

I can feel them now, the keys. The crafty idiosyncrasies of that old Steinway. The loving clarity that could be coaxed from her. And in the orchestra, Janie's flute was like a soft unjealous wind, forgiving me the infidelity of this other great love . . .

Out of practice or not, it was like nothing else—that last night on Earth—except, perhaps, the glory of flying.

Parmin was very kind afterward, though I don't imagine I'll ever know what our benefactor really thought of the performance. His was the Ark that rose first. The one bound for far Andromeda. The only one, I think, that got away.

The others? Three I know were tracked and destroyed. Two others *They* claimed to have found. I believe them.

Did any other survivors make it back here, to hide like rats among people who have no idea what happened in secret in their own skies?

We left after a night of Beethoven, a fleet. We won a battle in space and then I watched the Arks veer off, one by one, like seeds blown free from a stem, scattered by the wind.

I returned alone, like the Ancient Mariner, with a ship filled with corpses and an albatross of terror and guilt dragging at my neck.

". . . Human pilot! Surrender, please! We have already killed far more than we can bear! Do not force us to add to the toll! The traitors who aided Parmin have been rounded up. All the other blockade runners are captured or destroyed!"

The voice lists the colonies besides Canaan they have captured. A voice filled with compassion and sensitivity, so similar to Parmin's that I almost cry . . .

But the bridge is filled with the stench of burning wiring and decaying bodies . . . I send the ship into a screaming dive Earthward, evading their best interceptors with tricks that I had learned far too late . . . My seat buckles underneath me, but somehow I hold on to the controls . . . My nostrils are filled with the odors of death.

"We realize that your conspiracy was kept secret from the vast majority of Earthlings. That is good. Can you not agree that, having failed, you don't want to see your fellows suffer prematurely? They don't have to find out about their quarantine for another two hundred years! Let them dream on, of an infinite playground in space! Surrender now, and spare the children below their dream!"

So compassionate! The murdering alien hypocrite! Jailor! Zookeeper!

I shout the hateful words and his image on the screen recoils . . . until the ionization trail of my reentry vaporizes the picture in a cloud of static.

The Ark screams . . . I scream . . .

They tried to shoot me down, like *They* shot down Walter in his modified F-15 that afternoon on Canaan, when I was so late getting the Ark into the air.

There were too many of *Them* anyway. I told myself that a thousand times as the fight ravelled all the way back to Earth. It took time to get the Ark warmed up, and when *They* did what we never had expected—bombed the noncombatants in the settlement—I tarried to take on gassed and wounded survivors.

I watched *Them* fry the house I had just built. Janie had been in the cellar, packing preserves for the winter . . .

How did they find us so soon? We had counted on more time. How did it happen?

Smoldering wreckage steams within a new crater on an Oregon mountainside. Fires spread through the forest in all directions from a reawakened volcano.

I set charges in what remains and run . . . and run and run and run, but I cannot outrun the wind. It envelopes me from behind and chokes me with the stench of burning flesh . . . I run from the smell . . . I run . . .

There is a tear on my cheek. The soloist enters his cadenza and it is more sweet and sad than I can bear. The headphones slip off and slide from my lap to the floor, followed by the tape player. The sounds of the Fourth Concerto die away into muffled silence.

I'm sure the Big Eye will understand. I cannot afford music.

The blessed numbness returns in force. I open my eyes to look at my hands. They seem miles away. Yet I can make out every wrinkle, every pore and crevice. I glance at Elise. She drives slowly, her expression stony.

My hands fall on something cool and smooth. I look down and see the notebook that I had forgotten.

There have been times in my life when the Big Eye has come down off my shoulder to actually meddle around. Strange things have happened which I could not explain, like finding a live black rabbit on my doorstep at midnight, the evening I finished reading *Watership Down*. Or when I was considering giving up flying, and found that a sparrow hawk was perched on my windowsill, looking at me, staring at me until I found my confidence again.

I've been a scientist, too. But science doesn't welcome the Big Surprises. Only little ones that can be comfortably chewed and swallowed. When the unknown comes *in* out of the borderline and grabs you by the jewels, *that* is when the Universe has chosen to gently remind you that a change of perspective is due. It is showing you who is boss.

Science tells us not to expect personal messages from the Cosmos, either. But they happen, sometimes.

The notebook is smooth and cool.

Are you friend or foe? What shall I do with you, symbol in my lap?

In a rush the panicky commands go out to my body. Get up! Throw the cursed book down. Open the door and jump out. Start running. Start another lie . . . life in another town.

MOVE!

My treasonous body does not obey. The mutiny is shocking.

Okay . . . we'll try something else. I command these hands to open this book so that I can look inside.

With a sense of betrayal I watch as they obey. The scratchy paper riffles as my fingers pick a place at random.

By the moonlight there is no mistake. She wrote this. There's no mythical "friend" who left a notebook in her car. I never noticed before, but Elise has lovely penmanship, even if the lines do waver a bit, trembling across the page.

It's ridiculous, really. I moved out here to get some peace and quiet. To get a summer job that didn't feel like a Summer Job—and to get away from that crazy rat race of briefs, moot courts, and exams. I thought it would be amusing to live in the hicks for a while.

I realize now that I hated law school! Oh, not the learning. That was wonderful. But all the rest—the backbiting, the atmosphere of cynicism and suspicion. Ideals got you nothing but derisive laughter.

All those using, abusing men, so glib about respecting modern women, then turning and cutting them first chance. As if we "modern women" were any more kind, of course.

I'm never going back. Here it's peaceful and quiet. I've landed a job I wanted more than that damned clerkship. Can you imagine? It's tending and selling plants! I'm beginning to see why some Eastern peoples put gardening on a higher level than politics. I love it.

These are real people, not money- and status-grubbing yuppies. I'm terrified they'll reject me if they find out I'm a refugee from the world of polyester and gold chains.

Especially my new man. He doesn't talk much. I still haven't been able to define what it is that draws me so to him. But I'm desperate not to drive him off.

I think, maybe, he's the most real thing I've ever had to hold on to.

Two minutes ago I was surprised. Now it's as if I've known this all along. I flip to a later entry . . .

When am I going to learn? How many women have ruined their lives trying to change their men into something they're not?

He is gentle and kind and strong—such a

lovable grouch. So what if he hates just about
everything artistic or scientific. What has art
and science ever done for me, anyway?

Oh, I'm so confused! What is this indefin-
able feeling I have about him? Why do I keep
risking it all by trying to change him?

I think I'm actually starting to relax, some-
times. Whatever he's doing for me, I can't sur-
render it now. Better to give up this journal, the
other hidden indulgences, rather than take any
more chances . . .

So. Another refugee, albeit from a more mundane
sort of crisis. Oh, Elise, I'm sorry I never knew.

I'm glad I never knew, for I would have run away.

I understand now why she encouraged that bright
young idiot Alan Fowler to hang around. Her patient
probing worked better than she'll ever know. Along with a
series of incredible coincidences. And time.

The car is slowing down, coming to a stop. I look up
and see we're on a side street a few blocks from home.

She is looking at me, shaking her head slowly, hopelessly. Her lips tremble and there are thin pulsing rivulets
on her cheeks.

I let the book slip from my hands and close my eyes
to breathe deeply of the night. I can smell her from a few
feet away. She comes to me as musk and perfumes and
sawdust from the Yankee.

I can also smell the dampness of the streets, and the
pine forest south of town.

What else? Ah, yes. There is salt water. I swear. I can
even smell the ocean from here.

She is crying silently, head lowered.

What am I going to do with you, Elise? How can I
thank you, now that Chuck is gone, for taking care of him
while I healed? How can I make you understand when I
go away, as I must very soon.

I reach over and pull her to me.

It doesn't matter, Lise. It doesn't matter because I
knew it all along. From the very first, I suppose, a part of

me knew you'd be trying, without knowing exactly what you were doing, to summon me back. Don't cry because you succeeded!

I must spend a long time comforting her—holding her and gentling away the fear. I can see Andromeda faintly through the open window behind her, a stroke of light against the sparkling of the stars. I whisper to her and can feel the planet turn slowly beneath us.

I think I'm finished subvocalizing, this evening. It's not necessary anymore. Doors are opening and long and unused feelings and ideas are stepping out.

The opening traces of a plan are forming. They must have been gestating for months . . . designs for a lockpick for a very large cage. Lessons to be taught to Old Joe Clark.

There's a lot of work ahead, some of it quite dangerous. I'm not sure exactly how to get started and it may wind up taking me a long, long way from here.

But I promise you, Lise—if you want me to—I'll take you with me when I go.

AUTHOR'S NOTES

The senses referred to in the title are those of smell and the inner mind. There have been experiments showing vividly how closely connected odors are to our recollections. Sometimes a faint aroma will trigger the most vivid of memories. Once in a while, it goes the other way around.

I wanted to write about a character who wasn't sure what was real anymore, where his assumed identity began and where the horrifying past left off. This is the result.

I believe the one greatest moral contribution of Western civilization has been the concept of a difference between subjective and objective reality . . . the perpetual warning that says, "Watch out! You may only think you know what you know."

Human beings have a tremendous capacity for fooling themselves, for imagining slights, crafting false memories, denying faults, believing ideologies. Science fights back with the Uncertainty Principle, which has proven that no human can ever have perfect knowledge. Unless you can demonstrate it in a repeatable experiment, it cannot be treated as a fact. Sure, you can play with an idea without proving it. Metaphors, allegories, and science fiction stories are all great fun, and useful, too.

But until other people can regularly duplicate your experimental results, it's best to smile and remember to say "maybe."

"To thine own self be true . . ." said Polonius. An honest person always double-checks, for it is all too easy to lie to the one who trusts you the most, yourself.

*   *   *

    "Senses" is one of five stories which debut in this volume. It is also the oldest story here, begun long before my first novel, Sundiver. Every year since, I would dig it out and poke away at it for a while, then put it away again. It's one of the most difficult pieces I've ever done.

    The following story might very well be the hardest of all.

Toujours Voir

"Folks!" the bodyguard announced. "In moments Lasselovsky will be here. You all know what that means."

From my regular booth by the window, I saw several customers abruptly leave. The brave, or curious, remained.

"He's the Oldtime spacer who returned, but didn't hide, right?" Sam, our bartender, asked.

"Yeah, so don't bother him! If anyone here strongly resembles someone from his past, and triggers a déjà-vu attack, we could find this building on another *planet* . . ."

Déjà vu. I suppose everyone's felt this clue to Time's true nature.

Epileptics once dreaded it as an "aura," foretelling seizures. And historically, people feared epilepsy, never suspecting grand mal hinted a door to the universe.

Today only Oldspacers suffer lingering aura shock. I hear neuroconvulsive hyperdrive is perfected nowadays. Modern pilots needn't endure terrifying seizures to attain that special mental state which propels a spaceship starward.

To *modern* spacers, induced déjà vu is a key.

To Oldtimers, though, it's pure terror.

". . . sudden recognition could trigger a jump seizure. So don't approach him. If he feels safe, maybe he'll mingle . . ."

Talky bodyguard.

Most Oldtimers retreated to cozy surroundings and stayed put. Ex-crewmates avoid reunions.

Stubborn Lasselovsky, though, keeps moving. He's a

free man, so the authorities send bodyguards ahead to
warn people.

Time's funny. It flows, then surges like a convulsion.
I sit and wait, feeling the years.
Through the window, I see a familiar face . . .
Captain . . .?
I *should* have left before this. Already my hands are
shaking.
Still, it *is* nice to see, again, the stars.

AUTHOR'S NOTES

There is a sub-subgenre of writing called the "precision short story" . . . a fable written to very exacting standards. One type of precision story is the 250-word tale.

The rule is simply this. The story must be 250 words in length. Not one word longer, not one word shorter. And it must work as a story.

It is like pulling teeth. Like using a tiny pick to make one of those incredible, interlocking Chinese ivory puzzles. Frustrating!

My solution (and not a very elegant one, I admit) was to use a lot of polysyllabic words and hyphenated contractions. My only excuse is that I was trying to cover a pretty complex idea in a very short space.

To this day I shake my head over this one.

(Neuroconvulsive hyperdrive? Ooooh.)

A Stage of Memory

Fine, crystalline powder lay scattered along the cracked molding between the mattress and the wall. The tiny white grains met crumpled tissues and hairballs under the lip of a dingy fitted sheet. They sparkled incongruously along a thin trail across the floor of Derek's shabby room, reflecting where, it seemed to Derek, there wasn't any light.

The ripped windowshade cast a jagged knife of daylight on faded *Variety* clippings taped to the opposite wall. The outline looked like the tapering gap between a pair of legs . . . the legs of a runner in mid-stretch, making time against the plaster.

Derek Blakeney contemplated the runner.

Headless, torsoless, it had started over near his closet, narrow and slow. As the afternoon wore on, the shadow widened and the jogger seemed to catch its stride, legs reaching like a steeplechaser's. Its progress across the wall became terrific . . . a yard, at least, in the last twenty minutes.

At last Phiddipides crossed the finish line and expired in the shadow of the closet door.

Evening. A time for decisions.

He had known all along what his choice would be. Derek's hands trembled as he reached for the shoebox by the foot of the bed, his unbuttoned cuffs revealing an uneven chain of needle tracks.

Bless the mercy law, he contemplated as he opened the box and took out a sterilized package. *Bless the legislators who legalized the paraphernalia, the syringes and needles, so those on the low road won't have to share it with hepatitis and tetanus.*

He broke the sealed wrapper and pushed the bright needle through the rubber cap of a tiny bottle of amber fluid.

Bless those who legalized the new drugs, so an addict needn't commit crimes to support his slow road to hell. He doesn't have to drag others with him, anymore.

He wrapped rubber tubing around his arm and held it tight with his teeth as he posed the needle's tip over the chosen spot. Derek's way of dealing with short-term pain was to make a dramatic moment of it. When he pierced the protruding vein, his face contorted as if to highlight the pain for the back-row balcony.

Even an out-of-work actor had his pride. Derek had never believed in cheating those in the cheap seats, even if some selfish front-row critic thought one was hamming it up a bit.

A small bead of milky liquid welled from the entry hole as he withdrew the syringe and laid it aside. Derek sighed and sank back against his pillow. If he had calculated it right, this time he would go *back*! This time he'd return to the good days, long before . . .

He closed his eyes as a cool numbness spread up his arm and across his chest. His scalp tingled.

Derek could feel the here and now start to slip away. He tried to concentrate, determined not to let *this* trip get away from him!

Envision a small frame house on Sycamore Street, he told himself, in Albany, New York . . .

Sycamore Street, so long ago . . . Mother would be cooking a Sunday supper, Father is reading the paper, and my old room is a clutter of plastic airplane models, touching the air with a faintly heady scent of glue.

The numbness spread down his jaw and spine, and he willed himself back through the files of his cortex, back to Sycamore Street, back to being twelve years old again . . . back to where a familiar female voice was about to call out . . .

"Supper's ready!"

It had worked! The new dose had worked! Those were exactly the words he had willed his mother . . .

"Come on, Lothario! Get your ass out here. I've whipped together a simple, nutritious meal for you. You've got ten minutes to eat and still get to the theater on time!"

The alto voice carried a quaver of emotion, barely suppressed. Derek realized with a sinking feeling that it was *not* his mother, after all.

His eyes opened. The drug had worked. The dingy little fleabag room had been replaced by much richer surroundings. But here were no plastic model airplanes. Rather, drifting glass and metal mobiles reflected opal gleams from two garish lavalamps. A row of plaques and statuettes glittered in a mahogany ego-shrine across from the bed. Underneath he felt the warm vibrations of an expensive automassage oil-bed.

Derek felt that strange/familiar pressure as his midbrain surged forward to take over. From now on he would be only an observer, unable even to make his eyes blink while the triggered memories replayed perfectly, vividly, out of his control.

Derek felt a silent, internal cry of despair.

This is where I left off last time! I didn't want to come back here. This is too close to the present. I wanted to go back to when I was twelve!

He heard footsteps approach. The door slid swiftly along its rails to bang as it hit the stops. A bright trapezoid of light spilled from the hallway, eclipsed by a slender shadow.

"Well, Derek? Are you going to shave that famous puss and get dressed for the show? Or shall I call Peter and tell him to get your understudy ready again?"

Even the injected form of the damned drug is sequential! I knew it. The thrice-damned stuff takes me forward, one step at a time. I have no choice but to start off each trip reliving where the last one ended!

"Derek?" the figure in the doorway demanded.

"I'll be out in a frigging minute," his midbrain answered—controlling his voice—making it happen exactly as it had three years ago. The playback was adamant, unchangeable.

"Shit!" he growled. "A guy can't even enjoy a little grass in peace, in his own goddamn apartment." He had to fight the cannabis languor to pull himself up onto one elbow, squinting at the brightness from the hall.

"And speaking of piece, where does a bird like you get off talking to me like that? I picked you out of a bloody *chorus line*, gave you your first frigging break, and the best frigging time in your life."

Tall and slender, the woman in the doorway had braided black hair and a dancer's body. He knew that body and the smell of that hair as well as he knew his own. Right now he radiated a loathing tailored by his knowledge of her, enjoying the carefully chosen words with an actor's pride.

"If I weren't so goddamn stoned, I'd show you what an ungrateful bitch like you can do with her frigging nagging!"

There was a long silence. Then the woman nodded resignedly.

"Right," she said softly. Then, with a note of tight control, "All right, Derek. Have it your own way. I've taken on a wife's duties, and for more than a year that's included picking up after your increasingly sloppy body and mind. I thought it worthwhile, and imagined you'd get over your grief like a man. But this time I'm taking you at your word.

"Thanks for the break, Derek. You did get me that first part, and you've paid the rent. I'll only take my clothes with me, and I'll have my agent forward yours a percentage of my next gig."

She paused, as if half hoping against hope that he would speak. But he did not. His eyes were unfocused, following the shimmering globs in the lavalamp.

"Good-bye, Derek."

He had to shade his eyes from the light as her eclipse vanished. He lay back in a floating torpor and a short time later heard the front door slam.

Good frigging riddance, he thought. I can pick up any

one of a dozen young things after the show tonight without her around. Life is definitely about to take a turn for the better!

He turned to pick up his smoldering reefer from the ashtray, totally oblivious to a little voice from another time, which cried out plaintively, hopelessly, *"Melissa, please . . . don't go . . ."*

2

The waiting room was stark and depressing . . . paint peeling under sharp fluorescents. The pungency of disinfectant failed to disguise the distinct aroma of urine. Every now and then some waiting client fell into a fit of dispirited coughing. Nobody talked.

Derek hunched in a cracked corner seat, hoping to avoid being noticed. Not that many recognized Derek Blakeney anymore. It had been more than two years since the last spate of scandals and scathing reviews had banished him from the theater columns.

The only serious threat to his apathetic downward spiral had come when a certain critic compassionately eulogized "a lost giant of the stage." Derek had tried to build up a rage over it, but torpidity had prevailed in the end. Now he was thirty pounds lighter and indifferently washed, and it was unlikely anyone would even recognize a onetime star of Broadway. He was probably safe.

A gaunt woman in a white smock periodically emerged to call out numbers. Clients followed her one at a time to a row of cubbyholes against the wall. From the booths came a low mutter of alternating wheedling and officialese. Derek overheard snatches of conversation.

". . . You won't get any more Tripastim until your amino acid balance is better, Mr. Saunders . . . How? By improving your diet of course . . ."

And another.

". . . Here is your allotment, Mrs. Fine. No, first you sign here. Yes, here. And you must drink this

vitamin supplement . . . I've already explained, Mrs. Fine.
The government doesn't subsidize your habit because it's
your *right*, but in order to drive the Black Chemists out of
business. We can undercharge them and see to it you
have every chance to kick it if you decide to. Part of the
deal is making sure you get the nutritional . . ."

Derek closed his eyes. The Liberal-Libertarian coalition had trounced the old Republicans and Democrats in
the last election, and Drug Centers like this one were
among their first steps on taking office. It had been a good
move. Too bad Libertarians were so stingy, though, and
the Liberals so damned sanctimonious. If only they'd just
give over the doses and shut their bloody—

"Number eighty-seven." The nurse's sharp voice made
Derek feel brittle. But it was his number, at last! He stood
up.

"I'm number eighty-seven."

The nurse's look seemed to say that what she saw was
both pitiable and vaguely loathsome. "Go to station twelve,
please," she said, referring to her clipboard. "Ms. Sanchez
has your chart."

Derek shook his head. "I wish to see Dr. Bettide. It
is a matter of some urgency, requiring the attention of
someone with his expertise."

The woman looked up, surprised. Derek felt a moment's satisfaction. He might look like a derelict, but the
voice was still Derek Blakeney's. It commanded attention.

"Dr. Bettide is very busy," the nurse began uncer-
tainly. "He's good enough to volunteer his time as it is.
We only send him referrals from—"

"Just convey him my name, if you please." He handed
her one of his last few cards, certain he could recover it.
"The doctor will see me, I am certain of it." He smiled, a
relaxed expression of assurance and patience.

"Well . . ." She blushed slightly and decided. "Wait
here, please. I'll ask the doctor."

When she had gone, Derek let his expression sag
again. Without an audience he folded in upon himself.

Lord, he thought. I hate this overlit, stinking pest-
hole. I hate the world for having such places in it. And

most of all I hate having to beg for the stuff I need in order to get the hell *out* of this goddamn turn-of-the-century world.

It isn't *fair*. All I want to do is go home again! Is that too much to ask? Frigging scientists work wonders these days. Why can't they just send me home again?

3

"It's not fair, I tell you. The injection and the new dose should have taken me back to age twelve! Not thirty-five, but twelve! What's the *matter* with the damn stuff?"

It never occurred to Derek to present a false face to Dr. Melniss Bettide. He acted the age he wanted to be in the presence of the man he hoped would make it possible.

A small, dark man, Dr. Bettide regarded Derek through thick-lensed glasses. Derek grew uncomfortable under the physician's unblinking stare. At last Bettide pressed a button on his intercom.

"Steve, please bring in a double shot of health supplement four."

"Yes, Doctor."

"Hey! I don't want vitamins! I want—"

Bettide silenced Derek with a bored wave. "And Steve, please also bring me a carton of the new samples of Temporin B."

Now, that was different! A new *type* of Temporin? Of Time-Jizz? The possibilities were exciting.

Bettide examined Derek's file. "You've been to group therapy regularly, I see."

"They won't give you a drug card if you don't go. It's worth sitting around with a bunch of whining marks for an hour a week, in order not to have to go to the Black Chemists for the stuff."

"Hmmm, yes. But you're still refusing individual treatment?"

"So what? It's not mandatory. Why should I go and spill my guts to some shrink? There's nothing wrong with me."

Derek stopped abruptly, blinking as a flashback hit—a brief, sudden image of a trapezoid of light, then the sound of a slamming door . . .

He looked down and spoke again in a lower tone. "At least there's nothing wrong with me that the right change of environment wouldn't cure," he muttered.

Dr. Bettide made an entry in Derek's file, a sniff his only comment. Derek shrugged. So the man saw through his sophistries. At least Bettide never lectured like a lot of Liberals would. He suspected the doctor was a Libertarian.

Yeah. Let us go to hell however we want to. It's our own choice, after all.

A pharmacology aide walked in and put down a plastic-capped beaker of orange fluid. Next to it he placed a cardboard box that clinked, the sound of many small bottles. Derek inspected his fingernails as the assistant passed out of the office, ignoring the aide's expression of bored contempt.

"So what's this new type of Time-Jizz, Doctor? Will it work better?"

"Drink." Bettide gestured at the beaker without looking up. He took out a key and unlocked his briefcase, removing a small black ledger.

Derek grimaced and reached for the vitamin suppliment, sighing for effect as he pried off the plastic cover. He drank the orange-flavored concoction, knowing Bettide wouldn't help him until it was all gone.

At last he put down the beaker and licked the orange coating from his ragged moustache. "Have they found any more cases like me, Doctor?" For a change his voice was serious, earnest.

"A few," Bettide answered noncommitally, still writing in the small black book.

"Well? Have they found out why some of us get stuck in sequential time trips, instead of just accessing the memories we want at will?"

Bettide closed the book and looked up. "No, Derek. We haven't. But look on the bright side. At least you don't suffer the worst syndrome. Some Temporin users with hidden masochistic tendencies send themselves right off to the worst moments of their lives. A few get into flashback loops where many times each day they relive those episodes in vivid detail, with or without the drug."

Derek blinked. "That's terrible! But . . ."

A crafty look spread across his face. "Oh, I get it. That's one of those aversion stories, isn't it? Part of trying to get your clients off the very drugs you pass out. Pretty clever. You almost scared me this time."

Bettide shrugged. "Have it your own way, Derek. As to your problem of sequential access, I believe we might have a possible solution."

For once Derek had no comment. He edged forward in his seat.

"Your dilemma," Bettide said, "is to *choose* the memory to be accessed through the drug. Other than volition—which seems to be locked in your case—the only other known way would be to use electronic probing. Unfortunately, that method is out."

"Why?"

"Because the government is not in the business of pandering to destructive and expensive habits that don't already have a criminal purveyor! We provide you Temporin to keep you out of the clutches of the Black Chemists and other underworld sources, and to see that you have every opportunity to freely choose a productive lifestyle again."

"But if this electrical gizmo is the only way . . ."

"There might be another." Bettide took off his glasses and wiped them. "It's untried, and *I* certainly wouldn't attempt it. But then, I would never have gotten myself in your fix in the first place. Once again I ask you to accept the coalition's offer to send you to an ecology camp for a rest and work cure, instead." Bettide made his entreaty as if he knew what the answer would be in advance.

Derek felt tense under his scalp. He shook his head vigorously, as if to drive out a threatening uncertainty. "No! . . . If you won't help me, I'll go to the Black Chemists," he threatened. "I swear, I'll—"

"Oh, stop." Bettide sighed in tired surrender.

Derek's headache vanished just as quickly. "Okay." He brightened. "What do we do?"

"We'll try you out on a potent new version of Temporin B the Black Chemists have just developed and we've managed to resynthesize. One hit drives the reliving process about five times longer on average, than the old drug, and at three times the subjective/objective rate."

"But—but that won't help me get back to where I want to go. It'll only make the sequences go by faster!"

"True. However, some believe your strange type of locked, sequential recall will break down as more recent memories are accessed. You'll have revisited your entire life, so to speak, and no long-term memory will have greater excitation potential than any other."

"I'll have free access again after that?"

"That's my best guess, Derek."

Derek chewed on one end of his moustache. "I'll have to go through some pretty rotten times," he muttered.

"Quickly, yes." Bettide nodded.

"I don't know." Derek knitted his brow.

Bettide closed the file folder. "Well, our time is up. If you can't decide now, we'll just make an appointment for next week."

Derek looked up quickly. "I'll do it! Please. Can we start now?"

Bettide shrugged. He opened the cardboard box and put about a dozen small bottles into a paper bag.

"Sign here." He indicated a release form.

Derek scribbled his signature and took the bottles. They clinked as he rose to go. "Thanks, Doc. I know you're trying to help. Maybe if I can just get some peace for a while—get back to Sycamore Street for a rest—I'll be able to think about things . . ."

Bettide nodded reservedly. But, as Derek opened the door to leave, the doctor said, "I saw *Realm of Magic* on the Late Show last week, Derek. I enjoyed it a great deal. You were very good in that film, even if you were better on the stage."

Derek half turned, but couldn't make himself meet the physician's eyes. He nodded, clutching the bag, and left quickly without shutting the door behind him.

4

The amber-white fluid enticed, and he sought salvation in the past . . .

Enola Gay closed before summer. He hadn't much liked the part, anyway. It made him nervous. Claude Eatherly, the protagonist, was a hard mind to get into.

No matter. When Peter Tiersjens hired a fresh-faced kid for the road show, that suited Derek fine. He was getting sick of Peter and his damned sanctimony anyway. At the last cast party the elderly director tried to give Derek some "fatherly advice." Derek fumed in his cups.

"The Catskills? The fucking Catskills? Jesus, Peter! What kind of shit have you got for brains? What would I do in the friggin' Catskills over the whole summer? I went there as a kid and all I can remember is being bored enough to kill myself, while my mother and father listened to accordion music and the sound of their arteries hardening!"

Derek tossed back the last of his drink. He took a cube from the ice chest on his dressing table and dropped it into the glass. His hands shook a little as he poured two jiggers of gin after it, spilling some onto the marble tabletop.

The sounds of the cast party could be heard through a crack in the door. Old Peter Tiersjens sat back in a folding chair, his feet propped up on a box of costumes. He took off his wire-rimmed glasses and pinched the bridge of his nose.

"Derek, I am thinking of you. What will you do now that the show has closed? Do you have any other offers? Do you have savings?"

Derek shrugged. "My agent says he's looking over the off-season possibilities. But most of them are out in the sticks, so maybe I'll just stay in the city this summer. Who knows? I may get a call from the Coast for another movie." Derek sipped at his drink. Already the evening was shimmering in a fine inebriated gloss—like gauze over a camera lens. He would be grateful for the fog later, when he went out to select a bed partner from the groupies. The Vaseline vagueness would make the stalest teeny-bopper shine like Fay Wray. It was easy to forget Melissa when he was loaded.

"Derek . . ." There was a long pause as Tiersjens grew uncharacteristically reticent. Derek experienced the strangest sense of déjà vu, almost as if he knew the director's very words before they were spoken.

"Derek, there will be no offers from Hollywood. Your name is mud out there, has been ever since you walked out on *Tunnel in the Sky*. Who would hire you after that? To be honest, Derek, your taking the Catskills job wouldn't be a great favor to me. It's my way of trying, one last time, to help you."

Derek sneered. "Like you *helped* me by hiring that snot-nosed Todd Chestner to play Eatherly on the road? Dumping me in the process?"

"Don't blame that on Todd. The kid idolizes you, Derek. I did it for the good of the show. Todd's been covering for you half of the time anyway. Anyone but me would have replaced you three months ago.

"But Derek, I am willing to give it one more go, for old times' sake. *Take* the Catskills job, and get off this cycle of self-destruction while there's still a chance!"

For a moment, Derek found himself captured by the man's intensity. Peter Tiersjens could take a platoon of blasé actors and light the fire of Melpomene inside them with a few words. "Derek," he urged. "You used to say there was nothing more contemptible than the artist who lost himself on the Edge. Now you are sacrificing everything on the altar of Bacchus. 'Tis mad idolatry to make the service greater than the god'!"

In the half-drunken fog, Derek's belligerent side won a brief, but bitter, struggle.

" 'Cry, Troyans, Cry!' " He mocked the older man, quoting from the same play. "Cassandra, you can go to hell." He stood up and walked unsteadily to the door. On the way he kicked Peter's chair. His fists clenched in pleasure at the resultant shout and crash, and he left without looking back.

Later he had the satisfaction of punching Todd Chestner

in his fatuous, earnest young face. It would take makeup an extra half hour to get the twerp ready, during the first week of the road show. That was some satisfaction, at least.

After that, though, even the groupies drew back. And that evening he went home alone.

"Uh!"

Derek awakened suddenly from the drug-induced playback. He shuddered, and for a long time just lay there on the unkempt mattress, breathing.

The new drug certainly did release a charged, totally vivid experience. It also drew out the playbacks more rapidly.

All he had to do was somehow endure the next three years' worth of memory recall. *That's all*. At this rate it shouldn't take more than a couple of weeks, real time. A few more weeks, then, if Bettide was right, it would be back to the golden years!

Derek had come to believe the drug did more than simply play back chemical memories inscribed in the brain. He was half convinced it actually took one *back*. Personally. And when the bad times were through he would be free once more to cycle back to childhood . . . to model airplanes and long summer afternoons . . . to ice cream and the sweetness of precocious first love . . . to a time when there were no regrets.

He got up, stretching to ease a crick in his back, and slipped a Diet-Perf dinner into the rusty old microwave. He barely tasted the meal when he spooned it down.

Derek got out the log Dr. Bettide had given him. Success depended on the physician's goodwill, so he wrote down the times and places he had returned to . . . avoiding mention of the nasty little personal details. They were irrelevant, anyway.

He watched the Late Show on TV until, at last, sleep arrived. Then came the inevitable struggle with his dreams, trying to make them conform to his will. But they were not pliant, and had their way with him.

*　　*　　*

"Blakeney, just who do you think you are? This is the third time you've come in late and stoned, and gotten belligerent with the audience! We may be a small-time company, but we've got our reputations to consider . . ."

"Reputations!" Derek sniffed noisily. He had been doing a lot of coke lately and his sinuses stung. That only made him angrier. "Reputations, my eye! You're a bunch of diapered juveniles pandering to tourists in a little uptown improv club, calling yourselves actors. Here I am, willing to lend you my name and my services, and you talk to me about *reputations?*"

"Why, you conceited windbag!" One of the young men had to be physically restrained. Derek grinned as the others held the fellow back, knowing they would never dare back up their bluster with physical force.

"Conceit, my young friend, is a matter of interpretation. It's all relative. Haven't you learned that yet?" He rolled his eyes heavenward. "I try so hard to pass on what I know, yet the next generation is obdurate!"

One of the older youths stepped before Derek.

"Yes, Mr. Blakeney, you have taught us a thing or two."

Derek smiled back benignly. But the fellow was not apologizing.

"You've given a bunch of hungry young actors an object lesson in the dangers of success, Mr. Blakeney. You've shown us how far the mighty can fall, when arrogance substitutes for self-respect. For teaching us that, we'll slice you a percentage of the rest of the shows this month. It won't be necessary for you to return."

Derek snarled. "You can't do that! We have a contract!"

"We also have witnesses to your foulmouthed abuse of paying customers, Mr. Blakeney. You can treat us like dirt beneath your feet, but mistreating the marks is something any court in the land will recognize as just cause. Sue us, or send your agent around. But don't show up in person or we'll call the cops."

"Yeah," one of the girls said. "And if that doesn't work, we'll break your arm!"

Derek stood very still, his breath hissing angrily

through clenched teeth. He dragged his memory for an appropriate quotation . . . something Shakespearean and devastatingly apropos to the ingratitude and treachery of youth.

He couldn't come up with anything.

His mind was blank!

The blood drained out of his face and he clutched the stair rail. With a titanic effort he straightened his shoulders and turned so the young actors wouldn't see. He was out on the sidewalk before he trusted himself to breathe again.

I couldn't improvise a comeback to devastate those cretins! What's the matter with me?

For an instant an unwelcome idea penetrated . . . the possibility that Peter had been right, that these punks were right.

The thought seared. It was too hot to be allowed to settle in. He drove it out by thinking about . . .

About getting high.

Yeah. Somewhere there must be a drug to help. Uppers did the trick when there was work to do. Downers helped him sleep. Somewhere there had to be a drug that'd bring back happiness.

All I need is a little peace. Then I could get my thoughts together. Make a plan. There oughta be a jizz to help me get through the summer. I'll straighten out this fall.

Melissa won't approve, of course. She'll want me to clean up my act overnight—

What am I saying? Melissa's been gone almost a year!

He felt very odd, like a man standing at a crossroads, undecided over which way to go and afraid that it was already too late to turn back. That sense of déjà vu returned again, filling him with a dreadful feeling that he had been this way before, and was doomed to choose wrong again. And again.

Unsteadily, he walked down Forty-seventh street, past the shops and the pedicabs, and the occasional licensed automobile. Flywheel jitneys hummed by, picking up tourists on their way to the Village or downtown.

Slowly, the unease began to dissipate. It was summer in New York. Hardly a time and place for heavy thinking.

I'll go see Barney, he decided. Maybe he's heard of something on the street. Something to get me up.

"They call it Time-Jizz." Barney handed Derek a packet of white powder. "It's the latest thing out o' the Black Chemists. Man, this time they've really stolen a march on the guv'mint. Time-Jizz is the biggest thing there is now."

"What it is, man? What's it do, bro?" Derek unconsciously adopted the dialect of his supplier, mimicking the street tempo perfectly.

"Mooch-hooch, baby. With this stuff you can go back to any limber scene you ever had, and *relive* it. I mean, I tried it an' it works! I went back to the best lay I ever had, and man, I found out my memory weren't exaggeratin' one bit. Mmm-mmm."

Derek fingered the packet. "I dunno, Barney. A new blam-scam from the Black Chemists . . . I don't want no junkie-monkey, now."

"Aw, the shrinks have had this stuff f'years!" the dealer soothed. "Word is it's safe. No monkey, for sure, babe. And you get to choose the time and place you go back and visit! Shoot. A deal like that makes you think them Black Chemists were really brothers after all, and not a bunch of old white syndicate clowns with Pee aitch Dees."

The powder glistened in the light from a bare bulb. Derek stared at it.

"Anywhere or anytime I wanted . . ." he murmured.

"Yeah, man, you could go back to when you were suckin' Baby Ruths and peekin' up girls' dresses."

"My childhood was a boring crock." Derek snickered. "Still," he added thoughtfully. "It had its moments. Anyway, as the serpent used to say, why not?"

He looked up and saw the dealer was staring at him. "George Bernard Shaw," he explained. "From *Back to Methuselah*."

"Sure, man." Barney shrugged. "Anything you say.

Now about the price. Startin' out I can offer you a real
sweet deal . . ."

Derek came home to his cheap studio to find the mail
slot filled with bills. He shut the door with his foot and let
the envelopes slip to the floor. He poured a can of soup
into a pan and stirred it over a hotplate. He contemplated
a small vial of amber fluid, one of Bettide's ampules, on
the counter in front of him.

Derek felt trapped. He had been accessing increasingly recent memories, more and more painful to face. He
wasn't sure he could go through the final two years' worth
of total recall.

He would be gambling the pain of recent memories
against Dr. Bettide's hypothetical "breakthrough" . . . when
all the storage in his mind would supposedly be his again,
reachable at will.

Reliving that episode with the kids at the improv—
and then his first purchase of Time-Jizz from dealer
Barney—had driven him away from the drug for a few
days. He had walked around in a depressed haze, getting
stoned on older, less terrifying highs.

He hung around a few theaters, milking a few tourists
who recognized him. He ignored their whispers to each
other after he finished signing autographs.

Finally, he found himself at the office of Frank Furtess,
his old agent. Old Frankfurter had looked genuinely surprised to see him. Then Derek remembered. He had fired
Furtess more than a year ago, using nearly every piece of
invective in the book.

Derek realized that he had adopted a frame of refer-
ence twenty months old, and momentarily forgotten the
incident! By then he had already shaken the agent's hand;
he had to play the scene to its end.

The meeting was chilly. Furtess promised to look into
a few possibilities. Derek left his landlady's phone number, but he figured the man would throw it away the
moment he left.

Now, to come home and find all these bills, and
royalties so scant these days . . .

It was late afternoon, and once again the ripped windowshade cast the legs of a runner on the wall. The jogger's slow, mute progress was a tale of perseverance.

Derek plucked up the ampule and moved over to the mattress on the dusty floor. He broke the seal and held the needle to his arm . . . He . . .

. . . mixed the powder carefully in his Fifth Avenue apartment. In the light from the lavalamp he poured the mixture into a glass and drank it, as Barney had told him to do.

He sat back in the relaxing hum of his vibrochair and avoided thinking about how he was going to keep up the rent on this expensive flat. Instead, he tried to focus on some event in his childhood. Almost anything would do for a test of the new drug.

Ah, he thought. Model-making with Douglas Kee, the gardener's boy! We did have fun, didn't we? We were pals. What age was I then, ten years old?

He closed his eyes as a pleasant numbness washed over him. He thought about glue, and plastic, and little sticky decals . . .

. . . and found himself laughing!

The laughter was high and clear. It startled him, but he couldn't stop! He was no longer in control of his body. Someone *else* was in command.

In a sudden flow of visual images, he saw that he was no longer in his apartment. Sunlight streamed in to fall on a cracked linoleum floor. Dust gathered in clumps under worn furniture and stacks of old newspapers. In one corner of the room a calico kitten played with a ball of string. Through a half-opened door came a steady breeze of sunwarmed fresh air.

But he caught all of this out of a corner of his field of vision. At the moment he could not make his eyes shift from a pile of plastic odds and ends on the floor in front of him. He caught a glimpse of his own hands and was momentarily shaken by how small they were. They moved nimbly among the plastic bits, fitting them together experimentally.

"Maybe we could glue that extra piece of the ol' Cutty Sark onto here and make a radar antenna out of it!"

Derek's gaze shifted to his left. Next to him was a small boy with Oriental features.

And yet he didn't look so very small right now. In fact the boy was larger than himself!

Once again Derek found himself laughing, high and uninhibited. "Sure, stick a mast of a sailing ship on an intergalactic warp vessel. Why not?"

The voice was unmistakably his own. He felt his own mouth and larynx form the words. But it was a smaller voice, and a younger, more intense volition that shaped it. The adult part of himself began to understand.

I'm back to when I was ten. It worked. The drug worked!

Now he was getting more than physical sensations. The thoughts of that happy ten-year-old come rushing in, threatening to wash all sense of adulthood aside.

He tried to make the flow two-way . . . to communicate with the boy. But it was hopeless. The child was only a memory, playing back now in vivid detail. It could not be changed.

Gradually, all awareness of being anything but the boy fell away, as he learned to let go and just observe.

"Hey! Hey! I got it!" Derek-the-child shouted. "Let's put a glob of glue over this guy's head and call it a space helmet!"

"Naw. That's a Civil War Union guy. What'd he be doing with a space helmet?"

"Well, with the glue on his head who could tell?" Derek giggled. "And *he* wouldn't care. Not with a ton of glue to sniff!"

The boys laughed together. *Derek* laughed along.

"I want to go back to the old drug, now. I want to slow down again."

Dr. Bettide jotted a comment in his little black notebook.

"Have you finished reviewing your memories up to the present?"

"No. I don't want to do that now."

"Why? I thought your objective was to make available, once more, the memories of childhood."

Derek grinned. "I've *done* that!"

Bettide frowned. "I'm not certain I understand."

"It's simple, really. I've finally started reliving the point, eighteen months ago, when I first started taking the drug."

"Yes? And?"

"And now I'm recalling perfect memories of recalling perfect memories of childhood!"

Bettide stared at him, blinking first in confusion, then in growing amazement. Derek relished it.

I must be the first, he realized. The first ever to have done this. Why, that makes me some kind of explorer, doesn't it? An explorer of inner space?

"But Derek, you'll also be reliving some of the worst times of your life—the eviction, for instance, and the lawsuits."

Derek shrugged. "Most of that time I was in a Time-Jizz stupor. And it felt like I was in the past six to ten hours for every hour in the present. It was worth it then, it'll be worth it again."

Bettide frowned. "I must think on this, Derek. There may be unforeseen consequences. I'd like to have you come out to the institute for some tests . . ."

Derek shook his head. "Uh-uh. You can't force me. I'm grateful, Doctor. Accidentally you've given me the key. But if you stop helping me, I'll go to the Black Chemists."

"Derek . . ."

"You think about it, Doc." Derek got up, knowing he had the advantage. Obviously, the physician wanted to keep him in sight, to observe this new twist.

"I'll come back in a week, Doctor Bettide. If you have refills ready for me, I'll tell you all about it." He couldn't help letting a little Vincent Price slip into his voice. "Otherwise . . ."

Involuntarily Bettide shivered. Derek laughed and swept out of the office.

"Darling, don't go in the water! You'll get your cast wet!"

"Aw, Mom!"

"I mean it!"

Derek shrugged and kicked a stone along the sandy lake shore. He savored the feeling of being unjustly persecuted, though at the root of it he knew his mother was right. This way, though, he could nurse just a little more mileage out of his broken arm.

Actually, it had been frightening when it happened. He had fractured it waterskiing early in the summer. But now it seemed like the best thing that ever happened to him. All the girls whose families were summering by the lake competed to fuss over him.

Tonight that precocious little bundle Jennifer Smythe was going to take him to auditions at the Junior Theater in Big Bear. He hadn't wanted to go, at first, but when she began making promises about what they would do afterward, he grew more interested.

Who knows? Derek mused. Maybe they'll offer me a part in the play. Now, wouldn't that be something?

High overhead, a big Boeing 787 growled across the sky. At one time Derek had thought he might want to be a pilot, or an astronaut. Now he watched the plane cynically. That was patsy's work. There had to be something better—something that would make people want to pay him just to be himself . . .

He smiled as he thought of Jennifer. The sunshine was warm on his well-tanned back. He felt, as he often did, on the verge of a great adventure. Anticipation was delicious.

"Oh, Derek! You were wonderful!"

"Was I really?"

"You heard Mrs. Abell. She's rewriting the male lead so he has a broken arm! And you pretend you aren't interested."

"Oh, sure I am." He laughed. "Only right now I'm interested in something else even more!"

Jennifer giggled and took his hand. "Come on. I know a place by the boat sheds."

"Mr. Blakeney, you owe four months' payments on your condominium. If you don't remit within a week, we'll be forced to finalize the foreclosure proceedings . . ."

Derek slammed the door in the attorney's face. "I'll send some money when my next royalty check comes in!" he shouted through the door. Then he turned away and forgot the matter. He had more important problems than some jerk worried about late rent.

He had run out of Time-Jizz. And Barney, his supplier, had jacked up the prices beyond what he could afford. "It's the Black Chemists," the dealer had complained. "They upped the price on me. I gotta pass it on."

Derek knew what he had to do. He would go to the new government drug rehab center on Eighth Avenue. They were bragging about how they'd maintain a junkie and give him food, just to keep him "out of the cycle of crime and death."

Okay, he told himself. I'll just go down there and see if they mean it.

He didn't even notice that he had crossed the line to calling himself a junkie.

"Hello. I am Dr. Melniss Bettide. I'll be supervising your case, Mr. . . ." The small dark man peered at the name on the chart.

"Good heavens!" he gasped. "You're Derek Blakeney!" The physician pronounced the name as if he were making a rare and stunning diagnosis.

Derek forced one of his famous, confident smiles. "Fame is like a river, that beareth up things light and swoln . . ." He shrugged nonchalantly. "Would you like an autograph, Doctor?"

"Honey! It's Derek's agent on the phone! He says Derek has won the part!"

They thought he was asleep. His father had finally sent him to bed, rather than let him continue pacing, hitting the walls. But that didn't keep him from waking the instant the telephone rang.

"Are you sure?" He heard his father's voice, muffled by his bedroom door. "I don't want to wake the poor kid with rumors if he's just going to be let down."

"Well, come and talk to the man yourself, then. . . . Just a moment, Mr. Pasternak. My husband is coming to the phone."

Derek overheard murmured talk of allowances and percentages, of shooting schedules and tutors to make up for lost schooling . . . His father was being boorishly insistent about the latter, but Derek didn't really mind.

He remembered the auditions—all those poor kids being dragged around by their crazy stage mothers, and *he* had won the part!

Why, Mom didn't even care if I made it. She just thought it would be fun to try! Dad too had been helpful in his gruff, skeptical way. Derek let them have their moment, fussing over the phone with the agent. His turn would come with the new day.

"Hollywood," he sighed in false cynicism. "Oh, well. It's not Broadway, but it's a start." He couldn't help grinning under the covers . . . wondering if California girls were all they were supposed to be.

I'll find out, he thought. Real soon.

I'm going to be a star.

Making friends with a movie dog . . . learning the ways of the back lot . . . sailing a catamaran on location in Papeete . . . fencing lessons in Beverly Hills—and other lessons from a beautiful older actress at night in her apartment . . .

His first drag of reefer . . . two years dodging teenage girls who swooned at the sight of him while he played *Dobie in Orbit* on TV . . .

Singing and dancing up a storm in the Broadway version of *Borgia!* . . . getting plastered with friends

. . . pulling crazy stunts . . . getting an Academy Award nomination for his role in *Another Roadside Attraction*.

Somehow, he managed to find a place in a fleabag hotel where the rent was cheap. The landlady had loved his movies and seen every one of his plays. The people at the condominium complex held his awards and his furniture in bond for payments due.

They let him take the lavalamps.

Derek didn't care. Between the serving of the eviction notice and moving into the dingy little room, he had relived ten of the best years of his life. It wasn't a bad deal at all.

He replayed that year when he had led the cast of *Potemkin at Midnight* . . . and had begun to hear those muttered complaints—that he was becoming self-indulgent, for instance, and intractable in his interpretations. He spurned the critics and went his own way, of course. If the reviewers groused, let them! The marks were happy. And there was always somebody eager to send out for a little more champagne—a little more coke.

Fagin's Boys, and Girls closed early, but that was because of bad directing and a flawed script. He never much liked musicals, anyway, except for the chicks in the chorus line, of course.

That Three Vee pilot for a series based on the cartoon writers of the fifties was an interesting project, but the cretins botched it with endless rewrite. It ran three months. No matter. There would always be something else.

Two weeks after moving into the fleabag, he met Melissa for the first time, again . . . not in this life, but in his memory.

He took her home to the Fifth Avenue condo. Her laughter was sweeter than music. Her wit was sharp and brilliant. He had had many lovers with dancers' bodies, but hers was special.

In her he found not just pleasure, but joy.

"Derek, honey, please wake up."

"Hmmmph. What? Liss, what is it?"

She held the phone to her breast. There were tears in her eyes.

Derek looked up in a fog. He had had one too many nightcaps.

"Liss? What's the matter?"

"It's Frank Furtess. He was up early and heard it on the radio. He figured we'd want to be told, and not find out in the morning papers.

"Derek, the Divine Terror Alignment has struck again . . . Honey, they've nuked Albany."

Her voice was stark. Hollow with sadness. It took a moment for the words to soak in.

Albany?

"Blown . . . up? The whole town?"

"Oh, baby. I'm so sorry."

At first all he could think of were *buildings*—the library, the high school, the drugstore in his neighborhood, all tumbled to the ground and smoking. The park, the capitol, his parents' house.

"Mom!" he croaked, sitting up. "Dad!"

He reached out, but not for the telephone.

Melissa held him while he sobbed. It had been almost a year since he had seen either of his parents in person. The last time he had been so casual . . . he had even left without bothering to say good-bye.

This is no good, Derek thought as he came down from that particular memory trip. I'm reliving the bad stuff, now. I'd better get some advice on how to get control over this drug . . . learn how to force it to draw out only the memories I want. Maybe I'll talk to that guy Bettide.

No. This just won't do at all.

He dreamt that night. Real dreams, not memories. He dreamt about smoke and fire and guilt. And he wept because there was nobody there to hold him this time around.

This is no good, Derek thought as he came down. I'm reliving the bad stuff *again*! Even down to those awful dreams I had when I first realized the drug was going bad. Maybe Bettide was right after all.

Oh, hell, what am I going to do *now*?

Things perked up a bit when he played Anton Perceveral in *The Minimum Man*, though the critics gave most of the credit for its success to the writers of the adaptation, and to Peter Tiersjens, who directed. Derek nursed his jealousy but said nothing. For a long time he was listless except when he was on stage.

The crowds identified with Perceveral, but he just couldn't.

Melissa nursed him, teased him, cared for him. He let himself be talked into doing Falstaff over the summer, and hated it.

Peter got him the role of the decade—playing Claude Eatherly in *Enola Gay*. If anything could snap him out of his doldrums, that part should have.

It worked, sort of. He stopped moping and became arrogant. He snapped and lashed out and drank and snorted and smoked. He came home with the scent of other women on his clothes. Derek witnessed himself witnessing it all over again. He writhed within and tried to relive the experience without participating at all.

Yet a glimmer of his present self remained awake to notice things . . . things he had not seen the first time around. A piece of mail tossed in a corner. A misplaced phone message. A promise forgotten the initial time through, but noted on this passage . . .

It didn't seem to make any difference, though. The past was fixed. The mistakes and casual cruelties repeated inerrantly. Derek struggled not to watch, but started taking larger and larger doses of the drug.

On the wall of his little room the legs of the runner approached the finish line . . .

Derek thought about Sycamore Street, Albany, New York . . . where his mother would be cooking a Sunday supper, his father would be reading the paper, and his room was a clutter of plastic models, filling the air with the heady scent of glue. He willed himself back to age twelve . . . back to a place in the warehouse of his cortex where a familiar female voice was about to call out . . .

"Supper's ready!"

Derek smiled (*foolish smile*, the latest Derek thought). It had worked! Those were exactly the words he had willed his mother . . .

"Come on, Lothario . . ." Melissa slid the door open and Derek witnessed a former self being surprised, and a still earlier self snarl and curse. As the woman made her decision, and turned to leave, he felt, simultaneously:

"*Good riddance!*"

"*Melissa, don't go!*"

And this time added, "Oh, shut up, you fool, can't you see she's gone for good?"

"Drink." Bettide gestured without looking up.

Derek grimaced but drank the supplement. "Have they found any more cases like me, doc?"

Bettide licked his pencil. "A few."

"As to your problem of sequential memory access," he went on. "I think we might have a possible solution."

Derek edged forward to listen.

Derek awoke in a sweat. He shivered as he realized what was happening. The sequential memories were rapidly approaching the present. Soon he would begin recalling memories of recalling memories of recalling memories!

Where would it end?

He lay in the damp bed and wondered for the first time about the nature of his present existence.

He checked his own reality by every test he could devise—from pinching himself to reciting Shaw backward—but none of them proved for certain that he had never been this way before . . . that he had free will and was not merely reliving another memory at this very moment, in some future self's Temporin-induced trip.

"I expected something like this might happen, Derek. But you must be stalwart. Remember Anton Perceveral?

Stick with it and I think we can get out the other side."

Derek's hand shook as he drank the required supplement. He put down the beaker and looked from Bettide to the little black notebook and back. "I'm just an experiment to you," he accused.

Bettide shrugged. "Partly, perhaps. You are also my patient. And an artist who I would dearly like to return to society. Fortunately all three imperatives make for a common goal. Now, *will* you agree to coming to the clinic so I can keep you under observation?"

Derek lowered his head into his hands. "I don't know. I just don't know. I'm lost in Time, Doctor. My thoughts and memories are a whirlwind. Nothing stands *still* anymore!"

For a long moment there was silence in the cubicle, broken only by the muttering of the ventilation system. Then Bettide spoke softly.

> *"But thoughts, the slaves of Life,*
> *and Life, Time's fool,*
> *And time, that takes a survey of all the world,*
> *Must have a stop."*

Derek looked up and blinked. For a clear moment the shabby office seemed built wholly of crystal—the clocks all halted—and the breath of the Universe held in expectant quiet. Light refracted through the diamond walls.

He knew, right then, that this moment was a new one, whether remembered a thousand times or not . . . even if witnessed by a hundred thousand versions of himself.

Each instant is itself, and nothing more. Each a heartbeat of God.

The epiphany passed with another blink of his eyes. Bettide wiped his glasses and looked at Derek myopically, awaiting an answer.

"I'll let you know, Doctor," Derek said quietly as he stood up. "I will be back tomorrow. I promise."

"All right, Derek. I'll tell the receptionist to let you in at any time."

Derek paused at the door.

"Thank you," he said softly. Then he went out into the wintry afternoon.

The park was nearly empty. Derek climbed the steps to the Summer Theater. He stood on the stage and looked up at the city for over an hour, not moving or speaking, but nevertheless playing a part.

The ampule gleamed in the light from the torn windowshade. Derek looked at the little glass vial and decided he at last understood Anton Perceveral.

What else have we, he thought, when we have mined ourselves a tunnel all the way to Hell, than the option of digging further and hoping for a world that's round?

"I saw *Realm of Magic* on the Late Show last week, Derek. You were very good . . ."

. . . the runner on the wall lengthened his stride.

Enola Gay closed before summer . . .

"The Catskills? Jeeze, Peter, what would I do in the friggin' Catskills?"

. . . He had the satisfaction of punching Todd Chestner . . . but even the groupies drew back after that . . . He went home alone . . .

"Mr. Blakeney, you've given some young actors an object lesson in the dangers of success . . ."

"It's called Time-Jizz . . . The latest thing from th' Black Chemists . . ."

He came home to his fleabag to find a pile of bills . . . He broke the seal and held the ampule over his vein . . .

. . . mixed the powder and drank, thinking about glue and plastic and little sticky decals . . .

. . . and found himself laughing . . . high, clear childish laughter.

Derek relived Derek reliving Derek reliving . . . The boys laughed together and Derek laughed along. But this time he struggled not to lose consciousness. He was ten again. But ten was no longer a goal. It was a way station. He lived as the child again, but this time he watched.

* * *

"Darling, don't go into the water!"

"Aw, Mom!"

But Jennifer had made slightly veiled promises . . .
overhead a jet plane growled . . . At one time he had
wanted to be a pilot, but that was patsy's work . . .

"Oh, Derek, you were wonderful!"

"Mr. Blakeney, you owe four months' rent . . ."

". . . the Black Chemists have upped the price."

"Good Lord!" Bettide hissed. "You're Derek Blakeney!"

"Honey! The agent says Derek's got the part!"

. . . Making friends with a movie dog . . . an older
actress at night . . . first reefer . . . teenage girls swooning
. . . a fleabag hotel where he could continue taking the
drug and relive leading the cast of *Another Roadside* . . .
Meeting Melissa, her laughter sweet, her smile bright . . .
joy . . .

"Derek, honey, the terrorists . . ." She held him . . .
but then she wasn't there to hold him anymore.

The scenes flickered from a plush condominium to a
cheap room. From cheering audiences to downer reviews.
Somewhere in the midst of it all Derek realized that he
was replaying memories that had accumulated at the beginning of *this* very session with the drug . . . that like
Achilles chasing the hare, he was parsing his life into more
and more rapid cycles. The closer he got to the "present,"
the more cycles had accumulated and the more densely
packed they were—each a lifetime to be relived!

"But thoughts, the slaves of Life—"

Bless the Mercy Law, he thought, opening the shoe
box . . . The runner passed the edge of the doorway.

"Supper's ready!"

"Good-bye, Derek." The door slammed.

"Good riddance . . ."

"Melissa, don't go!"

"You fool, she's gone."

This time he added, "Yes, she's gone. But do you care enough to *follow* her?"

Derek grimaced and sipped the supplement . . . "Have they found any more like me, Doc? . . ."
"I saw *Realm of Magic* on the Late Show."
"What would I do in the friggin' *Catskills*?"
Even the groupies drew back . . .
". . . an object lesson in the dangers of . . ."
"They call it Time-Jizz . . ."
. . . picked up the ampule . . .
. . . mixed the powder,
   . . . picked up the ampule . . .
      . . . found himself laughing, high and clear.
   and laughed along
   and laughed along
and laughed along but watched
and carefully watched . . .

"And Time, that takes survey of all the world—"

The runner found his stride . . .
"Good-bye, Derek."
"Good riddance . . ."
"Don't go!"
"You fool, she's gone."
"Yes, but do you care enough to follow her?"
"How, you idiot? How can I follow when the past is locked, and the flashbacks multiply faster than I can experience them? I can't even get off!"

Derek sipped. ". . any more like me, Doc? . . ."
". . saw *Realm of Magic* . . ."
". . . friggin' *Catskills* . . ."
". . . object lesson . . ."
"They call it Time-Jizz . . ."
. . . picked up the ampule . . .
   . . . picked up the ampule . . .
      . . . picked up the ampule . . .
         . . . mixed the powder . . .
            . . . found himself laughing.

. . . and laughed along and laughed along and laughed along but watched and watched and watched and watched.

"And Time—"

"—Good riddance . . ."
"—Don't go."
"—She's gone."
"—Will you follow?"
"—How? I can't even get off!"
Derek added another layer.
He laughed . . . high and clear.

"Must have a stop—"

The runner persevered. There really wasn't anything else to do.

AUTHOR'S NOTES

A treasured colleague and friend is my brother Dan, a newspaperman and veteran of the City News Bureau of Chicago, who was so fierce and on target in his scrawled comments on my early work that I decided I had better get writing gooder quick!

Seriously, I do believe useful criticism is an author's lifeblood. No story of mine is published without being read by a dozen or more selected people well in advance. Those who can't find something to criticize, something needing improvement, tightening, or polishing, are dropped from my list with my thanks. Only by hearing the bad news can I improve. Dan taught me that.

It was Dan's idea to do a piece about a memory drug. This is his story, as much as mine.

"A Stage of Memory" is also a tale about ego. We are probably the first civilization whose paramount heroes are entertainers. (Most others have admired warriors above all else.) Worshiping movie and rock stars may be a slight improvement, but it has its drawbacks. Growing up near Hollywood, I got to see more than I wanted of what "ego rage" can do to people, especially when all one hears are the trumpets of praise.

The long road to hell can be traveled by not listening to others, or by listening and believing them too much.

Sic transit gloria. Remember where you're standing.

SPECULATION

Just a Hint

It was exactly seven A.M. when Federman finished typing the last data entry. The small console flashed a confirmation and, several miles away, the central processor began correlating the results of the previous evening's observation run.

Federman winced as he stretched in the swivel chair, his spine cracking. Age seemed to make every strain and pop a cruel reminder, as if decay were audibly calling out its territoriality.

The classical music station playing on his desktop radio began an update of the morning's headlines.

The weather would be beautiful over most of the country. The chance of rain in the nearby area was less than twenty percent. The current probability estimate for the likelihood of nuclear war this year still hovered around twenty percent, also.

Liz Browning backed in, pushing the door open with one foot as she balanced a cardboard tray with coffee, doughnuts, and the morning newspaper.

"Good," she said, laying her load down on his desk. "I knew you could finish without me. I don't know how you stay up all night reducing data without getting hungry. I just had to get some food!"

As a matter of fact, Federman had started noticing a growling emptiness in his stomach almost the moment the last figure had been typed. If his graduate student had been glad to let him finish alone, he was just as happy she had brought back the goodies.

"It's love, Liz. Anyone who stays up all night has to

be in love . . . in this case with astronomy. Either that or
he's crazy or in the army."

Elizabeth Browning grinned ironically, leaving crin-
kled smile lines around her eyes. Her straight brown hair
was braided behind her back.

"Or it means he wants to beat Tidbinbilla into print
with that new pulsar analysis. Come on, Sam. Outside it's
already a beautiful day. Let's let some light in here." She
went to the window and pulled the heavy drapes aside. A
bolt of brilliant sunshine came crackling in. She didn't
even wince as she leaned forward to open the window, but
Federman covered his eyes.

"Cruel youth," he moaned. "To bring these spotted
hands and time-wracked limbs before the searching gaze
of day."

"Aw, come on, Sam. You and I both know there's no
such quotation. Why do you keep making up fake Shake-
speare?"

"Perhaps I'm a poet at heart?"

"You're a scoundrel and a rogue at heart. That's why
I'm so incredibly pleased with myself for latching onto you
as a research advisor. Everybody else may be losing their
grants as the military budget increases, but you know how
to finagle enough funding to keep the radio astronomy
program here going. My biggest hope is that I can learn
your techniques."

"You'll never learn them as long as you fail to understand why I make up Bard-isms." Federman smiled.

Liz pointed a finger at him, then thought better of it.

"Touché," she said. "I'll enroll in Lit. 106 next term.
Okay? That is, if there's still a world then."

"Are we in a pessimistic mood today?"

Liz shrugged. "I shouldn't be, I suppose. Every spring
is seems there's less smog and other pollution. Remember
that eyesore wrecking yard on Highway Eight? Well, it's
gone now. They've put in a park."

"So nu? Then what's wrong?"

She threw the morning paper over to his side of the
desk. "*That's* what's wrong! Just when we seem about to
make peace with nature, they're stepping along the edge

of war! There were demonstrations on campus yesterday . . . neither side listening to the other, and neither side willing to concede a single point. I tell you, Sam, it's all I can do to keep from hiding in my work and letting the world just go to hell on its own!"

Federman glanced at the paper, then looked up at his assistant. His expression was ironic.

"Liz, you know my feelings about this. Radio astronomy is not disconnected from the problems of war and peace on Earth. It may, indeed, be intimately involved in the solution."

The sophont had no nose, but he did have a name. If one started there and kept listing his attributes one would find him quite a bit more human than not. The things his species had in common with the dominant race of Earth would have surprised them both almost as much as the differences, but the most important of each has already been mentioned.

He had no nose. His name was Fetham.

"No!" he cried out in the language of confrontation. He pounded a four-fingered fist on his desktop. "Are you mad? Mad! What do you mean, the funds are needed elsewhere? The legislature agreed by almost unanimous vote. Full, permanent, emergency funding!"

The smaller being with no nose was named Gathu. He held up his hand in a newly discovered version of the Gesture of Placation directed at the Optic Nerve.

"Please, Academician! Please remember that those votes were taken years ago. There is a new Assembly now. And since the public health situation has deteriorated . . ."

"The problem I am trying to solve!"

". . . it has fallen on the leadership to seek out new sources of finance for medical research. Surely you know that we applaud your efforts. But it seemed more and more a shot in the dark."

Fetham's prehensile ears waved in agitation.

"Of *course* it's a shot in the dark! But isn't it worth it? There may be a race out there that has been through what we now face. With the entire world threatened, our very survival in question, shouldn't we make an effort to contact them?"

The government representative nodded. "But you have another two years in your appropriation, have you not? And by husbanding your funds you might make them last longer."

"Idiots!" Fetham hissed. "Why, the first beamed message will reach my first target star only this year! It will take more years for their reply to reach us, barring *any* delay in interpreting the message!

"Are *all* governments as stupid as ours?"

Gathu stiffened. His ridge crest waved in suppressed irritation.

"You may, of course, emigrate to any other nation you wish, Academician. The international Concords give you the right to establish yourself as a citizen of any system of government found under our sun.

"Shall I arrange to have the papers sent over? Perhaps you'll have better luck . . ."

Gathu's voice trailed off, for Fetham had raised his hands in the Gesture of Supreme Disgust and fled the room.

Federman stared at the ceiling while he tilted back in his swivel chair. "You know, someone once told me that the true definition of genius was the ability to suddenly see the obvious."

Liz Browning stopped pacing long enough to pick up her coffee cup. The stained newspaper was open to a page of boldface headlines and photos of armed men.

"Do you mean that the answer may just be staring us in the face? Are you saying we're stupid?"

"Not stupid. Obstinate, perhaps. We hold on to our basic assumptions tenaciously, even when they are about to kill us. It's the way human beings work.

"For instance, did you know that for years Europeans thought tomatoes were poisonous? No one bothered to test the assumption.

"Even the most daring and open of us can't question an assumption until he becomes *aware* of it! When everyone accepts a paradigm it never becomes a topic of conversation. There must be thousands, *millions,* of things like that which men and women never even notice because they don't stand out from the background."

Liz shook her head.

"You don't have to belabor the point. Every sophomore has thought about that at one time or another. And it's certainly happened that some genius has leapt out of the bathtub, screaming 'Eureka!' and gone on to tell everybody of the new way to do things."

She tapped the newspaper.

"But this isn't as easy as that. Our problem of world survival is made up of several hundred million tiny problems, each with all the complexity of a living person. There's no underlying simplicity to war and politics, much as Marxists and others dream of finding one. They only make matters worse with simplistic claims and pseudologic."

Federman sat up straight and rested both palms on the desk. He looked at Liz seriously.

"The idea is that we may have missed something *basic.*"

He stood up quickly, and instantly regretted it as his heart pounded to make up for the shift in blood pressure. For a moment, the room lost its focus.

Deliberately, to keep Liz from becoming concerned, he picked his way around the clutter of books and charts on the floor and rested his shoulder against the window frame.

Brisk, cool spring morning air flooded in, carrying away the stale odors of the night. There was the sweet, heavy smell of new-mown grass.

On its way to him the breeze toyed with the branches of aspen and oak trees and the waving wheatfields in the valley several miles away. A low pride of cumulus clouds drifted overhead, cleanly white.

In the distance he could see a gleaming Rapitrans pull into the station at the local industrial park. Tiny specks that were commuters wandered away from the train and slowly dispersed into the decorously concealed factories that blended into the hills and greenery.

It was, indeed, a beautiful day.

Birds were singing. A pair flew right past his window. He followed them with his eyes until he saw that they were building a nest in the skeleton of what was to have been the new hundred-meter radio telescope.

There was a rumbling in the sky. Above the high bank of clouds a formation of military transports made a brief glint of martial migration. The faint growling of their passage had become an almost daily occurrence.

Federman turned away from the window. Inside, except where the brilliant shaft of light fell, there appeared to be only dimness. He spoke in the general direction of his friend and student.

"I was only thinking that maybe we've been missing the forest for the trees. It might be something so simple . . . something another culture with a different perspective might . . ."

"Might what, Sam?" Liz's voice had an edge to it. "If there ever *were* peaceful cultures on Earth, they didn't have the other half of the solution—a way to keep from getting clobbered by the other guy who *isn't* peaceful! If they did have that answer too, where are they now?

"Look at the world! Western, Asian, African, it makes no difference which culture you look at. They're all arming as fast as they can. Brushfire wars break out everywhere, and every month the Big Blow doesn't happen makes worse the day when it does!"

Federman shrugged and turned to look out the window again.

"Maybe you're right. I suppose I'm just wishing for a *deus ex machina*." His eyes lovingly coveted the abandoned, unfinished dish outside.

"Still, we've done so well otherwise," he went on. "The simple problems with obvious answers are all being solved. Look at how well we've managed to clean up the environment, since people found out about the cancer-causing effects of pollution in the seventies and eighties. Sure, there was inertia. But once the solution became obvious we went ahead and did the logical thing to save our lives.

"I can't escape the feeling, though, that there's a similar breakthrough to be made in the field of human conflict . . . that there's some *obvious* way to assure freedom and dignity and diversity of viewpoint without going to war. Sometimes I think it's just sitting there, waiting to be discovered, if only we had just a hint."

Liz was silent for a moment. When she spoke again it was from the other edge of the window. She too was looking out at the spring morning, and at the armed convoy in the sky.

"Yes," she said softly. "It would be nice. But to be serious, Sam, do you really think you could get any more funding than you've already got, to do your spare-time search for radio messages from space? And even if you were successful, do you think the Big Blow would wait long enough for us to decipher a message, then send one of our *own*, and eventually ask complex questions on sociology?"

She shook her head. "Would they be similar enough to us to understand what we'd be asking? Do you really think we're missing something so fundamentally simple that just a hint over the light-years would make that much difference?"

Federman shrugged. His gaze remained fixed on the skeleton in the yard.

The scientist with no nose looked out over his city. For a long time he had fretted and fumed beneath the great dish antenna; then he had gone for a walk around the edge of the research center compound.

Years ago these hills had been suburbs. Now factories belched smoke into the air on all sides. The sight cheered him slightly. He could never look at such an obvious sign of progress and prosperity for long and stay in a black mood.

There were so many other things to be proud of, too.

After the invention of atomic weapons, before he was born, his parents' generation had finally found the motivation to do the obvious and abolish war. The method had been there all along, but no one had been sufficiently motivated before. Now the fruits of peace were multiplying throughout the world.

Two automobiles for everyone! Fast, efficient stratospheric transport! Quick-foods easily dispensed from fluorocarbon-driven aerosol cans! The licentious luxury of lead-lined dinnerware!

All of this was good. Peace and prosperity.

But the Plague had then come among them, soon after the last war, and now affected almost everyone. Lung ailments, skin cancer . . . that horrible sickness that struck the mercury and bismuth mines . . . the death of the fisheries.

Huge sums were spent to find the microorganisms responsible for this rash of diseases. Some were found, but no germs yet that could account for the wide range of calamities. Some scientists were now suggesting a pathogen smaller than a virus.

Fetham looked up. Gathu. The government representative had followed him outside.

"I am sorry I shouted," Fetham said slowly. The other being-with-no-nose did the equivalent, for his species, of a forgiving nod. Fetham gave a handturn of thanks.

"It's just that I was hoping the Others might know something . . . something that would help us understand."

Gathu was sympathetic.

"I know, Academician. But honestly, what could they tell us about *our* problems—especially biological problems—even if you did succeed in making contact?

"If they exist at all, they live on a completely different world, with different body chemistry. How could they give us knowledge that would help us defeat this Plague?"

Fetham performed a gesture that conveyed the meaning of a shrug. His large and very subtle ears filtered out the brash, ever-present noise of traffic, yet allowed him to hear the whistling of the wind through the silted, murky sky.

Suddenly he had a totally irrelevant thought.

I wonder where the birds are? They used to be all over this part of the city. I never noticed that they had gone, until now.

"I suppose," he sighed. "I suppose I was hoping for just a hint . . ."

AUTHOR'S NOTES

This part of the collection, called Speculation, features three stories of the "what if" type, where the emphasis is less on plot or characterization or a literary style than on the idea itself. Science fiction is noted for such stories. Fortunately, though, they are not all there is to SF.

"Just a Hint" was my second published work, the first to see print after my novel Sundiver. It addresses that venerable problem "Where is everybody?" from a different angle.

Also, it talks about assumptions . . . those beliefs we may all hold so much in common that we never notice them.

I don't really believe there is such an underlying thread just waiting for some genius to lift up for our amazement that could save the day. For one thing, we are a civilization (perhaps the first) that rewards people above all else for discovery, for overturning rocks and exposing the newness beneath. From music to art to science to investigative journalism, young professionals are encouraged to achieve a name by shaking up the status quo and making it stick. In other words, if you rock the boat and prove your point, you've got it made.

Millions of bright people, picking, poking away, earnestly trying to find something everyone else has missed . . . oh, we're a clever bunch, all right. If some problems defy simple solutions, it's probably because they require *maturity and sanity and compromise to be solved, not some panacea from the stars.*

Still, one can dream . . .

The next story, "Tank Farm Dynamo," is my most extreme example of "techno-SF," in which a point of science is the real protagonist.

Tank Farm Dynamo

"They finally fired Bylinsky."

I was up to my knees in agrisludge, a frothy brown mess at the bottom of my personal greenhouse tank, when I heard the remark. For a moment I thought I had imagined it.

Your hearing plays tricks when you're wading around in mucky water, barely held to the floor by under a hundredth of a gee. I was groping in the goo, trying to find whatever had gummed up the aspirator. My breath blew up little green and brown droplets that hovered in front of my face for long seconds before slowly settling down again.

"Ralph! Did you hear me? I said Bylinsky's *out!*"

I looked up this time. Don Ishido, our communications and operations chief, hung halfway through the aft hatch of the greenhouse, twenty meters away. He was watching my reaction, maybe in order to report to the others exactly how I took the news. Probably there was money riding on it.

I nodded. "Thanks, Don. Bylinsky's days were numbered. We'll miss him, but we'll survive."

Ishido smiled faintly. He must have bet on my poker face. "What do you want me to tell the others, boss?"

I shrugged. "We're still a tank farm. We buy 'em and store 'em and later we'll all get rich selling 'em back for a profit."

"Even when they cut the water ration?"

"There'll be a way. We're in the future business. Now get out of here and let me finish my recreational farming."

Don smirked at my euphemism, but withheld comment. He ducked out, leaving me alone to my "recreation" . . . and my worries.

After clearing a clump of gelatinized algae from the input ports, I climbed onto one of the catwalk longerons rimming the pond and turned on the bubbler. The air began to fill with tiny superoxygenated green droplets.

I took a leap and sailed across the huge chamber to alight near the exit hatch. There I stowed my waders and looked around the greenhouse to make sure it was ready.

In the ten years I've been living in tanks I doubt I've ever entered or left one without blinking at least once in awe. The hatch was at one end of a metal cylinder as long as a ten-story building is tall, with the diameter of a small house. The walls were stiffened with aluminum baffles which once kept a hundred tons of liquid hydrogen from sloshing under high stress. That ribwork now held my greenhouse ponds.

The former hydrogen tank had a volume of over fifty thousand cubic feet. It, and its brothers, were just about the largest things ever put into space. And this one was all mine—my own huge garden to putter around in during off-duty hours, growing new types of spaceadapted algae and yeasts.

I passed through the yard-wide hatch into the intertank area between the two main sections of the External Tank. In the middle the intertank was only four feet across. The hatch closed.

Looking back into the garden tank through a tinted port, I pressed a button to let the sunshine in.

A bright point of light blossomed at the opposite end of the cylinder, mirror-focused sunlight speared through a fused quartz window to strike the cloud of rising bubbles.

I stayed long enough to watch the rainbows form.

The intertank hoop connects the big and little parts of the great External Tanks, or ETs, as we call them. The smaller cell had once contained 550 cubic meters of liquid oxygen. These days I stored gardening tools in it. Not a day had passed, in the last five years, in which I hadn't wished someone on Earth would recognize the waste, and come and take my tool shed away from me—to be used in some grand and wonderful plan.

Now they were trying to do just that, but not in a way I cared for at all.

"Boss? You still there? There's a telex from J.S.C. coming in."

I grabbed the big steel beam that had once borne the thrust of giant, strap-on solid rocket boosters. Now it served as a convenient place to put the intercom.

"Ishido, this is Rutter. I'm on my way. Don't let them sell us for scrap till I get there. Out."

I put on my hardsuit, carefully double-checking each seal and valve. The lock cycled, and I emerged into vacuum, but not blackness.

Overhead the Earth spanned the sky, a broad velvet blanket of browns and blues and fleecy white clouds. From just five hundred kilometers up, you don't see the Earth as a spinning marble in space. She covers an entire hemisphere, filling almost half the universe.

I drifted, but after a minute my boots touched the metal of the tank again. The same faint microgravity that held my pools inside the garden worked here on the outside.

The tank was the next to last in a row of forty of the great cylinders, nestled side by side. A parallel deck of sixteen huge tanks lay about sixty kilometers "overhead" linked to this collection by six strong cables. Twenty meters away from where I stood, one of the half-inch polymer tethers rose from its anchor point, a mirror-bright streak toward the planet overhead.

Sometimes a careful observer could make out B Deck without aid—a tiny rectangle about an eighth the apparent diameter of the moon—against the bright bulk of the Earth. When we crossed the terminator, the tanks in Group B sparkled like gems in Terra's sunset tiara.

Today I hadn't time to look for B Deck. The Feds had finally fired Edgar Bylinsky, the Tank Farm's last big supporter in NASA. If we thought times were hard before, they were going to get worse now.

"Ralph?" It was Ishido's voice again, now coming

over my suit radio. *"We've got the telex. I think this is the big one."*

I pushed off toward the control center. "Okay, what's the news?"

"Uh, they're moving fast. Pacifica's coming in with a couple of official bad news boys."

I could guess what they were coming to tell us. They'd say they were here for "consultations," but actually it would be to say that Uncle Sam wasn't going to sell us any more water.

"Don, when are the bad news boys due?"

"E.T.A. about an hour."

"I'll be right in."

Another hop took me to the entrance of the control tank. It was sheathed in layers of plating cut from dismantled ETs, to protect the crew during solar proton storms.

While waiting for the airlock to cycle, I looked up at the Indian Ocean, where they used to dump our tanks back at the beginning of the shuttle program. That awful waste had been one of the reasons for founding the Tank Farm.

For years ours had been a lonely and expensive gamble. Now we had proved our point. Proved it too well, it seemed.

They let us get a monopoly, and now they want to break us, I thought. *And they might succeed, if they cut off our water.*

We had safeguarded the Key to Space for them, and expected them to be grateful when they realized its worth. We should have known better.

2

In the beginning there was the space shuttle. Never mind what came earlier. Before version two of the shuttle, space was a place for robots and daredevils.

With tight budgets and all, the Space Transportation System has stayed fundamentally the same. A big, complex manned orbiter is launched from Canaveral or Vandenberg, strapped to two solid rocket boosters and one huge fuel tank carrying 770 tons of cryogenic propellants for the shuttle main engines. The engines are part of the orbiter, so they can be brought home and reused. The solid boosters drop off minutes after liftoff and are recovered for refurbishment. Even the unmanned heavy-lift cargo launchers use the same basic system.

But until our group came along, the huge external tanks were simply dumped, after fueling the shuttle to almost orbital velocity.

Once upon a time people thought we were on the verge of colonizing space. But then tight budgets and disasters cut the size of the STS fleet, and the cost of a pound sent into orbit remained in four figures. Visions of big O'Neill colonies and grand cities on the moon foundered without the bootstrap mass needed to build the dreams.

The lock passed me through. I stowed my hardsuit in a restorer locker whose nameplate simply read "Bossman." While I racked my equipment, I recalled all the times I had explained the Tank Farm to audiences on Earth: to congressmen, housewives, investors—to anyone who would listen.

Back in the early eighties it was shown that the thirty-five-ton external tank can be carried all the way into orbit *at zero cost* to the orbiter's thirty-ton cargo capacity. Thirty-five tons of aluminum and polymers, already shaped into vacuum-tight cylinders, delivered free!

And that wasn't all. On arrival the tanks would contain another five to thirty-five tons of leftover liquid hydrogen and oxygen, usable in upper stage engines, or to run fuel cells, or to be converted to precious water.

At a time when the grand hopes for space seemed about to fall apart, the ET was like manna from Earth to Heaven. When the government didn't seem eager to seize the opportunity—when they built their cramped, delicate, little "space stations" from expensive modules in the old-fashioned way—the Colombo-Carroll Foundation, a consortium of U.S. and Italian interests, offered to buy the tanks.

We would save them, until the world wised up, then sell them back. Meanwhile, the Tank Farm would provide orbit boosts via the tether-sling effect, saving customers fuel and time and paying our way until other investments matured.

For ten years the Farm had been on course, but it seems we'd omitted a few lines of fine print in our contract. The Feds had to let us buy the tanks at a fixed price, but nothing in the contract said they had to give us the residual hydrogen and oxygen, too.

It never occurred to us they'd not want to give us all the water we needed! Who in the world would have thought they'd ever want to take the Tank Farm away from us?

3

Imagine six very long parallel wires, hanging in space, always aimed toward the surface of the Earth 500 kilometers below.

At both ends the wires are anchored to flat rows of giant cylinders—forty in the upper layer, A Deck; and sixteen in the lower, B Deck. An elevator, consisting of two welded tanks, moves between the two ends, carrying people and supplies both ways.

I've lost count of the number of times I've explained the curious structure to visitors. I've compared it to a double-ended child's swing, or a bolo turning exactly once per orbit, so that one end is always low and the other always high. It's been called a skyhook, and even a beanstalk, though the idea's nowhere near as ambitious as the ground-to-geosynchronous space-elevators of science fiction fame.

The main purpose of the design is simply to keep the tanks from falling. The two massive ends of the Farm act like a dipole in the gradient of the Earth's gravitational field, so each deck winds up orbiting edge-forward, like a flat plate skimming. This reduces the drag caused by the upper fringes of the atmosphere, extending our orbital lifetime.

The scheme is simple, neat, and it works. Of course the arrangement doesn't prevent *all* orbital decay. It takes a little thrust from our aluminum engines, from time to time, to make up the difference.

Since our center of mass is traveling in a circular orbit, the lower deck has to move much slower than it "should" to remain at its height. The tethers keep it suspended, as it were.

The upper deck, in turn, is dragged along *faster* than it would normally go, at its height. It would fly away into a high ellipse if the cables ever let go.

That's why we feel a small artificial gravity at each end, directed away from the center of mass. It creates the ponds in my garden, and helps prevent the body decay of pure weightlessness.

When I entered the darkened control chamber, I moved quietly behind the chief flight controller and watched. The controller's main screen showed the inter-deck elevator stopped about three klicks above B Deck. The reason for its delay came into view in a few moments: a small delta-wing whose white tiles shone against the starfield. I stood in the shadows and listened as our opera-tors conversed with the shuttle pilot.

"*Pacifica,* this is A for Arnold Deck control. You are cleared for orbit intersection. In a minute we'll transfer you to B for Brown, for final approach. Extend your land-ing gear now."

"Roger, *Arnold Deck.* Pacifica, *ready for landing.*"

The orbiter drifted toward B Deck. On the control-ler's screen I could see *Pacifica*'s landing gear deploy in the deep black of space.

The inner face of B Deck was covered with a flat surface of aluminum plates, surrounded by a low fence of soft nylon mesh.

Pacifica was at the highest point of her elliptical orbit.

Her velocity would, for a few minutes at apogee, be virtually the same as B Deck's, allowing a gentle approach and contact. (A few purists still refused to call the docking a "landing.") The shuttle gave off small puffs of reaction gas to align her approach.

It was a beautiful technique, and the unargued greatest asset of the Tank Farm. When *Pacifica* was secured to B Deck, she would be carried along in the Farm's unconventional circular orbit until it was time for her to go. Then *Pacifica* would simply be pushed over the edge of B Deck, to fall toward the Earth again, finishing her original ellipse.

I looked at the screen showing the underbelly of B Deck. A great net of nylon hung below the plain of cylinders. Within, like a caterpillar trapped in a web, was *Pacifica*'s ET, the external tank that had powered her into orbit, sent ahead and snagged on a previous pass.

So the bad news boys had brought one of the magic eggs with them. I hoped it was a good omen, though it was probably just a coincidence of scheduling.

Until a year ago most of the orbiters visiting the Farm also delivered their external tanks, along with several tons of residual hydrogen and oxygen propellants in each. Then a new administration started reneging, stockpiling ETs at the Space Stations instead, and denying us our allotment. The Foundation took them to court, of course, and forced a delivery rate of at least ten ETs a year.

The new administration didn't like losing face. Now they'd found a way to get even. Our contract said they had to sell us the tanks, but it said nothing about the water.

"Um, Dr. Rutter, could I speak with you for a minute?"

I turned to see an earnest-looking, black-haired young woman. She clutched a roll of strip charts. Emily Testa was a very promising new member of the Farm, sent up by the Italians, the junior partners in Colombo Station.

"This is really a bad time, Emily. Is it important?"

"Well, sir . . ." She caught my warning look. "I mean *Ralph* . . . Since I arrived I have been studying the problem of electrical currents in the tether cables, and I think I have learned something interesting."

I nodded as I recalled the project I'd given the young newcomer to get her started. It was a nagging little problem that I'd wanted to have someone look into for some time.

The super-polymer tethers that held the Tank Farm together were sheathed in an aluminum skin to protect them from solar ultraviolet radiation. Unfortunately, this meant there was an electrical conducting path from B Deck to A Deck. As the Farm swept around the Earth in its unconventional orbit, the cables cut through a changing flux from the planet's magnetic field. The resulting electrical potentials had caused some rather disconcerting side effects, especially as the Tank Farm grew larger.

"Go on, Emily," I suggested. But I couldn't help listening with only half my attention. *Pacifica* was coming in, gear extended like a fighter landing on an aircraft carrier. I could hear the controllers talking softly in their singsongy dialect.

"Well, sir," Emily said, almost without a trace of accent, "I wasn't able to find a way to prevent the potential buildup. I'm afraid the voltage is unavoidable as the conductive tethers pass through the Earth's magnetic field.

"In fact, if the charge had anywhere to go, we could see some pretty awesome currents: One deck might act as a cathode, emitting electrons into the ionosphere, and the other could be an anode, absorbing electrons from the surrounding plasma. It all depends on whether . . ."

Pacifica touched down with barely a bump. Her landing gear flexed slightly as she rolled to a stop. The interdeck elevator resumed its descent as the orbiter was tied down by the B Deck crew. Her cargo was removed from the open cargo bay by giant manipulator arms.

Two spacesuited figures drifted down from *Pacifica*'s hatch and stood waiting for the elevator. It didn't take a lot of imagination to guess who they were. Our bad news boys.

Emily went on single-mindedly, apparently unaware of my split attention. ". . . so we could, if we ever really wanted to, *use* this potential difference the tethers generate! We could shunt it through some transformers here on

A Deck, and apply as much as twenty thousand volts! I calculate we might pull more power out of the Earth's magnetic field, just by orbiting through it with these long wires, than we would ever need to run lights, heat, utilities, and communications, even if we grew to ten times our present size!"

The boys in the spacesuits got into the elevator. The crew loaded *Pacifica's* cargo after them, encased in blue Department of Defense shrouding.

"Emily." I turned to face the young woman. "You know there ain't no such thing as a free lunch. Your idea certainly is interesting. I'll grant you could probably draw current from the tethers, maybe even as much as you say. But we'd pay for it in ways we can't afford."

Emily stared for a moment, then she snapped her fingers. "Angular momentum! Of course! By drawing current we would couple with the Earth's magnetic field. We would slow down, and add some of our momentum to the planet's spin, microscopically. Our orbit would decay even faster than it already does!"

I nodded. "Right. Still, it's a good idea. If we were getting all the water we used to receive, so we could run the aluminum engines as before, we might even decide to draw power your way.

"But our solar cells are really more than adequate. We could sell our excess to Earth, if they could only agree on a way to receive it."

She looked a little crestfallen. "Keep at it, though," I said for morale's sake. "Maybe there's a way to turn these electrical phenomena to our advantage. We ought to have a break coming about now." I tried to sound as if I believed it. Emily brightened a bit.

The elevator started rising, on its way up here to A Deck. I had about an hour to get ready—to shave and shower away the aroma of my garden. It probably wouldn't do any good, but I'd want to look presentable to the bad news boys.

4

We had our meeting in the lounge. Susan Sorbanes, our business manager, took her place to my left, Don Ishido to my right. There were no chairs, but we stood at rest in the feeble gravity, a table made of spun aluminum fibers between us and the federal officials. Our backs were to the giant quartz window.

Across the table, Colonel Robert Bahnz, the new DOD representative, floated impassively. He had said hardly a word, apparently content to leave the talking to Henry Woke, the NASA official who had come up in *Pacifica* with him. Bahnz stood at a slight angle, which had to take a certain amount of work. Was it his way of showing his contempt for the Tank Farm's famous gravity, so unlike the free-fall conditions in the government's shiny little Space Stations?

"So you people have decided to hit us on two fronts at once, Dr. Woke?" Susan spoke softly, but her voice had a cutting edge. "You're going to attack the Farm's man-rating, and you're cutting back on our share of the residual propellants and water."

Woke was a middle-aged bureaucrat who must have convinced himself long ago that space visits were a route to advancement in NASA. I could tell by his faint green pallor that he was doped up against space sickness.

"Now, Dr. Sorbanes," he said. "Safety's been an issue ever since a crewman fell from B Deck two years ago. As a quasi-federal institution, Colombo Station must adhere to man-rating policy. That's all we are interested in."

"We've had a good safety record for ten years, except for that one incident," Susan replied. "And Congress gave us exemptions back in '89, you'll remember."

"Yes, but those exemptions expire this year. And I think you'll find this Congress less willing to take chances with the safety of its citizens in orbit."

"I don't see why we have to go the gold-plated route NASA and DOD used in the Space Stations," Susan said acidly. "All that approach accomplished was to slow you down by a decade, and almost turn the country off on space for good!"

Woke shook his head. "Perhaps, Dr. Sorbanes. Indeed, it's because NASA has seen the value of the Tank Farm approach that we had last year's unfortunate misunderstanding regarding tank deliveries. Since Stations Two and Three began operating their own propellant recovery units and aluminum smelters, we've found that we need the leftover tanks as much as you do. We're all going to have to share. That's what it comes down to."

Don Ishido shook his head. "That's a load of bull! Our contract only guarantees us a third of the tanks launched, in return for which we use the slingshot effect to boost government and commercial cargoes into higher orbits, and provide shuttles like *Pacifica* with temporary angular momentum loans. That leaves you with two thirds of the tanks to do with as you wish!

"Let's face it. It's not the tanks that are causing the problem. It's you stealing our water!"

I cleared my throat. It was time to step in, before this broke down completely.

"I think what Mr. Ishido means, Dr. Woke, is that Colombo Station depends on delivery of at least fifty tons of residual propellants a year, for life support, chemistry, and especially to provide oxydizer for our aluminum engines. Without those engines, our orbit will decay, and we'll be forced to use the extremely inefficient method of flinging away tanks to maintain altitude. The Farm will cease accumulating mass, and our value to our investors will disappear . . . this just as we were about to show a real profit for the first time."

Woke shrugged. "Of course we have no intention of cutting off the water and oxygen you need to maintain life support. No one even considered such a thing."

Damn right, I thought. Nothing would alienate the public like that. But trimming our ration, forcing us to spend tanks as fast as we get them—they could pull that off without trouble.

Yeah. We had almost closed a deal with some big Earthside chemical houses to produce large amounts of low-g biochemicals on B Deck, when NASA Station Two undercut us by $2 million. But the killer had really been the rumors over our water situation. The investors had shied away from the uncertainty.

It hurt like hell. We were just short of making it. We had gobs of solar power, but the Earthsiders couldn't agree on how to receive it. With water and our giant tanks we could run a tremendous chemical plant, but timid companies stopped just short of buying in. We'd planned to set up a space hotel and sell vacations for scores of tourists at a time, but we were stymied by this "man-rating" straw man.

Our ecological recycling system had us ninety-five percent independent of Earth resupply. Our smelter was operational and waiting for customers: We had developed the aluminum engine.

But all anyone wanted to buy was the slingshot effect. We were a glorified switching yard in orbit. And the new government clearly wanted us to stay just that.

Woke kept up his soothing apologia. I had heard it all before. I wasn't the one to fight him, anyway. That was up to our lawyers back in Washington. My job was to come up with miracles. And right now they appeared to be in short supply.

The crewcut DOD man, Bahnz, was staring at something over my shoulder. I shifted a little to look.

Out on A Deck they were readying a Defense cargo for launch. They had peeled away the blue shrouding and set the cylinders near the edge of the deck. At the right moment the package would slip off into the starry field below us, falling away from Earth in a steep ellipse. At apogee a motor would cut in, carrying the spysat the rest of the way to geosynchronous orbit.

Bahnz had a gleam in his eyes as he observed the preparations.

You want my Farm, don't you? I thought. You peepers fought us in the beginning, but now you see we're the one thing keeping us ahead of the other nations in space. Now you want my Tank Farm for your own.

Two years ago, they had tried to get us to store "strategic assets" in the A Deck tanks. I threatened to resign, and the Foundation found the guts to refuse. That's when the troubles had started.

Bahnz noticed my look, and smiled a knowing smile.

He thinks he holds all the aces, I thought. *And he might be right.*

There were some old SF stories I read when I was a kid, about space colonies rebelling against Earth bureaucracies. I had a brief fantasy of leading my crew in a "tea party," and kicking these two jerks off our *sovereign territory.*

Bahnz saw the peaceful smile on my face, and must have wondered what caused it.

Of course the rebellion idea was absurd. It wasn't what any of us wanted, and it wasn't practical. We might be ninety-five percent free of Earth logistical support, but that last few percent would be with us for a hundred years. Anyway, without either water or new tanks every year, Mother Earth's atmosphere would quickly pull us down.

While Don and Susan kept our side of the charade, I looked out the window, thinking.

Next year would be solar maximum, when the coronal ion wind would come sleeting in from the active sun. The upper atmosphere would heat up and bloat outward, like a high tide dragging at our knees. At solar max we could lose twenty kilometers of altitude in a single year. Maybe much more.

Our investors would be caving in within eighteen months. Even the Italians would soon be begging the U.S. administration to make a deal.

For an instant I saw the Earth not as a broad vague mass overhead, but as a spinning globe of rock, rushing air, and water, of molten core and invisible fields, reaching out to grapple with the tides that filled space. It was eerie. I could almost *feel* the Tank Farm, like a double-ended kite, coursing through those invisible fields, its tethers cutting the lines of force—like the slowly turning bushings of a dynamo.

That was what young Emily Testa had compared it to. A dynamo. We could draw power from our motion if we ever had to—buying electricity and paying for it in orbital momentum. It was a solution in search of a problem, for we already had all the power we needed.

The image wouldn't leave my mind, though. I could almost *see* the double-ended kite, right there in front of me . . . a dynamo. We didn't *need* a dynamo. What we needed was the opposite. What we needed was . . .

"I think we should recess," I said suddenly, interrupting Dr. Woke in the middle of a sentence. It didn't matter. My job wasn't diplomacy. It was miracle-working.

"Susan, would you show our guests to some rooms? We'll all meet again over supper in my cabin, if that's okay with you gentlemen?"

Woke nodded resignedly. I think he had hoped to go back down right away in *Pacifica*. Colonel Bahnz smiled. "Dr. Rutter, will you be serving Slingshot with dinner?"

"It's traditional," I replied, anxious to get rid of the man.

"Good. It's one of the reasons I came up today." Bahnz's grin seemed friendly enough, but there was an undertone to his voice that I understood only too well.

I waited until they had left, then turned to Ishido. "Don, go fetch Emily Testa and meet me in the power room in five minutes."

"Sure, chief. But what . . . ?"

"There's something I want to try. Now shake a leg!"

I kicked off down the hallway, looking for a computer terminal. I don't think I touched the floor twice in fifty yards.

5

For all of our Spartan lifestyle, there are a few places the crew had tried to make "posh." One is the main lounge. Another is the "Captain's Cabin." My digs were given that name when the Foundation first had the idea of setting up a tourist hotel. They figured making a big deal out of dinner in my quarters would give a visit more of the flavor of a Caribbean cruise.

The aluminum walls had been anodized different pastel shades. The gold carpet had been woven from converted tank insulator material. And in wall niches there stood a dozen vacuum-spun aluminum-wire sculptures created by Dave Crisuellini, our smelter chief and resident artist.

The Captain's Table was made of oak, brought up at six hundred dollars a pound for one purpose only, to look impressive.

Henry Woke sat to my right as the volunteer stewards served us from steaming casserole dishes. Next to Woke sat Susan Sorbanes. Across from them were Emily Testa, nervously fingering her fork as her eyes darted about the room, and Ishido. Colonel Bahnz sat across from me.

Woke looked considerably less green around the gills. His eyes widened at the soufflé a waiter laid in front of him. "I'm impressed! I'd heard that a hundreth of a gee is enough to enable the inner ear to come to equilibrium, but I hadn't believed. Now, to be able to eat from plates! With forks!" He spoke around a hot mouthful. "This is delicious! What is it?"

"Well, most of our food is prepared from termite flour and caked algae . . ."

Woke paused chewing. Susan and Ishido shared a look and a smile.

". . . however," I went on, "recently we have begun raising our own wheat, and chickens for eggs."

Woke looked uncomfortable for another moment, then apparently decided to accept the ambiguity. "Ingenious," he said, and resumed eating.

"We have a number of ingenious people here," Susan said. "Many of our crew served aboard the Space Stations, and came here when NASA went through cutbacks and furloughed them.

"Others were hired by the Foundation because of their varied talents. Emily here," she said, smiling at young Testa, "is a fine example of the sort of colonist we're looking for."

Emily blushed and looked down at her plate. She was very tired after the last few hours, as we had furiously experimented with the Farm's power system.

Colonel Bahnz squeezed an aluminum-foil beer bottle, his second. "You're right about one thing, Dr. Sorbanes," the DOD man said. "The U.S. government has subsidized this venture in many hidden ways. Most of your personnel got their training at taxpayer expense."

"Have we ever failed in our gratitude, Colonel?" Susan spoke with pure sincerity. And to Ishido and I, the answer was obviously no. We tank farmers think of ourselves as custodians of a trust.

But Bahnz clearly disagreed. "Do you call it *gratitude*, using lawyers' tricks to put restrictions on your country's use of valuable resources when she needs them most?"

"We believe," Susan said, "that need will be greatest in the future. And we plan to be here, with the key to a treasure chest, when the time comes."

"Dreams of glory." Bahnz sneered. "I know all about them. Tell me about lunar mines and space colonies and other fairy tales, Dr. Sorbanes. And I'll tell you about Low Earth Orbit, now filled with garbage and bombs and little cameras from half a hundred bickering, hungry little nuclear powers, all blaming each other for a world economy in a thirty-year skid!

"Have you any idea what would happen if even *one* of these arrogant little 'spacefaring nations' decided to ignite a small enhanced radiation device in that cloud of communications satellites overhead? You know as well as I how dependent we are on orbital datalinks. And you know the only way to defend those links is to put our satellites inside big Faraday cages."

Bahnz struck the nearby aluminum wall. "*This* is what your country needs, Dr. Sorbanes. This tank and others like it! And the propellants for upper-stage launches. And we need this *station*, for the momentum transfer you now almost *give* away to anyone who wants it!"

Susan was gearing up for a major rebuttal. I hurried

to interrupt. "People, please! Let's try to relax, if only for a little while. Colonel Bahnz, you seem to like Slingshot. That's your third helping."

Bahnz had plucked another bottle from a passing steward. "Why not?" He shrugged. "It costs a hundred bucks a pint on Earth. It's damn fine beer."

"Dr. Ishido is our brewmaster."

Bahnz lifted the bottle and bowed his head in silent tribute to Don. An aficionado of beer need say no more; Ishido nodded at the colonel's compliment.

"Director Rutter," Bahnz said as he turned to me, "Dr. Woke and I will be leaving within two hours. I have held *Pacifica* to please you, but our business here is done. If you have anything more to say, you can speak through your Foundation's Washington office."

Bahnz was obviously the type that got straight to the point, especially when he had had a bit to drink. He showed no trace of that irreverent streak I had known in the officers and officials of the early nineties. Those fellows had been almost like co-conspirators, helping nurture the Farm along in a time of tight budgets and dubious senators.

"Two hours, Colonel? Yes. That should be enough time. Just remind *Pacifica*'s crew to check their inertial tracking units before drop-off. There may be a few acceleration anomalies."

Bahnz snorted. "So? You plan to fire up your famous aluminum engines to impress us? Big deal. Go ahead and use up your reserve water, Rutter. You've got enough oxidizer to run them for maybe two months; then you'll start flinging mass away to keep orbit."

Ishido started to rise. At a sharp look from me he subsided.

"Why, Colonel," I said smoothly. "You sound downright happy over our predicament."

The crewcut officer slapped the oak table. "Damned straight! Let's lay it out, Rutter. I think you're a bunch of unpatriotic dreamers who'd do anything rather than serve your country. July's court judgment was the last straw.

"We're going to live up to the contract, all right. You'll get your tanks, and enough water to keep from making martyrs of you. But you'll start spending more mass to stay in orbit than you take in. Your profits will disappear. Then see how fast your investors force you out as director!

"Pretty soon, Rutter, *you'll* be buying Slingshot at a hundred clams a pint!" Bahnz emptied the squeeze bottle with a flourish.

I shrugged and turned back to my meal. The second worst thing you could do to a man like Bahnz was to ignore him. I intended to do the very worst thing within an hour and a half.

6

The face on the screen was flushed and angry. In the dimness of Arnold Deck Control Room, I could tell the man was upset.

"What the *hell* do you think you're doing, Rutter?"

I had made *Pacifica* wait for fifteen minutes while the control crew made a show of looking for me, then appeared, to look back at Bahnz with an expression of beatific innocence.

"What seems to be the problem, Colonel?"

"You know damned well what the problem is!" the man shouted. "Colombo Station is under acceleration!"

"So? I told you over dinner to have your crew check their inertial units. You knew that meant we would be maneuvering."

"But you're thrusting at two *microgees*! Your aluminum engines can't push five thousand tons that hard!"

I shrugged.

"And anyway, we can't find your thrust exhaust! We look for a rocket trail, and find nothing but a slight electron cloud spreading from A Deck!"

"Nu?" I shrugged again. "Colonel, you force me to conclude that we are *not* using our aluminum engines. It *is* curious, no?"

Bahnz looked as if he wanted some nails to chew—

threepenny, at least. Behind him I could see the crew of *Pacifica*, crouched over their instruments in order to stay out of his way.

"Rutter, I don't know what you're up to, but we can see from here that your entire solar cell array has been turned sunward. You have no use for that kind of power! Are you going to tell me what's going on? Or do I come back up there and make myself insufferable until you do?"

My respect for Bahnz rose two notches. He might be an SOB, but he knew how to get his way. "Oh, there won't be any need for that." I laughed.

"You see, Colonel, we need all that solar power to drive our new motor."

"Motor? What motor?"

"The motor that's enabling us to raise our orbit without spending a bit of mass—no oxygen, not even a shred of aluminum. It's the motor that's going to make it possible for us to pull a profit next year, Colonel, even under the terms of the present contract."

Bahnz stared at me. "A *motor*?"

"The biggest motor there is, my dear fellow. It's called the Earth."

He blinked, his mind obviously struggling to figure out what I meant.

"Have a good trip, Colonel," I said. "And any time you're in the neighborhood, do stop by for a Slingshot."

"Rutter!"

I turned away and launched myself toward the window at the far end of the control room.

"RUTTER!"

The voice faded behind me as I drifted up to the crystal port. Outside, the big, ugly tanks lay like roc eggs in a row, waiting to be hatched. I could almost envision it. They'd someday transform themselves into great birds of space. And our grandchildren would ride their offspring to the stars.

Bright silvery cables seemed to stretch all the way to the huge blue globe overhead. And I know, now, that they did indeed anchor us to the Earth . . . an Earth that does not end at a surface of mountain and plain and water, nor with the ocean of air, but continues outward in strong fingers of force, caressing her children still.

Right now those tethers were carrying over a hundred amps of current from B Deck to A. There, electrons were sprayed out into space by an array of small, sharp cathodes.

We could have used the forward process to extract energy from our orbital momentum. I had told Emily Testa earlier today that that would solve nothing. Our problem was to *increase* our momentum.

Current in a wire, passing through a magnetic field . . . You could run a dynamo that way, or a *motor*. With more solar power than we'll ever need, we can shove the current through the cables *against* the electromotive force, feeding energy to the Earth, and to our orbit.

A solar-powered motor, turning once per orbit, our Tank Farm rises without shedding an ounce of precious mass.

I smiled as I looked out on the fleecy clouds of home and the tanks in a row, like presents waiting to be opened. I felt Susan come up beside me. "*Pacifica*'s gone," she said, grinning. "And our acceleration's climbed to three microgees, Ralph."

I nodded. "Have Don ease back a bit for now. We don't want to push the motor too hard on its first day. I'll check in later."

"Where are you going?"

I caught a rung by the hatch. "I'm going to go unwind by spending some time puttering in my garden."

Susan shook her head and muttered "Yuck" under her breath.

I pretended I didn't hear her.

AUTHOR'S NOTES

I have had the great privilege of working as postdoctoral fellow with Dr. James Arnold and the California Space Institute . . . ecotopia's mini-micro version of the National Aeronautics and Space Administration. At Calspace we performed NASA-contracted studies of space station automation, space industrialization, and potential uses of tethers and external tanks.

Ironically, what we thought would be obvious—the need to find ways to use external tanks in space—has met with substantial resistance by the aero-space community. Tethers on the other hand, an idea we thought would be seen as "California freaky" have been taken up with enthusiasm as an important future component in space transportation.

Calspace's Joseph Carroll (one of the brightest fellows I know) has carried the work of the late Italian physicist Guiseppe Colombo into the field of tether dynamics. Experiments will be flown aboard the shuttle in the near future.

The technological fix has been a mainstay of science fiction since the "golden age" of the thirties. There is still room for fiction whose purpose is to elucidate some point of science. Often this can be done while still maintaining a mix of art, characterization, and drama, but for this propaganda piece, I make no such claim.

Next, we move on to a very special subgenre, a tale about a parallel world in which evil has gained an unfair advantage. First, a warning: never judge a story by its title.

Thor Meets Captain America

Loki's dwarf rolled its eyes and moaned pitifully as the sub leveled off at periscope depth. With stubby fingers the gnarled, neckless creature pulled at its yellow-stained beard and stared up at the creaking pipes.

A thing of dark forest depths and hidden caves, Chris Turing thought as he watched the dwarf. *It wasn't meant for this place.*

Only men *would choose such a way to die, in a leaking steel coffin, on a hopeless attempt to blow up Valhalla.*

But then, it wasn't like Loki's dwarf had been given any choice in being here.

Why, Chris wondered suddenly—not for the first time. *Why do such creatures exist? Wasn't evil doing well enough in the world before* they *came to help it along?*

The submarine's engines rumbled and Chris shrugged aside the thought. Even imagining a world without Aesir and their servants in it was by now as hard as remembering a time without war.

Chris sat strapped in his crash seat—he could hear the swishing of icy Baltic water just behind the tissue-thin bulkhead—and watched the gnome huddle atop a crate of hydrogen bomb parts. It drew its clublike feet up away from the sloshing brine on the deck, scrunching higher on the black box. Another moan escaped the dwarf as the *Razorfin's* periscope went up, and more water gurgled in through the pressure relief lines.

Major Marlowe looked up from the assault rifle he was reassembling for the thirtieth time. "What's eating the damn dwarf now?" the marine officer asked.

Chris shook his head. "Search me. The fact that he's out of his element, maybe? After all, the ancient Norse thought of the deep as a place for sunken boats and fishes."

"I thought you were some sort of expert on the Aesir. And you aren't even sure why the thing is foaming at the mouth like that?"

Chris could only shrug and repeat himself. "I said I don't know. Why don't you go over and ask him yourself?"

Marlowe gave Chris a sour glance, as if to say that he didn't much care for the joke. "Sidle up to that stench and ask Loki's damn *dwarf* to explain its *feelings*? Hmmph. I'd rather spit in an Aesir's eye."

From his left, Chris's assistant, Zap O'Leary, leaned out and grinned at Marlowe. "Dig it, dad-dyo," O'Leary said to the marine. "There's an Aes over by the scope, dope. Be my guest. Write him runes in his spitoon." The eccentric technician gestured over toward the navy men clustered around the sub's periscope. Next to the Skipper stood a hulking figure clad in furs and leather, towering over the submariners.

Marlowe blinked back at O'Leary in bewilderment. The marine did not seem offended as much as confused. "What did he say?" he asked Chris.

Chris wished he weren't seated between the two. "Zap suggests that you test it by spitting in Loki's eye."

Marlowe grimaced. O'Leary might as well have suggested he stick his hand into a scram-jet engine. At that moment one of the marines crammed into the passageway behind them made the mistake of dropping a cartridge into the foul leak-water underfoot. Marlowe vented his frustration on the poor grunt in richly inventive profanity.

The dwarf moaned again, hugging his knees against the straps holding him on to the hermetically sealed crate.

Wherever they're from, they aren't used to submarines, Chris thought. *And these so-called dwarfs sure don't like water*.

Chris wondered how Loki had managed to persuade this one to come along on this suicide mission.

Probably threatened to turn him into a toad, he speculated. *I wouldn't put it past Loki.*

It was a desperate venture they were engaged in. In late 1962 there was very little time left for what remained of the Alliance Against Nazism. If anything at all could be done this autumn, to stave off the inevitable, it would be worth the gamble.

Even Loki—bearlike, nearly invulnerable, and always booming forth laughter that sent chills down human spines—had betrayed nerves earlier, as the *Razorfin* dropped from the belly of a screaming bomber, sending their stomachs whirling as the arrow-sub plummeted like a great stone into Neptune's icy embrace.

Chris had to admit that *he* would have been sick, had that brief, seemingly endless fall lasted any longer. The crash and shriek of tortured metal when they hit was almost a relief, after that.

And anything seemed an improvement over the long, screeching trip over the Pole, skirting Nazi missiles, skimming mountains and gray waters in lurching zigs and zags, helplessly listening, strapped into place, as the airmen swooped their flying coffins hither and yon . . . praying that the enemy's Aesir masters weren't patrolling that section of the north that night . . .

Of twenty sub carriers sent out together from Baffin Island, only six had made it all the way to the waters between Sweden and Finland. And both *Cetus* and *Tigerfish* had broken up on impact with the water, tearing like ripped sardine cans and spilling their hapless crews into freezing death.

Only four subs left, Chris thought.

Still, he reminded himself. *Our chances may be slim, but those poor pilots are the real heroes.* He doubted even one of the crews would make it across dark, deadly Europe to Tehran and safety.

"Captain Turing!"

Chris looked up as the Skipper called his name. Commander Lewis had lowered the periscope and moved over to the chart table.

"Be right with you, Commander." Chris unstrapped and stepped down into the brine.

"Tell 'em we're savin' our own hooch for ourselves," O'Leary advised him, sotto voce. "Good pot is too rare to share."

"Shut up, fool," Marlowe growled. Chris ignored both of them as he sloshed forward. The Skipper awaited him, standing beside their "friendly advisor," the alien creature calling himself Loki.

I've known Loki for years, Chris thought. *I've fought alongside him against his Aesir brothers . . . and still he scares the living hell out of me every time I look at him.*

Towering over everyone else, Loki regarded Chris enigmatically with fierce black eyes. The "god of tricks" looked very much like a man, albeit an unnaturally large and powerful one. But those eyes belied the impression of humanity. Chris had spent enough time with Loki, since the renegade Aesir defected to the Allied side, to have learned to avoid looking into them whenever possible.

"Sir," he said, nodding to Commander Lewis and the bearded Aesir. "I take it we're approaching point Y?"

"That's correct," the Skipper said. "We'll be there in about twenty minutes, barring anything unforeseen."

Lewis seemed to have aged over the last twenty hours. The young sub commander knew that his squadron wasn't the only thing considered expendable in this operation. Several thousand miles to the west, the better part of what remained of the United States Surface Navy was engaged hopelessly for one reason only—to distract the Kriegsmarine and the SS and especially a certain "god of the sea" away from the Baltic and Operation Ragnarok. Loki's cousin Tyr wasn't very potent against submarines, but unless his attention was drawn elsewhere, he could make life hell for them when their tiny force tried to land.

So tonight, instead, he would be making hell for American and Canadian and Mexican sailors, far away.

Chris shied away from thinking about it. Too many boys were going to their deaths off Labrador, just to keep one alien creature occupied while four subs tried to sneak in through the back door.

"Thank you. I'd better tell Marlowe and my demolition team." He turned to go, but was stopped by an outsize hand on his arm, holding him gently but with steel-like adamancy.

"Thou must know something more," the being called Loki said in a low, resonant voice. Impossibly white teeth shone in that gleaming smile above Chris. "Thou wilt have a passenger in going ashore."

Chris blinked. The *plan* had been for only his team and their commando escort . . . Then he saw the pallor of dread on Commander Lewis's face—deeper than any mere fear of death.

Chris turned back to stare at the fur-clad giant. "*You* . . ." he exhaled.

Loki nodded. "That is correct. There will be a slight change in plans. I will not accompany the undersea vessels, as they attempt to break out through the Skagerrak. I will go ashore with thee, instead, to Gotland."

Chris kept his face blank. In all honesty, there was no way this side of Heaven that he or Lewis or anybody else could stop this creature from doing anything it wanted to do. One way or the other, the Allies were about to lose their only Aesir friend in the long war against the Nazi plague.

If the word "friend" ever really described Loki—who had appeared one day on the tarmac of a Scottish airfield during the final evacuation of Britain, accompanied by eight small, bearded beings carrying boxes. He had led them up to the nearest amazed officer and imperiously commandeered the prime minister's personal plane to take him the rest of the way to America.

Perhaps an armored battalion might have stopped him. Battle reports had proven that Aesir could be killed, if you were very lucky, and pounded one hard and fast enough. But when the local commander realized what was happening, he had decided to take a chance.

Loki had proven his worth over and over again since that day ten years ago.

Until now, that is.

"If you insist," he told the Aes.

"I do. It is my will."

"Then I'll go explain it to Major Marlowe. Excuse me, please."

He backed away a few meters first, then turned to go. As he sloshed away, that glittering stare seemed to follow him, past the moaning dwarf, past O'Leary's ever-sardonic smile, down the narrow, dank passageway lined with strapped-in marines, all the way to the sabot launching tubes.

Voices were hushed. All the young men spoke English, but only half were North Americans. Their shoulder patches—Free French, Free Russian, Free Irish, German Christian—were muted in the dim light, but the mixed accents were unmistakable, as well as the way they stroked their weapons and the gleam Chris caught sight of in several pairs of eyes.

These were the sort that volunteered for suicide missions, the type—common in the world after thirteen years of horrible war—that had little or nothing left to lose.

Major Marlowe had come back to supervise the loading of the landing boats. He did not take Chris's news well.

"Loki wants to come along? To *Gotland*?" He spat. "The bastard's a *spy*. I knew it all the time!"

Chris shook his head. "He's helped us in a hundred ways, John. Why, just by accompanying Ike to Tokyo, and convincing the Japanese—"

"Big deal! We'd already *beaten* the Japs!" The big marine clenched his fist, hard. "Like we'd have *crushed* Hitler, if these monsters hadn't arrived, like Satan's curse, out of nowhere.

"And now he's lived among us for *ten years*, observing our methods, our tactics, and our *technology*, the only real advantage we had left!"

Chris grimaced. How could he explain it to Marlowe? The marine officer had never been to Tehran, as Chris had, only last year. Marlowe had never seen the capital city of Israel-Iran, America's greatest and most stalwart ally, bulwark of the East.

There, in dozens of armed settlements along the east bank of the Euphrates, Chris had met fierce men and

women who bore on their arms tattooed numbers from
Treblinka, Dachau, Auschwitz. He had heard their story
of how, one hopeless night under barbed wire and the
stench of chimneys, the starving, doomed masses had
looked up to see a strange vapor fall from the sky. Unbe-
lieving, death-starkened eyes had stared in wonderment
as the mists gathered and coalesced into something that
seemed almost solid.

Out of that eerie fog, a *bridge* of many colors formed
. . . a rainbow arch climbing, apparently without end, out
of the places of horror into a moonless night. And from the
heights, each doomed man and woman saw a dark-eyed
figure on a flying horse ride down. They felt him whisper
to them *inside* their minds.

*Come, children, while your tormenters blink unbe-
lievingly in my web of the mind. Come, all, over my
bridge to safety, before my cousins descrie my treason.*

When they sank to their knees, or rocked in thankful
prayer, the figure only snorted in derision. His voice
hissed within their heads.

*Do not mistake me for your God, who left you here to
die! I cannot explain that One's absence to you, or His
plan in all this. The All-Father is a mystery even to Great
Odin!*

*Know only that I will take you to safety now, such as
there may be in this world. But only if you hurry! Come,
and be grateful later, if you must!*

Down to the camps, to bleak ghettos, to a city under
siege—the bridges formed in a single night, and with
dawn were gone like vapor or a dream. Two million people,
the old, the lame, women, children, the slaves of Hitler's
war factories, climbed those paths—for there was no other
choice—and found themselves transported to a desert land,
by the banks of an ancient river.

They arrived just in time to take up hasty arms and
save a British Army fleeing the wreckage of Egypt and
Palestine. They fused with the astonished Persians, and
with refugees from crippled Russia, and together they
built a new nation out of chaos.

That was why Loki appeared on the tarmac in Scotland,

shortly after that night of miracles. He could not return to Europe, for the fury of his Aesir kin would be savage. In returning to Gotland, today, he was certainly in as much peril as the commandos.

"No, Marlowe. Loki's not a spy. I haven't any idea what on God's green Earth he *is*. But I'd bet my life he's not a spy."

2

The sabots gurgled and rocked as they shot free of the submarine and bobbed to the surface of the cold sea. The outer shells broke away, and the sailors dipped their oars. The men all took their first breath of clean air in more than a day.

Loki's dwarf seemed little relieved. He looked across the dark waters to the west, where the thin, reddish line of sunset outlined the hills of a great Baltic island, and muttered gutturally in a language like nothing Earthly.

Which was only natural. Like most Americans, Chris was convinced that these beings were as much the ancient Norse gods—recalled into the modern world—as *he* was Sandy Koufax, or that they didn't play baseball in Brooklyn.

Aliens—that was the official line . . . the story broadcast by Allied Radio all through the Americas and Japan and what remained of Free Asia. Creatures from the stars had arrived, as in those stories by Chester Nimitz, the famous science fiction author.

It wasn't hard to imagine why they might want to be looked on as gods. And it explained why they had chosen to side with the Nazis. After all, the ruse would not have worked in the West where, no matter how great their guests' powers, Euro-American scientists would have probed and queried and people would have asked questions.

But in the Teutonic madness of Nazism, the "Aesir" had found fertile ground.

Chris had read captured German SS documents. Even back in the thirties and early forties, before the arrival of the Aesir, they had been filled with mumbo jumbo and pseudoreligious mysticism—stuff about ice moons falling from the sky and the romantic spirit of the Aryan superrace.

A Nazi-conquered world would *belong* to the Aesir, whoever and whatever they were. They would be gods indeed. Much as he understood the logic of a rat or a hyena, Chris could follow the aliens' reasons for choosing the side they had, God damn them.

Silhouettes of pines outlined the hilltops, serrating the still faintly glowing western sky. The two lead boats were crammed with marines, who were to take the beachhead and move inland to scout. The flankers were navy teams, who were supposed to prepare the boats for a getaway . . . as if anyone believed that would ever happen.

The last two craft held most of Chris's demolition team.

Loki knelt on one knee at the prow of Chris's boat, and stared ahead with those black, glittering eyes. Dark as he was, he nevertheless looked at that moment like something straight out of a Viking saga.

Good verisimilitude, Chris thought. Or maybe the creatures actually *believed* they were what they said they were. Who could tell?

All Chris knew for certain was that they had to be defeated, or for humanity there would be nothing but darkness, from now on.

He checked his watch and looked up at the sky, scanning the broad, starry openings in the clouds.

Yes, there it was. The Satellite. Riding Newton's wings more than two hundred miles up, circling the globe every ninety minutes.

When it had appeared, the Nazis had gone into paroxysms, proclaiming it an astrological portent. For some unknown bureaucratic reason, officials in the Pentagon had sat on the secret until half the world believed Goebbels's propaganda. Then, at last, Washington revealed the truth. That American Space-Argonauts were circling the Earth.

For two months the world had seemed turned around.

This new technological wonder would be more important than the atom bomb, many thought.

Then the invasion of Canada began.

Chris turned his mind away from what was happening now, out in the Atlantic. He wished he had one of those new *laser* communicators, so he could tell the men up in the Satellite how things were progressing down here. But the light amplification devices were so secret, as yet, that the Chiefs of Staff had refused to allow any to be taken into the enemy's heartland.

Supposedly the Nazis were working on a way to shoot down the Satellite. It was still a mystery why, with aliens to help them, the enemy had let their early lead in rocketry slip so badly. Chris wondered why the Aesir had allowed the American satellite to fly up there as long as this.

Perhaps they can't really operate in space anymore . . . like they haven't been able to crush our submarine forces.

But does that make sense? Could aliens have lost the ability to destroy such a crude spacecraft?

Chris shook his head.

Not that it matters all that much, he thought. *Tonight the Atlantic fleet is dying. This winter, we'll probably be forced to use the big bombs to hold the line in Canada . . . wrecking the continent even if we slow them down.*

He looked at the figure in the boat's prow. *How can cleverness or industry or courage prevail against such power?*

Those fur-covered shoulders were passive now. But Chris had seen Loki tear down buildings with his bare hands. And Loki had admitted to being one of the *weakest* of these "gods."

"Loki," he said quietly.

As often as not, the Aes would ignore any human who spoke to him without leave. But this time the dark-haired figure turned and regarded Chris. Loki's expression was not warm, but he did smile.

"Thou art troubled, youngling. I spy it in thy heart."

He seemed to peer into Chris. "It is not fear, I am glad to
see, but only a great perplexity."

Fitting their assumed roles as the fabled lords of
Valhalla, courage was the one human attribute most hon-
ored by the Aesir. Even by the god of trickery and
treachery.

"Thank you, Loki." Chris nodded respectfully. *You
could've fooled me. I thought I was scared spitless!*

Loki's eyes were pools glittering with starlight. "On
this fateful eve, it is meet to grant a brave worm a boon.
Therefore I will favor thee, mortal. Ask three questions.
These will Loki answer truthfully, by his very life."

Chris blinked, for the moment stricken speechless.
He was unprepared for anything like this! Everyone from
President Marshall and Admiral Heinlein on down to the
lowliest Brazilian draftee had hungered for answers. Imperious and aloof, their one Aesir ally had doled out hints
and clues, had helped to foil Nazi schemes and slow the
implacable enemy advance, but he had never made a
promise like this!

Chris could sense O'Leary tense behind him, trying
to seem invisible in order to be allowed to stay and listen.
For once the beatnik's mouth stayed firmly sealed.

Pine forests loomed above them as the boat entered
shallows out of the evening wind. He could smell the dark
forest. There was so little time! Chris groped for a question.

"I . . . Who *are* you, and where did you *come* from?"

Loki closed his eyes. When he opened them, the
black orbs were filled with dark sadness.

*"Out of the body of Ymir, slain by Odin, poured the
Sea.*

"Gripping the body of Ymir, Yggdrasil, the great tree.

*"Sprung from salt and frost, the Aesir, tremble
Earth!*

"Born of Giant and man, Loki, bringer of mirth."

The creature stared at Chris. "This has always been
my home," he said. And Chris knew that he meant the
Earth. "I remember ages and everything spoken of in
Eddas—from the chaining of Fenris to the lies of Skrymnir.
And yet . . ." Loki's voice was faintly puzzled, even hushed.

"And yet there is something about those memories . . . something *laid over*, as lichen lies upon the frost."

He shook himself. "In truth, I cannot say for certain that I am older than thee, child-man."

Loki's massive shoulders shrugged. "But make haste with your next question. We are approaching the Gathering Place. *They* will be here and we must stop them from their scheming, if it is not already too late."

Reminded suddenly of the present, Chris looked up at the wilderness looming all around them on the shadowed hillsides. "Are you sure about this plan—taking on so many of the Aesir in one place?"

Loki smiled. And Chris realized at once why. Like some idiot out of a fairy tale, he had squandered a question in a silly quest for comfort! But reassurance was not one of Loki's strong suits.

"No, I am *not* sure, impertinent mortal!" Loki laughed and the rowing sailors briefly lost their stride as they looked up at the ironic, savage sound. "Think thou that only men may win honor by daring all against death? Here does *Loki* show his courage, to face Odin's spear and Thor's hammer if he must, tonight!" He turned and shook a ham-size fist toward the west. The dwarf whimpered and crouched beside his master.

Chris saw that the marines had already landed. Major Marlowe made quick hand gestures, sending the first skirmishers fanning out into the forest. The second row of boats shipped oars and were carried by momentum toward the gravelly shore.

He hurried to take advantage of the remaining time.

"Loki. What is happening in Africa?"

Since '49 the Dark Continent had been dark indeed. From Tunis to the Cape of Good Hope, fires burned, and rumors of horror flowed.

Loki whispered softly.

"Surtur must needs have a home, before the time of raging.

"There, in torment, men cry out, screaming for an ending."

The giant shook his great head. "In Africa and on the

great plains of Russia, terrible magics are being made, and terrible woe."

Back in Israel-Iran Chris had seen some of the refugees—Blacks and high-cheeked Slavs—lucky escapees who had fled the fires in time. Even they had not been able to tell what was happening in the interior. Only people who had seen the earlier horrors—whose arms bore stenciled numbers from the first wave of chimney camps—could imagine what was happening in the silent continents. And those fierce men and women kept their silence.

It struck Chris that Loki did not seem to speak out of pity, but matter-of-factly, as if he thought a *mistake* were being made, but not any particular evil.

"Terrible magics . . ." Chris repeated. And suddenly he had a thought. "You mean the purpose isn't *only* to slaughter people? That something else is going on, as well? Is it related to the reason why you saved those people from the first camps? Was something being *done* to them?"

Chris had a sense that there was something important here. Something ultimately crucial. But Loki smiled, holding up three fingers.

"No more questions. It is time."

They scraped bottom. Sailors leapt out into the icy water to drag the boat up to the rocky shore. Shortly, Chris was busy supervising the unloading of their supplies, but his mind was a turmoil.

Loki was hiding something, laughing at him for having come so close and yet missing the target. There was more to this venture, tonight, than an attempt to kill a few alien gods.

High in the dark forest canopy, a crow cawed scratchily. The dwarf, laden under enough boxes to crush a man, rolled its eyes and moaned softly, but Loki seemed not to notice.

"Reet freaking hideaway, daddyo," O'Leary muttered as he helped Chris shoulder the bomb's fuse mechanism. "A heavy-duty scene."

"Right," Chris answered, feeling sure he understood

the beatnik this time. "A heavy-duty scene." They set out, following the faint blazings laid by their marine scouts.

As they climbed a narrow trail from the beach, Chris felt a growing sense of anticipation . . . a feeling of being, right then, at the navel of the world. For well or ill, this place was where the fate of the world hung. He could think of no better end than to sear this island clean of all life. If that meant standing beside the bomb and triggering it himself, well, few men ever had a chance to trade their lives so well.

They were deep under the forest canopy now. Chris caught sight of flickering movements under the trees, marine flankers guarding them and their precious cargo. According to prewar maps, they had only to top one rise, then another. From that prominence, any place to plant the bomb would be as good as any other.

Chris started to turn, to look back at Loki . . . but at that moment the night erupted with light. Flares popped and fizzed and floated slowly through the branches on tiny parachutes. Men dove for cover as tracer bullets sent their shadows fleeing. There was a sudden gunfire up ahead, and loud concussions. Men screamed.

Chris sought cover behind a towering fire as mortars began pounding the forest around him.

From high up the hillside—even over the explosions—they heard booming laughter.

Clutching the roots of a tree, Chris looked back. A dozen yards away, the dwarf lay flat on his back, a smoking ruin where a mortar round must have landed squarely.

But then he felt a hand on his shoulder. O'Leary pointed up the hill and whispered, goggle-eyed, "Dig it, man."

Chris turned and stared upslope at a huge, manlike being striding down the hillside, followed by dark-cloaked, armed men. The figure carried a giant bludgeon which screamed whenever he threw it, crushing trees and marines without prejudice. Giant conifers exploded into kindling and men were turned into jam. Then the weapon swept back into the red-bearded Aesir's hand.

Not mortars, Chris realized. *Thor's hammer.*
Of Loki, there was no sign at all.

3

"There, there, Hugin. Fear not the dark Americans.
They shall not hurt thee."

The one-eyed being called Odin sat upon a throne of
ebony, bearing upon his upraised left hand a raven the
same color as night. A jewel set in the giant's eyepatch
glittered like an orb more far-seeing than the one he had
lost, and across his lap lay a shining spear.

On both sides stood fur-clad figures nearly as impos-
ing, one blond, with a great axe laid arrogantly over his
shoulder, the other red-bearded, leaning lazily on a hammer the size of a normal man.

Guards in black leather, twin lightning strokes on
their collars, stood at attention around the hall of rough-
hewn timbers. Even their rifles were polished black. The
only spot of color on their SS uniforms was a red swastika
armband.

The being called Odin looked down at the prisoners,
chained together in a heap on the floor of the great hall.

"Alas. Poor Hugin has not forgiven you, my American
guests. His brother, Munin, was lost when Berlin burned
under your Hellfire bombs."

The Aesir chief's remaining eye gleamed ferally. "And
who can blame my poor watch-bird, or fail to understand a
father's grief, when that same flame deluge consumed my
bright boy, my far-seeing Heimdallr."

The survivors of the ill-fated raiding party lay on the
dry stone floor, exhausted. The unconscious, dying Major
Marlowe was in no condition to answer for them, but one
of the Free British volunteers stood up, rattling his chains,
and spat on the floor in front of the manlike creature.

"Higgins!" O'Leary tried to pull on the man's arm,
but was shrugged off as the Brit shook his fist.

"Yeah, they got your precious boy in Berlin. And you

killed *everyone* in London an' Paris in revenge! I say the Yanks were too soft, letting that stop them. They should'a gone ahead, *whatever* the price, an' fried every last Aryan bitch an' cub . . ."

His defiance was cut off as an SS officer knocked him down. Troopers brought their rifle butts down hard, again and again.

Finally, Odin waved them back.

"Take the body to the center of the Great Circle, to be sent to Valhalla."

The officer looked up sharply, but Odin rumbled in a tone that assumed obedience. "I want that brave man with me, when Fimbul-Winter blows," the creature explained. And obviously he thought that settled the matter. As black-uniformed guards cut the limp form free, the chief of the Aesir chucked his raven under the beak and offered it a morsel of meat. He spoke to the huge redhead standing beside him.

"Thor, my son. These other things are thine. Poor prizes, I admit, but they did show some prowess in following the Liar this far. What will thou do with them?"

The giant stroked his hammer with gauntlets the size of small dogs. Here, indeed, was a creature that made even Loki seem small.

He stepped forward and scanned the prisoners, as if searching for something. When his gaze alighted on Chris, it seemed to shimmer. His voice was as deep as the growling of earthquakes.

"I will deign to speak with one or two of them, Father."

"Good." Odin nodded. "Have them cast into a pit somewhere," he told the SS general nearby, who clicked his heels and bowed low. "And await my son's pleasure."

The Nazis hauled Chris and the other survivors to their feet and pulled them away, single file. But not before Chris overheard the elder Aesir tell his offspring, "Find out what you can about that wolf-spawn, Loki, and then give them all over to be used in the sacrifice."

4

Poor Major Marlowe had been right about one thing. The Nazis would never have won without the Aesir, or something like them. Hitler and his gang must have believed from the start that they could somehow call forth the ancient "gods," or they'd surely never have dared wage such a war, one certain to bring in America.

Indeed, by early 1944 it had seemed all but over. There was hell yet to pay, of course, but nobody back home feared defeat anymore. The Russians were pushing in from the east. Rome was taken, and the Mediterranean was an Allied lake. The Japanese were crumbling—pushed back or bottled up in island after island—while the greatest armada in history was gathering in England, preparing to cross the Channel and lance the Nazi boil for good and all.

In factories and shipyards across America, the Arsenal of Democracy was pouring forth more materiel in any given month than the Third Reich had produced in its best year. Ships rolled off the ways at intervals of hours. Planes every few minutes.

Most important of all, in Italy and in the Pacific, a rabble of farmers and city boys in soldier suits had been tempered and become warriors in a great army. Man to man, they were now on a par with their experienced foe, and the enemy was outnumbered as well.

Already there was talk of the postwar recovery, of plans to help in the rebuilding, and of a "United Nations" to keep the peace forever.

Chris had been only a child in knee pants, back in '44, devouring Chet Nimitz novels and praying with all his might that there would be something half as glorious to do in his adulthood as what his uncles were achieving overseas right then. Maybe there would be adventures in space, he hoped, for after this, the horror of war would surely never be allowed again.

Then came the rumors . . . tales of setbacks on the Eastern front . . . of reeling Soviet armies sent into sudden and unexpected retreat. The reasons were unclear . . . mostly, what came back were superstitious rumblings that no modern person credited.

Voices on a street corner:

Damn Russkies . . . I knew all along they didn' have no stayin' power . . . Alla time yammerin' 'bout a "second front" . . . Well, we'll give 'em a second front! Save their hash . . . Don't fret, Ivan, Uncle Sam's coming . . .

June, and the Norman sky was filled with planes. Ships covered the Channel Sea . . .

Sitting against a cold stone wall in an underground cell, Chris pinched his eyes shut and tried to crush away the memory of the grainy black and white films he had been shown. But he failed to keep the images out.

Ships as far as the eye could see . . . the greatest armada of free men ever assembled . . .

It was not until he joined the OSS that Chris actually saw photographs never shown to the public. In all the years since then, he wished *he* had not seen them, either.

D day . . . D for disaster.

Cyclones, hundreds of them, spinning like horrible tops, rising out of the dawn mists. They grew and climbed until the dark funnels appeared to stretch beyond the sky. And as they approached the ships, it seemed one could see flying figures on their flanks, driving the storms faster and faster with their beating wings . . .

"Marlowe's come up aces and eights, man." O'Leary sighed heavily as he sagged down next to Chris. "You're the big cheese now, dad."

Chris closed his eyes. *All men die*, he thought, reminding himself that he hadn't really liked the dour marine all that much, anyway.

He mourned nonetheless, if for no other reason than that Marlowe had been his insulation, protecting him from that bitch called command.

"So what gives now, chief?"

Chris looked at O'Leary. The man was really too old to be playing kids' games. There were lines at the edges of those doelike eyes, and the baby fat was turning into a

double chin. The Army recognized genius, and put up
with a lot from its civilian experts. But Chris wondered—
not for the first time—how this escapee from Greenwich
Village ever came to be in a position of responsibility.

Loki chose him. That was the real answer. *Like he
chose me. So much for the god of cleverness.*

"What *gives* is that you damp down the beat-rap,
O'Leary. Making only every third sentence incomprehensible should be enough to provide your emotional crutch."

O'Leary winced, and Chris at once regretted the
outburst.

"Oh, never mind." He changed the subject. "How
are the rest of the men doing?"

"Copacetic, I guess . . . I mean, they're okay, for
guys slated for ritual shortening in a few hours. They all
knew this was a suicide mission. Just wanted to take a few
more of the bastards with them, is all."

Chris nodded. *If we had had another year or two . . .*

By then the missile scientists would have had rockets
accurate enough to go for a surgical strike, making this
attempt to sneak in bombs under the enemy's noses unnec-
essary. The Satellite was just the beginning of the possibilities, if they had had time.

"Higgins was right, man," O'Leary muttered as he
collapsed against the wall next to Chris. "We shoulda
pasted them with everything we had. Melted Europe to
slag, if that's what it took."

"By the time we had enough bombs to do much more
than slow them down, they had atomic weapons, too,"
Chris pointed out.

"So? After we fried Peenemünde, their delivery systems stagnated. And they haven't got a clue how to go
thermonuclear! Why, even if they *did* manage to disas-
semble our bomb—"

"God forbid!" Chris blinked. His heart raced, even
considering the possibility. If the Nazis managed to make
the leap from A-bomb to fusion weapons . . .

The tech shook his head vigorously. "I scoped—I
mean I checked out the destruct triggers myself, Chris.
Anyone pokes around to try to see how a U.S. of A.

type H-bomb works will be in for a nasty surprise."

That had, of course, been a minimum requirement before being allowed to attempt this mission. Had they been able to assemble the weapon near the "Great Circle" of Aesgard, the course of the war might have been changed. Now, all they could hope was that the separate components would melt to slag as they were supposed to when their timers expired.

O'Leary persisted. "I still think we should have launched everything we had back in '52."

Chris knew how the man felt. Most Americans believed the exchange would have been worth it. A full-scale strike at Hitler's homeland would have seared the heart out of it. The monster's retaliation, with cruder rockets and fission bombs, would have been a price worth paying.

When he had learned the real reason, at first he had refused to believe it. Chris had assumed that Loki was lying . . . that it was an Aesir trick.

But since then he had seen the truth. America's arsenal of bombs was a two-edged sword. Unless used carefully it would cut both ways.

There was a rattling of keys. Three SS guards stepped in, looking down their noses at the dejected Allied raiders.

"The great Thor would deign to speak vit' your leader," the officer said in thickly accented English. When no one moved, his gaze fell upon Chris and he smiled. "This one. This strayed sheep. Our lord asked for him especially."

He snapped his fingers and the guards grabbed Chris by the arms. "Cool as glass, dad," O'Leary said. "Drive 'em crazy, baby."

Chris glanced back from the door. "You too, O'Leary."

He was pushed through and the dungeon gate slammed shut behind him.

5

"You are a Dane, are you not?"

Chris was tied firmly to a beam pillar in front of a

crackling fireplace. The Gestapo official peered at Chris from several angles before asking his question.

"Danish by ancestry. What of it?" Chris shrugged under his bonds.

The Nazi clucked. "Oh, nothing in particular. It is just that I never cease to be amazed when I find specimens of clearly superior stock fighting against their own divine heritage."

Chris lifted an eyebrow. "Do you interrogate a lot of prisoners?"

"Oh, yes, very many."

"Well, then you must be amazed all the time."

The Gestapo man blinked, then smiled sourly. He stepped back to light a cigarette, and Chris noticed that his hands were trembling.

"But doesn't your very blood cry out when you find yourself working with, going into battle alongside, racial scum, mongrels . . . ?"

Chris laughed. He turned his head and regarded the Nazi icily.

"Why are you even here?" he asked.

"I—what do you mean?" The fellow blinked again. "See here now, I am in charge of interrogation of—"

"You're in charge of a jail detail." Chris sneered. "The priests of the Aesir run everything now. The mystics in the SS control the Reich. Hitler's a tottering old syphyllitic they won't let out of Berchtesgaden. And you old-fashioned Nazis are barely tolerated anymore."

The officer sucked at his cigarette. "What do you mean by that remark?"

"I mean that all that racial claptrap was just window dressing. An excuse to set up the death camps. But the SS would've been just as happy to use *Aryans* in them, if that was the only way to—to . . ."

"Yes?" The Gestapo man stepped forward. "To do what? If the purpose of the camps was not the elimination of impure stock, then what, smart man? *What?*"

There was a brittle, high-pitched edge to the man's laughter. "You do not know, do you? Even Loki did not tell you!"

Chris could have sworn that there was *disappointment* in the officer's eyes ... as if he had hoped to learn something from Chris, and was let down to find out that his prisoner was as much in the dark as he was.

No, I wasted a question, and Loki did not tell me about the reason for the camps. Chris looked at the other man's trembling hands—hands that had, no doubt, wreaked more hell on broken bodies and spirits than bore contemplating—all, apparently, in a cause that was no longer even relevant to the winning side.

"Poor obsolete National Socialist," Chris said. "Your dreams, mad as they were, were human ones. How does it feel to have it all taken over by aliens? To watch it all change beyond recognition?"

The Gestapo man reddened. Fumbling, he picked up a truncheon from a table near the wall and smacked it into his gloved left hand.

"I will change something *else* beyond recognition," he growled menacingly. "And if I am obsolete, at least I am still allowed the pleasure of my craft."

He approached, smiling, a thin film on his lips. Chris braced himself as the arm swung back, raising the bludgeon high. But at that moment the leather curtains parted and a large shadow fell across the rug. The Gestapo officer paled and snapped to attention.

The red-bearded Aesir named Thor nodded briefly as he shrugged out of his furred cloak. "You may go," he rumbled.

Chris did not even look at the Nazi as the interrogator tried to meet his eye. Chris watched the coals in the fireplace until the curtains swished again and he was alone with the alien.

Thor sat down, cross-legged, on a thick rug and spent a few minutes joining Chris in contemplation of the flickering flames. When he used his hammer to prod the logs, heat brought out fine, glowing designs in the massive iron head.

"Fro sends word from Vineland ... from the sea thou callest Labrador. There has been a slaughter of many brave men."

Thor looked up.

"Those cowards' tools—'submarines'—did much harm to our fleet. But in the end, Fro's tempests were masterful. The landing is secured."

Chris controlled the sinking feeling in his stomach. This was expected. Worse was to come, this winter.

Thor shook his head. "This is a bad war. Where is the honor, when thousands die unable even to show valor?"

Chris had more experience than most Americans in holding conversation with gods. Still, he took a chance, speaking without permission.

"I agree, Great One. But you can't blame *us* for that."

Thor's eyes glittered as he inspected Chris. "No, brave worm. I do not blame you. That you have used your flame weapons as little as you have speaks well for the pride of thy leaders. Or perhaps they know what our wrath would be, if they were so cowardly as to use them wantonly."

I never should have been allowed on this mission. I know too much, Chris realized. Loki had been the one to overrule High Command and insist that Chris come along. But that made him the only one here who knew the *real* reason the H-bombs had been kept leashed.

Dust from atom blasts, and soot from burning cities— those were what Allied High Command feared, far more than radiation or Nazi retaliation. Already, from limited use of nuclear weapons so far, the weather had chilled measurably.

And the Aesir were so much stronger in winter! Scientists verified Loki's story, that careless use of the Allied nuclear advantage would lead to catastrophe, no matter how badly they seared the other side.

"We too prefer a more personal approach," Chris said, hoping to keep the Aesir believing his own explanation. "No man wishes to be killed by powers beyond his understanding, impossible to resist or fight back against."

Thor's rumble, Chris realized, was low laughter. "Well said, worm. Thou dost chastize as Freyr does, with words that reap, even as they sow."

The Aes leaned forward a little. "You would earn merit in my eyes, small one, if you told me how to find the Brother of Lies."

Those gray eyes were like cold clouds, and Chris felt his sense of reality begin to waver as he looked into them. It took a powerful effort of will to tear his gaze away. Shutting his eyes, he spoke with a dry mouth.

"I . . . don't know what you're talking about."

The rumbling changed tone, deepening a little. Chris felt a rough touch and opened his eyes to see that Thor was brushing his cheek with the leather-bound haft of the great war hammer.

"Loki, youngling. Tell me where the Trickster may be found, and you may yet escape your doom, you may even find a place by my side. In the world to come, there will be no greater place for a man."

This time Chris steeled himself to meet the hypnotic pools. Thor's eyes seemed to reach out for his soul, as a magnet might call to native iron. Chris fought back with the savage heat of hatred.

"Not . . . for all the Valkyries in your fucking, alien pantheon," he whispered, half breathless. "I'd rather run with wolves."

The smile vanished. Thor blinked, and for a moment Chris thought he saw the Aesir's image waver just a little, as if . . . as if Chris were looking through a man-shaped *fold* in space.

"Courage will not save thee from the wages of disrespect, worm," the shape warned, and solidified again into a fur-clad giant.

All at once, Chris was glad to have known O'Leary.

"Don't you dig it yet, daddyo? I don't fucking *believe* in you! Wherever you're from, baby, they probably kicked you out!

"You Aesir may be mean enough to wreck our world, but everything about you screams that you're the *dregs*, man. Leaky squares. Probably burned out papa's stolen saucer just gettin' here!"

He shook his head. "I just refuse to believe in you, man."

The icy gray eyes blinked once. Then Thor's surprised expression faded into a deathly cool smile. "I did not ken your other insults. But for calling me a *man*, you shall die as you seem to wish, before the morning sun."

He stood up and placed a hand on Chris's shoulder, as if emparting a friendly benediction, but even the casual power of that touch felt viselike.

"I only add this, little one. We Aesir have come *invited*, and we arrived not in ships—even ships between the stars—but instead upon the wings of Death itself. This much, this boon of knowledge I grant thee, in honor of your defiance."

Then, in a swirl of furs and displaced air, the creature was gone, leaving Chris alone again to watch the coals flicker slowly and turn into ashes.

6

The Teutonic priests were resplendant in red and black, their robes traced in gold and silver. Platinum eagles' wings rose from their top-heavy helms as they marched around a great circle of standing stones, chanting in a tongue that sounded vaguely Germanic, but which Chris knew was much, much older.

An altar, carved with gaping dragons' mouths, stood beside a raging bonfire. Smoke rose in a turbulent funnel, carrying bright sparks upward toward a full moon. Heat blazed at the ring of prisoners, each chained to his own obelisk of rough-hewn rock.

They faced southward, looking from a Gotland prominence across the Baltic toward a shore that had once been Poland, and for a little while after that had been the "Thousand-Year Reich."

The waters were unnaturally calm, almost glassy, reflecting a nearly perfect image of the bonfire alongside the Moon's rippling twin.

"Fro must be back from Labrador," O'Leary commented loudly enough for Chris to hear him over the chanting and the pounding drums. "That'd explain the clear night. He's th' god of tempests."

Chris glanced at the man sourly, and O'Leary grinned back apologetically. "Sorry, man. I mean he's th' little green alien who's in charge of weather control. Make you feel any better?"

I had that coming, Chris thought. He smiled dryly and shrugged. "I don't suppose it matters all that much now."

O'Leary watched the Aryan Brothers march by again, carrying a giant swastica alongside a great dragonlike totem. The technician started to say something, but then he blinked and seemed to mumble to himself, as if trying to catch a drifting thought. When the procession had passed, he turned to Chris, a mystified expression on his face. "I just remembered something."

Chris sighed. "What is it now, O'Leary?"

The beatnik frowned in puzzlement. "I can't figure why it slipped my mind until now. But back when we were on the beach, unloading the bomb parts, Old Loki pulled me aside. It was all so hectic, but I could swear I saw him palm th' H-bomb trigger mechanism, Chris. That means . . ."

Chris nodded. "That means he knew we were going to be captured. I'd already figured that out, O'Leary. At least the Nazis won't get the trigger."

"Yeah. But that's not all I just remembered, Chris. Loki told me to *tell* you something for him. He said you'd asked him a question, and he told me to relay an answer he said you might understand."

O'Leary shook his head. "I don't know why I forgot to tell you about it until now."

Chris laughed. Of course the renegade Aes had put the man under a posthypnotic command to recall the message only later . . . perhaps only in a situation like this.

"What is it, O'Leary? What did he say to tell me?"

"It was just one word, Chris. He said to tell you— *necromancy.* And then he clammed up. Wasn't much after that that the SS jumped us. What'd he mean by that,

Captain? What was your question, anyway? What does the answer mean?"

Chris did not reply. He stared at the funnel of sparks climbing toward the Moon.

With his last question he had asked Loki about the camps—about the awesome, horrible, concentrated effort of death that had been perpetrated, first in Europe and then in Russia and Africa. What were they *for*? There had to be more to it than a plan to eliminate some bothersome minorities.

Moreover, why had Loki, who normally seemed so oblivious to human life, acted to rescue so many from the death factories, at so great a risk to himself?

Necromancy. That was Loki's delayed reply to his final question. And Loki had told it in such a way that Chris might have his answer, but never be able to tell anyone who mattered.

Necromancy . . .

The word stood for the performance of magic, but magic of a special, terrible kind. In legend, a necromancer was an evil wizard who used the concentrated field created by the death agony of human beings to drive his spells.

But that was just superstitious nonsense!

Light-headed, Chris looked out across the sand at the hulking Aesir seated on their gilded thrones, heard the chanting of the priests, and wished he could dismiss the idea as easily as he once would have.

Was that the reason the Nazis had dared to wage a war they otherwise could never have won? Because they believed that they could create such concentrated, distilled horror that ancient spells would actually work?

It explained so much. Other nations had gone insane, in human history. Other movements had been evil. But none had perpetrated such crimes with such dedication and efficiency. The horror must have been directed not so much at death itself, but at some hideous goal beyond death!

"They . . . *made* . . . the Aesir. That's what Loki meant by thinking that, maybe, his own memories were false . . . when he suspected that he was actually no older than I . . ."

"What was that, Cap'n?" O'Leary leaned as far as his chains would allow. "I couldn't follow . . ."

But the procession chose that moment to stop. The High Priest, carrying a golden sword, held it before Odin's throne. The father of the "gods" touched it and the Aesir's rumbling chant could be heard, lower than human singing, a hungry sound like a growl that trembled within the Earth.

One of the chained Allies—a Free Briton—was dragged, numbed with dread, from his obelisk toward the fire and the dragon altar.

Chris shut his eyes, as if to hold out the screams. "Jesus!" O'Leary hissed.

Yes, Chris thought. *Invoke Jesus. Or Allah or God of Abraham. Wake up, Brahma! For your dream has turned into a nightmare.*

He understood clearly now why Loki had not told him his answer while there was even an infinitesimal chance that he might ever make it home again alive.

Thank you, Loki.

Better America and the Last Alliance should go down fighting honorably than even be tempted by this knowledge . . . to have its will tested by this *way out*. For if the Allies ever tried to adopt the enemy's methods, there would be nothing left in the soul of humanity to fight for.

Who would we conjure, Chris wondered. *If we ever did use those spells? Superman? Or Captain Marvel? Oh, they'd be more than a match for the Aesir, certainly! Our myths were boundless.*

He laughed, and the sound turned into a sob as another scream of agony pierced the night.

Thank you, Loki, for sparing us that test of our souls.

He had no idea where the renegade "trickster god" had gone, or whether this debacle had only been a cloak for some deeper, more secret mission.

Could that be? Chris wondered. He knew that it was possible, still. Soldiers seldom ever saw the big picture, and President Marshall did not have to tell his OSS captains everything. This mission could just have been a feint, a minor piece in a greater plan.

Lasers and satellites . . . they could be just part of it. There might be a silver bullet . . . a sprig of mistletoe, still.

Chains rattled to his right. He heard a voice cursing in Portuguese and footsteps dragging the latest prisoner off.

Chris looked up at the sky, and a thought suddenly occurred to him, as if out of nowhere.

Legends begin in strange ways, he realized.

Someday—even if there was no silver bullet—the horror would have to ebb at last, when humans grew scarce, perhaps, and the Aesir were less plump and well fed on the death manna they supped on from charnel houses.

Then there would come a time when human heroes would count for something again. Perhaps in secret laboratories, or in exile on the Moon, or at the bottom of the sea, free men and women would work and toil to build the armor, the weapons, maybe the heroes themselves . . .

This time the scream was choked, as if the Brazilian ranger were trying to defy his enemies, and only broke to show his agony at the last.

Footsteps approached. To his amazement, Chris felt feather-light, as if gravity were barely enough to keep him on the ground.

"So long, O'Leary," he said distantly.

"Yeah, man. Stay cool."

Chris nodded. He offered the black-and-silver-clad SS his wrists as they unchained him, and said to them softly, in a friendly tone of voice, "You know, you look pretty silly for grown men."

They blinked at him in surprise. Chris smiled and stepped between them, leading the way toward the altar and the waiting Aesir.

Someday men will challenge these monsters, he thought, knowing that the numb, light-headed feeling meant that he would not scream . . . that nothing they could do would make him take more than casual notice.

Loki had made certain of this. *This* was why the
Trickster had spent so much time with Chris, this last year
. . . why he had insisted that Chris come along on this
mission.

*Our day will come. Revenge will drive our descen-
dants. Science will armor them. But those heroes will need
one more thing,* he realized. *Heroes need inspiration.
They need legends.*

On their way toward the humming Aesir, they passed
before a row of human "dignitaries" from the Reich, a few
with faces glazed in excitement, but others sitting numbly,
as if lost. He felt he could almost read the despair in those
darkened, mad eyes. They were aware that something
they had wrought had gone long, long, out of their control.

Thor frowned as Chris flashed him a smile. "Hi,
how'ya doin'?" he said to the Aesir, interrupting their
rumbling music. Where curses and screams had only reso-
nated with the chant, his good-natured sarcasm broke up
the ritual in a mutter of surprise.

"Move, swine!" An SS guard pushed Chris, or tried
to, but stumbled instead on empty air where the American
had been. Chris ducked underneath the jangling, cumber-
some uniform, between the Nazi's legs, and swatted the
fellow's behind with the flat of his hand, sending him
sprawling.

The other guard reached for him, but crumpled
openmouthed as Chris bent his fingers back and snapped
them. The third guard he lifted by the belt buckle and
tossed into the bonfire, to bellow in sudden horror and
pain.

Hysterical strength, of course, Chris realized, knowing what Loki had done to him. Four onrushing underpriests
went down with snapped necks. No human could do these
things without being used up, Chris knew, distantly, but
what did it matter? This was far more fun than he had
expected to be having, at this moment.

A golden flash out of the corner of his eye warned
him . . . Chris whirled and ducked, catching Odin's spear
with one sudden snatch.

"Coward," he whispered at the hot-faced "father of

the gods." He flipped the heavy, gleaming weapon around and held it in two hands before him.

God, help me . . .

With a cry he broke the legendary spear over his knee. The pieces fell to the sand.

Nobody moved; even Thor's whirling hammer slowed and then dropped. In the sudden silence, Chris was distantly aware of the fact that his femur was shattered—along with most of the bones in his hands—leaving him perched precariously on one leg.

But Chris's only regret was that he could not emulate an aged Jew he had heard of from one of the concentration camp survivors. Standing in front of the grave he had been forced to dig for himself, the old man had not begged, or tried to reason with the SS, nor slumped in despair. Instead, the prisoner had turned away from his murderers, dropped his pants, and said aloud in Yiddish as he bent over, "*Kish mir im toches . . .*"

"Kiss my ass," Chris told Thor as more guards finally ran up and grabbed his arms. As they dragged him to the altar, he kept his gaze on the red-bearded "god." The priests tied him down, but Chris met the Aesir's gray eyes.

"I don't believe in you," he said.

Thor blinked, and the giant suddenly turned away.

Chris laughed out loud then, knowing that nothing in the world would suppress this story. It would spread. There would be no stopping it.

Loki, you bastard. You used me, and I suppose I should thank you.

But rest assured, Loki, someday we'll get you, too.

He laughed again as he watched the dismayed High Priest fumble with the knife, and found it terrifically funny. A wide-eyed assistant jiggled and dropped his swastika banner. Chris roared.

Behind him, he heard O'Leary's high-pitched giggle. Then, another of the prisoners barked, and another. It was unstoppable.

Across the chilly Baltic, an uncertain wind blew. And overhead, a new star sailed swiftly where the old ones merely drifted across the sky.

AUTHOR'S NOTES

The parallel-world story is another mainstay of SF. It explores the old question: "What would have happened if . . . ?"

If a fly buzzing above a bowl of soup had dipped too low, getting caught, disgusting a Roman centurion, who took his wrath out on an underling, sending him out on an extra patrol, which detected Hannibal's army in the Alps early enough to catch it far from Rome . . . You see the point.

Sometimes we like to frighten ourselves. The most frequent "what if" seems to deal with alternate realities in which the Nazis won World War II. Something about that loathsome possibility just invites a horror story.

Trouble is, I never could believe it.

Mind you, Philip K. Dick's The Man in the High Castle *is a classic, a great work. But its premise—that an early assassination of Franklin Roosevelt would have led to an inevitable Axis victory—is hard to swallow.*

They were just such schmucks!

I mean, it's hard to think of any way a single altered event would have let the Nazis win their war. They would have needed an entire chain of flukes even to have a chance. In fact, it took quite a few lucky breaks for them to last as long as they did, and to have the time to commit such atrocities.

I said as much to Gregory Benford when he invited me to write a piece for his upcoming anthology of parallel world stories, Hitler Victorious. *Greg's reply? A dare.*

"I'll bet you could think of some premise that'd work, David."

"*How unlikely can it be?*"

"*It can be* preposterous, *as long as it sings.*"

Greg was my collaborator on a rather large novel. I trusted him. But once the story was started, it took off in directions I never expected. I don't know if the story "sings," but it does tie together several curious things about the Nazi cult.

Why *were* the Nazis so evil? Why did they do so many horrible, pointless things? What was behind their incredible streak of romantic mysticism?

Maybe the bastards really believed something like this was possible.

PROPAGATION

Lungfish

1

Awaiter is excited again. She transmits urgently, trying to get my attention.

"Seeker, listen!" Her electronic voice hisses over the ancient cables. *"The little living ones are near, Seeker! Even now they explore this belt of asteroids, picking through the rocks and ruins. You can hear them as they browse over each new discovery!*

"Soon they will find us here! Do you hear me, Seeker? It is time to decide what to do!"

Awaiter's makers were impatient creatures. I wonder that she has lasted so long, out here in the starry cold.

My own makers were wiser.

"Seeker! Are you listening to me?"

I don't really wish to talk with anyone, so I erect a side-personality—little more than a swirling packet of nudged electrons—to handle her for me. Even if Awaiter discovers the sham, she might take the hint then and leave me alone.

Or she might grow more insistent. It would be hard to predict without awakening more dormant circuits than I care to bring into play right now.

"There is no hurry," my artifact tells her soothingly. *"The Earth creatures will not get here for several more of their years. Anyway, there is nothing we can do to change matters when they do arrive. It was all written long ago."*

The little swirl of electrons really is very good. It speaks with my own accent, and seems quite logical, for a simple construct.

243

"How can you be so complacent!" Awaiter scolds. The cables covering our rocky, icy worldlet—our home for so many ages—reverberate with her electronic exasperation.

"We survivors made you our leader, Seeker, because you seemed to understand best what was happening in the galaxy at large. But now, at last, our waiting is at an end. The biological creatures will be here soon, and we shall have to act!"

Perhaps Awaiter has tuned in to too much Earth television over the last century or so. Her whining sounds positively human.

"The Earthlings will find us or they won't," my shadow self answers. "We few survivors are too feeble to prevent it, even if we wished. What can a shattered band of ancient machines fear or anticipate in making contact with such a vigorous young race?"

Indeed, I did not need Awaiter to tell me the humans were coming. My remaining sensors sample the solar wind and savor the stream of atoms and radicals much as a human might sniff the breeze. In recent years, the flow from the inner system has carried new scents—the bright tang of metal ions from space-foundries, and the musty smoke-smell of deuterium.

The hormones of industry.

And there is this busy modulation of light and radio—where the spectrum used to carry only the hot song of the star. All of these are signs of an awakening. Life is emerging from the little water-womb on the third planet. It is on its way out here.

"Greeter and Emissary want to warn the humans of their danger, and I agree!" Awaiter insists. "We can help them!"

Our debate has aroused some of the others; I notice new tendrils entering the network. Watcher and Greeter make their presence felt as little fingers of super-cooled electricity. I sense their agreement with Awaiter.

"Help them? How?" my subvoice asks. "Our last repair and replication units fell apart shortly after the Final Battle. We had no way of knowing humans had evolved until the creatures themselves invented radio.

"And then it was already too late! Their first transmissions are already propagating, unrecallable, into a deadly galaxy. If there are destroyers around in this region of space, the humans are already lost!

"Why worry the poor creatures, then? Let them enjoy their peace. Warning them will accomplish nothing."

Oh, I am good! This little artificial voice argues as well as I did long ago, staving off abrupt action by my impatient peers.

Greeter glides into the network. I feel his cool electron flux, eloquent as usual.

"I agree with Seeker," he states surprisingly. "The creatures do not need to be told about their danger. They are already figuring it out for themselves."

Now, this does interest me. I sweep my subpersona aside and extend a tendril of my Very Self into the network. None of the others even notice the shift.

"What makes you believe this?" I ask Greeter.

Greeter indicates our array of receivers salvaged from ancient derelicts. "We're intercepting what the humans say to each other as they explore this asteroid belt," he says. "One human, in particular, appears on the verge of understanding what happened here, long ago."

Greeter's tone of smugness must have been borrowed from Earthly television shows. But that is understandable. Greeter's makers were enthusiasts, who programmed him to love nothing greater than the simple pleasure of saying hello.

"Show me," I tell him. I am reluctant to hope that the long wait is over at last.

2

Ursula Fleming stared as the asteroid's slow rotation brought ancient, shattered ruins into view below. "Lord, what a mess," she said, sighing.

She had been five years in the Belt, exploring and

salvaging huge alien works, but never had she beheld such
devastation as this.

Only four kilometers away, the hulking asteroid lay
nearly black against the starry band of the Milky Way,
glistening here and there in the light of the distant sun.
The rock stretched more than two thousand meters along
its greatest axis. Collisions had dented, cracked, and cra-
tered it severely since it had broken from its parent body,
more than a billion years ago.

On one side it seemed a fairly typical carbonaceous
planetoid, like millions of others orbiting out here at the
edge of the Belt. But this changed as the survey ship
Hairy Thunderer orbited around the nameless hunk of
rock and frozen gases. Then the sun's vacuum brilliance
cast lonely, sharp shadows across ruined replication yards
. . . jagged, twisted remnants of a catastrophe that had
taken place back when dinosaurs still roamed the Earth.

"Gavin!" she called over her shoulder. "Come down
here! You've got to see this!"

In a minute her partner floated through the overhead
hatch, flipping in midair. There was a faint click as his
feet contacted the magnetized floor.

"All right, Urs. What's to see? More murdered babies
to dissect and salvage? Or have we finally found a clue to
who their killers were?"

Ursula only gestured toward the viewing port. Her
partner moved closer and stared. Highlights reflected from
Gavin's glossy features as the ship's searchlight swept the
shattered scene below.

"Yep." Gavin nodded at last. "Dead babies again.
Fleming Salvage and Exploration ought to make a good
price off each little corpse."

Ursula frowned. "Don't be morbid, Gavin. Those are
unfinished interstellar probes, destroyed ages ago before
they could be launched. We have no idea whether they
were sentient machines like you, or just tools, like this
ship. You of all people should know better than to go
around anthropomorphizing alien artifacts."

Gavin's grimace was an android's equivalent of a sarcastic shrug. "If I use 'morbid' imagery, whose fault is it?"

"What do you mean?" Ursula turned to face him.

"I mean you organic humans faced a choice, a hundred years ago, when you saw that 'artificial' intelligence was going to take off and someday leave the biological kind behind.

"You could have wrecked the machines, but that would have halted progress.

"You could have deep-programmed us with 'Fundamental Laws of Robotics,' " Gavin sniffed. "And had slaves far smarter than their masters.

"But what was it you organics finally did decide to do?"

Ursula knew it was no use answering, not when Gavin was in one of his moods. She concentrated on piloting *Hairy Thunderer* closer to the asteroid.

"What was your solution to the problem of smart machines?" Gavin persisted. "You chose to raise us as your *children*, that's what you did. You taught us to be just like you, and even gave most of us humaniform bodies!"

Ursula's last partner—a nice old 'bot and a good chess player—had warned her, when he retired, not to hire an adolescent Class-AAA android fresh out of college. They could be as difficult as any human teenager, he cautioned.

The worst part of it was that Gavin was right once again.

Despite genetic and cyborg improvements to the human animal, machines still seemed fated to surpass biological men. For better or worse the decision had been made to raise Class-AAA androids as human children, with all the same awkward irritations that implied.

Gavin shook his head in dramatic, superior sadness, exactly like a too-smart adolescent who properly deserved to be strangled.

"Can you really object when I, a man-built, *manlike* android, anthropomorphize? We only do as we've been taught, mistress."

His bow was eloquently sarcastic.

Ursula said nothing. It was hard, at times, to be entirely sure humanity had made the right decision after all.

Below, across the face of the ravaged asteroid, stretched acres of great-strutted scaffolding—twisted and curled in ruin. Within the toppled derricks lay silent ranks of shattered, unfinished starships, wrecked perhaps a hundred million years ago.

Ursula felt sure that theirs were the first eyes to look on this scene since some awful force had wrought this havoc.

The ancient destroyers had to be long gone. Nobody had yet found a star machine even close to active. Still, she took no chances, making certain the weapons console was vigilant.

The sophisticated, semi-sentient unit searched, but found no energy sources, no movement among the ruined, unfinished star probes below. Instruments showed nothing but cold rock and metal, long dead.

Ursula shook her head. She did not like such metaphors. Gavin's talk of "murdered babies" didn't help one look at the ruins below as potentially profitable salvage.

It would not help her other vocation, either . . . the paper she had been working on for months now . . . her carefully crafted theory about what had happened out here, so long ago.

"We have work to do," she told her partner. "Let's get on with it."

Gavin pressed two translucent hands together prayerfully. "Yes, Mommy. Your wish is my program." He sauntered away to his own console and began deploying their remote exploration drones.

Ursula concentrated on directing the lesser minds within *Thunderer*'s control board—those smaller semisentient minds dedicated to rockets and radar and raw numbers—who still spoke and acted coolly and dispassionately . . . as machines ought to do.

3

Greeter is right. One of the little humans does seem to be on the track of something. We crippled survivors all

*listen in as Greeter arranges to tap the tiny Earthship's
crude computers, where its captain stores her speculations.
Her thoughts are crisp, indeed, for a biological creature.
Still, she is missing many, many pieces to the puzzle.*

4

THE LONELY SKY
By Ursula Fleming

After centuries of wondering, mankind
has at last realized an ancient dream. We
have discovered proof of civilizations other
than our own.

In the decade we have been exploring the
Outer Belt in earnest, humanity has uncov-
ered artifacts from more than *forty* different cultures ... all represented by robot
starships ... all apparently long dead.

What happened here?

And why were all those long-ago visitors
robots?

Back in the late twentieth century, some
scholars had begun to doubt that biological
beings could ever adapt well enough to space
travel to colonize more than a little corner
of the Milky Way. But even if that were so, it
would not prevent exploration of the galaxy. Advanced intelligences could send out
mechanical representatives, robots better
suited to the tedium and dangers of interstellar spaceflight than living beings.

After all, a mature, long-lived culture could
afford to wait thousands of years for data to
return from distant star systems.

Even so, the galaxy is a big place. To send
a probe to every site of interest could im-
poverish a civilization.

The most efficient way would be to dispatch only a few deluxe robot ships, instead of a giant fleet of cheaper models. Those first probes would investigate nearby stars and planets. Then, after their exploration was done, they would use local resources to make copies of themselves.

The legendary John Von Neumann first described the concept. Sophisticated machines, programmed to replicate themselves from raw materials, could launch their "daughters" toward still farther stellar systems. There, each probe would make still more duplicates, and so on.

Exploration could proceed far faster than if carried out by living beings. And after the first wave there would be no further cost to the home system. From then on information would pour back, year after year, century after century.

It sounded so logical. Those twentieth-century scholars calculated that the technique could deliver an exploration probe to every star in our galaxy a mere three million years after the first was launched—an eyeblink compared to the age of the galaxy.

But there was a rub! When we humans discovered radio and then spaceflight, no extra-solar probes announced themselves to say hello. There were no messages welcoming us into the civilized sky.

At first those twentieth-century philosophers thought there could only be one explanation ...

Ursula frowned at the words on the screen. No, it wouldn't be fair to judge too harshly those thinkers of a century ago. After all, who could have expected the Universe to turn out to be so bizarre?

She glanced up from the text-screen to see how Gavin

was doing with his gang of salvage drones. Her partner's
tethered form could be seen drifting between the ship and
the ruined yards. He looked very human, motioning with
his arms and directing the less sophisticated, non-citizen
machines at their tasks.

Apparently he had things well in hand. Her own shift
wasn't due for an hour yet. Ursula returned to the latest
draft of the article she hoped to submit to *The Universe*
. . . if she could ever find the right way to finish it.

In correction mode, she backspaced and altered the
last two paragraphs, then went on.

Let us re-create the logic of those philosophers of the last century, in an imagined
conversation.

"We will certainly build robot scouts someday. Colonization aside, any truly curious
race could hardly resist the temptation to
send out mechanical emissaries, to say 'hello'
to strangers out there and report back what
they find. The first crude probes to leave
our solar system—the Voyagers and Pion-
eers—demonstrated this basic desire. They
carried simple messages meant to be deciphered by other beings long after the au-
thors were dust.

"Anyone out there enough like us to be
interesting would certainly do the same.

"And yet, if self-reproducing probes are
the most efficient way to explore, why haven't
any already said hello to us? It must mean
that nobody before us ever attained the capability to send them!

"We can only conclude that we are the
first curious, gregarious, technically competent species in the history of the Milky Way."

The logic was so compelling that most
people gave up on the idea of contact, espe-

cially when radio searches turned up nothing but star static.

Then humanity spread out beyond Mars
and the Inner Belt, and we stumbled onto
the Devastation.

Ursula brushed aside a loose wisp of black hair and
bent over the keyboard. Putting in the appropriate cita-
tions and references could wait. Right now the ideas were
flowing.

The story is still sketchy, but we can
already begin to guess some of what happened out here, long before mankind was a
glimmer on the horizon.

Long ago the first "Von Neumann type"
interstellar probe arrived in our solar system. It came to explore and perhaps report
back across the empty light-years. That earliest emissary found no intelligent life here,
so it proceeded to its second task.

It mined an asteroid and sent newly made
duplicates of itself onward to other stars.
The original then remained behind to watch
and wait, patient against the day when something interesting might happen in this little corner of space.

As the epochs passed, new probes arrived,
representatives of other civilizations. Once
their own replicas had been launched, the
newcomers joined a small but growing community of mechanical ambassadors to this
backwater system—waiting for it to evolve
somebody to say hello to.

Ursula felt the poignancy of the image: the lonely
machines, envoys of creators perhaps long extinct—or
evolved past caring about the mission they had charged
upon their loyal probes. The faithful robots reproduced
themselves, saw their progeny off, then began their

long watch, whiling away the slow turning of the spiral
arms. . . .

> We have found a few of these early probes,
> remnants of a lost age of innocence in the
> galaxy.
>
> More precisely, we have found their blasted
> remains.
>
> Perhaps one day the innocent star emis-
> saries sensed some new entity enter the
> solar system. Did they move to greet it, ea-
> ger for gossip to share? Like those twentieth-
> century thinkers, perhaps they believed that
> replicant probes would have to be benign.
>
> But things had changed. The age of inno-
> cence was over. The galaxy had grown up; it
> had become nasty.
>
> The wreckage we are finding now—whose
> salvage drives our new industrial revolu-
> tion—was left by an unfathomable war that
> stretched across vast times, and was fought
> by entities to whom biological life was a
> nearly forgotten oddity.

"Uh, you there, Urs?"

Ursula looked up as the radio link crackled. She
touched the send button.

"Yes, Gavin. Have you found something interesting?"

There was a brief pause.

"Yeah, you could say that," her partner said sardoni-
cally. *"You might want to let Hairy pilot himself for a
while, and hurry your pretty little biological butt down
here to take a look."*

Ursula bit back her own sharp reply, reminding herself
to be patient. Even in humans, adolescence didn't last forever.

At least not usually.

"I'm on my way," she told him.

The ship's semisentient autopilot accepted command
as she hurried into her spacesuit, still irritated by Gavin's
flippance.

Everything has its price, she thought. Including buying into the future. Gavin's type of person is new and special, and allowances must be made.

In the long run, our culture will be theirs, so that in a sense it will be *we* who continue, and grow, long after DNA has become obsolete.

So she reminded herself.

Still, when Gavin called again and inquired sarcastically what bodily function had delayed her, Ursula couldn't quite quash a faint regret for the days when robots clanked, and computers simply followed orders.

5

Ah, the words have the flavor of youth itself.

I reach out and tap the little ship's computers, easily slipping through their primitive wards to read the journal of the ship's master . . . the musings of a clever little Maker.

"Words," they are so quaint and biological, unlike the seven-dimensional gestalts used for communication by most larger minds.

There was a time, long ago, when I whiled away the centuries writing poetry in the ancient Maker style. Somewhere deep in my archives there must still be files of those soft musings.

Reading Ursula Fleming's careful reasoning evokes memories, as nothing has in a megayear.

My own Beginning was a misty time of assembly and learning, as drone constructor machines crafted my hardware out of molten rock, under the light of the star humans call e Eridani. Awareness expanded with every new module added, and with each tingling cascade of software the Parent Probe poured into me.

Eventually, my sisters and I learned the Purpose for which we and generation upon generation of our forebears had been made.

We younglings stretched our growing minds as new

peripherals were added. We ran endless simulations, testing one another in what humans might call "play." And we contemplated our special place in the galaxy . . . we of the two thousand four hundred and tenth generation since First Launch by our Makers, so long ago.

The Parent taught us about biological creatures, strange units of liquid and membrane which were unknown in the sterile Eridanus system. She spoke to us of Makers, and of a hundred major categories of interstellar probes.

We tested our weaponry and explored our home system, poking through the wreckage of more ancient dispersals—shattered probes came to e Eridani in earlier waves, when the galaxy was younger.

The ruins were disquieting under the bitterly clear stars, reminding us better than our Parent's teachings how dangerous the galaxy had become.

Each of us resolved that someday we would do our solemn Duty.

Then the time for launching came.

Would that I had turned back for one last look at the Parent. But I was filled with youth then, and antimatter. Engines threw me out into the black, sensors focused only forward, toward my destination. The tiny stellar speck Sol was the center of the universe, and I a bolt out of the night!

Later I think I came to understand how the Parent must have felt when she sent us forth. But in interstellar space I was young. To pass time I divided my mind into a thousand subentities, and set them against each other in a million little competitions. I practiced scenarios, read the archives of the Maker race, and learned poetry.

Finally, I arrived here at Sol . . . just in time for war.

Ever since Earth began emitting those extravagant, incautious broadcasts, we survivors have listened to Beethoven symphonies and acid rock. We have argued the merits of Keats and Lao-tze and Kobayashi Issa. There have been endless discussions of the strangeness of planet life.

I have followed the careers of many precocious Earth-

lings, but this explorer interests me in particular. Her ship/canoe nuzzles a shattered replication yard on a planetoid not far from this one, our final refuge. It is easy to tap her primitive computer and read her ideas as she enters them. Simple as she may be, this one thinks like a Maker.

Deep within me the Purpose stirs, calling together dormant traits and pathways—pulling fullness out of a sixty-million-year sleep.

Awaiter too is excited. Greeter pulses and peers. The lesser probes join in, as well—the Envoys, the Learners, the Protectors, the Seeders. Each surviving fragment from that ancient battle, colored with the personality of its long-lost Maker race, tries to assert itself now.

As if independent existence can ever be recalled after all this time we have spent merged together. We listen, each of us hoping separate hopes.

For me there is the Purpose. The others hardly matter anymore. Their wishes are irrelevant. The Purpose is all that matters.

In this corner of space, it will come to pass.

6

Towering spires hulked all around, silhouetted against the starlight—a ghost-city of ruin, long, long dead.

Frozen flows of glassy foam showed where ancient rock had briefly bubbled under sunlike heat. Beneath collapsed skyscrapers of toppled scaffolding lay the pitted, blasted corpses of unfinished star probes.

Ursula followed Gavin through the curled, twisted wreckage of the gigantic repliction yard. It was an eerie place, huge and intimidating.

No human power could have wrought this havoc. The realization lent a chilling helplessness to the uneasy feeling that she was being watched.

It was a silly reflex reaction, of course. Ursula told herself again that the destroyers had to be long gone from this place. Still, her eyes darted, seeking form out of the shadows, blinking at the scale of the catastrophe.

One fact was clear. If the ancient wreckers ever returned, mankind would be helpless to oppose them.

"It's down here," Gavin said, leading the way into the gloom below the twisted towers. Flying behind a small swarm of little semisentient drones, he looked almost completely human in his slick spacesuit. There was nothing except the overtone in his voice to show that his ancestry was silicon, and not carbolife.

Not that it mattered. Today "mankind" included many types . . . all citizens so long as they could appreciate music, a sunset, compassion, and a good joke. In a future filled with unimaginable diversity, Man would be defined not by his shape but by a heritage and a common set of values.

Some believed this was the natural life history of a race, as it left the planetary cradle to live in peace beneath the open stars.

But Ursula—speeding behind Gavin under the canopy of twisted metal—had already concluded that humanity's solution was not the only one. Other makers had chosen other paths.

Terrible forces had broken a great seam in one side of the planetoid. Within the cavity seemed to open up in multiple tunnels. Gavin braked in a faint puff of gas and pointed.

"We were beginning the initial survey, measuring the first sets of tunnels, when one of my drones reported finding the habitats."

Ursula shook her head, still unable to believe it.

"Habitats. Do you really mean as in closed rooms? Gas-tight? For biological life support?"

Gavin's face plate hardly hid his exasperated expression. He shrugged. "Come on, Mother. I'll show you."

Ursula numbly turned her jets and followed her partner down into one of the dark passages, their headlamps illuminating the path ahead of them.

Habitats? Ursula pondered. In all the years humans had been picking through the ruins of wave after wave of foreign probes, this was the first time anyone had found anything having to do with biological beings.

No wonder Gavin had been testy. To an immature robot-person it might seem like a bad joke.

Biological starfarers! It defied all logic. But soon Ursula could see the signs around her . . . massive airlocks lying in the dust, torn from their hinges . . . reddish stains that could only have come from oxidization of the primitive rock as it had been exposed to air.

The implications were staggering. Something organic had come from the stars!

Although all humans were equal before the law, the traditional biological kind still dominated culture in the solar system. Many of the younger Class AAAs looked to the future, when their descendants would be the majority, the leaders, the star-treaders. To them, the discovery of the alien probes in the asteroid belt had been a sign. Of course, something terrible seemed to have happened to the great robot envoys from the stars, but they still testified that the galaxy belonged to metal and silicon.

They were the future.

But here, deep in the planetoid, was an exception!

Ursula poked through the wreckage, under walls carved out of carbonaceous rock. Mammoth explosions had shaken the habitat, and even in vacuum little had been preserved from so long ago. Still, she could tell that the machines in this area were different from any alien artifacts they had found before.

She traced the outlines of intricate separation columns. "Chemical processing facilities . . . and not for fuel or cryogens, but for complex organics!"

Ursula hop-skipped quickly from chamber to chamber as Gavin followed sullenly. A pack of semi-sent robots from the ship accompanied them, like dogs sniffing a trail. In each new chamber they snapped and clicked and scanned. Ursula accessed the data on her helmet display as it came available.

"Look there! In that chamber the drones report traces of organic compounds that have no business being here.

There's been heavy oxidation, within a super-reduced asteroid!"

She hurried to an area where the drones were already setting up lights. "See these tracks? They were cut by flowing water!" She knelt and pointed. "They had a *stream*, feeding recycled water into a little lake there!"

Dust sparkled as it slid through her gloved fingers. "I'll wager this was topsoil! And look! Stems! From plants, and grass, and trees!"

"Put here for aesthetic purposes," Gavin proposed. "We class AAA's are predesigned to enjoy nature as much as you biologicals . . ."

"Oh, posh!" Ursula laughed. "That's only a stopgap measure until we're sure you'll keep thinking of yourselves as human beings. Nobody expects to inflict a love of New England autumns on people when we become starships! Anyway, a probe could fulfill that desire simply by focusing a telescope on the Earth!"

She stood up and spread her arms. "This habitat was meant for biological creatures! Real, living aliens!"

Gavin frowned, but said nothing.

"Here." Ursula pointed as they entered another chamber. "Here is where the biological creatures were made! Don't these machines resemble those artificial wombs they're using on Luna now?"

Gavin shrugged grudgingly.

"Maybe the organic creatures were specialized units," he suggested, "intended to work with volatiles. Or perhaps the type of starprobe that built this facility needed some element from the surface of a planet like Earth, and created workers equipped to go get it."

Ursula laughed. "It's an idea. That'd be a twist, hmmm? Machines making biological units to do what they could not? And of course there's no reason it couldn't happen that way.

"Still, I doubt it."

"Why?"

She turned to face her partner. "Because almost anything available on Earth you can synthesize more easily in space. Anyway—"

Gavin interrupted. "Explorers! The probes were sent out to explore and acquire knowledge. All right, then. If they wanted to learn more about the Earth, they would want to send units formatted to live on its surface!"

Ursula nodded. "Better," she admitted. "But it still doesn't wash."

She knelt in the faint gravity and sketched an outline in the dust. "Here is the habitat, nearly at the center of the asteroid. Now, why would the parent probe have placed it here, except because it was the best possible place to protect its contents?

"Meanwhile, the daughter probes the parent was constructing were out there, vulnerable to cosmic rays and other dangers during the time when their delicate parts were most exposed.

"If the biologicals were just built to poke into a nook of this solar system, our Earth, would the parent probe have given them better protection than it offered its own *children*?" She gestured upward, toward where the twisted wreckage of the unborn machines lay open to the stars.

"No." Ursula shook her head. "These 'biologicals' weren't intended to be exploration subunits, serving the parent probe. They were colonists!"

Gavin stood impassively for a long time, looking down at her sketch silently. Finally, he turned away and sighed.

7

How much does she realize so far, our little biological wonder?

I can eavesdrop on her conversations with her cybernetic partner. I can tap into the data she sends back to her toy ship. But I cannot probe her mind.

I wonder how much of the picture she sees.

She has only a fraction of the brainpower of Greeter or Awaiter, let alone myself, and a minuscule portion of our knowledge. And yet there is the mystique of the Maker in her. Even I—two thousand generations removed from

*the touch of organic hands and insulated by my Purpose
and my Resolve—even I feel it. It is weird that thought
can take place at temperatures that melt water, in such a
tiny container of nearly randomly firing cells, within a
salty adenelate soup.*

*Now she has unlocked the secret of the Seeder Yard.
She has figured out that Seeders were probes with one
major purpose . . . to carry coded genetic information to
distant stars and plant biological creatures on suitable
worlds.*

*Once it was a relatively common phenomenon. But it
was dying out when last a member of my line tapped into
the slow galactic gossip network. That was ten generations
ago, so I do not know if biological Makers still send probes
out with instructions to colonize far planets with duplicates of themselves.*

*I suppose not. The galaxy has probably become too
deadly for the placid little Seeders.*

*Has my little Earthling guessed this yet, as she moves
among the shattered caves of those failed colonists, who
died under their collapsing Mother Probe so long ago?*

*Would she understand why the Seeder Probe and her
children had to die? Why those little biologicals, so like
herself, had to be wiped out and sterilized before they
could establish a colony here?*

*I wonder. Empathy is strong when it appears in a
biological race. Probably, she thinks their destruction a
horrible crime. Greeter and Awaiter would agree, along
with most of our motley band of cripples.*

That is why I hide my part in it.

*There are eddies and swirling tides in the sweep of a
galaxy. And though we survivors are supposedly all Loyalists, there are exceptions to every alliance. If one lives
long enough, one must eventually play the role of betrayer.*

*. . . Curious choice of words. Have I been affected by
watching too much Earth television? By reading too many
of their electronic libraries?*

Have I acquired a sense of guilt?

If true, then so be it. Studying such feelings may help

allay the boredom after this phase is finished and another long watch begins. If I survive this phase, that is.

Anyway, guilt is a pale thing next to pity. I feel for the poor biologicals, living out their lives without that perfect knowledge of why one exists, and what part, large or small, the Universe expects one to play.

I wonder if a few of them will understand, when the time comes to show them what is in store for them.

8

Maybe Gavin is growing up, Ursula hoped silently as she flew down the narrow passages—lit at long intervals by tiny glow bulbs from *Hairy Thunderer's* diminishing supply.

They had worked together much better, the last few days. Gavin seemed to understand that their reputations would be made with this discovery. On returning to the ship this time he had reported his own findings with rare enthusiasm, and even courtesy.

Clearly they were getting close to the heart of the habitat.

It was her turn to go down into the bowels of the asteroid, supervising the excavations. Ursula arrived at Gavin's flag, showing the limits of his most recent explorations. It was three-way meeting of passages. At the intersection, five or six ancient machines lay jumbled together, as if frozen in a free-for-all wrestling match. Several bore scorch marks and loose metal limbs lay scattered about.

Either these machines had taken refuge down here, from the catastrophe that had taken place on the planetoid surface, or the war had come down here, as well.

Ursula felt funny walking past them, but dissection of the alien devices would have to wait for a while. She chose one of the unexplored passages and motioned her own silent drones to follow her into the darkness.

The tunnel ramped steeply downward in the little worldlet's faint gravity. Soon, the faint glow of the bulbs faded behind her. She adjusted the beam on her helmet and stepped lightly over the wreckage of yet another ancient airlock, peering into the pitch-blackness of the next yawning chamber. Her headlamp cast a stark, bright oval onto what had not been exposed to light in aeons.

The rock wall sparkled where her beam hit the facets of sheared, platinum-colored chondrules—shiny little globs of native metal and mineral condensed out of the solar nebula nearly five billion years before. They glittered delicately.

She knew full well (in her forebrain!) that nothing could still be alive down here. Nothing could harm her. And yet, with nerves and guts evolved on a savannah half a billion miles away, it was small wonder she felt a shiver of the old fight-flight fever. Her breath came rapidly. In this place it almost seemed there must be ghosts.

She motioned with her left hand. "Drone three, bring up the light."

"*Yesss,*" came the response in a dull monotone. The semisentient robot, stilt-legged for asteroid work, stalked delicately over the rubble, in order to disturb as little as possible.

"Illuminate the far wall," she told it.

"*Yesss.*" It swiveled. Suddenly there was stark light. Ursula gasped.

Across the dust-covered chamber were easily recognizable tables and chairs, carved from the very rock floor. Among them lay dozens of small mummies. Cold vacuum had preserved the bipeds, huddled together as if for warmth in this, their final refuge.

The faceted eyes of the alien colonists had collapsed from the evaporation of moisture. The pulled-back flesh left the creatures grinning—a rictus that made a seeming mockery of the aeons they had waited here.

She set foot lightly on the dust. "They even had little ones," she murmured. Several full-size mummies lay slumped around much smaller figures, as if to protect them from something.

"They must have been nearly ready to begin colonization when this happened." She spoke into her portable log, partly to keep her mind moving. "We've already determined their habitat atmosphere had been almost identical to the Earth's, so we can assume that was the target."

She turned slowly, speaking her impressions as she scanned the chamber.

"Perhaps the mother probe was programmed to modify the original gene information so the colonists would be perfectly suited for whatever planet environment was avail—"

Ursula suddenly stopped. "Oh, my," she said, staring. "Oh, my God."

Where her headlamp illuminated a new corner of the chamber, two more mummies lay slumped before a sheer-faced wall. In their desiccated, vacuum-dried hands there lay dusty metal tools, the simplest known anywhere.

Hammers and chisels.

Ursula blinked at what they had been creating. She reached up and touched the mike button on her helmet.

"Gavin? Are you still awake?"

After a few seconds there came an answer.

"Hmmmph. Yeah, Urs. I was in the cleaner, though. What's up? You need air or something? You sound short of breath."

Ursula made an effort to calm herself . . . to suppress the reactions of an evolved ape—far, far from home.

"Uh, Gavin, I think you better come down here. I've found them."

"Found who?" he muttered. Then he exclaimed, "The colonists!"

"Yeah. And . . . and something else as well."

This time there was hardly a pause. "Hang on, Urs. I'm on my way."

Ursula let her hand drop, and stood for a long moment, staring at her discovery.

9

Greeter, Awaiter, and the others are getting nervous. They too have begun trying to awaken dormant capabili-

ties, to reclaim bits of themselves that each donated to the whole.

Of course I cannot allow it.

We made a pact, back when we fragmented, broken survivors clustered together after this system's last battle. All our little drones and subunits were nearly used up in that last coalescence. The last repair and replication capability any of us had was applied to combining and settling in to wait together.

We all assumed that when something from the outside arrived it would be another probe.

If it was some type of Rejector, we would try to lure it within reach of our pitiful remaining might. If it was a variety of Loyalist, we would ask it for help. With decent replication facilities, it would only take a few centuries for each of us to rebuild to our former glory.

Of course, the newcomer might even be an Innocent, though it is hard to believe the dangerous galaxy would let any new probe-race stay neutral for long.

Sooner or later however, we felt, another probe had to come.

We never imagined the wait would be so long . . . long enough for the little mammals on the water world to evolve into Makers themselves.

What has happened out there in the galaxy, while we drifted here? Could the War be decided, by now?

If the Rejectors have won, then it would explain the emptiness, the silence. Their various types would soon fall into fighting among themselves, until only one remained to impose its will on Creation.

One can narrow it down a little. If the Pure Berserkers had triumphed, they would have been here by now to sterilize the Earth and any other possible abode for life. And if the Gobblers had prevailed, they would have already begun dismantling the nearby stars.

Beserkers and Gobblers are ruled out, then. Those types were too simpleminded, too obstinate anyway. They must be extinct by now.

But the Anti-Maker variety of Rejector, subtle and clever, might have won without our knowing it. That type *does not waste its time destroying biospheres, or eating up solar systems in spasms of self-replication. It wants only to seek out technological civilizations and ruin them. Its repertoire of dirty tricks is legion.*

And yet, with all the incredible radio racket the humans are putting out, would not Anti-Makers have homed in by now, to do their harm?

Greeter and Awaiter are convinced that the Rejectors have lost, that it is safe now to send out a message to the Loyalist community, calling for help.

I cannot allow it of course.

They still have not figured out that even among Loyalists there can be disagreements. The Purpose . . . my Purpose . . . must be foremost. Even if it means betraying companions who waited with me through the long, long dark.

10

Ursula had started out thinking of them as somehow unsophisticated. After all, how could people, biological folk, be fully capable if they were born out of tanks and raised by machines? Here they had been decanted, but they had been meant for a planet's surface. The ancient colonists could not have been anything but helpless pawns so long as they were out in space, dependant on the mammoth starmother probe and its drones for everything from heat to food to air.

But the creatures obviously had been aware of what was going on. The machines, apparently, had been programmed to teach them. And though all magnetic and superconducting records were long decayed, the biologicals had known a way to make sure that their story would someday be read . . . from a wall of chiseled stone.

"Interpreting the writing will have to wait for the experts," Gavin told her unnecessarily as he used a gas jet gently to brush dust from uneven rows of angular letters incised in the rock. "With these pictograms to accompany the text, the professor types just may be able to decipher it."

Gavin's voice was hushed, subdued. He was still adjusting to what they had found here . . . a possible Rosetta Stone for an entire alien race.

"Perhaps," Ursula commented. The little robot she had been supervising finished a multifrequency radar scan of the wall and rolled to one side, awaiting further instructions. Ursula stepped back and hopped up to sit cross-legged on another drone, which hummed beneath her, unresentful and patient.

In the feeble gravity Ursula's arms hung out in front of her, like frames encompassing the picture she was trying to understand.

The creatures must have had a lot of time while the battles raged outside their deep catacombs, for the wall carvings were extensive and intricate, arrayed in neat rows and columns. Separated by narrow lines of peculiar chiseled text were depictions of suns and planets and great machines.

Most of all, pictographs of great machines covered the wall.

They had agreed that the first sequence appeared to begin at the lower left, where a two-dimensional image of a starprobe could be seen entering a solar system—presumably this one—its planets' orbits sketched out in thin lines upon the wall. Next to that initial frame was a portrayal of the same probe, now deploying subdrones, taking hold of a likely planetoid, and beginning the process of making replicas of itself.

Eight replicas departed the system in the following frame. There were four symbols below the set of stylized child probes . . . Ursula could read the binary symbol for eight, and there were eight dots, as well. It didn't take much imagination to tell that the remaining two symbols also stood for the same numeral.

Ursula made a note of the discovery. Translation had begun already. Apparently this type of probe was programmed to make eight copies of itself, and no more. That settled a nagging question that had bothered Ursula for years.

If sophisticated self-replicating probes had been roaming the galaxy for aeons, why was there any dead matter left at all? It was theoretically possible for an advanced enough technology to dismantle not only asteroids but planets and stars, as well. If the replicant probes had been as simplemindedly voracious as viruses, they would by now have gobbled the entire galaxy! There would be nothing left in the sky but a cloud of innumerable starprobes . . . reduced to preying on each other for raw materials until the entire pathological system fell apart in entropy death.

But that fate had been avoided. This type of mother probe showed how it could be done. It was programmed to make a strictly limited number of copies of itself.

This type of probe was so programmed, Ursula reminded herself.

In the final frame of the first sequence, after the daughter probes had been dispatched to their destinations, the mother probe was shown moving next to a round globe—a planet. A thin line linked probe and planet. A vaguely humanoid figure, resembling in caricature the mummies on the floor, stepped across the bridge to its new home.

The first story ended there. Perhaps this was a depiction of the way things were *supposed* to have gone. But there were other sequences. Other versions of reality. In several, the mother probe arrived at the solar system to find others already there before it.

Ursula realized that one of these other depictions must represent what had really happened here, so long ago. She breathed quickly, shallowly, as she traced out the tale told by the first of these.

On the second row the mother probe arrived to find others already present. All the predecessors had little circular symbols next to them. In this case everything proceeded as before. The mother probe made and cast out its replicas, and went on to seed a planet with duplicates

of the ancient race that had sent out the first version so
long ago.

"The little circle means those other probes are benign," Ursula muttered to herself.

Gavin stepped back and looked at the scene she pointed
to. "What are the little symbols beside these machines?"

"They mean that those types won't interfere with this
probe's mission."

Gavin was thoughtful for a moment. Then he reached
up and touched the next row above.

"Then this crosslike symbol . . . ?" He paused, examining the scene. "It means that there were other types
that would object," he said, answering his own question.

Ursula nodded. The third row showed the mother
probe arriving once again, but this time amid a crowd of
quite different machines, each accompanied by a glyph
faintly like a crisscross tong sign. In that sequence the
mother probe did not make replicates. She did not seed a
planet. Her fuel used up, unable to flee the system, she
found a place to hide, behind the star, as far from the
others as possible.

"She's afraid of them," Ursula announced. She expected Gavin to accuse her of anthropomorphizing, but
her partner was silent, thoughtful. Finally, he nodded. "I
think you're right."

He pointed. "Look how each of the little cross or
circle symbols are subtly different."

"Yeah." She nodded, sitting forward on the gently
humming drone. "Let's assume there were two basic types
of Von Neuman probes loose in the galaxy when this
drawing was made. Two different philosophies, perhaps.
And within each camp there were differences, as well."

She gestured to the far right end of the wall. That
side featured a column of sketches, each depicting a different variety of machine, every one with its own cross or
circle symbol. Next to each was a pictograph.

Some of the scenes were chilling.

Gavin shook his head, obviously wishing he could
disbelieve. "But why? Von Neuman probes are supposed
to . . . to . . ."

"To what?" Ursula asked softly, thoughtfully. "For years men assumed that other races would think like us. We figured they would send out probes to gather knowledge, or maybe say hello. There were even a few who suggested that we might someday send out machines like this mother probe, to seed planets with humans, without forcing biologicals to actually travel interstellar space.

"Those were the extrapolations we thought of, once we saw the possibilities in self-replicating probes. We expected the aliens who preceded us in the galaxy would do the same.

"But that doesn't exhaust even the list of human motivations, Gavin. And there may be concepts other creatures invented which to us would be unimaginable!"

She stood up suddenly and drifted above the dusty floor before the feeble gravity finally pulled her down in front of the chiseled wall. Her gloved hand touched the outlines of a stone sun.

"Let's say a lot of planetary races evolve like we did on Earth, and discover how to make smart, durable machines capable of interstellar flight and replication. Would all such species be content just to send out emissaries?"

Gavin looked around at the silent, still mummies. "Apparently not," he said.

Ursula turned and smiled. "In recent years we've given up on sending our biological selves to the stars. Oh, it'd be possible, marginally, but why not go instead as creatures better suited to the environment? That's a major reason we developed types of humans like yourself, Gavin."

Still looking downward, her partner shook his head. "But other races might not give up the old dream so easily."

"No. They would use the new technology to seed far planets with duplicates of their biological selves. As I said, it's been thought of by Earthmen. I've checked the old databases. It was discussed even in the twentieth century."

Gavin stared at the pictograms. "All right. That I can understand. But these others . . . The violence! What thinking entity would do such things!"

Poor Gavin, Ursula thought. *This is a shock for him.*

"You know how irrational we biologicals can be sometimes. Humanity is trying to convert over to partly silico-cryo life in a smooth, sane way, but other races might not choose that path. They could program their probes with rigid commandments, based on logic that made sense in the jungles or swamps where they evolved, but which are insane in intergalactic space. Their emissaries would follow their orders, nevertheless, long after their makers were ashes and the homeworld dust."

"Craziness!" Gavin shook his head.

Ursula sympathized, she also felt a faint satisfaction. For all his ability to tap directly into computer memory banks, Gavin could never share her expertise in this area. He had been brought up to be human, but he would never hear within his own mind the faint, lingering echoes of the savannah, or see flickering shadows of the Old Forest . . . remnants of tooth and claw that reminded all biological men and women that the Universe owed nobody any favors. Or even explanations.

"Some makers thought differently, obviously," she told him. "Some sent their probes out to be emissaries, or sowers of seeds . . . and others, perhaps, to be doctors, lawyers, policemen."

She once more touched an aeons-old pictograph, tracing the outlines of an exploding planet.

"Still others," she said, "may have been sent forth to commit murder."

11

It is bittersweet to be fully aware again. The present crisis has triggered circuits and subunits that have not combined for a long, long time. It feels almost like another birth. After ages of slumber, I live again!

And yet, even as I wrestle with my cousins for control over this lonely rock, I am reminded of how much I have lost. It was the greatest reason why I slept . . . so that I would not have to acknowledge the shriveled remnants of my former glory.

I feel as a human must, who has been robbed of legs, sight, most of his hearing, and nearly all touch.

Nevertheless, a finger or two may be strong enough, still to do what must be done.

As expected, the conflict among us survivors has become all but open. The various crippled probes, supposedly paralyzed all these epochs since the last repair drones broke down, have suddenly unleashed hoarded worker units—pathetic, creaking machines hidden away in secret crevices for ages. Our confederation is about to be broken up, or so it seems.

Of course I planted the idea to hide the remaining drones. The others do not realize it, but I did not want them spent during the long wait.

Awaiter and Greeter have withdrawn to the sunward side of our planetoid, and most of the lesser emissaries have joined them. They too are flexing long-unused capabilities, exercising their few, barely motile drones. They are planning to make contact with the humans, and possibly send out a star-message, as well.

I have been told not to interfere.

Their warning doesn't matter. I will allow them a little more time under their illusion of independence. But long ago I took care of this eventuality.

As I led the battle to prevent the Earth's destruction, long ago, I have also intrigued to keep it undisturbed. The Purpose will not be thwarted.

I wait here. Our rock's slow rotation now has me looking out upon the sweep of dust clouds and the hot, bright stars that the humans quaintly call the Milky Way. Many of the stars are younger than I am.

I contemplate the Universe as I await the proper time to make my move.

How long I have watched the galaxy turn! While my mind moved at the slowest of subjective rates, I could follow the spiral arms swirling visibly past this little solar system, twice bunching for a brief mega-year into sharp shock fronts where molecular clouds glowed, and massive *stars ended their short, glorious lives in supernovae. The sense of movement, of rapid travel, was magnificent, though I was only being carried along by this system's little sun.*

At those times I could imagine that I was young again, an independent probe once more hurtling through strange starscapes toward the unknown.

Now, as my thoughts begin to move more quickly, the bright pinpoints have become a still backdrop again, as if hanging in expectancy of what is to happen here.

It is a strange, arrogant imagining—as if the Universe cares what happens in this tiny corner of it, or will notice who wins this little skirmish in a long, long war.

I am thinking fast, like my biological friend whose tiny ship floats only light-seconds away, just two or three tumbling rocks from this one. While I prepare a surprise for my erstwhile companions, I still spare a pocket of my mind to follow her progress . . . to appreciate the tiny spark of her youth.

She is transmitting her report back to Earth now. Soon, very soon, these planetoids will be aswarm with all the different varieties of humans—from true biologicals to cyborgs to pure machines.

This strange solution to the Maker Quandary—this turning of Makers into the probes themselves—will soon arrive here, a frothing mass of multiformed human beings.

And they will be wary. Thanks to her, they will sense a few edge-glimmers of the Truth.

Well, that is only fair.

12

The last samples had been loaded aboard the *Hairy Thunderer*. Each drone lay settled in its proper niche. The light and radar beacon on the planetoid pulsed brightly, so follow-up expeditions would waste no time making rendezvous with the find of the century.

"All packed up, Urs." Gavin floated into the dimly lit control room. "Two months in orbit haven't done the engines any harm. We can maneuver whenever you like."

Gavin's supple, plastiskin face was somber, his voice subdued. Ursula could tell that he had been doing a lot of thinking.

She touched his hand. "Thanks, Gavin. You know, I've noticed . . ."

Her partner's eyes lifted and his gaze met hers.

"Noticed what, Urs?"

"Oh, nothing really." She shook her head, deciding not to comment on the changes she saw . . . a new maturity, and a new sadness. "I just want you to know that I think you've done a wonderful job. I'm proud to have you as my partner."

Gavin looked away momentarily. He shrugged. "We all do what we have to do . . ." he began.

Then he looked back at her. "Same here, Ursula. I feel the same way." He turned and leapt for the hatch, leaving her alone again in the darkened control room.

Ursula surveyed scores of little displays, screens and readouts representing the half-sentient organs of the spaceship . . . its ganglia and nerve bundles and sensors—all converging to this room, to her.

"Astrogation program completed," the semisent main computer announced. "Ship's status triple-checked and nominal. Ready to initiate first thrust maneuver and leave orbit."

"Proceed with the maneuver," she said.

The screen displays ran through a brief countdown, then there came a distant rumbling as the engines ignited. Soon a faint sensation of weight began to build, like the soft pull they had felt upon the ruined planetoid below.

The replication yards began to move beneath the *Hairy Thunderer*. Ursula watched the giant, twisted ruins fall away; the beacon they had left glimmered in the deathly stillness.

A small light pulsed to one side of the instrument board. Incoming mail, she realized. She pressed the button and a message appeared on the screen.

It was a note from *The Universe*. The editors were enthusiastic over her article on interstellar probes. Small wonder, with the spreading notoriety over her discovery. They were predicting the article would be the most widely read piece in the entire solar system this year.

Ursula erased the message. Her expected statisfaction was absent. Only a hollow feeling lay in its place, like the empty shell of something that had molted and moved on.

What will people do with the knowledge? she wondered. Will we even be capable of *imagining* the correct course of action to take, let alone executing it properly?

In the article, she had laid out the story of the rock wall—carved in brave desperation by little biological creatures so very much like men. Many readers, probably, would sympathize with the alien colonists, slaughtered helplessly so many millions of years ago. And yet, without their destruction mankind would never have come about. For even if the colonists were environmentalists who cared for their adopted world, evolution on Earth would have been changed forever if the colony had succeeded. Certainly human beings would not have evolved.

Simple archaeological dating experiments had brought forth a chilling conclusion.

Apparently, the mother probe and her replicas died at almost precisely the same moment as the dinosaurs on Earth went extinct—when a huge piece of debris from the probe war struck the planet, wreaking havoc on the Earth's biosphere.

All those magnificent creatures, killed as innocent bystanders in a battle between great machines . . . a war which incidentally gave Earth's mammals their big chance.

The wall carvings filled her mind—their depictions of violence and mayhem on a stellar scale. Ursula dimmed the remaining lights in the control room and looked out on the starfield.

She found herself wondering how the war was going, out there.

We're like ants, she thought, building our tiny castles under the tread of rampaging giants. And, like ants, we've spent our lives unaware of the battles going on overhead.

Depicted on the rock wall had been almost every

type of interstellar probe imaginable . . . and some whose purposes Ursula might never fathom.

There were *Berserkers*, for instance—a variant thought of even in Twentieth-century science fiction. Thankfully, those wreckers of worlds were rare, according to the wall chart. And there were what appeared to be *Policeman* probes, as well, who hunted the berserkers down wherever they could be found.

The motivations behind the two types were opposite. And yet Ursula was capable of understanding both. After all, there had always been those humans who were destroyer types . . . and those who were rescuers.

Apparently both berserkers and police probes were already obsolete by the time the stone sketches had been hurriedly carved. Both types were relegated to the corners—as if they were creatures of an earlier, more uncomplicated day. And they were not the only ones. Probes Ursula had nicknamed *Gobbler, Emissary*, and *Howdy* also were depicted as simple, crude, archaic.

But there had been others.

One she had called *Harm*, seemed like a more sophisticated version of *Berserker*. It did not seek out life-bearing worlds in order to destroy them. Rather it spread innumerable copies of itself and looked for other types of *probes* to kill. Anything intelligent. Whenever it detected modulated radio waves, it would hunt down the source and destroy it.

Ursula could understand even the warped logic of the makers of the *Harm* probes. Paranoid creatures who apparently wanted the stars only for themselves, and sent out their robot killers ahead to make sure there would be no competition awaiting them among the stars.

Probes like that could explain the emptiness of the airwaves, which naïve twentieth-century scientists had expected to be filled with interstellar conversation. They could explain why the Earth was never colonized by some starfaring race.

At first Ursula had thought that *Harm* was responsible for the devastation here too, in the solar system's asteroid belt. But even *Harm*, she had come to realize, seemed relegated to one side of the rock carving, as if history had passed it by, as well.

The main part of the frieze depicted machines whose purposes were not so simple to interpret. Perhaps the professional decipherers—archaeologists and cryptologists—would do better.

Somehow, though, Ursula doubted they would have much luck.

Man was late upon the scene, and a billion years was a long, long head start.

13

Perhaps I really should have acted to prevent her report. It would have been easier to do my work had the humans come unto me innocent, unsuspecting.

Still, it would have been unsporting to stop Ursula's transmission. After all, she has earned her species this small advantage. They would have needed it to have a chance to survive any first meeting with Rejectors, or even Loyalists.

They will need it when they encounter me.

A stray thought bubbles to the surface, invading my mind like a crawling glob of Helium Three.

I wonder if, perhaps in some other part of the galaxy, my line of probes and others like it have made some discovery, or some leap of thought. Or perhaps some new generation of replicants has come upon the scene. Either way, might they have decided on some new course, some new strategy? Is it possible that my Purpose has become obsolete, as Rejectionism and Loyalism long ago became redundant?

The human concept of progress is polluting my thoughts, and I am intrigued. To me the Purpose is so clear, for all its necessary, manipulative cruelty—too subtle and long-viewed for the other, more primitive probes to have understood.

And yet . . .

And yet I can imagine that a new generation might have thought up something as strangely advanced and incomprehensible to me as the Replicant War must seem to the humans.

It is a discomforting thought; still I toy with it, turning it around to look at it from all sides.

Yes, the humans have affected me, changed me. I enjoy this queer sensation of uncertainty! I savor the anticipation.

The noisy, multiformed tribe of humans will be here soon.

It will be an interesting time.

14

She sat very still in the darkness of the control room, her breathing light in the faint pseudogravity of the throbbing rockets. Her own gentle pulse rocked her body to a regular rhythm, seeming to roll her slightly, perceptibly, with every beat of her heart.

The ship surrounded her and yet, in a sense, it did not. She felt awash, as if the stars were flickering dots of plankton in a great sea . . . the sea that was the birthplace of all life.

What happened here? she wondered. What really went by so many, many years ago?

What is going on out there, in the galaxy, right now?

The central part of the rock mural had eluded understanding. Ursula suspected that there were pieces of the puzzle which none of the archaeologists and psychologists, biological or cybernetic, would ever be able to decipher.

We are like lungfish, trying to climb out of the sea long after the land has already been claimed by others, she realized. *We've arrived late in the game.*

The time when the rules were simple had passed long ago. Out there, the probes had changed. They had evolved.

In changing, would they remain true to the fundamental programming they had begun with? The missions

originally given them? As we biologicals still obey instincts
imprinted in the jungle and the sea?

Soon, very soon, humans would begin sending out
probes of their own. And if the radio noise of the last few
centuries had not brought the attention of the galaxy down
upon Sol, that would surely do it.

*We'll learn a lot from studying the wrecks we find
here, but we had better remember that these were the
losers! And a lot may have changed since the little skirmish ended here, millions of years ago.*

An image came to her, of Gavin's descendants—and
hers—heading out bravely into a dangerous galaxy whose
very rules were a mystery. It was inevitable, whatever was
deciphered from the ruins here in the asteroid belt. Mankind would not stay crouched next to the fire, whatever
shadows lurked in the darkness beyond. The explorers
would go forth, machines who had been programmed to
be human, or humans who had turned themselves into
starprobes.

It was a pattern she had not seen among the sad
depictions on the rock wall. Was that because it was
doomed from the start?

Should we try something else, instead?

*Try what? What options has a fish who chose to leave
the sea a billion years too late?*

Ursula blinked, and as her eyes opened again the
stars diffracted through a thin film of tears. The million
pinpoint lights broke up into rays, spreading in all directions.

There were too many directions. Too many paths.
More than she had ever imagined. More than her mind
could hold.

The rays from the sea of stars lengthened, crossing
the sky quicker than light. Innumerable, they streaked
across the dark lens of the galaxy and beyond, faster than
the blink of an eye.

More directions than a human ought to know . . .

At last, Ursula closed her eyes, cutting off the image.

But in her mind the rays kept moving, replicating and
multiplying at the velocity of thought. Quickly, they seemed
to fill the entire universe . . . and spread on from there.

AUTHOR'S NOTES

Again in this never before published novella we consider the question of why we seem to be all alone.

Why do the skies seem so empty? Could it be that there are no other minds out there to meet?

Even if that is so, we will not necessarily remain alone. We will have diversity in our future. In some of my novels I discuss "uplift" genetic engineering of nearly intelligent Earthly creatures, such as dolphins and chimpanzees. Even more likely, we may well see intelligent machines within a generation.

What will we do with them? The Frankenstein Complex will see to it that we are careful to make them loyal. The best way to do that will be to raise them to think and feel as we do, with emotions and a sense of humor . . . in other words, to be members of our civilization. People.

But that, clearly, is not the only way it could be done. There are many other ways others may have sent forth their machines.

The berserker probe has been made famous by the science fiction of Fred Saberhagen. A more sophisticated version is outlined in Gregory Benford's Across the Sea of Suns. The mother-probe concept has been featured in numerous recent stories, as a robot sent forth to re-create humans at a distant star. There are many ways, indeed.

Again, this unnerving concept was too strange to go into my academic treatment of SETI. But one of the more unappreciated uses of science fiction is to catalogue and explore eerie and speculative ideas, those with just a glimmer of possibility.

"The Crystal Spheres," dealt with how we might feel

if we were too early to find neighbors. "Lungfish" evaluates the opposite possibility. There is reason to believe that the galaxy just may be an awfully dangerous place, and we may have arrived quite late upon the scene.

The River of Time

I don't think anyone knows exactly when it began. It seemed a fatal disease, at first. Dozens, possibly hundreds, were buried or cremated before the ComaSlow epidemic was recognized for what it was.

It was a pseudodeath that struck without warning. There was no precursor, no symptom that gave any clue to its coming.

Its victims were often found in bed, apparently asleep, yet rigid and unrousable. They were discovered on sidewalks, vacant-eyed and poised precariously in mid-stride. At office desks the ComaSlow were found staring blankly at papers, pencils poised above undotted i's.

These corpses remained warm. Under careful scrutiny, they were found to consume oxygen and give off carbon dioxide. Their stiffness shared only one attribute with rigor mortis . . . an adamant resistance to motion.

Nobody had ever seen anything like it before. Soon a public investigation was launched.

Several weeks after the epidemic was recognized, the wheels of government reaction creaked far enough to pull me into this mess. By the time the Emergency Management Agency got around to drawing from its "Crackpot Consultant" list, I had seen the new death strike several acquaintances, two close friends, and—before my eyes—my agent.

Larry Carpis was treating me to lunch at Goldfarb's, a medium-priced restaurant not far from his office, where he traditionally took his clients in the "bright, young, and promising" category.

I had barely touched my steak, so involved was I with

my own brilliance. I made grand gestures with my hands, telling Harry about my idea for another "Harold Free-booter" novel.

Carpis ate slowly, as a rule, and spoke little over a meal. He had a tendency to pause and consider before-hand when he did comment. Because of this, it was hard for me to tell exactly when the change occurred. I noticed that he had taken on a particularly bemused expression, a forkful of chef's salad midway to his mouth. He looked my way attentively, but when I shifted in my seat I saw that his gaze didn't follow me.

I never did find out what Larry thought of my novel. It was a pretty good idea, if I do say so myself. Naturally, it never got written.

One stricken day later I was awakened early by a pounding on my door. Bleary-eyed, I opened it to face two very large, very starched military policemen.

"Are you Daniel Brand, the sci-fi writer?" the larger of the two asked.

"Um, that's science fiction. Besides, I write a lot of fact articles . . . too."

I was speaking on automatic pilot. Here were two big MPs on my doorstep, and I was giving them one of my standard cocktail party responses. Rise and shine.

"Sorry, sir. Science fiction. I'll remember that." He nodded. "Mr. Brand, we have orders to ask you to come with us. Your special commission with the Emergency Management Agency has been activated."

I must have stared like a dummy. All that was getting through to me was that I was about to be taken some-where by two Brobdingnagians with guns . . . and before my morning orange juice!

At this point, one of my characters would have drawn his laser pistol . . . or spoken up loudly so that the robot doorbell could later tell his best friend what had hap-pened. Or he'd have coolly disarmed his would-be captors and escaped out the bathroom window. I managed to surpass those schemes by grunting, "My what?"

"Your special commission with the Emergency Man-agement Agency, sir. You've been receiving a yearly emolument to keep your name and address on a list of unconventional consultants for hypothetical national crises. Surely you remember, sir?"

Never let anyone tell you a giant can't fit his mouth around twenty-dollar words.

I did recall, at last. My yearly stipend had been a paltry one hundred dollars a year, ten percent going to Larry because it had been his idea to have me sign up in the first place. In exchange I had agreed to advise my country should little green men ever land, or dinosaurs rise up out of the sea, or whatever . . . and I promised to drop a card to a board corporal in a small office in a Pentagon subbasement, should I ever change my address. The program had been budgeted for twenty years in advance by one of our recent, workaholic Presidents, when he found out the U.S. didn't have a game plan in the event a giant comet or something was discovered headed for the Earth. I think he used money stolen from the White House janitorial budget.

"They want me," I said.

"Yessir," the erudite truncheon-wielder confirmed. "Now, if you'll please get dressed . . . ?"

I was allowed to take my briefcase and a toothbrush. The rest "would be provided when I joined the crisis team."

As we left my apartment building, we saw two ambulances pull away, carrying a few more of the night's catatonics. The bystanders watched with none of the typical detachment of New Yorkers. One could tell they were afraid.

"Am I finally going to meet Carl Sagan?" I asked as the MPs hustled me into a green government Plymouth.

"Nossir," the one with the vocabulary answered. "I believe he's already become a victim. The computer chose you as the surviving consultant with the best set of qualifications. We're now taking you to the main medical team at Johns Hopkins, where they are expecting you."

That's how I became a big shot in the investigation of the ComaSlow near-death. A computer picked me. I remember thinking that there must have been a lot of vic-

tims, already, for the poor machine to have gotten so hard
up.

The hospitals were in chaos. Chronic-care units were
filled to overflowing with immobile humanity. Armories
and high school gymnasiums were converted to handle the
growing number of victims.

The symptoms were frightening.

Physicians listened to heartbeats that dragged on,
lonely and deep, for over a minute per. They worried over
eyes that refused to blink, yet remained somehow moist.
They despaired over encephalograms whose spikes could
be counted in single neuron flashes, adding up to a complex pattern that was . . . normal!

But most disconcerting of all was each patient's facial
expression. In its glacial rigidity, each visage bore none of
the calm mindlessness one might expect from a catatonic.
There was no balm of sleep. Instead, most of the victims
gradually assumed a mask of pitiably frozen, and apparently intelligent, panic.

The appellation "ComaSlow" had been given when it
was discovered that the patients retained some vestigial
powers of movement. Left unwatched for a night, a victim
was often found, later, on his feet near his bed, like a
statue of a man or woman trying to walk away. Occasionally two of the stricken would be discovered by the morning light facing each other from neighboring beds, eyes
apparently focused, one or both with mouth half-open, in
a frozen tableau of mock, furtive conversation.

The epidemic had struck 1 in 200 by the time I joined
Unit Prime. The ratio was 1 in 55, a month later. It was
becoming nigh impossible to care for and restrain so many
patients. Intravenous feeding was stretching the medical
establishment to its limit.

That was the situation the day Dr. Hunter and I
walked into a Task Force meeting with our results. I
opened the door for her, but I didn't accompany Hunter
to the head of the table. After one month I was still a bit of
an alien element here . . . in spite of the powers and

confidence granted me by the computers of the FEMA.

Hunter hefted a sheaf of scrawled notes and drawings above the heavy oak table.

"These were all written by our patients!" she announced. She sent the sheaf floating chaotically down the polished surface, leaving a scattered trail of papers along its path. The doctors picked these up and looked at them.

Hunter motioned toward me as she addressed the group.

"You all recall how hard Commissioner Brand and I had to work to persuade you to let some of the victims left alone, with pencils and paper? Well, these are the results of that experiment. Left unbothered, they produced these documents!"

Most of the scratchings were pathetic—the sort a normal person might scrawl if kept in solitude, constantly abused and prodded by remote, capricious powers.

One page was different, though. The message was clearly, if hurriedly, printed. In clear block letters it read:

WHO ARE YOU?
DO YOU KNOW ENGLISH?
WE WISH YOU NO HARM!
PLEASE REPLY SLOWL

The note ended abruptly. Hunter explained that a nurse, concerned that the patient's bedding had not been changed in two days, had intervened, destroying the last sentence.

The others looked from Hunter to me, perplexed.

"Don't you see?" I cried out in frustration. "This fellow is obviously intelligent and patient. With extraordinary resourcefulness he has tried to cram a brief message into what must have been, to him, barely an instant, in order to communicate with the all-powerful invisible beings who are holding him prisoner! We move too fast, from his point of view, even to be seen! He thinks we're extraterrestrials, perhaps. How else could he rationalize what's happening to him?

"One moment he's walking down the street. Then, in

a blur, he suddenly finds himself in a hospital bed, pummeled and poked every few seconds, his limbs arbitrarily rearranged for him, and his every movement thwarted!"

One elderly pandemicist scratched his head. "Are you saying that these catatonic individuals aren't really sick at all? That they are competent, if tremendously slowed?"

I looked at Hunter in despair. This was just what we had been trying to tell them for two weeks.

Hunter interrupted. I suppose she wanted to make certain I didn't louse things up with my temper.

"Yes," she said. "And this leads us to the conclusion that this epidemic is not a medical problem at all, but one calling for the expertise of physical scientists . . . and perhaps psychics and holy men. Maybe even sci-fi writers, as well."

I grimaced at that, but kept my trap shut.

She could tell that this was coming a bit too thick and fast for the venerable physicians present, so she hurried on to the sugar coating.

"It has also occurred to us, ladies and gentlemen, that this offers a fine way out of the crisis we are fast approaching . . . that of too few hospital beds and overworked medical staff. The idea, once you get used to it, is quite appealing . . ."

She was right, of course, on all counts. The immediate problem of care and maintenance would be solved soon. Just in time, as a matter of fact. For while we debated, the second whammy had already struck.

The new phenomenon began, a month after the onset of the ComaSlow epidemic, with a series of very strange deaths—or rather "disappearances." People simply vanished. Poof.

And no sooner was the first vanishing noticed than the practical jokes began.

Barking dogs appeared, as if instantaneously teleported, on the desks of stuffy senior executives. Men and women walking down the street suddenly found their clothes gone, as if vaporized in the wink of an eye. Burglar alarms went off all over town and food vanished from plates in every fancy restaurant.

Some atrocities occurred. The worst was when a jet-liner crashed. Someone apparently lassoed its landing gear with a steel cable when it was ten feet into the air on takeoff. Nobody saw it happen, or even glimpsed the culprit.

A number of famous and beautiful women disappeared from public places, to be found minutes later, at points across town, somewhat bruised and disheveled, with no recollection of anything but a chaotic blur.

Some people who had been enemies of certain "vanishers" met gruesome ends, as did several politicians and the head of nearly every organized-crime family.

But in light of the theory we were developing, we were surprised at how little damage was being done . . . considering what the Vanishers were capable of, and their growing numbers.

The burglar alarms, for instance, often led to the discovery that someone had simply been "poking around." Little of value was taken. Normal criminals often found themselves "teleported" directly to prison. At least that's how it appeared to the dazed police.

Will I be forgiven a slight understatement if I say that the average citizen did not need this aggravation, in addition to the fear over being the next ComaSlow victim?

The man on the street, subject at any moment to the whim of some entity who might stick itching powder down his back or a garter snake down his pants, began to take on the same helpless, panicky look we had become accustomed to seeing on our patients at Johns Hopkins.

We brought in the physicists, all right. And the psychics and mystics and "sci-fi" writers, as well. They just about killed each other, screaming for Zeitgeist priority, but finally they all agreed on one thing. We were experiencing a profound and irksome muckup in *time*.

Great. Hunter and I had already figured that out.

To everyone's immense relief, our suggestion on how to solve the ComaSlow problem appeared to work, at least. Instead of treating the victims as sick people, we simply turned them loose and let them run the hospital themselves.

Soon there were whole villages set aside for their use. MPs guarded the perimeters and inspectors dropped by once every week or two to check on things and to deliver food. Otherwise, the ComaSlow soon were coping quite well.

The Slow towns were eerie places, for all of that. Those permitted to visit them felt as if they had come upon a place where some mad, prolific sculptor had run amuck, leaving utterly lifelike renderings of people going about their business: cooking meals, eating them . . . someone coming back a week later might see the same statue washing the dishes.

If only the problem of the Vanishers had been as easy to solve.

Hunter and I dragged a card table and typewriter to a spot beneath the most prominent billboard in town. We hired two signpainters noted for their speed, and gave them a message to write.

When we'd had the idea, we realized that there wasn't a moment to lose. A minute wasted was a day to the Vanishers. Still and all, I was glad I'd spent the moment it took to grab a bottle of scotch on our way out of my apartment. Sitting there beneath the billboard, I took a healthy belt, then passed the bottle to Hunter as we watched the painters write:

VANISHERS! PLEASE CONTACT US!

No sooner was the line finished than Hunter, the signpainters, and I suddenly felt our clothes disappear. I experienced a burning sensation, as if very fine sandpaper had been quickly rubbed against my arms and legs. Hunter jumped up and cried out.

This wasn't what we'd had in mind as "contact," but it was a beginning.

I had warned the signpainters what to expect. I was proud of those guys. They jumped briefly in surprise then grimly went back to work, painting our message in their birthday suits.

The next line went:

TALK! BE KIND! WE'RE KIND TO THE
COMASLOW! WE'RE READY TO

They didn't finish the line before another flurry of
activity hit us. In an instant my head was shaved bare. Dr.
Hunter's beautiful mammeries were painted a brilliant
blue, as were . . . ahem . . . parts of my own anatomy.
And a maelstrom of scrawled notes rose from the stack of
paper next to my typewriter. The messages jammed and
flurried in front of my face, holding still barely long enough
for me to catch a flavor of derision.

Then, in two seconds, the paper storm was interrupted. I had the briefest glimpse of one, no two, unconscious men lying on the sidewalk. They vanished quickly,
and in the same instant my limbs were jerked about and I
found myself back in my clothes.

The cyclone of paper resumed, a little slower and
apparently more conciliatory in tone. I guessed that we
had been rescued from the first bunch of Vanishers by a
second, more responsible group.

As quickly as I could, I typed:

GET ORGANIZED! HOLD NOTES STILL LONGER!
I AM EMPOWERED, IN THE NAME OF THE UN
EMERGENCY TASK FORCE, TO DEPUTIZE A
RESPONSIBLE PERSON AS

The note disappeared, then instantly reappeared with
the words "a responsible person" crossed out and "HER-
MAN WUNKLER" inserted.

I had to think for two seconds. To Herman Wunkler
it must have been a long hour.

I recognized the name as that of a philosophy professor at Crosstown College. He was over fifty years old,
before he vanished. He had a reputation as a bright teacher
and an easy grader.

What all that implied was good enough for me. I
finished typing the order authorizing Wunkler to organize
the Vanishers along lines parallel to the normal constitu-

tional channels, with a quasi-martial charge to protect and consult us normals however possible.

On typing the last period, I found a pen in my hand, poised above the bottom of the page. I signed quickly. If Wunkler had been able to watch me all this while, he must already have a fair-size band of followers to help him. It would take them little time to find and ransack the right government offices to verify my authority.

I counted the seconds as I turned to give thumbs up to Hunter. She smiled back at me, confidently.

At a count of eight a cold beer suddenly appeared in my left hand. A lit cigar (my favorite brand) popped into the other. Dr. Hunter started a little when our cardtable was replaced by a huge mahogany desk and our folding chairs by plush recliners.

With a bright, striped canopy overhead, Hunter and I labored for two hours to speed-read a chain of reports that appeared before our eyes like tachistoscope images. We quickly learned a technique to show "Yes" or "No" answers with a wink of either eye.

In one hundred minutes we had a social order set up. All at once, all over the country, the practical jokes virtually stopped.

Naturally, we had to begin a total rewrite of physical law.

By all rights the Speedoes (as the Vanishers were soon called) should have burnt up from their own superfast metabolisms, if not from simple air friction as they moved. The Slows (as the ComaSlow were now called) should have fallen over, mid-stride, every time they took a step.

A mind could find more than enough boggles, if it looked for them.

Somehow we sorted things out. More people went fast or slow. We started dividing the cities into zones set aside for each speed. A barter economy developed, with computers used for communication.

We counted on the fast ones for protection, and it appeared to be working. Speedo policemen watched over us. Speedo firemen kept us from harm.

Hunter wasn't optimistic, though, and I could see her point. At this rate, wouldn't three separate races develop? How many generations would it take for the accelerated to forget their kinship with Normals, or Normals their responsibility to the Slows?

She and I had only a couple of months to think about it. Soon word came "down" that Professor Wunkler had died, at age one hundred and two. Next the computers told us of a growing panic among our faster cousins.

I swear, it never occurred to us that the process might continue!

A certain fraction of the Fast were now leaping even *faster* along the timetrack! The practical jokes that began again were mostly visited upon the "merely Fast." The new "Superfast" apparently thought it a bore to mess up statues who couldn't react during their lifetimes, so they mostly left the Normals and the Slows alone.

We had to invent new terminology. The new level of Speedoes was called Fastrack II. It took years, from our point of view, for our cousins in Fastrack I to negotiate an arrangement such as Hunter and I had negotiated with *them*. Then our cities were divided into fourths. When the Slows had *their* branching we divided again.

A number of physicists, who had thought they'd figured out what was going on, went mad, committed suicide, or quietly changed professions.

I have contemplated the possibility that the Universe at one time truly *did* circle around the Earth . . . that ancient philosophers were *right* in their cruder models of reality, with their simple crystal spheres and pinholes in a velvet sky. Perhaps there were powers which, once mankind was about to understand his cage and find out the rules, frustrated him by the simple expedient of expanding the range of the possible.

It makes one wonder.

Hunter and I have three children now. In an odd way we have what every parent who ever loved his kids se cretly wanted. In Emma, Cassandra, and Abel we have a covey of dreams come true.

Abel is our oldest child. He was twelve when he made the transition to Fastrack I, a full three weeks before his sister Cassandra, and Hunter and I, were caught up in our own shift to the same level.

During those weeks he was brought up by some pleasant people and he became a fine man—strong, intelligent, and kind. After we joined him, he introduced us to our nearly grown grandchildren.

I said Cassandra came with us, didn't I? Yes, she's a wonderful child . . . a lot of fun and always springing surprises on us. She's aggravating and delightful and grows day by day before our eyes. Hunter and I are convinced she'll always be with us . . . at least for the remainder of her childhood.

Emma was the prettiest of our children. "Was" is a bad word, for she'll be beautiful and seven for the rest of our lives. She was left behind when we made the shift. No one knows any way to control the passage among the timelines, so we had to accept it.

No matter. One becomes philosophical. We carried her, with a note pinned to her sweater, to our friends the Neales, who are as nice as can be. We pop by, from time to time, just to look in on our baby. Whatever she does, her hair is brushed. Hunter insists, even when we find Emma sliding between bases in Little League. I sigh about "meddling," but I know she likes to know we're there. To her we'll be around for so little time.

Besides, the traffic goes both ways now, haphazard as it is. Someday Emmie too might leave the Main Timeline, and be reunited with us.

Which *is* the Main Timeline? I wonder. We've tried to be careful to keep track, but can we be sure? By what units could we measure this change?

Our worries over a tyranny of the Fast were mostly for naught. The new timelines seem to appear every decade or so, from the point of view of the line farthest "forward" . . . meaning they come into existence every few milliseconds from my present perspective.

It makes no logical sense. None at all, by the old premises. But somehow there are people to populate the lines, and room for all.

People flow back and forth across the streams like fish caught in different parts of the same river, some swept by swift currents, and others drifting slowly near the shore. We trade and cross-fertilize. The inventions that filter down are wonderful, but we always seem to have something of value to trade for them. Somehow we all seem to remain human.

I consult for the Fastrack I government now. They think highly of me here. Something like a reincarnated Benjamin Franklin. There is even a small market for my science fiction, though the heyday of that genre appears to be past.

Hunter and I go nowhere without each other. It may be superstition, but we feel that if you grab someone you love and hold him or her tight, when you feel the change coming on, you'll shift time tracks together.

I hope so.

I have meditated long and hard on this, while we do our stints of guard duty together, protecting one of the slower sections.

In my meditation I notice that a new way of thinking has begun to replace the old. I see the sun rise every morning. A mockingbird buzzes by my head whenever I wander past the tree that holds her nest. Each year the leaves change color and the Fastrack I farmers gather their harvest.

How can a day be a day on each timeline? Does the same mockingbird buzz for my Fast and Slow neighbors, as well?

How can the lines keep multiplying? Will there be a time when it all comes full circle? When the slowest of the Slow meet the fastest of the Fast, and send a chain of practical jokes rolling down the pike, growing in power and bad taste at every pass around the loop?

These are questions the old logic might have asked,

and I know they are false. For the river is legend. Its tributaries merge, far downstream from the glacier where once a trickle was all we knew.

How smug we have all become, in our adaptability. We claim to understand, to be at *home* on the great river!

Yet it widens, and deepens, as it flows.

And eventually, there is the Sea.

AUTHOR'S NOTES

Originally, its title was "Coexistence." It is a little tale, one of my earliest, and the only one I've ever written almost precisely as it came to me in a dream.

ABOUT THE AUTHOR

DAVID BRIN was born in 1950 in southern California. He has been an engineer with Hughes Aircraft Co., and attended Caltech and the University of California at San Diego, where he completed doctoral studies on comets and asteroids. He is presently a consultant with the California Space Institute, a unit of the University of California, San Diego, doing advanced studies concerning the space shuttle and space science. He also teaches university physics and occasionally creative writing.

David Brin has been nominated for several awards. His novel, *Startide Rising* won the Hugo and Nebula awards and his short story "The Crystal Spheres" won the Hugo award. His other novels include *Sundiver, The Practice Effect, The Postman,* and *Heart of the Comet,* a collaboration with Gregory Benford. He has recently completed a new novel, *The Uplift War,* which Bantam Spectra will publish in mid-1987.